FORTNIGHT OF FEAR

FORTNIGHT OF FEAR

Graham Masterton

This first world edition published in Great Britain 1994 by
SEVERN HOUSE PUBLISHERS LTD of
9–15 High Street, Sutton, Surrey SM1 1DF.
First published in the USA 1994 by
SEVERN HOUSE PUBLISHERS INC., of
425 Park Avenue, New York, NY 10022.

British Library Cataloguing in Publication Data
Masterton, Graham
  Fortnight of Fear
  I. Title
  823.914 [FS]

  ISBN 0-7278-4438-5 [cased]
  ISBN 0-7278-9016-6 [paper]

Typeset by Hewer Text Composition Services, Edinburgh.
Printed and bound in Great Britain by
Redwood Books, Trowbridge, Wiltshire.

CONTENTS

INTRODUCTION

The horror writer is cursed with one terrible curse. No matter where he travels, no matter how blissful the scenery or how congenial the accommodation, he soon begins to think of darker possibilities.

The sun may be shining, the sea may be sparkling. But in the horror writer's mind, a chilly shadow is already passing across the landscape.

Imagine your two weeks' vacation . . . fourteen nights of relaxation and fun. But wherever you are, some terrible doubt is always lurking.

Look at this picturesque Yorkshire village, with its mellow stone walls and its cobbled steps. Who would think that a dark, rushing, carnivorous creature could be waiting around the next corner?

Look at this warm, curving bay on the island of Jersey. Who would guess that something nameless could rise from the very sand beneath your feet?

Look at this peaceful farm in Connecticut, or this handsome Scottish estate. Look at this tasteful apartment on Central Park South, in New York, or this brash and glittering casino in Las Vegas.

Who would guess that here, night after night, for fourteen nights, there are heart-clutching terrors?

Come with me now on a two week holiday, with each night spent in a different locale. Each of these stories is set in a different location – a place that I have lived in or visited. Each story is a study in how my imagination slowly distorted each visit into something nightmarish.

From California to Northern England, from Nevada to the South Pole, this is a travel-guide to the uncivilized terrors of the civilized world.

You are invited to join me for a fortnight's travelling – a fortnight without sleep.

You need no luggage. You need no passport. The runway is deserted, and the dock has long since fallen into disrepair.

You will need only the courage to take my hand, and let me lead you into the darkness. To paraphrase Chairman Mao, the journey into two weeks of total terror begins with a single step.

Graham Masterton.

Hurry Monster

Great Ayton, Yorkshire, England

Beneath the northern ridges of the Yorkshire Moors nestles the village of Great Ayton (pronounced, locally, "Yatton"), one of the prettiest in Cleveland. A shallow river flows through the middle of the village, spanned by stone and wooden bridges; and it is this river, where my three sons played and fished, that gave me the dark inspiration for *Hurry Monster*.

Captain James Cook went to school in Great Ayton. The cottage where he once lived was shipped stone by stone to Australia in 1934, to be replaced by an obelisk chiseled out of the rocks close to Point Hicks, the first point in Australia to be sighted by Cook on his voyage of discovery (1768–71).

Hurry Monster was originally commissioned by Bill Munster, as an illustrated chapbook for his Footsteps Press, based at Roundtop, New York. Since then, it has appeared in many different forms – most notably in comic format, illustrated by the incomparable Dan Day.

HURRY MONSTER

Under a sky the color of corroded copper Kevin came running down the path beside the river, his school satchel slap-slap-slapping against the back of his gaberdine raincoat. Spots of rain were beginning to rustle threateningly into the grass, and to draw hundreds of compass-circles on the surface of the river.

But Kevin wasn't running because of the rain. He was running because of the Hurry Monster, which was hurrying close behind him. He thought that he could hear the echoing castanets of its claws, as it rushed shapeless and dark through the alleyways and down the narrow steps, and along the muddy track beside the river.

Just behind him, just out of sight – just behind the pie-shop, just behind the bushes.

Hurrying, with nothing on its mind but blood.

Kevin was already gasping for breath, but he knew what would happen if he slowed down. The Hurry Monster would snatch hold of him and bite into his body, and worry him ferociously from side to side, the same way that Orlando worried the mice she caught. Screaming – then pumping blood; then tearing muscle and stringy guts; then *crunch-crunch-crunch* and *ggllommp*! – swallowed.

He didn't dare to look back. He had left the playground more than five minutes late because he had been playing a last-minute game of cigarette-cards with Herbert Thorpe. The Hurry Monster had gained all that time already, and if he hesitated even for a second to look back –

3

He passed the sweetie-shop on the corner. He hesitated for one agonizing second, because he still had tuppence in his pocket from this morning, and he could see through the window that the sweetie-shop lady had opened up a fresh box of flying saucers.

But there wasn't time. He couldn't risk it. The Hurry Monster might catch up with him, and be lying in wait for him when he came out of the sweetie-shop. Then – *gnarrgghh!* – and his blood would be spattered all over the York-stone pavement.

He rushed across the main road. A coal-lorry honked its horn at him, and the driver said something he couldn't hear. It was ten past four already! Ten past four! His cheeks burned with the panic of being so late.

His mother had warned him about the Hurry Monster, last October, after Robert Browne had disappeared. Her face had been white and serious. That calm, almost featureless face, with black eyes that always reminded him of fresh glittering raisins. *Boys who dawdle on their way home from school get eaten by the Hurry Monster. So hurry, when you're coming home! Hurry! Hurry! Hurry!*

The first day after she had told him about the Hurry Monster, Kevin hadn't been sure whether he ought to believe it or not. After all, he had never seen the Hurry Monster, even when he had taken off his shoes and socks and fished under the footbridge for frogspawn, for almost an hour.

But on the second day, after he had crossed the main road, and walked past the gates to Ayton Hall, he was sure that he had heard footsteps very close behind him. Scratchy footsteps, like a large dog walking on stone; and *breathing*.

He had stopped; and he had turned around, but there had been nobody there. No dogs, no Hurry Monster. Only the shadows of the elderly oaks; only the whispering of the afternoon wind and the hollow-jar rushing of the river.

He had shivered, and then he had run on; across the narrow wooden footbridge that took him past the pub and down the lane and home.

But every day since then, on his way home from school, he had gradually become convinced that the Hurry Monster was close behind him. He had heard it, just out of sight. It had taken its shape from shadows and stray reflections. It had taken its breathing from the wind and the trees and the sound of the traffic. He hadn't dared to mention it to his schoolfriends, because it wasn't true in the same way that aniseed balls were true, or school dinners were true. But it wanted him. He knew that it wanted him. It was waiting every afternoon behind the high stone wall opposite Captain Cook's old schoolroom, and when he ran for home it came after him.

Every day he ran home faster. He ran like the wind. The Hurry Monster was after him! And he knew that it must be real because his mother had never lied to him ever; she had always told him that lying was the gravest sin of all. And didn't she always turn and smile with such warm relief when he came bursting out of breath through the kitchen door, into that safe aroma of pastry and lardy-cakes?

Didn't she always hug him tight, as if he had just managed to escape from the most vicious of demons?

The Hurry Monster even began to lurk on the edges of his nightmares. He dreamed he was running home from school and it caught up with him, and savaged him to death. The tearing of sinews; the crackling of pulled-apart fat.

It was after him today, and he was five minutes late.

School sandals pattering along the river-bank; torn-off grass catching in the metal buckles. He was sure that he could hear the Hurry Monster's claws, ripping into the earth as it ran. He was sure that he could feel its urgent breath. *Hah! hah! hah! hah!*

Once he reached the footbridge, he would be safe.

5

The Hurry Monster was too heavy to cross the footbridge.

He was only five or six yards away from the footbridge when he thought he heard somebody shout. *Kevin!* the smallest of cries, as small as a man shouting into an empty tin mug. He stopped, panicking, hesitated, turned. The day was so dark that he could scarcely see.

Kevin! the voice cried out.

There was something in the shadows by Ayton Hall. Something black; something that flickered. He ran on, and reached the footbridge, and rushed halfway across it before he dared to stop.

Then he turned around again, a small boy in a school cap and short trousers, on a wooden footbridge, with the shallow river sliding beneath his feet. Only a few yards away, vans and lorries passed on their way to Guisborough or Harrogate. North Yorkshire, on a thundery night in March.

The Hurry Monster had gone. Vanished, as it always did, when he reached the footbridge. He had outrun it again; and he was safe.

He was just about to continue on his way home when he saw something floating towards him in the river. It was dark, and heavy, and it left behind a trail of arrow-shaped ripples. He climbed up on the wooden handrail to stare at it. He didn't like the river that ran through Great Ayton, even though he often fished in it. All he had ever caught was frogspawn and peculiar fish that looked as if they had arms and legs.

But this was different, this thing that was floating towards him this afternoon. This was sinister and dark and very big. He stepped down from the handrail, and unconsciously retreated from it.

It slid slowly beneath the footbridge. As it passed through the shadow of the bridge itself, Kevin could see for the first time what it was. He was chilled with

6

terror, but all he could do was utter the tiniest of whimpers.

It was the body of a man, floating face up, staring. Behind him he stained the water with a deep crimson fog; and Kevin could see that the front of his suit had been torn open, and that bloody coils were lazily floating in the man's lap.

Worst of all, though, the man was still alive. Only just. But enough to look up at Kevin and give him the wannest of smiles. Then the current had carried him away, and he was gone, over the weir, through the deeper pools where Kevin usually swam, over the second weir, and round the bend in the river between the pollards.

Kevin was still standing on the footbridge when his mother appeared in her apron, her hands dusty-white with flour.

"Kevin?"

He stared at her as if he didn't know who she was. "There was a man. He was floating in the river and he smiled at me."

He sat on the high wooden stool in the police-station for nearly an hour. He had described the man, and even drawn him, in crayon. At half-past six his mother took him home. They walked hand-in-hand beside the river, and across the footbridge. Round the bend in the river, two policemen in shirt-sleeves were still poking at the weeds with long sticks, watched by a crowd of Kevin's schoolfriends and some old men who had come across from the pub with their pints of beer.

After tea, one of the old men came and knocked at their kitchen door. "Thought you'd like to know that they found 'im, poor bugger. Two miles down the river, caught in the weeds. They can't work out who 'e is, though. No wallet, nothin'. And nobody's ever seen 'im before. But 'e was fair ripped to pieces, no mistake. Stummick ripped out. Terrible. That tea still fresh?"

Kevin sat at the kitchen table. He felt very cold, very *compressed*, as if the shock of seeing the dying man had somehow made him smaller than he already was.

Why had the man smiled at him? What can a drowning man with his stomach all ripped out – what can he possibly find to smile about?

He went into the sweetie-shop for twenty Rothman's and he was pleasantly surprised how little it had changed. The glass-fronted counter with the flying saucers and the aniseed-balls and the licorice-whips was still there; much lower down and much tinier than he remembered; but still the same.

There was a different woman behind the counter – red-haired, this one, with freckles all over her arms; and there was a television on the back shelf, switched to racing from Redcar. But the *smell* was the same; and even though the main road was ten times busier, they hadn't widened it; and the river still ran as dark and reflective as it always had when he was a boy.

"I used to live here, years ago," he told the red-haired woman. "Just across the river, Number Three Brownlow Lane."

The red-haired woman smiled. "I'm from Barnsley, myself."

He left the sweetie-shop and the doorbell jangled behind him. Outside he smelled rain in the air. He crossed the road and stood beside the river, and lit a cigarette. He wondered if those peculiar fish that looked as if they had arms and legs still bred beneath the weir.

Thirty years, first time back to Great Ayton in thirty years. His mother had met the captain of a merchant-ship soon after he had left home, and she had died in Hull of all places. He had stood beside the captain while his mother had disappeared into the crematorium furnace to the strains of *The Old Rugged Cross*. The captain had smelled strongly of Vick chest-rub. They had shaken hands, and then Kevin had taken the first train back to London, and his job at Pearl Assurance, and his single flat in Islington, just round the corner from the Angel.

This week, he had been taking care of an insurance claim in Middlesborough. He hated Middlesborough, a gray dreary industrial wasteland, butcher's shops with nothing but belly-pork and working-men's clubs with off-key rock'n'roll groups and pints of bitter in straight-sided glasses. He had driven out to Great Ayton for the afternoon just to smell the moors and feel the creamy warmness of the Yorkshire village stone.

He finished his cigarette and flicked it into the river. He looked at his watch. He had a final meeting with the assessors at five, he'd better be getting back. Besides, it was beginning to rain quite hard now, whispering in the grass, drawing compass-circles on the surface of the river.

He was about to cross the road when he saw a small boy running along the pavement, really running. The boy was wearing a school cap and flannel shorts, and a school satchel joggled up and down on his back. *Look at that poor little chap*, he thought to himself. *Running home at full steam just like I used to.*

The boy passed the sweetie-shop, hesitated for a second, then darted across the main road. A coal-lorry blew its horn at him, and the driver shouted out of the window, "Silly young bugger! You could have been killed!"

It was then – to Kevin's horror – that he saw the reason why the boy was running so fast. Out of a shadowy alleyway not far behind him rushed a huge dark creature that billowed like a conjuror's cape. It flew along the pavement with a soft clashing noise, crossed the road, and began to pursue the boy along the bank of the river.

Kevin froze. Then he started running, too. He was out of condition, he had been smoking too much, but he sprinted as hard and as fast as he could. The creature had almost caught up with the boy, and one dark arm was lifted, with claws that gleamed in the coppery gloom like razors.

"Kevin!" Kevin shouted out. *"Kevin!"*

The creature rumbled and billowed and immediately turned around. Kevin ran headlong into it. It was black and it was cold and its breath hit him like opening up a freezer.

Kevin saw eyes that were malevolent and narrow and yellow as pus. Eyes which had stared at him before, in nightmares. He heard a soft roar of triumph; a scissoring of teeth.

"Oh God," he said. "It's true."

The claws sliced through waistcoat, shirt, Aertex vest, skin, fat, muscle. They were so sharp that Kevin didn't even feel them. He was hooked up in the air, sickeningly spun around. He dropped heavily on to the river bank, on to the grass. Rolled, blindly, helpless, into the river.

The water was intensely cold. He was glad of that, because it anesthetized the pain, although he didn't like the feeling of it pouring into his sliced-open abdomen.

He was lying on his back. He knew that he was dying. He floated gradually downstream, hearing the river gurgle in his ears.

He passed under the footbridge. A horizontal bar of darkness in front of his eyes. Then he saw a small face staring down at him, wide-eyed, horrified.

Don't be frightened, he thought to himself, as the current carried him away. *You will do the same one day. You will save Kevin yet again. And yet again. And yet again.*

He closed his eyes. He slid over the weir as lifeless as a

10

sack. Then he floated around the bend of the river where his mother was waiting for him.

He was sure that he could hear her whisper, *Hurry, Kevin. Hurry!*

Changeling

Amsterdam, The Netherlands

Amsterdam is always best out of season, when the wind cuts along the *grachten* (canals) like a craft knife. The chill always give me a good excuse to stop at a cafe for steaming mussels and fried fish, or an Indonesian restaurant for *rijstafel*. In March, the light in Amsterdam is strange and gray, so that you have a sense of being in a black-and-white movie about the life of Rembrandt. They still have hippies in Amsterdam, and trams. They also have the Nieuwe Kerk with its stunning stained-glass windows; and the Rijksmuseum, which is crammed with Flemish and Dutch masters. Less than an hour south of Amsterdam is the seaside resort of Scheveningen, with flat sandy beaches and a pier, and a curiously 1950s atmosphere, even today. During World War Two, captured German spies who were pretending to be Dutchmen were always asked by their British inquisitors to pronounce "Scheveningen" as a test of their Dutchness. Almost all of them failed.

CHANGELING

The elevator door opened and there she was, looking directly into his eyes as if she had known that he was standing on the other side. Tall, beautiful, dressed utterly in white. He hesitated for a moment and then stepped back one half-shuffle to allow her to pass.

"*Pardon mivrouw,*" he acknowledged. She smiled briefly but didn't reply. She passed him in a pungent swirl of Calvin Klein's Obsession, and he turned around and watched her walk across the marble lobby and out through the revolving door. Her long brunette hair was lifted for a moment by the April wind out on the hotel steps. Then the doorman came forward to salute her and she was gone.

"You're going up?" asked an irritated American who was waiting for him in the elevator, his finger pressed on the Doors Open button.

"I'm sorry? Oh, no. I've changed my mind."

He heard the man growl, "For Chrissakes, some people . . ." and then he found himself hurrying across the lobby and out through the door, just in time to see her climbing into the back of a taxi.

The doorman approached him and touched his cap. "Taxi, sir?"

"No, no thank you." He stood holding his briefcase, the skirts of his raincoat flapping, watching the woman's taxi turn into Sarphatistraat, feeling abandoned and grainy and weird, like a character in a black-and-white art movie. The doorman stood beside him, smiling uneasily.

"Do you happen to know that lady's name?" he asked. His voice sounded blurry in the wind. The doorman shook his head.

"Is she a guest here?"

"I'm sorry, sir. It is not permissible for me to say."

Gil reached into his inside pocket and for one moment considered bribery; but there was something in the doorman's smile that warned him against it. He said, "Oh, okay, sure," and retreated awkwardly back through the revolving door. The two elderly hall porters beamed and nodded at him as he returned to the elevator. Stan and Ollie, one thin and one fat. They were obviously quite accustomed to irrational behaviour.

Gil stood in the oak-paneled elevator as it took him up to the third floor and scrutinized himself in the brass-framed mirror with as much intensity as if he were a business partner whom he suspected of cracking up. He had never done anything in years as spontaneous as chasing after that woman. What the hell had come over him? He was married, with two children, he was right on top of his job. He had a six-bedroom house in Working, a new Granada Scorpio, and he had been profiled in *Business Week* as one of the new breed of "totally committed" young entrepreneurs.

And yet he had hurried after that unknown woman as gauche and panicky as an adolescent autograph-hunter.

He closed the door of his suite behind him and stood for a long time in the middle of the room with his briefcase still in his hand, thinking. Then he set the briefcase down and slowly took off his coat. *"Pity about Gil, he's thrown a wobbly."* He could almost hear them talking about him in the office. *"He was absolutely fine until that Amsterdam business. Probably suffering from overwork."*

He went to the window and opened it. The hotel room overlooked the Amstel River, wide and gray, where it was crossed by the wide elevating bridge called the

16

Hogesluis. Trams rumbled noisily over the sluis, their bells ringing, on their way to the suburbs. The wind blew so coldly through the window that the net curtains were lifted, shuddering, and Gil found that there were tears in his eyes.

He checked his pulse. It was slightly too fast, but nothing to take to the doctor. He didn't feel feverish, either. He had been working for four days, Tuesday to Friday, sixteen to eighteen hours a day, but he had been careful not to drink too much and to rest whenever he could. Of course, it was impossible to judge what effect this round of negotiations might have had on his brain. But he *felt* normal.

But he thought of her face and he thought of her hair and he thought of the way in which she had smiled at him; a smile that had dissolved as quickly as soluble aspirin; and then was gone. And against all the psychological and anthropological logic in the world, he knew that he had fallen in love with her. Well, maybe not in *love*, maybe not actually in *love*, not the way he loved Margaret. But she had looked into his eyes and smiled at him and wafted past in beguiling currents of Obsession, and in ten seconds he had experienced more excitement, more curiosity, more plain straightforward *desire* than he had in the last ten years of marriage.

It's ridiculous, he said to himself. It's just a moment of weakness. I'm tired, I'm suffering from stress. I'm lonely, too. Nobody ever understands how lonely it can be, traveling abroad on business. No wonder so many businessmen stay in their hotel rooms, drinking too much whiskey and watching television programmes they can't understand. There is no experience so friendless as walking the streets of a strange city, with nobody to talk to.

He closed the window and went to the mini-bar

17

to find himself a beer. He switched on the television and watched the news in Dutch. Tomorrow morning, after he had collected the signed papers from the Gemeentevervoerbedrijf, he would take a taxi straight to Schiphol and fly back to London. Against ferocious competition from Volvo and M.A.N. Diesel, he had won an order for twenty-eight new buses for Amsterdam's municipal transport system, all to be built in Oxford.

On the phone, Brian Taylor had called him "a bloody marvel." Margaret had squealed in delight, like she always did.

But the way the wind had lifted up that woman's hair kept running and re-running in his mind like a tiny scrap of film that had been looped to play over and over. The revolving door had turned, her hair had lifted. Shining and dark, the kind of hair that should be spread out over silk pillows.

It began to grow dark and the lights began to dip and sparkle in the river and the trams began to grind their way out to Oosterpark and the farther suburbs. Gil consulted the room-service menu to see what he could have for supper, but after he had called up to order the smoked eel and the veal schnitzel, with a half-bottle of white wine, he was taken with a sudden surge of panic about eating alone, and he called back and canceled his order.

"You don't *want* the dinner, sir?" The voice was flat, Dutch-accented, polite but curiously hostile.

"No thank you. I've . . . changed my mind."

He went to the bathroom and washed his face and hands. Then he straightened his necktie, shrugged on his coat, picked up his key, and went down to the hotel's riverside bar for a drink. The bar was crowded with Japanese and American businessmen. Only two women, and both of them were quite obviously senior executives, one lopsidedly beautiful, the other as hard-faced as a man. He sat up on a bar-stool and ordered a whiskey-and-soda.

18

"Cold wind today, hmh?" the barman asked him.

He drank his whiskey too quickly, and he was about to order another one when the woman came and sat just one stool away from him, still dressed in white, still fragrant with Obsession. She smiled to the barman and asked for a Bacardi, in English.

Gil felt as if he were unable to breathe. He had never experienced anything like it. It was a kind of panic, like claustrophobia, and yet it had an extraordinary quality of erotic compulsion, too. He could understand why people half-strangled themselves to intensify their sexual arousal. He stared at himself glassy-eyed in the mirror behind the Genever gin-bottles, trying to detect any signs of emotional breakdown. But did it show, when you finally cracked? Did your face fall apart like a broken jug? Or was it all kept tightly inside of you? Did it snap in the back of your brain where nobody could see?

He glanced covertly sideways, first at the woman's thigh, then more boldly at her face. She was looking straight ahead, at the mirror. Her nose was classically straight, her eyes were cobalt-blue, slightly slanted, very European. Her lips were glossed with crimson. He noticed a bracelet of yellow-and-white gold, intertwined, that must have cost the equivalent of three months of his salary, including expenses, and a gold Ebel wristwatch. Her nails were long and crimson and perfect. She moved slightly sideways on her stool and he noticed the narrowness of her waist, and the full sway of her breasts. She's naked underneath that dress, he thought to himself, or practically naked. She's just too incredibly sexy to be true.

What could he say to her? Should he say anything? *Could* he say anything? He thought dutifully for a moment about Margaret, but he knew that he was only being dutiful. This woman existed on a different planet from

19

Margaret, she was one of a different species. She was feminine, sexual, undomesticated, elegant, and probably dangerous, too.

The barman approached him. "Can I fix you another drink, sir?"

"I – unh –"

"Oh, go ahead," the woman smiled. "I can't bear to drink alone."

Gil flushed, and grinned, and shrugged, and said, "All right, then. Yes." He turned to the woman and asked, "How about you?"

"Thank you," she acknowledged, passing her glass to the barman, although there was a curious intonation in her voice which made it sound as if she were saying thank you for something else altogether.

The barman set up the drinks. They raised their glasses to each other and said, *"Prost!"*

"Are you staying here?" Gil asked the woman. He wished his words didn't sound so tight and high-pitched.

"In Amsterdam?"

"I mean here, at the Amstel Hotel."

"No, no," she said. "I live by the sea, in Zandvoort. I only came here to meet a friend of mine."

"You speak perfect English," he told her.

"Yes," she replied. Gil waited, expecting her to tell him what she did for a living, but she remained silent.

"I'm in transportation," he volunteered. "Well, buses, actually."

She focused her eyes on him narrowly but still she said nothing. Gil said, "I go back to London tomorrow. Job's over."

"Why did you come running after me?" she asked. "You know when – this afternoon, when I was leaving the hotel. You came running after me and you stood outside the hotel and watched me go."

Gil opened and closed his mouth. Then he lifted both

20

hands helplessly, and said, "I don't know. I really don't know. It was – I don't know. I just did it."

She kept her eyes focused on him as sharply as a camera. "You desire me," she said.

Gil didn't reply, but uncomfortably sat back on his barstool.

Without hesitation, the woman leaned forward and laid her open hand on his thigh. She was very close now. Her lips were parted and he could see the tips of her front teeth. He could smell the Bacardi on her breath. Warm, soft, even breath.

"You desire me," she repeated.

She gave him one quick, hard squeeze, and then sat back. Her face was filled with silent triumph. Gil looked at her with a mixture of excitement and embarrassment and disbelief. She had actually reached over and touched him – not touched him, *caressed* him, this beautiful woman in the white dress, this beautiful woman whom every businessman in the bar would have given his Christmas bonus just to sit with.

"I don't even know your name," said Gil, growing bolder.

"Is that necessary?"

"I don't really suppose it is. But I'd like to. My name's Gil Batchelor."

"Anna."

"Is that all, just Anna?"

"It's a palindrome," she smiled. "That means that it's the same backwards as it is forwards. I try to live up to it."

"Could I buy you some dinner?"

"Is *that* necessary?"

Gil took three long heartbeats to reply. "Necessary in what sense?" he asked her.

"In the sense that you feel it necessary to court me somehow. To buy me dinner; to impress me with your taste in wine; to make witty small-talk. To tell me all those humorous anecdotes which I am sure your colleagues have heard one hundred times at least. Is all that necessary?"

Gil licked his lips. Then he said, "Maybe we should take a bottle of champagne upstairs."

Anna smiled. "I'm not a prostitute, you know. The barman thinks I'm a prostitute, but of course prostitutes are good for business, provided they are suitably dressed and behave according to the standards expected by the hotel. If you take me up to your room now, let me tell you truthfully that you will be only the second man I have ever slept with."

Gil gave Anna a complicated shrug with which he intended to convey the feeling that he was flattered by what she had said, but couldn't take her seriously. A woman with Anna's style and Anna's body and Anna's sexual directness had slept in the whole of her life with only one man?

Anna said, "You don't believe me."

"I don't have to believe you, do I? That's part of the game." Gil thought that response was quite clever and sophisticated.

But Anna reached out toward him and gently picked a single hair from the shoulder of his coat and said very quietly, "It's not a game, my love."

She undressed in silence, close to the window, so that her body was outlined by the cold glow of the streetlights outside, but her face remained in shadow. Her dress slipped to the floor with a sigh. Underneath, she was naked except for a tiny *cache-sexe* of white embroidered cotton. Her breasts were large, almost too large for a woman with such a narrow back, and her nipples were wide and pale as sugar-frosting.

Gil watched her, unbuttoning his shirt. He could sense her smiling. She came over and buried the fingers of one hand into the curly brown hair on his chest, and tugged at it. She kissed his cheeks, then his lips. Then she reached down and started to unfasten his belt.

Gil thought: *this is morally wrong, damn it. I'm cheating the woman who gave me my children; the woman who's waiting for me to come home tomorrow. But how often does a man run into a sexual dream like this? Supposing I tell her to get dressed and leave. I'll spend the rest of my life wondering what it could have been like.*

Anna slid her hands into the back of his trousers. Her sharp fingernails traced the line of his buttocks, and he couldn't help shivering. "Lie down on the bed," she whispered. "Let me make love to you."

Gil sat on the edge of the bed, and struggled out of his trousers. Then Anna pushed him gently backwards. He heard the softest plucking of elastic as she took off her cache-sexe. She climbed astride his chest, and sat in the semi-darkness smiling at him, her hair like a soft and mysterious veil. "Do you like to be kissed?" she asked him. "There are so many ways to be kissed."

She lifted herself up, and teasingly lowered her vulva so that it kissed his lips. Her pubic hair was silky and long, and rose up in a plume. Gil kissed her, hesitantly at first, then deeper, holding her open with his fingers.

She gave a deep, soft murmur of pleasure, and ran her fingers through his hair.

They made love four times that night. Anna seemed to be insatiable. When the first slate-gray light of morning began to strain into the room, and the trams began to boom over Hogesluis again, Gil lay back in bed watching her sleep, her hair tangled on the pillow. He cupped her breast in his hand, and then ran his fingers gently all the way down the flatness of her stomach to her dark-haired sex. She was more than a dream, she was irresistible. She was everything that anybody could desire. Gil kissed her lightly on the forehead, and when she opened her eyes and looked up at him and smiled, he knew that he was already falling in love with her.

"You have to go back to England today," she said, softly.

"I don't know. Maybe."

"You mean you could stay a little longer?"

Gil looked at her, but at the same time he made a conscious effort to picture Margaret, as if he were watching a movie with a split screen. He could imagine Margaret sitting on the sofa sewing and glancing at the clock every few minutes to see if it was time for him to be landing at Gatwick Airport. He could see her opening the front door and smiling and kissing him and telling him what Alan had been doing at playschool.

"Maybe another day," Gil heard himself saying, as if there were somebody else in the room who spoke just like him.

Anna drew his head down and kissed him. Her tongue slipped in between his teeth. Then she lay back and whispered, "What about two days? I could take you to Zandvoort. We could go to my house, and then we could spend all day and all night and all the next day, making love."

"I'm not sure that I can manage two days."

"Call your office. Tell them you may be able to sell the good burghers of Amsterdam a few more of your buses. A day and a night and a day. You can go home on Sunday night. The plane won't be so crowded then."

Gil hesitated, and then kissed her. "All right then. What the hell. I'll call the airline after breakfast."

"And your wife? You have to call your wife."

"I'll call her."

Anna stretched out like a a beautiful sleek animal. "You are a very special gentle man, Mr Gil Batchelor," she told him.

"Well, you're a very special lady."

*　　*　　*

Margaret had sniffled: that had made him feel so guilty that he had nearly agreed to come back to England straight away. She missed him, everything was ready for him at home, Alan kept saying, "Where's daddy?" And *why* did he have to stay in Holland for another two days? Surely the Dutch people could telephone him, or send him a telex? And why *him*? George Kendall should have been selling those extra buses, not him.

In the end, it was her whining that gave him the strength to say, "I have to, that's all. I don't like it any more than you do, darling, believe me. I miss you too, and Alan. But it's only two more days. And then we'll all go to Brighton for the day, what about that? We'll have lunch at Wheeler's."

He put down the phone. Anna was watching him across the room. She was sitting on a large white leather sofa, wearing only thin pajama trousers of crêpe silk. Between her bare breasts she held a heavy crystal glass of Bacardi. The coldness of the glass had made her nipples tighten. She was smiling at him in a way that he found oddly disturbing. She looked almost triumphant, as if by persuading him to lie to Margaret, she had somehow captured a little part of his soul.

Behind her, through the picture window that was framed with cheese-plants and ivy, he could see the concrete promenade, the wide gray beach, the gray overhanging clouds, and the restless horizon of the North Sea.

He came and sat down beside her. He touched her lips with his fingertip and she kissed it. His hand followed the warm heavy curve of her breast, and then he gently rolled her nipple between finger and thumb. She watched him, still smiling.

"Do you think you could ever fall in love with somebody like me?" she asked him, in a whisper.

"I don't think there is anybody like you. Only you."

"So could you fall in love with me?"

He dared to say it. "I think I already have."

She set her drink down on the glass and stainless steel table next to her, and knelt up on the sofa. She tugged down her pajama trousers so that she was naked. She pushed Gil on to his back, and climbed on top of him. "You like kissing me, don't you?" she murmured. He didn't answer, but lifted his head slightly, and saw her looking at him with that same disturbing smile.

The house was always silent, except when they spoke, or when they played music. Anna liked Mozart symphonies, but she always played them in another room. The walls were white and bare, the carpets were gray. The inside of the house seemed to be a continuation of the bleak coastal scenery that Gil could see through the windows. Apart from the houseplants there were no ornaments. The few pictures on the walls were lean, spare drawings of naked men and women, faceless most of them. Gil had the feeling that the house didn't actually belong to Anna, that it had been occupied by dozens of different people, none of whom had left their mark on it. It was a house of no individuality whatsoever. An anxious house, at the very end of a cul-de-sac that fronted the beach. The gray brick sidewalks were always swirled with gritty gray sand. The wind blew like a constant headache.

They made love over and over again. They went for walks on the beach, the collars of their coats raised up against the stinging sand. They ate silent meals of cold meat and bread and cold white wine. They listened to Mozart in other rooms. On the third morning Gil woke up and saw that Anna was awake already, and watching him. He reached out and stroked her hair.

"This is the day I have to go home," he told her, his voice still thick from sleeping.

She took hold of his hand and squeezed it. "Can't you

manage one more day? One more day and one more night?"

"I have to go home. I promised Margaret. And I have to be back behind my desk on Monday morning."

She lowered her head so that he couldn't see her face. "You know that – if you go – we will never be able to see each other any more."

Gil said nothing. It hurt too much to think that he might never sleep with Anna again in the whole of his life. He eased himself out from under the quilt, and walked through to the bathroom. He switched on the light over the basin and inspected himself. He looked tired. Well, anybody would be, after two days and three nights of orgiastic sex with a woman like Anna. But there was something else about his face which made him frown, a different look about it. He stared at himself for a long time but he couldn't decide what it was. He filled the basin with hot water and squirted a handful of shaving-foam into his hand.

It was only when he lifted his hand toward his face that he realized he didn't need a shave.

He hesitated, then he rinsed off the foam and emptied the basin. He must have shaved last night, before he went to bed, and forgotten about it. After all, they had drunk quite a lot of wine. He went to the toilet, and sat down, and urinated in quick fits and starts. It was only when he got up and wiped himself by passing a piece of toilet-paper between his legs that he realized what he had done. *I never sit down to pee. I'm not a woman.*

Anna was standing in the bathroom doorway watching him. He laughed. "I must be getting old, sitting down to pee."

She came up to him and put her arms around his neck and kissed him. It was a long, complicated, yearning kiss. When he opened his eyes again she was staring at him very close up. "Don't go," she whispered. "Not yet, I

27

couldn't bear it. Give me one more day. Give me one more night."

"Anna . . . I can't. I have a family; a job."

With the same directness she had exhibited in the bar of the Amstel Hotel, she came up to him and put her arms around him, kissing his neck and his shoulders. His reaction was immediate. "Don't go," she repeated, "I've been waiting so long for somebody like you . . . I can't bear to lose you just yet. One more day, one more night. You can catch the evening flight on Monday and be back in England before nine."

He kissed her. He knew that he was going to give in.

That day, they walked right down to the edge of the ocean. A dog with wet bedraggled fur circled around and around, yapping at them. The wind from the North Sea was relentless. When they returned to the house, Gil felt inexplicably exhausted. Anna undressed him and helped him up to the bedroom. "I think I'm feeling the strain," he smiled at her. She leaned over and kissed him. He lay with his eyes open listening to Mozart playing in another room, and looking at the way the gray afternoon light crossed the ceiling and illuminated the pen-and-ink drawing of a man and a woman entwined together. The drawing was like a puzzle. It was impossible to tell where the man ended and where the woman began.

He fell asleep. It started to rain, salty rain from the sea. He slept all afternoon and all evening, and the wind rose and the rain lashed furiously against the windows.

He was still asleep at two o'clock in the morning, when the bedroom door opened and Anna came in, and softly slipped into bed beside him. "My darling," Anna murmured, and touched the smoothness of his cheek.

He dreamed that Anna was shaking him awake, and lifting his head so that he could sip a glass of water. He dreamed that she was caressing him and murmuring to him. He dreamed that he was trying to run across the

28

beach, across the wide gray sands, but the sands turned to glue and clung around his ankles. He heard music, voices.

He opened his eyes. It was twilight. The house was silent. He turned to look at his watch on the bedside table. It was 7:17 in the evening. His head felt congested, as if he had a hangover, and when he licked his lips they felt swollen and dry. He lay back for a long time staring at the ceiling, his arms by his sides. He must have been ill, or maybe he had drunk too much. He had never felt like this in his life before.

It was only when he raised his hand to rub his eyes that he understood that something extraordinary had happened to him. His arm was obstructed by a huge soft growth on his chest. He felt a cold thrill of complete terror, and instantly yanked down the quilt. When he saw his naked body, he let out a high-pitched shout of fright.

He had breasts. Two heavy, well-rounded breasts, with fully developed nipples. He grasped them in his hands and realized they weren't tumorous growths, they weren't cancers, they were actual female breasts, and very big breasts, too. Just like Anna's.

Trembling, he ran his right hand down his sides, and felt a narrow waist, a flat stomach, and then silky pubic hair. He knew what he was going to feel between his legs, but he held himself back for minute after minute, his eyes closed, not daring to believe that it had gone, that he had been emasculated. At last, however, he slipped his fingers down between his hairless thighs, and felt the moist lips of his vulva. He hesitated, swallowed, and then slipped one finger into his vagina.

There was no question about it. His body was completely female, inside and out. In appearance at least, he was a woman.

"None of this is real," he told himself, but even his voice

29

was feminine. He climbed slowly out of bed and his breasts swayed, just the way that Anna's had swayed. He walked across the room and confronted the full-length mirror beside the dressing-table. There was a woman looking back at him, a beautiful naked woman, and the woman was him.

"This isn't real," he repeated, cupping his breasts in his hands and staring intently at the face in the mirror. The eyes were his, the expression was his. He could see himself inside that face, his own personality, Gil Batchelor the bus salesman from Woking. But who else was going to be able to see what he saw? What was Brian Taylor going to see, if he tried to turn up for work? And, God Almighty, it seemed absurd, but what was Margaret going to say, if he came back home looking like this?

Without a sound, he collapsed on to the floor, and lay with his face against the gray carpet, in total shock. He lay there until it grew dark, feeling chilled, but unwilling or unable to move. He wasn't sure which and he wasn't going to find out.

At last, when the room was completely dark, the door opened, and a dim light fell across the floor. Gil heard a voice saying, "You're awake. I'm sorry. I should have come in earlier."

Gil lifted his head. Unconsciously, he drew his long tangled hair out of his eyes, and looked up. A man was silhouetted in the doorway, a man wearing a business-suit and polished shoes.

"Who are you?" he asked, hoarsely. "What the hell has happened to me?"

The man said, "You've changed, that's all."

"For Christ's sake, look at me. What the hell is going on here? Did you do this with hormones, or what? I'm a man! I'm a *man*, for Christ's sake!" Gil began to weep, and the tears slid down his cheeks and tasted salt on his lips.

The man came forward and knelt down beside him

30

and laid a comforting hand on his shoulder. "It wasn't hormones. If I knew how it happened, believe me, I'd tell you. But all I know is, it happens. One man to the next. The man who was Anna before me – the man who took the body that used to be mine – he told me everything about it, just as I'm telling you – and just as *you'll* tell the next man that you pick."

At that moment, the bedroom door swung a little wider, and the man's face was illuminated by the light from the hallway. With a surge of paralyzing fright, Gil saw that the man was him. His own face, his own hair, his own smile. His own wristwatch, his own suit. And outside in the hallway, his own suitcase, already packed.

"I don't understand," he whispered. He wiped the tears away from his face with his fingers.

"I don't think any of us ever will," the man told him. "There seems to be some kind of pattern to it; some kind of reason why it happens; but there's no way of finding out what it is."

"But you knew this was going to happen all along," said Gil. "Right from the very beginning. You *knew*."

The man nodded. Gil should have been violent with rage. He should have seized the man by the throat and beaten his head against the wall. But the man was him, and for some inexplicable reason he was terrified of touching him.

The man said, quietly, "I'm sorry for you. Please believe me. But I'm just as sorry for myself. I used to be a man like you. My name was David Chilton. I was thirty-two years old, and I used to lease executive aircraft. I had a family, a wife and two daughters, and a house in Darien, Connecticut."

He paused, and then he said, "Four months ago I came to Amsterdam and met Anna. One thing led to another, and she took me back here. She used to make me make love to her, night after night. Then one morning I woke up and *I* was Anna, and Anna was gone."

Gil said, "I can't believe any of this. This is madness. I'm having a nightmare."

The man shook his head. "It's true; and it's been happening to one man after another, for years probably."

"How do you know that?"

"Because Anna took my passport and my luggage, and it seemed to me that there was only one place that she could go – *he* could go. Only one place where he could survive in my body and with my identity."

Gil stared at him. "You mean – your own home? He took your body and went to live in your own home?"

The man nodded. His face was grim. Gil had never seen himself look so grim before.

"I found Anna's passport and Anna's bank-books – don't worry, I've left them all for you. I flew to New York and then rented a car and drove up to Connecticut. I parked outside my own house and watched myself mowing my own lawn, playing with my own daughters, kissing my own wife."

He lowered his head, and then he said, "I could have killed him, I guess. Me, I mean – or at least the person who looked like me. But what would that have achieved? I would have made a widow out of my own wife, and orphans out of my own children. I loved them too much for that. I love them still."

"You left them alone?" Gil whispered.

"What else could I do? I flew back to Holland and here I am."

Gil said, "Couldn't you have *stayed* like Anna? Why couldn't you stay the way you were? Why did you have to take *my* body?"

"Because I'm a man," David Chilton told him. "Because I was brought up a man, and because I think like a man, and because it doesn't matter how beautiful a woman you are, how rich a woman you are . . . well, you're going to find out what it's like, believe me. Not even the poorest most down-trodden guy in the whole wide world has to endure what women have to endure. Supposing every time that a woman came up to a man, she stared at his crotch instead of his face, even when they were supposed to be having a serious conversation? You don't think that happens? You did it to me, when we met at the hotel. Eighty per cent of the time, your eyes were ogling my tits, and I know what you were thinking. Well, now it's going to happen to you. And, believe me, after a couple of months, you're going to go pick up some guy not because you want to live like a man again but because you want your revenge on all those jerkoffs who treat you like a sex object instead of a human being."

Gil knelt on the floor and said nothing. David Chilton checked Gil's wristwatch – the one that Margaret had given him on their last anniversary – and said, "I'd better go. I've booked a flight at eleven."

"You're not –" Gil began.

David Chilton made a face. "What else can I do? Your wife's expecting me home. A straight ordinary-looking man like me. Not a voluptuous brunette like you."

"You can't do this," Gil told him. "It's theft!"

"Theft? How can a man steal something which everybody in the whole world will agree is his?"

"Then it's murder, for God's sake! You've effectively killed me!"

"Murder?" David Chilton shook his head. "Come on, now, Anna, I really have to go."

"I'll kill you," Gil warned him.

"I don't think so," said David Chilton. "Maybe you'll think about it, the way that I thought about killing the guy who took my body. But there's a diary in the living room, a diary kept by most of the men who have changed

33

into Anna. Read it, before you think of doing anything drastic."

He reached out and touched Gil's hair, almost regretfully. "You'll survive. You have clothes, you have a car, you have money in the bank. You even have an investment portfolio. You're not a poor woman. Fantasy women never are. If you want to stay as Anna, you can live quite comfortably for the rest of your life. Or . . . if you get tired of it, you know what to do."

Gil sat on the floor incapable of doing anything at all to prevent David Chilton from leaving. He was too traumatized; too drained of feeling. David Chilton went to the end of the hallway and picked up his suitcase. He turned and smiled at Gil one last time, and then blew him a kiss.

"So long, honey. Be good."

Gil was still sitting staring at the carpet when the front door closed, and the body he had been born with walked out of his life.

He slept for the rest of the night. He had no dreams that he could remember. When he woke up, he lay in bed for almost an hour, feeling his body with his hands. It was frightening but peculiarly erotic, to have the body of a woman, and yet to retain the mind of a man. Gil massaged his breasts, rolling his nipples between finger and thumb the way he had done with "Anna". Then he reached down between his legs and gently stroked himself, exploring his sex with tension and curiosity.

He wondered what it would be like to have a man actually inside him; a man on top of him, thrusting into him.

He stopped himself from thinking that thought. *For God's sake, you're not a queer.*

He showered and washed his hair. He found the length of his hair difficult to manage, especially when it was wet, and it took four attempts before he was able to wind a towel around it in a satisfactory turban. Yet Margaret always did it without even looking in the mirror. He decided that at the first opportunity he got, he would have it cut short.

He went to the closet and inspected Anna's wardrobe. He had liked her in her navy-blue skirt and white loose-knit sweater. He found the sweater folded neatly in one of the drawers. He struggled awkwardly into it, but realized when he looked at himself in the mirror that he was going to need a bra. He didn't want to attract *that* much attention, not to begin with, anyway. He located a drawerful of bras, lacy and mysterious, and tried one on. His breasts kept dropping out of the cups before he could fasten it up at the back, but in the end he knelt down beside the bed and propped his breasts on the quilt. He stepped into one of Anna's lacey little G-strings. He found it irritating, the way the elastic went right up between the cheeks of his bottom, but he supposed he would get used to it.

Get used to it. The words stopped him like a cold bullet in the brain. He stared at himself in the mirror, that beautiful face, those eyes that were still his. He began to weep with rage. *You've started to accept it already. You've started to cope. You're fussing around in your bra and your panties and you're worrying which skirt to wear and you've already forgotten that you're not Anna, you're Gil. You're a husband. You're a father. You're a man, damn it!*

He began to hyperventilate, his anger rising up unstoppably like the scarlet line of alcohol rising up a thermometer. He picked up the dressing-stool, and heaved it at the mirror. The glass shattered explosively, all over the carpet. A thousand tiny Annas stared up at him in uncontrollable fury and frustration.

He stormed blindly through the house, yanking open drawers, strewing papers everywhere, clearing ornaments off table-tops with a sweep of his arm. He wrenched open the doors of the cocktail cabinet, and hurled the bottles of liquor one by one across the room, so that they smashed against the wall. Whiskey, gin, Campari, broken glass.

Eventually, exhausted, he sat down on the floor and sobbed. Then he was too tired even to cry.

In front of him, lying on the rug, were Anna's identity card, her social security papers, her passport, her credit cards. *Anna Huysmans*. The name which was now his.

On the far side of the room, halfway under the leather sofa, Gil saw a large diary bound in brown Morocco leather. He crept across the floor on his hands and knees and picked it up. This must be the diary that David Chilton had been talking about. He opened it up to the last page.

He read, through eyes blurry with tears, *"Gil has been marvelous . . . he has an enthusiastic, uncluttered personality . . . It won't be difficult to adapt to being him . . . I just hope that I like his wife Margaret . . . she sounds a little immature, from what Gil says . . . and he complains that she needs a lot of persuading when it comes to sex . . . Still, that's probably Gil's fault . . . you couldn't call him the world's greatest lover."*

Gil flicked back through the diary's pages until he came to the very first entry. To his astonishment it was dated July 16, 1942. It was written in German, by a Reichswehr officer who appeared to have met Anna while driving out to Edam on military business. "Her bicycle tire was punctured . . . she was so pretty that I told my driver to stop and to help her . . ."

There was no way of telling, however, whether this German Samaritan had been the first of Anna's victims, or simply the first to keep a diary. The entries went on page after page, year after year. There must have been more than seven hundred of them; and each one told a different story of temptation and tragedy. Some of the

36

men had even essayed explanations of what Anna was, and why she took men's bodies.

"She has been sent to punish us by God Himself for thinking lustful thoughts about women and betraying the Holy Sacrament of marriage . . ."

"She does not actually exist. There is no 'Anna', because she is always one of us. The only 'Anna' that exists is in the mind of the man who is seducing her, and that perhaps is the greatest condemnation of them all. We fall in love with our own illusions, rather than a real woman."

"To me, Anna is a collector of weak souls. She gathers us up and hangs us on her charm-bracelet, little dangling victims of our own vicissitudes."

"Anna is a ghost . . ."

"Anna is a vampire . . ."

"If I killed myself, would it break the chain? Would Anna die if I died? Supposing I tried to seduce the man who was Anna before me . . . could I reverse the changing process?"

Gil sat on the floor and read the diary from cover to cover. It was an extraordinary chorus of voices – real men who had been seduced into taking on the body of a beautiful woman, one after the other – and in their turn had desperately tried to escape. Business executives, policemen, soldiers, scientists, philosophers – even priests. Some had stayed as Anna for fewer than two days; others had managed to endure it for months. But to every single one of them, the body even of the plainest man had been preferable to Anna's body, regardless of how desirable she was.

By two o' clock, Gil was feeling hungry. The icebox was almost empty, so he drove into Amsterdam for lunch. The day was bright but chilly, and so he wore Anna's black belted raincoat, and a black beret to cover his head. He tried her high-heels, but he twisted his ankle in the hallway, and sat against the wall with tears in his eyes saying, "Shit, shit," over and over, as if he *ought* to have been able to walk in them quite naturally. He limped back to the bedroom and changed into black court shoes.

He managed to find a parking-space for Anna's BMW on the edge of the Singel canal, close to the Muntplein, where the old mint-building stood, with its clock and its onion-dome. There was an Indonesian restaurant on the first floor of the building on the corner: one of the executives of the Gemeentevervoerbedrijf had pointed it out to him. He went upstairs and a smiling Indonesian waiter showed him to a table for one, overlooking the square. He ordered rijstafel for one, and a beer. The waiter stared at him, and so he changed his order to a vodka and tonic.

The large restaurant was empty, except for a party of American businessmen over on the far side. As he ate his meal, Gil gradually became aware that one of the businessmen was watching him. Not only watching him, but every time he glanced up, *winking* at him.

Oh shit, he thought. *Just let me eat my lunch in peace.*

He ignored the winks and the unrelenting stares; but after the business lunch broke up, the man came across the restaurant, buttoning up his coat, and smiling. He was big and red-faced and sweaty, with wavy blond hair and three heavy gold rings on each hand.

"You'll pardon my boldness," he said. "My name's Fred Oscay. I'm in aluminum tubing, Pennsylvania Tubes. I just couldn't take my eyes off you all during lunch."

Gil looked up at him challengingly. "So?" he replied.

"Well," grinned Fred Oscay, "maybe you could take that as a compliment. You're some looker, I've got to tell you. I was wondering if you had any plans for dinner tonight. You know – maybe a show, maybe a meal."

Gil was trembling. Why the hell was he trembling? He was both angry and frightened. Angry at being stared at

38

and winked at and chatted up by this crimson-faced idiot; frightened because social convention prevented him from being as rude as he really wanted to be – that, and his weaker physique.

It was a new insight – and to Gil it was hair-raising – that men used the threat of their greater physical strength against women not just in times of argument and stress – but *all the time*.

"Mr Oscay," he said, and he was still trembling. "I'd really prefer it if you went back to your party and left me alone."

"Aw, come along now," Fred Oscay grinned. "You can't mean that."

Gil's mouth felt dry. "Will you please just leave me alone?"

Fred Oscay leaned over Gil's table. "There's a fine concert at the Kleine Zaal, if it's culture you're after."

Gil hesitated for a moment, and then picked up a small metal dish of Indonesian curried chicken and turned it upside-down over Fred Oscay's left sleeve. Fred Oscay stared down at it for a very long time without saying anything, then stared at Gil with a hostility in his eyes that Gil had never seen from anybody before. Fred Oscay looked quite capable of killing him, then and there.

"You tramp," he said. "You stupid bitch."

"Go away," Gil told him. "All I'm asking you to do is go away."

Now Fred Oscay's voice became booming and theatrical, intended for all his business colleagues to hear. "You were coming on, lady. You were coming on. All through lunch you were giving me the glad-eye. So don't you start getting all tight-assed now. What is it, you want money? Is that it? You're a professional? Well, I'm sorry. I'm really truly sorry. But old Fred Oscay never paid for a woman in his life, and he aint about to start just for some sorry old hooker like you."

He picked up a napkin and wiped the curry off his sleeve with a flourish, throwing the soiled napkin directly into Gil's plate. The other businessmen laughed and stared. One of them said, "Come on, Fred, we can't trust you for a minute."

Gil sat where he was and couldn't think what to do; how to retaliate; how to get his revenge. He felt so frustrated that in spite of himself he burst into tears. The Indonesian waiter came over and offered him a glass of water. "Aroo okay?" he kept asking. "Aroo okay?"

"I'm all right," Gil insisted. "Please – I'm all right."

He was standing on the corner of the street as patient as a shadow as David Chilton emerged from his front door right on time and began walking his cocker spaniel along the grass verge. It was 10:35 at night. David and Margaret would have been watching *News At Ten* and then *South East News* just as Gil and Margaret had always done. Then David would have taken down Bondy's leash, and whistled, "Come on, boy! Twice round the park!" while Margaret went into the kitchen to tidy up and make them some cocoa.

He was wearing the same black belted raincoat and the same black beret that he had worn in Amsterdam; only now he had mastered Anna's high heels. His hair was curly and well-brushed and he wore make-up now, carefully copied from an article in a Dutch magazine.

Under his raincoat he carried a stainless steel butcher knife with a twelve-inch blade. He was quite calm. He was breathing evenly and his pulse was no faster than it had been when he first met Anna.

Bondy insisted on sniffing at every bush and every garden gatepost, so it took a long time for David to come within earshot. He had his hands in his pockets and he was whistling under his breath, a tune that Gil

40

had never known. At last, Gil stepped out and said, "David?"

David Chilton stood stock-still. "Anna?" he asked, hoarsely.

Gil took another step forward, into the flat orange illumination of the streetlight. "Yes, David, it's Anna."

David Chilton took his hands out of his pockets. "I guess you had to come and take a look, didn't you? Well, I was the same."

Gil glanced toward the house. "Is he happy? Alan, I mean."

"Alan's fine. He's a fine boy. He looks just like you. I mean me."

"And Margaret?"

"Oh, Margaret's fine too. Just fine."

"She doesn't notice any difference?" said Gil, bitterly. "In bed, perhaps? I know I wasn't the world's greatest lover."

"Margaret's fine, really."

Gil was silent for a while. Then he said, "The job? How do you like the job?"

"Well, not too bad," grinned David Chilton. "But I have to admit that I'm looking around for something a little more demanding."

"But, apart from that, you've settled in well?"

"You could say that, yes. It's not Darien, but it's not Zandvoort, either."

Bondy had already disappeared into the darkness. David Chilton whistled a couple of times, and called, "Bondy! Bondy!" He turned to Gil and said, "Look – you know, I understand why you came. I really do. I sympathize. But I have to get after Bondy or Moo's going to give me hell."

For the very first time, Gil felt a sharp pang of genuine jealousy for Margaret. "You call her Moo?"

"Didn't you?" David Chilton asked him.

41

Gil remained where he was while David Chilton went jogging off after his dog. His eyes were wide with indecision. But David had only managed to run twenty or thirty yards before Gil suddenly drew out the butcher knife and went after him.

"David!" he called out, in his high, feminine voice. "David! Wait!"

David Chilton stopped and turned. Gil had been walking quickly so that he had almost reached him. Gil's arm went up. David Chilton obviously didn't understand what was happening at first, not until Gil stabbed him a second time, close to his neck.

David Chilton dropped, rolled away, then bobbed up on to his feet again. He looked as if he had been trained to fight. Gil came after him, his knife upraised, silent and angry beyond belief. *If I can't have my body, then nobody's going to. And perhaps if the man who took my body – if his spirit dies – perhaps I'll get my body back. There's no other hope, no other way. Not unless Anna goes on for generation after generation, taking one man after another.*

Gil screamed at David and stabbed at his face. But David seized Gil's wrist and twisted it around, skin tearing, so that Gil dropped the knife on to the pavement. Gil's high heel snapped. He lost his balance and they both fell. Their hands scrabbled for the knife. David touched it, missed it, then managed to take hold of it.

The long triangular blade rose and fell five times. There was a sound of muscle chopping. The two rolled away from each other, and lay side by side, flat on their backs, panting.

Gil could feel the blood soaking his cotton blouse. The inside of his stomach felt cold and very liquid, as if his stomach had poured its contents into his whole abdominal cavity. He knew that he couldn't move. He had felt the knife slice sharply against his spine.

David knelt up on one elbow. His hands and his face

42

were smeared in blood. *"Anna . . ."* he said, unsteadily. *"Anna . . ."*

Gil looked up at him. Already, he was finding it difficult to focus. "You've killed me," he said. "You've killed me. Don't you understand what you've done?"

David looked desperate. "You *know*, don't you? You *know*."

Gil attempted to smile. "I don't know, not for sure. But I can feel it. I can feel you – you and all the rest of them – right inside my head. I can hear your voices. I can feel your pain. I took your souls. I took your spirits. That's what you gave me, in exchange for your lust."

He coughed blood, and then he said, "My God . . . I wish I'd understood this before. Because you know what's going to happen now, don't you? You know what's going to happen now?"

David stared at him in dread. "Anna, listen, you're not going to die. Anna, listen, you can't. Just hold on, I'll call for an ambulance. But hold on!"

But Gil could see nothing but darkness. Gil could hear nothing but the gray sea. Gil was gone; and Anna was gone, too.

David Chilton made it as far as the garden gate. He grasped the post, gripped at the privet-hedge. He cried out, "Moo! Help me! For Christ's sake help me!" He grasped at his throat as if he were choking. Then he collapsed into the freshly-dug flower-bed, and lay there shuddering, the way an insect shudders when it is mortally hurt. The way any creature shudders, when it has no soul.

All over the world that night, men quaked and died. Over seven hundred of them: in hotels, in houses, in restaurants, in the back of taxis. A one-time German officer collapsed during dinner, his face blue, his head lying in his salad-plate, as if it were about to be served

43

up with an apple in his mouth. An airline pilot flying over Nebraska clung to his collar and managed to gargle out the name *Anna!* before he pitched forward on to his controls.

A 60-year-old Member of Parliament, making his way down the aisle in the House of Commons for the resumption of a late-night sitting, abruptly tumbled forward and lay between the Government and the Opposition benches, shuddering helplessly at the gradual onset of death.

On I-5 just south of San Clemente, California, a 55-year-old executive for a swimming-pool maintenance company died at the wheel of his Lincoln sedan. The car swerved from one side of the highway to the other before colliding into the side of a 7-Eleven truck, overturning, and fiercely catching fire.

Helplessly, four or five Mexicans who had been clearing the verges stood beside the highway and watched the man burn inside his car, not realizing that he was already dead.

The civic authorities buried Anna Huysmans at Zandvoort, not far from the sea. Her will had specified a polished black marble headstone, without decoration. It reflected the slowly-moving clouds as if it were a mirror. There were no relatives, no friends, no flowers. Only a single woman, dressed in black, watching from the cemetery boundary as if she had nothing to do with the funeral at all. She was very beautiful, this woman, even in black, with a veil over her face. A man who had come to lay flowers on the grave of his grandfather saw her standing alone, and watched her for a while.

She turned. He smiled.

She smiled back.

Laird of Dunain

Inverness, Scotland

The charming Scottish county town of Inverness is situated on the River Ness, at the head of the Caledonian Canal. It is calm and clear and peaceful in the summer, with the spires of St Mary's Church and the High Church reflected in the river, although you always feel a bracing sense of dramatic history when you walk its streets. Not far away, to the east, a cairn marks the spot where the hopes of Bonnie Prince Charlie were finally crushed at the Battle of Culloden in 1746. Over 1,200 Highlanders were killed around Leanach Cottage, which still stands today. Most were brought down by the English army's opening cannonade, and then by the English tactic of ignoring the charging Scotsman in front of him, and bayoneting the exposed side of the Scotsman to the right.

Laird of Dunain is dedicated to Ann Nicoll, of Dunain Park hotel and restaurant, on which the setting for this story is loosely based. If you haven't eaten Ann Nicoll's saddle of lamb in tawny port sauce; or her pigeon breast stuffed with pecan nuts and apples; then you don't deserve to be a carnivore, like the laird himself.

LAIRD OF DUNAIN

"The tailor fell thro' the bed, thimbles an' a'
"The blankets were thin and the sheets they were sma'
"The tailor fell thro' the bed, thimbles an' a'

Out onto the lawns in the first gilded mists of morning
came the Laird of Dunain in kilt and sporran and thick
oatmeal-colored sweater, his face pale and bony and
aesthetic, his beard red as a burning flame, his hair as
wild as a thistle-patch.

Archetypal Scotsman; the kind of Scotsman you saw on
tins of shortbread or bottles of single malt whisky. Except
that he looked so drawn and gaunt. Except that he looked
so spiritually hungry.

It was the first time that Claire had seen him since her
arrival, and she reached over and tapped Duncan's arm
with the end of her paintbrush and said, "Look, there he
is! Doesn't he look *fantastic?*"

All nine members of the painting class turned to stare
at the Laird as he fastidiously patroled the shingle path
that ran along the back of Dunain Castle. At first,
however, he appeared not to notice them, keeping his
hands behind his back and his head aloof, as if he
were breathing in the fine summer air, and surveying
his lands, and thinking the kind of things that Highland
lairds were supposed to think, like how many stags
to cull, and how to persuade the Highlands Devel-
opment Board to provide him with mains electricity.

"I wonder if he'd sit for us?" asked Margot, a rotund frizzy-haired girl from Liverpool. Margot had confessed to Claire that she had taken up painting because the smocks hid her hips.

"We could try asking him," Claire suggested – Claire with her straight dark bob and her serious well-structured face. Her husband, her *former* husband, had always said that she looked "like a sensual schoolmistress." Her painting smock and her Alice-band and her moon-round spectacles only heightened the impression.

"He's so *romantic*," said Margot. "Like Rob Roy. Or Bonnie Prince Charlie."

Duncan sorted through his box of watercolours until he found the half-burned nip-end of a cigarette. He lit it with a plastic lighter with a scratched transfer of a topless girl on it. "The trouble with painting in Scotland," he said, "is that *everything* looks so fucking romantic. You put your heart and your soul into painting Glenmoriston, and you end up with something that looks like a Woolworth's dinner-mat."

"I'd still like him to sit for us," said Margot.

The painting class had arranged their easels on the sloping south lawn of Dunain Castle, just above the stone-walled herb gardens. Beyond the herb gardens the grounds sloped grassy and gentle to the banks of the Caledonian Canal, where it cut its way between the north-eastern end of Loch Ness and the city of Inverness itself, and out to the Moray Firth. All through yesterday, the sailing-ships of the Tall Ships Race had been gliding through the canal, and they had appeared to be sailing surrealistically through fields and hedges, like ships in a dream, or a nightmare.

Mr Morrissey called out, "Pay particular attention to the light; because it's golden and very even just now; but it'll change."

Mr Morrissey (bald, round-shouldered, speedy, fussy)

was their course-instructor; the man who had greeted them when they first arrived at Dunain Castle, and who had showed them their rooms ("You'll *adore* this, Mrs Bright . . . such a view of the garden . . .") and who was now conducting their lessons in landscape-painting. In his way, he was very good. He knew how to sketch; he knew how to paint. He wouldn't tolerate sentimentality.

"You've not come to Scotland to paint The Monarch of the Glen," he had told them, when he had collected them from the station at Inverness. "You're here to paint life, and landscape, in light of unparalleled clarity."

Claire returned to her charcoal-sketching but she could see (our of the corner of her eye) that the Laird of Dunain was slowly making his way across the lawns. For some reason, she felt excited, and began to sketch more quickly and more erratically. Before she knew it, the Laird was standing only two or three feet away from her, his hands still clasped behind his back. His aura was prickly and electric, almost as if he were already running his thick ginger beard up her inner thighs.

"Well, well," he remarked, at last, in a strong Inverness accent. "You have all of the makings, I'd say. You're not one of Gordon's usual giglets."

Claire blushed, and found that she couldn't carry on sketching. Margot giggled.

"Hech," said the Laird, "I wasn't flethering. "You're good."

"Not really," said Claire. "I've only been painting for seven months."

The Laird stood closer. Claire could smell tweed and tobacco and heather and something else, something cloying and sweet, which she had never smelled before.

"You're good," he repeated. "You can draw well; and I'll lay money that ye can paint well. Mr Morrissey!"

Mr Morrissey looked up and his face was very white.

49

"Mr Morrissey, do you have any objection if I fetch this unback'd filly away from the class?"

Mr Morrissey looked dubious. "It's supposed to be landscape, this morning."

"Aye, but a wee bit of portraiture won't harm her now, will it? And I'm dying to have my portrait painted."

Very reluctantly, Mr Morrissey said, "No, I suppose it won't."

"That's settled, then," the Laird declared; and immediately began to fold up Claire's easel and tidy up her box of watercolours.

"Just a minute –" said Claire, almost laughing at his impertinence.

The Laird of Dunain stared at her with eyes that were green like emeralds crushed with a pestle-and-mortar. "I'm sorry," he said. "You don't *object*, do you?"

Claire couldn't stop herself from smiling. "No," she said. "I don't object."

"Well, then," said the Laird of Dunain, and led the way back to the castle.

"Hmph," said Margot, indignantly.

He posed in a dim upper room with dark oak paneling all around, and a high ceiling. The principal light came from a leaded clerestory window, falling almost like a spotlight. The Laird of Dunain sat on a large iron-bound trunk, his head held high, and managed to remain completely motionless while Claire began to sketch.

"You'll have come here looking for something else, apart from painting and drawing," he said, after a while.

Claire's charcoal-twig was quickly outlining his left shoulder. "Oh, yes?" she said. She couldn't think what he meant.

"You'll have come here looking for peace of mind, won't you, and a way to sort everything out?"

She thought, briefly, of Alan, and of Susan, and of

doors slamming. She thought of walking for miles through Shepherd's Bush, in the pouring April rain.

"That's what art's all about it, isn't it?" she retorted. "Sorting things out."

The Laird of Dunain smiled obliquely. "That's what my father used to say. In fact, my father believed it quite implicitly."

There was something about his tone of voice that stopped Claire from sketching for a moment. Something very serious; something *suggestive*; as if he were trying to tell her that his words had more than one meaning.

"I shall have to carry on with this tomorrow," she said.

The Laird of Dunain nodded. "That's all right. We have all the time in the world."

The next day, while the rest of the class took a minibus to Fort Augustus to paint the downstepping locks of the Caledonian Canal, Claire sat with the Laird of Dunain in his high gloomy room and started to paint his portrait. She used designer's colours, in preference to oils, because they were quicker; and she sensed that there was something mercurial in the Laird of Dunain which she wouldn't be capable of catching with oils.

"You're a very good sitter," she said, halfway through the morning. "Don't you want to take a break? Perhaps I could make some coffee."

The Laird of Dunain didn't break his rigid pose, even by an inch. "I'd rather get it finished, if you don't mind."

She carried on painting, squeezing out a half a tube of red. She was finding it difficult to give his face any colour. Normally, for faces, she used little more than a palette of yellow ochre, terra verte, alizarin crimson and cobalt blue. But no matter how much red she mixed into her colours, his face always seemed anemic – almost deathly.

"I'm finding it hard to get your flesh-tones right," she confessed, as the clock in the downstairs hallway struck two.

The Laird of Dunain nodded. "They always said of the Dunains of Dunain that they were a bloodless family. Mind you, I think we proved them wrong at Culloden. That was the day that the Laird of Dunain was caught and cornered by half-a-dozen of the Duke of Cumberland's soldiers, and cut about so bad that he stained a quarter of an acre with his own blood."

"That sounds awful," said Claire, squeezing out more alizarin crimson.

"It was a long time ago," replied the Laird of Dunain. "The sixteenth day of April, 1746. Almost two hundred and fifty years ago; and whose memory can span such a time?"

"You make it sound like yesterday," said Claire, busily mixing.

The Laird of Dunain turned his head away for the very first time that day. "On that day, when he lay bleeding, the laird swore that he would have his revenge on the English for every drop of blood that he had let. He would have it back, he said, a thousandfold; and then a thousandfold more.

"They never discovered his body, you know, although there were plenty of tales in the glens that it was hurried away by Dunains and Macduffs. That was partly the reason that the Duke of Cumberland pursued the Highlanders with such savagery. He made his own promise that he would never return to England until he had seen for himself the body of Dunain of Dunain, and fed it to the dogs."

"Savage times," Claire remarked. She sat back. The laird's face was still appallingly white, even though she had mixed his skin-tones with almost two whole tubes of crimson. She couldn't understand it. She ran her hand back through her hair and said, "I'll have to come back to this tomorrow."

"Of course," said the Laird of Dunain.

On her way to supper, she met Margot in the oak-panelled corridor. Margot was unexpectedly bustling and fierce. "You didn't come with us yesterday and you didn't come with us today. Today we sketched sheep."

"I've been –" Claire began, inclining her head toward the Laird of Dunain's apartments.

"Oh, yes," said Margot. "I thought as much. We *all* thought as much." And then she went off, with wig-wagging bottom.

Claire was amazed. But then she suddenly thought: *she's jealous. She's really jealous*.

All the next day while the Laird of Dunain sat composed and motionless in front of her, Claire struggled with her portrait. She used six tubes of light red and eight tubes of alizarin crimson, and still his face appeared as starkly white as ever.

She began to grow more and more desperate, but she refused to give up. In a strange way that she couldn't really understand, her painting was like a battlefield on which she and the Laird of Dunain were fighting a silent, deadly struggle. Perhaps she was doing nothing more than struggling with Alan, and all of the men who had treated her with such contempt.

Halfway through the afternoon, the light in the clerestory window gradually died, and it began to rain. She could hear the raindrops pattering on the roof and the gutters quietly gurgling.

"Are you sure you can see well enough?" asked the laird.

"I can see," she replied, doggedly squeezing out another glistening snake of red gouache.

"You could always give up," he said. His voice sounded almost sly.

"I can *see*," Claire insisted. "And I'll finish this bloody portrait if it kills me."

She picked up her scalpel to open the cellophane wrapping around another box of designers' colours.

"I'm sorry I'm such an awkward subject," smiled the laird. He sounded as if it quite amused him, to be awkward.

"Art always has to be a challenge," Claire retorted. She was still struggling to open the new box of paints. Without warning, there was a devastating bellow of thunder, so close to the castle roof that Claire felt the rafters shake. Her hand slipped on the box and the scalpel sliced into the top of her finger.

"Ow!" she cried, dropping the box and squeezing her finger. Blood dripped onto the painting, one quick drop after another.

"Is anything wrong?" asked the laird, although he didn't make any attempt to move from his seat.

Claire winced, watching the blood well up. She was about to tell him that she had cut herself and that she wouldn't be able to continue painting when she saw that her blood had mingled with the wet paint on the laird's face *and had suffused it with an unnaturally healthy flush.*

"You've not hurt yourself, have you?" asked the laird.

"Oh, no," said Claire. She squeezed out more blood, and began to mix it with her paintbrush. Gradually the laird's face began to look rosier, and much more alive. "I'm fine, I'm absolutely fine." Thinking to herself: *now I've got you, you sly bastard. Now I'll show you how well I can paint. I'll catch you here for ever and ever; the way that I saw you; the way that I want you to be.*

The laird held his pose and said nothing, but watched her with a curious expression of satisfaction and contentedness, like a man who has tasted a particularly fine wine. That night, in her room overlooking the grounds, Claire dreamed of men in ragged cloaks and feathered bonnets; men with gaunt faces and hollow eyes. She dreamed of smoke and blood and screaming. She heard a sharp, aggressive rattle of drums – drums that pursued her through one dream and into another.

When she woke up, it was still only five o'clock in the morning, and raining, and the window-catch was rattling and rattling in time to the drums in her dreams.

She dressed in jeans and a blue plaid blouse, and then she quiet-footedly climbed the stairs to the room where she was painting the laird's portrait. Somehow she knew what she was going to find, but she was still shocked.

The portrait was as white-faced as it had been before she had mixed the paint with her own blood. Whiter, if anything. His whole expression seemed to have changed, too, to a glare of silent emaciated fury.

Claire stared at the portrait in horror and fascination. Then, slowly, she sat down, and opened up her paintbox, and began to mix a flesh tone. Flake white, red and yellow ochre. When it was ready, she picked up her scalpel, and held her wrist over her palette. She hesitated for only a moment. The Laird of Dunain was glaring at her too angrily; too resentfully. She wasn't going to let a man like him get the better of her.

She slit her wrist in a long diagonal, and blood instantly pumped from her artery onto the palette, almost drowning the watercolours in rich and sticky red.

When the palette was flooded with blood, she bound her paint-rag around her wrist as tightly as she could, and gripped it with her teeth while she knotted it. Trembling, breathless, she began to mix blood and gouache, and then she began to paint.

She worked with her brush for almost an hour, but as fast

as she applied the mixture of blood and paint, the faster it seemed to drain from the laird's chalk-white face.

At last – almost hysterical with frustration – she sat back and dropped her brush. The laird stared back at her – mocking, accusing, belittling her talent and her womanhood. Just like Alan. Just like every other man. You gave them everything and they still treated you with complete contempt.

But not this time. Not this time. She stood up, and unbuttoned her blouse, so that she confronted the portrait of the Laird of Dunain bare-breasted. Then she picked up her scalpel in her fist, so that the point pricked the plump pale flesh just below her navel.

"The sleepy bit lassie, she dreaded nae ill; the weather was cauld and the lassie lay still. She thought that the tailor could do her no ill."

She cut into her stomach. Her hand was shaking but she was calm and deliberate. She cut through skin and layers of white fat and deeper still, until her intestines exhaled a deep sweet breath. She was disappointed by the lack of blood. She had imagined that she would bleed like a pig. Instead, her wound simply glistened, and yellowish fluid flowed.

"There's somebody weary wi' lying her lane; there's some that are dowie, I trow wad be fain . . . to see that bit tailor come skippin' again."

Claire sliced upward, right up to her breastbone, and the scalpel was so sharp that it became lodged in her rib. She tugged it out, and the tugging sensation was worse than the pain. She wanted the blood, but she hadn't thought that it would hurt so much. The pain was as devastating as the thunderclap had been, overwhelming. She thought about screaming but she wasn't sure that it would do any good; and she had forgotten how.

With bloodied hands she reached inside her sliced-open stomach and grasped all the hot slippery heavy things she found there. She heaved them out, all over her painting of the Laird of Dunain, and wiped them around, and wiped them around, until the art-board was smothered in blood, and the portrait of the laird was almost completely obscured.

Then she pitched sideways, knocking her head against the oak-boarded floor. The light from the clerestory window brightened and faded, brightened and faded, and then faded away forever.

They took her to the Riverside Medical Centre but she was already dead. Massive trauma, loss of blood. Duncan stood in the car-park furiously smoking a cigarette and clutching himself. Margot sat on the leatherette seats in the waiting-room and wept.

They drove back to Dunain Castle. The laird was standing on the back lawn, watching the light play across the valley.

"She's dead, then?" he said, as Margot came marching up to him. "A grousome thing, no doubt about it."

Margot didn't know what to say to him. She could only stand in front of him and quake with anger. He seemed so self-satisfied, so calm, so pleased; like the cat who has swallowed the last dollop of cream.

"Look," said the Laird of Dunain, pointing up to the birds that were circling overhead. "The hoodie-craws. They always know when there's a death."

Margot stormed up to the room where – only two hours ago – she had found Claire dying. It was bright as a church. And there on its board was the portrait of the Laird of Dunain, shining and clean, without a single smear of blood on it. The smiling, triumphant, rosy-cheeked Laird of Dunain.

"Self-opinionated chauvinist sod," she said, and she seized the art-board and ripped it in half, top to bottom.

Out of temper. Out of enraged feminism. But, more than anything else, out of jealousy. Why had *she* never met a man that she would kill herself for?

And out in the garden, on the sloping lawns, the painting class heard a scream. It was a scream so echoing and terrible that they could scarcely believe that it had been uttered by one man.

In front of their eyes, the Laird of Dunain literally burst apart. His face exploded, his jawbone dropped out, his chest came bursting through his sweater in a crush of ribs and a bucketful of blood. There was so much blood that it sprayed up the walls of Dunain Castle, and ran down the windows.

They sat, open-mouthed, their paintbrushes poised, while he dropped onto the gravel path, and twitched, and lay still, while blood ran down everywhere, and the hoodie-craws circled and cried and cried again, because they always knew when there was a death.

"Gie me the groat again, canny young man; the day it is short and the night it is lang; the dearest siller that ever I wan.

"The tailor fell thro' the bed, thimbles an' a'."

Ever, Ever After

New York, New York

The locale of *Ever, Ever After* is Central Park South, which has always fascinated me because of its history. Walking along it now, it's almost impossible to conceive that until as recently as the 1860s it was one of the ugliest and least desirable areas on Manhattan – a swash of garbage dumps, shantytowns and decrepit taverns, all punctuated by slabby outcroppings of rock. As the *Herald* said in the 1850s, "these things all looked bad, and some of them smelt bad." Only with millions of dollars and thousands of laborers was the park transformed by Frederick Law Olmsted and Calvert Vaux into what it is today. Even if you're not very well-heeled, you can still enjoy the foyer and the Palm Court of the Plaza Hotel; and there are few pleasures that better improve a snappy Sunday morning than a hot toddy in the Oak Bar and a walk in the park. Maybe the "poverty, misery, beggary, starvation, crimes, filth and licentiousness" that was rife in the 1850s has been replaced by "swank, perfume and a view that costs a thousand dollars a square inch", but I could still conceive of something unsettling happening here . . .

EVER, EVER AFTER

The road was greasy; the light was poor; and the truck's braking-lights were caked in dirt. Robbie saw it pull up ahead of him only ten feet too late; but those ten feet were enough to send a scaffolding-pole smashing through the windshield of his Porsche and straight into his chest.

The medical examiner told me that he never would have known what hit him. "I'm truly sorry, Mr Deacon; but he never would have known what hit him." Instant death; painless.

Painless, that is, to Robbie. But not to Jill; and not to me; and not to anybody who had known him. Jill was his wife of thirteen weeks; and I was his brother of 31 years; and his humor and vivacity had won him more friends than you could count.

For a whole month afterward I kept his photograph on my desk. Broad-faced, five years younger than me, much more like Dad than I was; laughing at some long-forgotten joke. Then one morning in early October I came into the office and put the photograph away in my middle desk-drawer. It was then that I knew it was over; that he was really gone for ever.

That same afternoon, as if she had been affected by the same feeling of finality, Jill called me. "David? Can I meet you after work? I feel like talking."

She was waiting for me in the lobby, at the Avenue of the Americas entrance. Already the sidewalks were crowded with homegoing workers; and there wasn't a chance of finding a cab. The air was frosty, and sharp with the smell of bagels and chestnuts.

She looked pale and tired, but just as beautiful as ever. She had a Polish mother and a Swedish father, and she had inherited the chiseled face of one and the snow-white blondness of the other. She was tall, almost five feet nine, although her dark mink coat concealed most of her figure, just as her dark mink hat concealed most of her face.

She kissed me. She smelled of Joy, and cold October streets.

"I'm so glad you could come. I think I'm beginning to go mad."

"Well, I know the feeling," I told her. "Every day, when I wake up, I have to remind myself that he's dead; and that I'm never going to see him again, ever."

We went into the Brew Burger across the street for a drink. Jill ordered tomato-juice; I ordered Four Roses, straight up. We sat by the window while torrents of people passed us by.

"That's my trouble," Jill told me, picking at her freshly-lacquered fingernails. "I'm sad; I keep crying; but I can't really believe that he's dead."

I sipped my whiskey. "Do you know what he and I used to play when we were younger? We used to pretend that we were wizards, and that we were both going to live for ever. We even made up a spell."

Jill stared at me; and her her wide gray-green eyes were glistening with tears. "He was always full of dreams. Perhaps he went the best way, without even knowing what was going to happen."

"*Immortooty, immortaty – ever, ever after!*" I recited. "That was the spell. We always used to recite it when we scared."

"I loved him, you know," Jill whispered.

I finished my whiskey. "Haven't you talked about it with anybody else?"

She shook her head. "You know my family. They practically disowned me when I started dating Robbie, because he was still married to Sara. It was no use my telling them that he and Sara were already on the rocks; and that he despised her; and that they would have been divorced anyway, even if I hadn't shown up on the scene. Oh, no, it was all my fault. I broke up a healthy marriage. I was the scarlet woman."

"If it's any consolation," I told her, "I don't think you're scarlet at all. I never saw Robbie so happy as when he was with you."

I walked her back to her apartment on Central Park South. Thunder echoed from the skyscrapers all along Sixth Avenue; flags flapped; and it was beginning to rain. In spite of the swanky address, the flat that Jill and Robbie had shared together was very small, and sublet from a corporate lawyer called Willey, who was away in Minnesota for most of the time, something to do with aluminum tubing.

"Won't you come up?" she asked me, in the brightly-lit entrance lobby, which was graced with a smart black doorman in a mushroom-colored uniform, and a tall vase of orange gladioli.

"I don't think so," I told her. "I have a heap of work to finish up at home."

There were mirrors all around us. There were fifty Jills, curving off into infinity, fifty doormen, and fifty mes. A thousand spears of gladioli.

"You're sure?" she persisted.

I shook my head. "What for? Coffee? Whiskey? More breast-beating? There was nothing we could have done to save him, Jill. You took care of him like a baby. I just loved him like a brother. There was no way that either of us could have saved him."

"But to die that way. So quickly; and for no reason."

I grasped her hand. "I don't believe everything has to have a reason."

The doorman was holding the elevator for her. She lifted her face to me, and I realized that she expected me to kiss her. So I kissed her; and her cheek was soft and cold from walking in the wind; and somehow something happened between us that made both of us stand for a moment looking at each other, eyes searching, not speaking.

"I'll call you," I told her. "Maybe dinner?"

"I'd like that."

That was how our affair began. Talking, to begin with; and spending weekends together with a bottle of California chardonnay; listening to Mendelssohn's violin concertos; while Christmas approached, our first Christmas without Robbie.

I bought Jill a silver Alfred Durante cuff watch and a leather-bound book of poems by John Keats. I left a silk marker in the page which said,

"*Love! Thou art leading me from wintry cold,*
Lady! Thou leadest me to summer clime."

She cooked wild duck for me on Christmas Day, and Robbie's photograph watched us smiling from the chiffonier while we drank each other's health in Krug champagne.

I took her to bed. The white wintry light arranged itself across the sheets like a paper dress-pattern. She was very slim, narrow-hipped, and her skin was as smooth as cream. She didn't speak; her hair covered her face like a golden mask. I kissed her lips, and her neck. Her oyster-colored silk panties had tucked themselves into a tight crease between her legs.

Afterwards we lay back in the gathering twilight and listened to the soft crackle of bubbles in our champagne, and the sirens of Christmas echoing across Central Park.

"Are you going to ask me to marry you?" said Jill.

I nodded.

"It's not against the law or anything, is it? For a widow to marry her late husband's brother."

"Of course not. In Deuteronomy, widows are *ordered* to marry their late husband's brothers."

"You don't think Robbie would have minded?"

"No," I said, and turned over to pick up my glass, and there he was, still smiling at me. *Immortooty, Immortaty, ever, ever after.*

Robbie, in Paradise, may have approved, but our families certainly didn't. We were married in Providence, Rhode Island, on a sharp windy day the following March, with nobody in attendance but a justice of the peace and two witnesses whom we had rounded up from the local bookstore, and a gray-haired old lady who played the wedding march and *Scenes from Childhood*.

Jill wore a cream tailored suit and a wide-brimmed hat with ribbons around it and looked stunning. The old lady played and smiled and the spring sunshine reflected from her spectacles like polished pennies on the eyes of an ivory-faced corpse.

On our wedding night I woke up in the early hours of the morning and Jill was quietly crying. I didn't let her know that I was awake. She was entitled to her grief; and I couldn't be jealous of Robbie, now that he had been dead for over a year.

But I lay and watched her; knowing that by marrying me she had at last acknowledged that Robbie was gone. She wept for almost twenty minutes, and then leaned across and kissed my shoulder, and fell asleep, with her hair tangled across my arm.

Our marriage was cheerful and well-organized. Jill left her apartment on Central Park South and moved in to my big airy loft on 17th Street. We had plenty of money: Jill worked as a creative director for Palmer Ziegler Palmer, the advertising agency, and in those days I was an accountant for Henry Sparrow the publishers. Every weekend we compared Filofaxes and fitted as much leisure time together as we could; even if it was only a lunchtime sandwich at Stars on Lexington Avenue, or a cup of coffee at Bloomingdale's.

Jill was pretty and smart and full of sparkle and I loved her more every day. I suppose you could have criticized us for being stereotypes of the Perrier-water generation, but most of the time we didn't take ourselves too seriously. In July I traded in my old BMW for a Jaguar XJS convertible in British racing green, and we drove up to Connecticut almost every weekend, a hundred and ten miles an hour on the turnpike, with Beethoven on the stereo at top volume.

Mega-pretentious, *n'est-ce pas*? but it was just about the best fun I ever had in my whole life.

On the last day of July, as we were sitting on the old colonial verandah of the Allen's Corners hotel where we used to stay whenever we weekended in Connecticut, Jill leaned back in her basketwork chair and said dreamily, "Some days ought to last for ever."

I clinked the ice in my vodka-and-tonic. "This one should."

It was dreamily warm, with just the lightest touch of breeze. It was hard to imagine that we were less than two hours' driving from downtown Manhattan. I closed my eyes and listened to the birds warbling and the bees humming and the sounds of a peaceful Connecticut summer.

"Did I tell you I had a call from Willey on Friday?" Jill remarked.

I opened one eye. "Mr Willey, your old landlord? What did he want?"

"He says I left some books round at the apartment, that's all. I'll go collect them tomorrow."

"Don't mention tomorrow. I'm still in love with today."

"He said he hasn't re-let the apartment yet, because he can't find another tenant as beautiful as me."

I laughed. "Is that bullshit or is that bullshit?"

"It's neither," She said. "It's pure flattery."

"I'm jealous," I told her.

She kissed me. "You can't possibly be jealous of Willey. He's about seventy years old, and he looks just like a koala bear with eyeglasses."

She looked at me seriously. "Besides," she added, "I don't love anybody else but you; and I never will."

It thundered the following day; and the streets of New York were humid and dark and strewn with broken umbrellas. I didn't see Jill that lunchtime because I had to meet my lawyer Morton Jankowski (very droll, Morton, with a good line in Polish jokes); but I had promised to cook her my famous *pesce spada al salmoriglio* for dinner.

I walked home with a newspaper over my head. There was no chance of catching a cab midtown at five o'clock on a wet Monday afternoon. I bought the swordfish and a bottle of Orvieto at the Italian market on the corner, and then walked back along 17th Street, humming Verdi to myself. Told you I was mega-pretentious.

Jill left the office a half-hour earlier than I did, so I expected to find her already back at the loft; but to my surprise she wasn't there. I switched on the lights in the sparse, tasteful sitting-room; and then went through to the bedroom to change into something dry.

By six-thirty she still wasn't back. It was almost dark outside, and the thunder banged and echoed relentlessly. I called her office, but everybody had left for the day. I sat in the kitchen in my striped cook's apron, watching the news and drinking the wine. There wasn't any point in starting dinner until Jill came home.

By seven I was growing worried. Even if she hadn't managed to catch a cab, she could have walked home by now. And she had never come home late without phoning me first. I called her friend Amy, in SoHo. Amy wasn't there but her loopy boyfriend said she was over at her mother's place, and Jill certainly wasn't with her.

At last, at a quarter after eight, I heard the key turn in the door and Jill came in. The shoulders of her coat were dark with rain, and she looked white-faced and very tired.

"Where the hell have you been?" I demanded. "I've been worried bananas."

"I'm sorry," she said, in a muffled voice, and hung up her coat.

"What happened? Did you have to work late?"

She frowned at me. Her blonde fringe was pasted wetly to her forehead. "I've said I'm sorry! What is this, the third degree?"

"I was concerned about you, that's all."

She stalked through to the bedroom, with me following close behind her. "I managed to survive in New York before I met you," she said. "I'm not a child any more, you know."

"I didn't say you were. I said I was concerned, that's all."

She was unbuttoning her blouse. "Will you just get the hell out and let me change!"

"I want to know where you've been!" I demanded.

Without hesitation, she slammed the bedroom door in my face, and when I tried to catch the handle, she turned the key.

"Jill!" I shouted. "Jill! What the hell is going on?"

She didn't answer. I stood outside the bedroom door for a while, wondering what had upset her so much; then

I went back to the kitchen and reluctantly started to cook dinner.

"Don't do any for me!" she called out, as I started to chop up the onions.

"Did you eat already?" I asked her, with the knife poised in my hand.

"I said, don't do any for me, that's all!"

"But you have to eat!"

She wrenched open the bedroom door. Her hair was combed back, and she was wrapped in her toweling bathrobe. "What are you, my mother or something?" she snapped at me. Then she slammed the door shut again.

I stabbed the knife into the butcher-block and untied my apron. I was angry now. "Listen!" I shouted. "I bought the wine, and the swordfish, and everything! And you come home two hours late and all you can do is yell at me!"

She opened up the bedroom door again. "I went to Mr Willey's, that's all. Now, are you satisfied?"

"So you went to Willey's place? And what were you supposed to be doing at Willey's place? Collecting your books, if my memory serves me. So where are they, these precious books? Did you leave them in the cab?"

Jill stared at me and there was an expression in her eyes that I had never seen before. Pale, cold, yet almost *shocked*, as if she had been involved in an accident, and her mind was still numb.

"Jill . . ." I said, more softly this time, and took two or three steps towards her.

"No," she whispered. "Not now. I want to be alone for just a while."

I waited until eleven o'clock, occasionally tapping at the bedroom door, but she refused to answer. I just didn't know what the hell to do. Yesterday had been idyllic; today had turned into some kind of knotty, nasty conundrum. I put on my raincoat and shouted through the bedroom door that I was going down to the Bells of Hell for a drink. Still she didn't answer.

My friend Norman said that women weren't humans at all, but a race of aliens who had been landed on earth to keep humans company.

"Imagine it," he said, lighting a cigarette and blowing out smoke. "If you had never seen a woman before tonight, and you walked out of here and a woman was standing there . . . wearing a dress, with blonde hair, and red lipstick, and high-heel shoes . . . and you had never seen a woman before – then, *then*, my friend, you would understand that you had just made a close encounter of the worst kind."

I finished up my vodka, and dropped a twenty on the counter. "Keep the cha-a-ange, my man," I told the barkeep, with a magnanimous W.C. Fieldsian wave of my hand.

"Sir, there is no change. That'll be three dollars and seventy-five cents more."

"That's inflation for you," Norman remarked, with a phlegmy cough. "Even oblivion is pricing itself out of the market."

I left the bar and walked back up to 17th Street. It was unexpectedly cool for July. My footsteps echoed like the footsteps of some lonely man in some 1960s spy movie. I wasn't sober but I wasn't drunk, either. I wasn't very much looking forward to returning home.

When I let myself in, the loft was in darkness. Jill had unlocked the bedroom door, but when I eased it open, and looked inside, she was asleep. She had her back to me, and the quilt drawn up to her shoulders, but even in the darkness I could see that she was wearing her pajamas. Pajamas meant we're not talking, stay away.

I went into the kitchen and poured myself the dregs from a chilled bottle of Chablis, and switched the television on low. It was a 1940s black-and-white movie called *They Stole Hitler's Brain*. I didn't want to sit there watching it; and at the same time I didn't want to go to bed either.

At a little after two, however, the bedroom door opened and Jill was standing there pale and puffy-eyed.

"Are you coming to bed?" she asked, in a clogged-up whisper. "You have work tomorrow."

I looked at her for a long time with my lips puckered tight. Then I said, "Sure," and stood up, and switched off the television.

In the morning, Jill brought me coffee and left my Swiss muesli out for me, and kissed me on the cheek before she left for the agency, but there were no explanations for what had happened the previous evening. The only words she spoke were, "Good morning," and, "Goodbye."

I called, "Jill?" but the only response I got was the loft door closing behind her.

I went to the office late and I brooded about it all morning. Around eleven-thirty I telephoned Jill's secretary and asked if Jill were free for lunch.

"No, Mr Deacon, I'm sorry. She had a last-minute appointment."

"Do you happen to know where?"

"Hold on, I'll check her Filofax. Yes . . . here it is. One o'clock. No name, I'm afraid. No address, either. It just says 'Apt.'"

"All right, Louise, thank you."

I put down the phone and sat for a long time with my hand across my mouth, thinking. My assistant Fred Ruggiero came into my office and stared at me.

"What's the matter? You look like you're sick."

"No, I was thinking. What does the word 'apt' mean to you?"

Fred scratched the back of his neck. 'I guess it means

like 'appropriate,' you know. Or 'fitting.' Or 'suitable.' You doing a crossword?"

"No. I don't know. Sheila!"

One of our younger secretaries was bouncing along the corridor in beaded dreadlocks and a shocking-pink blouse. "Yes, Mr Deacon?"

I wrote 'apt' on my notepad and showed it to her. "Does that mean anything to you?"

She grinned. "Is this a trick? If you'd been looking for someplace to rent as long as I have, you'd know what that meant."

"What do you mean?"

"Apt. Don't you read the classifieds? Apt equals apartment."

Apartment. And whenever Jill mentioned "apartment", she meant one apartment in particular. Willey's apartment.

Fred and Sheila stared at me. Fred ventured, "Are you okay? You look kind of glassy if you don't mind my saying so."

I coughed, and nodded. "I guess I do feel a little logie."

"Hope you haven't stopped a dose of the Sichuan 'flu," Sheila remarked. "My cousin had it, said it was like being hit by a truck."

She suddenly realized what she had said. Everybody in the office knew how Robbie had died. "Oh, I'm sorry," she said. "That was truly dumb." But I was too busy thinking about Jill round at Willey's apartment to care.

It was still raining; a steady drenching drizzle; but I went out all the same. All right, I told myself, I'm suspicious. I have no justification; I have no evidence; and most of all I have no moral right. Jill made a solemn promise when she married me; to have and to hold, from this day forth.

A promise was a promise, and it wasn't up to me to police her comings and goings, in order to make sure that she kept it.

Yet here I was, standing on the corner of Central Park South and the Avenue of the Americas, the shoulders of my Burberry dark with rain, waiting for Jill to emerge from her apartment building, so that I could prove that she was cheating on me.

I waited over half an hour. Then, quite suddenly, Jill appeared, in the company of a tall dark-haired man in a blue raincoat. Jill immediately hailed a passing taxi, and climbed into it, but the man began to walk at a brisk pace toward Columbus Circle, turning his collar up as he did so.

I hesitated for a moment, and then I went after him.

He turned south on Seventh Avenue, still walking fast. The sidewalks were crowded, and I had a hard time keeping up with him. He crossed 57th St just as the lights changed, and I found myself dodging buses and taxis and trying not to lose sight of him at the same time. At last, a few yards short of Broadway, I caught up with him. I snatched at his sleeve and said, "Hey, fellow. Pardon me."

He turned to stare at me. He was olive-skinned, almost Italian-looking. Quite handsome if you had a taste for Latins.

He said nothing, but turned away again. He must have thought that I was excusing myself for having accidentally caught at his raincoat. I grabbed him again, and said, "Hey! Pardon me! I want to talk to you!"

He stopped. "What is this?" he demanded. "Are you hustling me, or what?"

"Jill Deacon," I replied, my voice shaking a little.

"What?" he frowned.

"You know what I'm talking about," I replied. "I'm her husband."

"So? Congratulations."

"You were with her just now."

The man smiled in exasperation. "I said hallo to her in the lobby, if that's what you mean."

73

"You know her?"

"Well, sure. I live along the hall. I've known her ever since she moved in. We say good morning and good evening in the lobby, and that's it."

He was telling the truth. I knew damn well he was telling the truth. Nobody stands there smiling at you at a busy intersection in the pouring rain and tells you lies.

"I'm sorry," I told him. "I guess it was a case of mistaken identity."

"Take some advice, fellow," the man replied. "Lighten up a bit, you know?"

I went back to the office feeling small and neurotic and jerkish; like a humorless Woody Allen. I sat at my desk staring at a heap of unpaid accounts and Fred and Sheila left me very well alone. At four o'clock I gave up, and left, and took a cab down to the Bells of Hell for a drink.

"You look like shit," Norman told me.

I nodded in agreement. "Alien trouble," I replied.

Maybe my suspicions about the Latin-looking man had been unfounded, but Jill remained irritable and remote, and there was no doubt that something had come adrift in our marriage, although I couldn't quite work out what.

We didn't make love all week. When I tried to put my arm around her in bed, she sighed testily and squirmed away. And whenever I tried to talk to her about it, she went blank or scratchy or both.

She came home well after ten o'clock on Friday evening without any explanation about why she was late. When I asked her if everything was all right, she said she was tired, and to leave her alone. She showered and went straight to bed; and when I looked in at the bedroom door only twenty minutes later, she was fast asleep.

I went to the bathroom and wearily stripped off my shirt. In the laundry basket lay Jill's discarded panties. I hesitated for a moment, then I picked them out and

74

held them up. They were still soaked with another man's semen.

I suppose I could have been angry. I could have dragged her out of bed and slapped her around and shouted at her. But what was the use? I went into the sitting-room and poured myself a large glass of Chablis and sat disconsolately watching Jackie Gleason with the volume turned down. *The Honeymooners*, blurred with tears.

Maybe the simple truth was that she had married me because I was Robbie's brother; because she had hoped in some distracted and irrational way that I would somehow become the husband she had lost. I knew that she had been nuts about him, I mean truly nuts. Maybe she hadn't really gotten over the shock. Robbie would live for ever; at least as far as Jill was concerned.

Maybe she was punishing me now for not being him. Or maybe she was punishing *him* for dying.

Whatever the reason, she was cheating on me, without making any serious effort to hide it. She might just as well have invited her lover into our bed with us.

There was no question about it: our marriage was over, even before it had started. I sat in front of the television with the tears streaming down my cheeks and I felt like curling myself up into a ball and going to sleep and never waking up.

You can't cry for ever, however; and after about an hour of utter misery I wiped my eyes on my sleeve and finished my glass of wine and thought: right, okay. I'm not giving Jill up without a fight. I'm going to find out who this bum is who she's been sleeping with, and I'm going to confront him, face to face. She can choose between him and me, but she's going to have to do it right out in front of us, no sneaking, no hiding, no hypocrisy.

I went to the bedroom and opened the door and Jill was lying asleep with her mouth slightly parted. She was

75

still beautiful. I still loved her. And the pain of still loving her twisted inside me like a corkscrew.

I hope you live for ever, I thought to myself. I hope you live to know how much you've hurt me. Immortooty, immortaty. Ever, ever, after.

On the dressing-table her key ring lay sprawled. I looked at it for a long moment, then quietly picked it up.

Next day it was windy and bright. I sat in the coffee shop opposite Jill's agency building, drinking too much coffee and trying to chew a bagel that tasted of nothing but cream cheese and bitterness. At a few minutes after twelve, I saw Jill march smartly out of the front of the building, and lift her arm to call a taxi. Immediately I ducked out of the coffee shop, and called another taxi.

"Follow that cab," I told the driver. He was a thin Puerto Rican boy with beads round his neck and a black straggly mustache.

"Wheesh cab?" he wanted to know.

"That Checker, follow that Checker."

"You thin this some kinda movie or somethin? I aint follnin nuttn."

I pushed a crumpled-up fifty into his hand. "Just follow that Checker, okay?"

"Whatever you say man. Your fewnral."

As it turned out, I paid fifty dollars plus the fare to follow Jill back to Willey's apartment on Central Park South, where I should have known she was going anyway. The Puerto Rican boy saw Jill climb out of the cab ahead of us. Those long black-stockinged legs, that smart black-and-white suit. "Hey man she's *worth* fifty, that one. She's worth a hundud."

Jill walked without hesitation into the apartment building. I allowed her five clear minutes, pacing up and down on the sidewalk, watched with stony-eyed curiosity by an old man selling balloons. Then I went into

76

the building after her, through the lobby to the elevators.

"You're looking for somebody, sir?" the black doorman wanted to know.

"My wife, Mrs Deacon. She arrived here just a few minutes ago."

"Oh, sure," the doorman nodded. "You go on up."

I went upward in the small gold-mirrored elevator with my heart beating against my ribcage like a fist. I could see my reflection, and the strange thing was that I looked quite normal. Pale-faced, tired, but quite rational. I certainly didn't look like a husband trying to surprise his wife *in flagrante* with another man. But then who does? People die with the strangest expressions on their faces. Smiles, scowls, looks of total surprise.

I reached the third floor and stepped out. The corridor was overheated and silent and smelled of lavender polish. I hesitated for a moment, holding the doors of the elevator open. Then I let them go; and they closed with a whine, and the elevator carried on upward.

What the hell am I going to say, if I actually find her with somebody? I thought to myself. *Supposing they turn around and laugh at me, what can I possibly do then?*

Reason told me that I should walk away – that if I was sure that Jill was cheating on me, I should call a lawyer and arrange a divorce. But it wasn't as simple as that. My ego was large enough to want to see what dazzling hero could possibly have attracted Jill away from me, after such a short marriage. Such a passionate marriage, too. If I was lacking in any way, I wanted to know why.

I reached the door with the name-card which read *Willey*. I pressed my ear against the door and listened; and after a moment or two I was sure that I could hear voices. Jill's, high-pitched, pleading. And a deeper voice; a man's voice. The voice of her lover, no less.

I took out the extra key which they had made for me

at American Key & Lock the previous evening. I licked my lips, and took a deep breath, and then I slid it into the door. I turned it, and the door opened.

You can still go back. You don't have to face this if you don't want to. But I knew that it was too late; and that my curiosity was overwhelming.

I quietly closed the door behind me and stood in the hallway listening. On the wall beside me were framed Deccan paintings of the 18th century, showing women having intercourse with stallions. Highly appropriate, I thought. And sickening, too. Maybe Jill *was* having an affair with Willey, after all. He seemed to have a pretty libidinous turn of mind.

I heard murmurings from the bedroom. The door was slightly ajar, and I could see sunlight and pale blue carpet. The sheets rustled. Jill said, "You're marvelous; you're magic; if only I'd known."

God, I thought, *I shouldn't have come. This is almost more than I can stand. And what am I going to look like if they discover me? A creeping cuckold; a jealous husband who couldn't satisfy his wife.*

"Promise me," said Jill. "Promise me you'll never leave me."

The man said something indistinct.

"All right," Jill replied, with tart satisfaction. "In that case – I'll get the champagne out of the icebox, and we'll – "

I hadn't realized, listening to her talking, that she had climbed out of bed, and crossed the bedroom floor. She opened the door, naked, flushed in the face, and caught me, standing in the hall.

"Oh my God!" she exclaimed. The color emptied out of her face like ink spilled from a bottle.

Without a word, I pushed past her, and threw open the bedroom door.

"All right, you bastard!" I roared, in a voice so hoarse

that it was almost insane. "Get up, and get dressed, and get the fuck out!"

The man on the bed turned, and stared at me; and then I froze.

He was very pale. He was almost gray. His eyes had a stony far-away look that was more like a statue than a man. He was naked, his gray penis still glistened from sex. His chest was bound tightly with wide white bandages.

"Robbie," I whispered.

He drew the sheet right up to his neck, but he didn't take his eyes away from me once.

"*Robbie?*" I repeated.

"That's right," he nodded. "I was hoping you wouldn't find out."

When he spoke, his words came out in a labored whisper. *Massive chest injuries*, that's what the doctors had told me. *He didn't feel a thing.*

I managed one mechanical step forward. Robbie continued to stare at me. He was dead; and yet here he was, staring at me. I had never been so frightened of anything in my entire life.

"What happened?" I asked him. "They told us you were killed instantly. That's what the doctors said. Don't worry, he didn't feel a thing. He was killed instantly."

Robbie managed a tight, reflective smile. "It's the words, George. They work!"

"Words?" I demanded. "What words?"

"Don't you remember? *Immortooty, immortaty, ever, ever after.* I saw the truck coming toward me and I shouted them out. The next thing I knew, it was dark, and I was buried alive."

He raised his hand, and turned it this way and that, frowning at it, as if it didn't really belong to him. "I don't know, maybe 'alive' is the wrong word. Immortal, sure. I'm immortal. I'm going to live for ever, whatever that means."

"You got out of your casket?" I asked him, in disbelief. "It was solid Cuban mahogany."

"The one you paid for might have been solid Cuban mahogany. The one I kicked my way out of was pine, tacked together with two-inch nails." He gave me a grim smile. "You should sue your mortician. Or then again, maybe you shouldn't."

"Jesus." I was trembling. I couldn't believe it was him. But it was really him. My own brother, gray-faced and dead, but still alive.

"Jill!" I shouted. "Jill!"

Jill came back into the room, wrapped in a red toweling robe.

"Why didn't you tell me?" I asked her, in a whisper, although I couldn't stop myself from staring at Robbie. He remained where he was, wrapped in his sheet, his eyes fixed on me with an expression that was as cold as glass. God Almighty, he *looked* dead, he *looked* like a corpse. How could Jill have – ?

"I love him," Jill told me, her voice small and quiet.

"You love him?" I quaked. "Jill, he's dead!"

"I love him," she repeated.

"I love him, too, for Christ's sake!" I screamed at her. "I love him, too! But he's dead, Jill! He's dead!"

I snatched hold of her wrist but she yanked herself angrily away from me. "He's not dead!" she shrieked. "He's not! He makes love to me! How can he be dead?"

"How the hell should I know? Because of a rhyme, because of a wish! Because of who knows what! But the doctors said he was dead and they buried him, and he's *dead*, Jill!"

Robbie slowly drew back the sheet from the bed, and eased himself up. His skin was almost translucent, like dirty wax. From the bandages around his chest, I could hear a whining inhalation and exhalation. The scaffolding poles had penetrated his lungs; he hadn't stood a chance.

"I dug my way out of the soil with my bare hands," he told me; and there was a certain kind of terrible pride in his voice. "I rose out of the earth at three o'clock in the morning, filthy with clay. Then I walked all the way to the city. *Walked!* Do you know how difficult that is, how far that is? And then I called Jill from a public telephone in Brooklyn; and she came to rescue me."

"I remember the night," I told him.

He came up close. He exuded a strange, elusive smell; not of decomposition, but of some preservative chemical. It suddenly occurred to me that embalming fluid must be running through his veins, instead of blood. He was my brother; I had loved him when he was alive. But I knew with complete certainty now that he was dead; and I loved him no longer.

Jill whispered, "You won't tell, will you? You won't tell anybody?"

For a very long moment I couldn't think what to do. Jill and Robbie watched me without saying a word, as if I were a hostile outsider who had deliberately set out to interfere, and to destroy their lives.

But at last I grinned, and nodded, and said to Robbie, "You're back, then! You're really back! It's a miracle!"

He smiled lopsidedly, as if his mouth were anesthetized. "I knew you'd understand. Jill said you never would; but I said bull. You always did, didn't you? You son-of-a-gun."

He rested his hand on my shoulder; his dead gray hand; and I felt the bile rise up in my throat. But I had already decided what I was going to do, and if I had betrayed any sign of disgust, I would have ruined it.

"Come on through to the kitchen," I told him. "I could use a beer after this. Maybe a glass of wine."

"There's some champagne in the icebox," said Jill. "I was just going to get it."

"Well, why not let's open it together," I suggested.

"Why not let's celebrate. It isn't every day that your brother comes back from the dead."

Jill dragged the sheet from the bed and wrapped it around Robbie like a toga. Then they followed me into the small green-tiled kitchen. I opened up the icebox, took out the bottle of champagne, and offered it to Robbie.

"Here, you were always better at opening up bottles of wine than I was."

He took it, but looked at me seriously. "I don't know. I'm not sure I've got the strength any more. I'm alive, you know, but it's kind of *different*."

"You can make love," I retorted, dangerously close to losing my temper. "You should be able to open a bottle of champagne."

His breath whined in and out of his bandages. I watched him closely. There was doubt on his face; as if he suspected that I was somehow setting him up, but he couldn't work out how.

"Come on, sweetheart," Jill coaxed him.

I turned around and opened one of the kitchen drawers. String, skewers, nutmeg grater. "Yes, come on, Robbie. You always were a genius at parties."

I opened the next drawer. Tea-towels. Jill frowned and said, "What are you looking for?"

Robbie began to unwind the wire muzzle around the champagne cork. "My fingers feel kind of *numb*, you know? It's hard to describe."

I opened a third drawer, trying to do it nonchalantly. Knives.

Jill knew instantaneously what I was going to do. Maybe it was genuine intuition. Maybe it was nothing more than heightened fear. But I turned around so casually that she didn't see the nine-inch Sabatier carving-knife in my hand, she was looking at my eyes; and it had penetrated Robbie's bandages right up to the hilt before she understood that I meant to kill him. I meant to *kill* him. He was my brother.

The champagne bottle smashed on the floor in an explosion of glass and foam. Jill screamed but Robbie said nothing at all. He turned to me, and grasped my shoulder, and there was something in his eyes which was half panic and half relief. I pulled the knife downwards and it cut through his flesh as if it were over-ripe avocado; soft, slippery, no resistance.

"Oh, God," he breathed. His gray intestines came pouring out from underneath his toga, and on to the broken glass. "Oh God, get it over with."

"No!" screamed Jill; but I stared at her furiously and shouted, "You want him to live for ever? He's my brother! You want him to live for *ever*?"

She hesitated for a second, then she pushed her way out of the kitchen, and I heard her retching in the toilet. Robbie was on his knees, his arms by his sides, making no attempt to pick up his heavy kilt of guts.

"Come on," he whispered. "Get it over with."

I was shaking so much that I could hardly hold the knife. He tilted his head back, passive and quiet, his eyes still open, and like a man in a slowly-moving nightmare I cut his throat from one side to the other; so deeply that the knife-blade wedged between his vertebrae.

There was no blood. He collapsed backward on to the floor, shuddering slightly. Then the unnatural life that had illuminated his eyes faded away, and it was clear that he was truly dead.

Jill appeared in the doorway. Her face was completely white, as if she had covered herself in rice powder. "What have you done?" she whispered.

I stood up. "I don't know. I'm not sure. We'll have to bury him."

"No," she said, shaking her head. "He's still alive . . . we could bring him back to life again."

"Jill –" I began, moving toward her; but she screamed, "Don't touch me! You've killed him! Don't touch me!"

I tried to snatch at her wrist, but she pulled herself away, and ran for the door.

"Jill! Jill, listen!"

She was out in the corridor before I could stop her, and running toward the elevator. The elevator doors opened and the Italian-looking man stepped out, looking surprised. Jill pushed her way into the elevator and hammered wildly at the buttons.

"No!" she screamed. "No!"

I went after her, but the Italian-looking man deliberately blocked my way.

"That's my wife!" I yelled at him. "Get out of my goddamned way!"

"Come on, friend, give her some breathing-space," the man told me, and pushed me in the chest with the flat of his hand. Desperately, I saw the elevator doors close and Jill disappear.

"For God's sake," I snarled at the man. "You don't know what you've done!"

I shoved my way past him and hurtled down the stairs, three stairs at a time, until I reached the lobby. The doorman said, "Hey, man, what's going on?" and caught at my arm.

He delayed me for only a second; but it was a second too long. The swing doors were just closing and Jill was already halfway across the sidewalk, running into Central Park South.

"Jill!" I shouted at her. She couldn't possibly have heard me. She didn't even hear the cab that hit her as she crossed the road, and sent her hurtling over its roof, her arms spread wide as if she were trying to fly. I pushed open the swing doors and I heard her fall. I heard screams and traffic and the screeching of brakes. Then I didn't hear anything, either.

It was a strange and grisly task, removing Robbie's body

from Willey's apartment. But there was no blood, no evidence of murder, and nobody would report him missing. I buried him deep in the woods beyond White Plains, in a place where we used to play when we were boys.

We buried Jill a week later, on a warm sunny day when the whole world seemed to be coming to life. Her mother wouldn't stop sobbing. Her father wouldn't speak to me. The police report had exonerated me from any possible blame, but grief knows no logic.

I took two weeks away from work after the funeral and went to stay at a friend's house in the Hamptons, and got drunk most of the time. I was still in shock; and I didn't know how long it was going to take me to get over it.

Down on the seashore, with the gulls circling all around me, I suppose I found some kind of unsteady peace of mind. I returned to the city on a dark threatening Thursday afternoon. I felt exhausted and hung-over, and I planned to spend the weekend quietly relaxing before returning to work on Monday. Maybe I would go to the zoo. Jill had always liked going to the zoo, more to look at the people than the animals.

I unlocked the door of my apartment and tossed my bag into the hallway. Then I went through to the kitchen and took a bottle of cold Chablis out of the icebox. Hair of the dog, I thought to myself. I switched on the television just in time to see the end credits of *As The World Turns*. I poured myself some wine; and then, whistling, went through to the bedroom.

I said, "Oh Christ," and dropped my full glass of wine on to my foot.

She was lying on top of the comforter naked, not smiling, but her thighs provocatively apart. Her skin had a grayish-blue sheen, as if it would be greasy to touch, but it wasn't decayed. Her hair was brushed and her lips were painted red and there was purple eye-shadow over her eyes.

"Jill?" I breathed. I felt for one implosive instant that I was going mad.

"I used the spare key from the crack in the skirting," she said. Her voice was hoarse, as if her chest were crushed. I had seen her hurtling over the taxi, I had seen her fall.

"You said the words," I told her, dully. "You said the words."

She shook her head. But it was then that I remembered watching her asleep, and reciting that childish rhyme. *Immortooty, immortaty, ever, ever after.*

She raised her arms, stiffly. The fingers of her left hand were tightly curled around, as if they had been broken.

"Make love to me," she whispered. "Please, make love to me."

I turned around and walked straight through to the kitchen. I pulled open one drawer after another, but there wasn't a single knife anywhere. She must have hidden them all, or thrown them away. I turned back again, and Jill was standing in the bedroom doorway. This time she was smiling.

"Make *love* to me," she repeated.

Pig's Dinner

Bakewell, Derbyshire

Bakewell lies on the River Wye, in a valley between the high ridges of mid-Derbyshire. The town's name was derived from the Saxon *bad-quell*, meaning "bath-well", but these days Bakewell is better known for the Bakewell Tart, which is a pastry filled with strawberry preserve and glazed with egg. The Derbyshire Dales are some of the most peaceful and beautiful countryside in England, which made them a natural (for me) for one of the most horrifying stories I have ever written.

Bakewell has a splendid arched and buttressed bridge, nearly 700 years old; and its brownstone buildings are unusually warm in appearance for a Peakland town. Just as warm are Bakewell's springs, which were known in Roman times, and still feed the Bath House, built in 1697 for the Duke of Rutland.

Pig's Dinner caused a considerable stir when it made its first appearance in the American magazine *Cemetery Dance* and is being recreated both as a graphic novel and a television movie.

PIG'S DINNER

David climbed tiredly out of the Land Rover, slammed
the ill-fitting door, and trudged across the yard with his
hands deep in the pockets of his donkey-jacket. It had
stopped raining at last, but a coarse cold wind was blowing
diagonally across the yard, and above his head the clouds
rushed like a muddy-pelted pack of mongrel dogs.

Today had been what he and Malcolm always sardoni-
cally called "a pig of a day."

He had left the piggery at half-past five that morning,
driven all the way to Chester in the teeming rain with a
litter of seven Landrace piglets suffering from suspected
swine erysipelas. He had waited two and a half hours for
a dithering young health inspector who had missed his
rail connection from Coventry. Then he had lunched on
steak-and-kidney pudding with a deputy bank manager
whose damp suit had reeked like a spaniel, and who had
felt himself unable to grant David the loan that he and
Malcolm desperately needed in order to repair the roof
of the old back barn.

He was wet, exhausted and demoralized. For the first
time since they had taken over the piggery from their
uncle four and a half years ago, he could see no future for
Bryce Prime Pork, even if they sold half of their livestock
and most of their acreage, and remortgaged their huge
Edwardian house.

He had almost reached the stone steps when he noticed
that the lights in the feed plant had been left burning.

Damn it, he thought. Malcolm was always so careless. It was Malcolm's over-ambitious investment in new machinery and Malcolm's insistence on setting up their own slaughtering and deep-freezing facilities that had stretched their finances to breaking-point. Bryce Prime Pork had been caught between falling demand and rising costs, and David's dream of becoming a prosperous gentleman farmer had gradually unraveled all around him.

He crossed the sloping yard toward the feed plant. Bryce Prime Pork was one of the cleanest piggeries in Derbyshire, but there was still a strong smell of ammonia on the evening wind, and the soles of David's shoes slapped against the thin black slime that seemed to cover everything in wet weather. He opened the door to the feed plant and stepped inside. All the lights were on; but there was no sign of Malcolm. Nothing but sacks of fish meal, maize, potatoes, decorticated ground-nut meal, and gray plastic dustbins filled with boiled swill. They mixed their own pig-food, rather than buying proprietary brands – not only because it cost them three or four percent less, but because Malcolm had developed a mix of swill, cereal and concentrate which not only fattened the pigs more quickly, but gave them award-winning bacon.

David walked up and down the length of the feed plant. He could see his reflection in the night-blackened windows: squatter, more hunched than he imagined himself to be. As he passed the stainless-steel sides of the huge feed grinder, he thought that he looked like a Golem, or a troll, dark and disappointed. Maybe defeat did something to a man's appearance, squashed him out of shape, so that he couldn't recognize himself any longer.

He crossed to the switches by the door, and clicked them off, one after another, and all along the feed plant the fluorescent lights blinked out. Just before he clicked the last switch, however, he noticed that the main switch which isolated the feed-grinder was set to 'off.'

He hesitated, his hand an inch away from the light-switch. Neither Malcolm nor Dougal White, their fore-man, had mentioned that there was anything wrong with the machinery. It was all German, made in Dusseldorf by Muller-Koch, and after some initial teething troubles with the grinder blades, it had for more than two years run with seamless efficiency.

David lifted the main switch to 'on' – and to his surprise, with a smooth metallic scissoring sound, like a carving-knife being sharpened against a steel, the feeding grinder started up immediately.

In the next instant, he heard a hideously distorted shriek – a gibbering monkey-like yammering of pain and terror that shocked him into stunned paralysis – unable to understand what the shriek could be, or what he could do to stop it.

He fumbled for the 'off' switch, while all the time the screaming went on and on, growing higher and higher-pitched, racketing from one side of the building to the other, until David felt as if he had suddenly gone mad.

The feed-grinder gradually minced to a halt, and David crossed stiff-legged as a scarecrow to the huge conical stainless steel vat. He clambered up the access ladder at the side, and while he did so the screaming died down, and gave way to a complicated mixture of gurgles and groans.

He climbed up to the lip of the feed vat, and saw to his horror that the entire shining surface was rusty-colored with fresh blood – and that, down at the bottom of the vat, Malcolm was standing, staring up at him wild-eyed, his hands braced tightly against the sloping sides.

He *appeared* to be standing, but as David looked more closely, he began to realize that Malcolm had been churned into the cutting-blades of the feed grinder right up to his waist. He was surrounded by a dark glutinous pool of blood and thickly-minced bone, its surface still punctuated by occasional bubbles. His brown plaid shirt was soaked in blood, and his face was spattered like a map.

David stared at Malcolm and Malcolm stared back at David. The silent agony which both joined and fatally separated them at that instant was far more eloquent than any scream could have been.

"Oh, Christ," said David. "I didn't know."

Malcolm opened and closed his mouth, and a huge pink bubble of blood formed and burst.

David clung tightly to the lip of the feed-grinding vat and held out his hand as far as he could.

"Come on, Malcolm. I'll pull you up. Come on, you'll be all right."

But Malcolm remained as he was, staring, his arms tensed against the sides of the vat, and shook his head. Blood poured in a thick ceaseless ribbon down his chin.

"Malcolm, come on, I can pull you out! Then I'll get an ambulance!"

But again Malcolm shook his head: this time with a kind of dogged fury. It was then that David understood that there was hardly anything left of Malcolm to pull out – that it wasn't just a question of his legs being tangled in the machinery. The grinder blades had consumed him up to the hip – reducing his legs and the lower part of his body to a thick smooth paste of bone and muscle, an emulsion of human flesh that would already be dripping down into the collecting churn underneath.

"Oh God, Malcolm, I'll get somebody. Hold on, I'll call for an ambulance. Just hold on!"

"No," Malcolm told him, his voice muffled with shock.

"Just hold on, for Christ's sake!" David screamed at him.

But Malcolm repeated, "No. I want it this way."

"What?" David demanded. "What the hell do you mean?"

Malcolm's fingers squeaked against the bloody sides of

92

the vat. David couldn't begin to imagine what he must be suffering. Yet Malcolm looked up at him now with a smile – a smile that was almost beatific.

"It's wonderful, David. It's wonderful. I never knew that pain could feel like this. It's better than anything that ever happened. Please, switch it back on. Please."

"Switch it *back on*?"

Malcolm began to shudder. "You must. I want it so much. Life, love – they don't count for anything. Not compared with this."

"No," said David. "I can't."

"David," Malcolm urged him, "I'm going to die anyway. But if you don't give me this . . . believe me, I'm never going to let you sleep for the rest of your life."

David remained at the top of the ladder for ten long indecisive seconds.

"Believe me," Malcolm nodded, in that voice that sounded as if it came straight from hell, "it's pure pleasure. Pure pleasure. Beyond pain, David, out of the other side. You can't experience it without dying. But David, David, what a way to go!"

David stayed motionless for one more moment. Then, without a word, he climbed unsteadily back down the ladder. He tried not to think of anything at all as he grasped the feed-grinder's main power switch, and clicked it to 'on.'

From the feed-grinder came a cry that was partly naked agony and partly exultation. It was a cry that made David rigid with horror, and his ill-digested lunch rose in the back of his throat in a sour, thick tide.

He was gripped by a sudden terrible compulsion that he needed to *see*. He scrambled back up the access ladder, gripped the rim of the vat, and stared down at Malcolm with a feeling that was almost like being electrocuted.

The grinding-blades scissored and chopped, and the entire vat surged with blood. Malcolm was still bracing

93

himself at the very bottom, his torso tensed as the grinder blades turned his pelvis and his lower abdomen into a churning mixture of blood, muscle and shredded cloth.

His face was a mask of concentration and tortured ecstasy. He was enjoying it, reveling in it, relishing every second of it. The very extinction of his own life; the very destruction of his own body.

Beyond pain, he had told David. *Out of the other side.*

Malcolm held his upper body above the whirling blades as long as he could, but gradually his strength faded and his hands began to skid inch by inch down the bloody metal sides. His screams of pleasure turned into a cry like nothing that David had ever heard before – piercing, high-pitched, an ullulation of unearthly triumph.

His white stomach was sliced up; skin, fat, intestines; and he began a quivering, jerking last descent into the maw of the feed-grinder.

"David!" he screamed. "David! It's won – "

The blades locked into his ribs. He was whirled around with his arms lifted as if he were furiously dancing. Then there was nothing but his head, spinning madly in a froth of pink blood. Finally, with a noise like a sink-disposal unit chopping up chicken bones, his head was gone, too, and the grinder spun faster and faster, without any more grist for its terrible mill.

Shaking, David climbed down the ladder and switched the grinder off. There was a long, drying whine, and then silence, except for the persistent worrying of the wind.

What the hell was he going to do now? There didn't seem to be any point in calling for an ambulance. Not only was it pointless – how was he going to explain that he had switched the feed-grinder back on again, with Malcolm still inside it?

The police would realize that the grinder didn't have the capacity to chop up Malcolm's entire body before David had had the opportunity to switch it off. And he doubted very much if they would understand that Malcolm had been beyond saving – or that even if he *hadn't* begged David to kill him – even if he hadn't said how ecstatic it was – finishing him off was probably the most humane thing that David could have done.

He stood alone in the shed, shivering with shock and indecision. He and Malcolm had been arguing a lot lately – everybody knew that. Only two weeks ago, they had openly shouted at each other at a livestock auction in Chester. It would only take one suggestion that he might have killed Malcolm deliberately, and he would face arrest, trial, and jail. Even if he managed to show that he was innocent, a police investigation would certainly ruin the business. Who would want to buy Bryce Pork products if they thought that the pigs had been fed from the same grinder in which one of the Bryce brothers had been ground up?

Unless, of course, nobody found out that he *had* been ground up.

Unless nobody found him at all.

He seemed to remember a story that he had read, years ago, about a chicken-farmer who had murdered his wife and fed her to the chickens, and then fed the chickens to other chickens, until no possible traces of his wife remained.

He heard a glutinous dripping noise from the feed-grinder. It wouldn't be long before Malcolm's blood would coagulate, and become almost impossible for him to wash thoroughly away. He hesitated for just one moment; then he switched on the lights again, and went across to the sacks of bran, middlings and soya-bean meal.

Tired and fraught and grief-stricken as he was, tonight he was going to make a pig's dinner.

He slept badly, and woke early. He lay in bed for a long time, staring at the ceiling. He found it difficult to believe now that what had happened yesterday evening had been real. He felt almost as if it had all been a luridly-colored film. But he felt a cold and undeniable difference inside his soul that told him it had actually happened. A change in himself that would affect him for the rest of his life – what he thought, what he said, what people he could love, what risks he was prepared to take.

Just after dawn, he saw the lights in the pig-houses flicker on, and he knew that Dougal and Charlie had arrived. He dressed, and went downstairs to the kitchen, where he drank half a pint of freezing-cold milk straight out of the bottle. He brought some of it directly back up again, and had to spit it into the sink. He wiped his mouth on a damp tea-towel and went outside.

Dougal was tethering a Landrace gilt and fixing up a heater for her piglets in a "creep", a boxlike structure hanging alongside her. Piglets under four weeks needed more heat than their mother could provide. Charlie was busy in a pen further along, feeding Old Jeffries, their enormous one-eyed Large Black boar. They bred very few Large Blacks these days: the Danish Landraces were docile and prolific and gave excellent bacon. But Malcolm had insisted on keeping Old Jeffries for sentimental reasons. He had been given to them by their uncle when they took over the business, and had won them their first rosette. "Old Jeffries and I are going to be buried in the same grave," he always used to say.

"Morning, Mr David," said Dougal. He was a sandy-haired Wiltshireman with a pudgy face and protuberant eyes.

"Morning, Dougal."

"Mr Malcolm not about yet?"

David shook his head. "No . . . he said something about ·going to Chester."

"Oh . . . that's queer. We were going to divide up the weaner pool today."

"Well, I can help you do that."

96

"Mr Malcolm didn't say when he'd be back?"

"No," said David. "He didn't say a word."

He walked along the rows of pens until he came to Old Jeffries' stall. Charlie had emptied a bucketful of fresh feed into Old Jeffries' trough, and the huge black boar was greedily snuffling his snout into it; although his one yellow eye remained fixed on David as he ate.

"He really likes his breakfast today," Charlie remarked. Charlie was a young curly-haired teenager from the village. He was training to be a veterinarian, but he kept himself in petrol and weekly Chinese takeaways by helping out at Bryce Pork before college.

"Yes . . ." said David. He stared in awful fascination as Old Jeffries snorted and guzzled at the dark red mixture of roughage, concentrate and meat meal that (in two horrific hours of near-madness) he had mixed last night out of Malcolm's soupy remains. "It's a new formula we've been trying."

"Mr Malcolm sorted out that bearing on the feed-grinder, then?" asked Charlie.

"Oh . . . oh, yes," David replied. But he didn't take his eyes off Old Jeffries, grunting into his trough; and Old Jeffries didn't for one moment take his one yellow eye off David.

"What did the health inspector say?" asked Charlie.

"Nothing much. It isn't erysipelas, thank God. Just a touch of zinc deficiency. Too much dry food."

Charlie nodded. "I thought it might be that. But this new feed looks excellent. In fact, it smells so good, I tasted a little bit myself."

For the first time, David took his eyes off Old Jeffries. "You did what?"

Charlie laughed. "You shouldn't worry. You know what Malcolm says, he wouldn't feed anything to the pigs that he wouldn't eat himself. I've never come across anybody who loves his livestock as much as your brother. I mean, he really puts himself into these pigs, doesn't he? Body and soul."

Old Jeffries had finished his trough, and was enthusiastically cleaning it with his long inky tongue. David couldn't help watching him in fascination as he licked the last fragments of meat meal from his whiskery cheeks.

"I'm just going to brew up some tea," he said, clapping Charlie on the back.

He left the piggery; but when he reached the door, he could still see Old Jeffries staring at him one-eyed from the confines of his pen, and for some inexplicable reason it made him shudder.

You're tired, shocked, he told himself. But as he closed the piggery door he heard Old Jeffries grunt and whuffle as if he had been dangerously roused.

The telephone rang for Malcolm all day; and a man in a badly-muddied Montego arrived at the piggery, expecting to talk to Malcolm about insurance. David fended everybody off, saying that Malcolm had gone to Chester on business and no, he didn't know when he was coming back. Am I my brother's keeper?

That night, after Dougal had left, he made his final round of the piggery, making sure that the gilts and the sows were all tethered tight, so that they didn't accidentally crush their young; checking the "creeps" and the ventilators; switching off lights.

His last visit was to Old Jeffries. The Large Black stood staring at him as he approached; and made a noise in his throat like no noise that David had ever heard a boar utter before.

"Well, old man," he said, leaning on the rail of the pen. "It looks as if Malcolm knew what he was talking about. You and he are going to be buried in the same grave."

Old Jeffries curled back his lip and grunted.

"I didn't know what else to do," David told him. "He

was dying, right in front of my eyes. God, he couldn't have lived more than five minutes more."

Old Jeffries grunted again. David said, "Thanks, O.J. You're a wonderful conversationalist." He reached over to pat the Large Black's bristly head.

Without any warning at all, Old Jeffries snatched at David's hand, and clamped it between his jaws. David felt his fingers being crushed, and teeth digging right through the palm of his hand. He shouted in pain, and tried to pull himself away, but Old Jeffries twisted his powerful sloped-back neck and heaved David bodily over the railings and into his ammonia-pungent straw.

David's arm was wrenched around behind him, and he felt his elbow crack. He screamed, and tried to turn himself around, but Old Jeffries' four-toed trotter dug into his ribcage, cracking his breastbone and puncturing his left lung. Old Jeffries weighed over 300 kilograms, and even though he twisted and struggled, there was nothing he could do to force the boar off him.

"Dougal!" he screamed, even though he knew that Dougal had left over twenty minutes ago. "Oh God, help me! Somebody!"

Grunting furiously, Old Jeffries trampled David and worried his bloody hand between his teeth. To his horror, David saw two of his fingers drop from Old Jeffries' jaw, and fall into the straw. The boar's bristly sides kept scorching his face: taut and coarse and pungent with the smell of pig.

He dragged himself backwards, out from under the boar's belly, and grabbed hold of the animal's back with his free hand, trying to pull himself upright. For a moment, he thought he had managed it, but then Old Jeffries let out a shrill squeal of rage, and burrowed his snout furiously and aggressively between David's thighs.

"No!" David screamed. "No! Not that! Not that!"

But he felt sharp teeth tearing through corduroy, and

then half of his inside thigh being torn away from the bone, with a bloody crackle of fat and tissue. And then Old Jeffries ripped him between the legs. He felt the boar's teeth puncture his groin, he felt cords and tubes and fats being wrenched away. He threw back his head and he let out a cry of anguish, and wanted to die then, right then, with no more pain, nothing but blackness.

But Old Jeffries retreated, trotting a little way away from him with his gory prize hanging from his mouth. He stared at David with his one yellow eye as if he were daring him to take it back.

David sicked up blood. Then, letting out a long whimpering sound, he climbed up to his feet, and cautiously limped to the side of the pen. He could feel that he was losing pints of blood. It pumped warm and urgent down his trouser-leg. He knew that he was going to die. But he wasn't going to let this pig have him. He was going to go the way that Malcolm had gone. Beyond pain, out on the other side. He was going to go in the ultimate ecstasy.

He opened the pen, and hobbled along the piggery, leaving a wide wet trail of blood behind him. Old Jeffries hesitated for a few moments, and then followed him, his trotters clicking on the concrete floor.

David crossed the yard to the feed buildings. He felt cold, cold, cold – colder than he had ever felt before. The wind banged a distant door over and over again, like a flat-toned funeral drum. Old Jeffries followed him, twenty or thirty yards behind, his one eye shining yellow in the darkness.

To market, to market, to buy a fat pig
Home again, home again, jiggety-jig.

Coughing, David opened the door of the feed building. He switched on the lights, leaning against the wall for support. Old Jeffries stepped into the doorway and watched him, huge and black, but didn't approach any closer. David switched the feed-grinder to 'on' and heard the hum of machinery and the scissoring of precision-ground blades.

It seemed to take him an age to climb the access ladder to the rim of the vat. When he reached the top, he looked down into the circular grinder, and he could see the blades flashing as they spun around.

Ecstasy, that's when Malcolm had told him. *Pleasure beyond pain.*

He swung his bloodied legs over the rim of the vat. He closed his eyes for a moment, and said a short prayer. Dear God, forgive me. Dear mother, please forgive me.

Then he released his grip, and tumble-skidded down the stainless steel sides, his feet plunging straight into the grinder blades.

He screamed in terror; and then he screamed in agony. The blades sliced relentlessly into his feet, his ankles, his shins, his knees. He watched his legs ground up in a bloody chaos of bone and muscle, and the pain was so intense that he pounded at the sides of the vat with his fists. This wasn't ecstasy. This was sheer nerve-tearing pain – made even more intense by the hideous knowledge that he was already mutilated beyond any hope of survival – that he was as good as dead already.

The blades cut into his thighs. He thought he had fainted but he hadn't fainted, *couldn't* faint, because the pain was so fierce that it penetrated his subconscious, penetrated every part of his mind and body.

He felt his pelvis shattered, crushed, chopped into paste. He felt his insides drop out of him. Then he was caught and tangled in the same way that Malcolm had been caught and tangled, and for a split-second he felt himself whirled around, a wild Dervish dance of sheer agony. Malcolm had lied. Malcolm had lied. Beyond pain there was nothing but more pain. On the other side of pain was a blinding sensation that made pain feel like a caress.

101

The blades bit into his jaw. His face was obliterated. There was a brief whirl of blood and brains and then he was gone.

The feed-grinder whirred and whirred for over an hour. Then – with no feed to slow down its blades – it overheated and whined to a halt.

Blood dripped; slower and slower.

Old Jeffries remained where he was, standing in the open doorway, one-eyed, the cold night wind ruffling his bristles.

Old Jeffries knew nothing about retribution. Old Jeffries knew nothing about guilt.

But something that Old Jeffries didn't understand had penetrated the black primitive knots of his cortex – a need for revenge so powerful that it had been passed from a dead soul to a bestial brain. Or perhaps he simply acquired a taste for a new kind of feed.

Old Jeffries trotted back to his pen and waited patiently for the morning, and for Charlie to arrive, to fill up his trough with yet another pig's dinner.

Heart of Stone

New Preston, Connecticut

I can still smell the woodsmoke and the leaves of New Preston, twenty years after my wife and I visited the Housatonic and East Aspetuck valleys looking for a house. It was almost Hallowe'en, and the skies were blue and the wooded hills were yellow and red and every color in between. New Preston is a quiet, isolated community – and like most of the rural hamlets in Litchfield County, it now has a smaller population (less than 800) than it did in the 18th century. There is a wonderfully witchy atmosphere here. When you drive through those silent woods, and arrive at those old tumbledown coaching inns, you feel that you have taken the wrong fork again, folks, and unknowingly entered an H.P. Lovecraft novel, where whippoorwhills cry from the hills, and retarded offspring sulkily stare at you from half-collapsed dwellings with gambreled roofs.

We found a white house on a wooded hill that was our heart's desire. But the day before we were due to complete the sale, my New York agent told me that my green card had been refused. So, for me, New Preston remains nothing more than a happy/regretful memory, and the setting for this story, *Heart of Stone*.

HEART OF STONE

Ron Maccione the contractor stood looking at the meadow for almost five minutes without saying anything, the peak of his Budweiser cap pulled low over his forehead, his tattooed forearms intertwined like the trunks of two gnarled old trees on to which long-dead lovers had carved hearts and flowers and secret messages.

"Tennis courts, you say?" he commented, as if anybody who wanted to turn over five-and-a-half acres of perfectly good agricultural land to the playing of ball games was either mad, or a faggot, or both.

"Six of them," said Richard, confidently. "Six international class asphalt courts. But I'm bringing in Fraser and Fairmont to lay out the courts themselves. All I want you to do is to level the site off."

Ron Maccione sniffed. "Site slopes off to the northwest more than you think. One in eight, maybe one in six. Have to bring in the heavy earthmover. Then you got all them stones to clear. A whole hell of a lot of stones. Always was a hell of a locality for stones, Preston. Reckon I've spent two-thirds of my working life clearing away stones."

Richard said, "How about it? You want to quote me a price?"

"Have to do some pretty close figuring first," Ron Maccione told him. "But I can call you Friday for sure. Ballpark, I'd say three thousand."

"That's about a third more than I had in mind."

"Sure. But you have to pick up all these goddamned

105

stones. You can't just turn 'em over and bury 'em. They always rise up to the surface again. Laws of natural physics. Cereal-box syndrome."

Richard looked around the weedy, triangular meadow. It was edged on its two far sides by dry-stone walls; and on the nearer side by a sparse screen of pine trees. Through the pines, he could just make out the paleness of the house, like a skull that had been hidden all summer in a hedge, only to be revealed by the onset of fall.

He laid his hand on Ron Maccione's shoulder, trying to act like a buddy. "Okay, whatever you say. I'll wait to hear from you."

He turned and began to walk back to the house. Ron Maccione hesitated for a moment, sniffed, and then followed him.

"Nobody thought we'd ever see a Palen back in Preston," said Ron Maccione. "The Sturgeons are all gone now, so's the Mitchells, and there hasn't been a Nugent since sixty-one."

"I never meant to come back," Richard told him, double-kicking his left ankle to help himself up the dry-stone steps that led to the house. "I always thought I'd retire to Palm Springs. Even had the plans drawn up. The Richard Palen Tennis Center. Ten tennis courts, six air-conditioned squash courts, health club, beauty parlor, restaurant. Nineteen-and-a-half million dollars."

They passed through the screen of pines, and crossed the overgrown garden. Huge rank cabbages grew amongst the grass. Artichokes stood as tall as giant thistles. The silence was complete, like a closed purse. At the end of the garden the huge weatherboarded house stood mean and miserable, a huge raft of dried-up wisteria hanging precariously from the roof of its conservatory.

"Well, you had your good years," remarked Ron Maccione.

Richard stopped in the garden with his hand over his

106

mouth as if he had forgotten something. Then he looked at Ron Maccione and said, "Yes, sure. I had my good years."

He stood by the front porch watching the red tail-lights of Ron Maccione's pickup truck winking through the trees. Then he went back into the house and closed the door.

The hallway was dark and smelled strongly of Black Flag. Everything that Richard remembered from his boyhood had disappeared; the long-case clock, the chair by the door. The last owners had left vestiges of jaundiced linoleum and multicolored venetian blinds, thick with grease and clinging fluff.

Richard stood with his back to the door, listening. The house was so silent that it seemed as if it were dead. Even houses can be killed. Appropriate, really, since Richard had been killed, too, in almost every respect except that he was still walking, talking, breathing, and waking up each morning with the knowledge that he was faced with yet another day.

A day in which he would have to make his way in the world without wealth, without glory, and without any of the glamor of being Richard Palen, international tennis champion. A day in which he would have to survive alone, without his friends, without his children, without Sara, his wife.

Withdrawn, tight-lipped, scarcely speaking to anybody from the moment he opened his eyes in the early morning to the second he closed them at night, numb with vodka and the exhaustion of trying to forget.

But almost every hour of every day that split-second, as abrupt and vivid as if it were really happening – as if it would *always* be happening. Turning in the driver's seat to smile at Sara, triumphant after winning the California Open. Then, instantly, a smash that he hadn't even seen coming, straight into the front of an oncoming Safeway truck.

He had spent that split-second in hell. Sara had dived beneath the glove-box in a spray of blood and ripped-apart upholstery, as if there were somewhere beneath the glove-box for her to go. Joanna and Davie had screamed like whistles. Then all he had heard was cracking glass, and the extraordinary crushed-sugar noise of his legs breaking, and somebody saying very close to his ear – maybe later, maybe immediately afterwards, *"Jesus Christ."*

The months that had followed had been an eternal calendar of pain, of white hospital laundry, of flowers that quivered in the afternoon sunlight, and friends with sympathetic, distracted expressions. Then fewer friends, and fewer flowers, but just as much pain.

After almost a year he had sat in the offices of Weinman, Westlake & Calloway, on Nob Hill, with the whole of San Francisco invisible in the fog, and his lawyer had said, "Technically, Rick, you're flat-busted."

That was why he was here, this pale gray October day, in Preston, Connecticut, in the home that his great-grandfather had passed to his grandfather, and his grandfather had passed to his father. It was here that he had met Sara Nugent, only eleven years ago, and fallen in love with her. It was here that his mother had died of cancer.

His father had sold the house in 1977 to some strange people whose eyes like blowflies had refused to settle in the same place for more than an instant, the Millers. But it had always remained Richard's home. He always thought of the house as his.

After the Millers had left, the house had stood empty for over two years – too far from New York to interest a daily commuter, too large for a weekend cottage, dilapidated, expensive to heat, a casualty of an ageing community that had dwindled to fewer now than had lived here in the 1700s.

But the house had been priced almost embarrassingly low, and perhaps more importantly it had offered Richard a familiar home when everything familiar had been taken away from him. He planned to lay out tennis courts, renovate the house, and open it up as the Richard Palen Professional Country Club. Five guest suites, a bar, and professional coaching for vengeful executives who wanted to wipe out their senior colleagues on the tennis-court.

It had taken Richard's last $58,000; plus as much money as he had been able to borrow from the New Milford Savings Bank (another $75,000) plus the peculiarly cheerless determination that only the recently-bereaved can sustain.

He went through to the sitting-room, and sat in solitary splendor on a huge damp Sears armchair in coffee-colored velour, and unscrewed a fifth of Jack Daniel's, forbidden by his consultant.

"Nazdravye," he told the house, lifting his glass to the damp-jigsawed ceiling.

He didn't know when he fell asleep; but when he woke up it was raining, and the first light of dawn was straining into the room, the color of cold tea. The phone was ringing.

He picked up the receiver and said, "Yes?" into the wrong end. It was Ron Maccione, the contractor. He said, "Sorry to call you so early, Mr Palen. Got to get down to Danbury by nine. Worked your price out, thought you'd like to know it."

"All right," Richard replied, smearing his face with his hand. "What do you think?"

"Well . . . seeing as how your family are Preston folk from way back, and there's not too many Preston folk left, and seeing how the county's just canceled my contract for asphalting the parking-lot down at the schoolhouse . . . well, I guess I can clear that meadow for you for two-and-a-half; two-two-fifty for cash."

Richard stood alone and hungover in the middle of the sitting-room. "All right," he agreed. "Go ahead."

It wasn't really the price that decided him. It was the fact that somebody had welcomed him home.

The earth-movers arrived the following Monday, three of them, and churned up and down the field all day, while Ron Maccione came and went, and yelled instructions, and opened one can of Miller Draft after the other. Richard stood by the window feeling detached but somehow more complete, like the day they had taken the plaster off his smashed left ankle.

Around noon, the doorbell chimed, and Richard went to the door to find a tall milky-faced woman standing on the step, holding a dish draped in a red gingham cloth.

"I guess you could say I'm the welcome wagon," she said. She was white-blonde, Scandinavian-looking, and she wore a thick old-fashioned woollen dress, gray, the color of rubbed charcoal. She held up the dish. "It's a peach pie," she told him.

"Well, thank you," said Richard. "Listen – why don't you come on in? You'll have to excuse the mess."

She stepped inside, looking cautiously and curiously all around her. "I've never been inside before," she explained. "The Millers weren't sociable folk."

He took the pie and set it down on the windowsill. "I was brought up here," he explained. "Do you want the cloth back?"

"Oh, later will do." She stepped across the sitting-room like a woman in a Bergman movie; unsmiling, self-possessed. "It's strange to think of all the history that you and I share."

"I'm sorry?" asked Richard.

She didn't turn around. "My name's Greta Reuter these days. But I used to be Greta Sturgeon. My family came here in sixteen-eighty, same as yours."

"Oh, really?"

She turned at last, with a smile that looked as if it had

110

been cut out of a magazine and held in front of her face. "Not that the Palens and the Sturgeons were ever friends. Not in those days."

"I didn't know that," said Richard, feeling as if he ought to apologize for something, but not knowing what.

"Well," she said, "the Palens accused the Sturgeons of witchcraft, back in the old days; and Nathan Nugent, too, although they withdrew that accusation when it finally came to a trial. But George Sturgeon was pressed to death; and Missie Sturgeon was burned to death; and neither the Sturgeons nor the Nugents forgave the Palens for more than a hundred years."

"My late wife was a Nugent," said Richard.

"Yes . . . Sara Nugent, I knew her."

"I'm surprised I never met you when I was younger," Richard told her.

"I wasn't allowed to mix with Palens. Stay away from them Palens, that's what my mother always used to say. Palens is poison."

Richard smiled. "Would you like a drink? Maybe we can patch things up after all these years."

Greta Reuter pursed her lips, and thought about it, but then she shook her head. "I'd best be getting back. I have chores to do. Baking, cleaning."

"Whatever you like," said Richard, not sure if he had made a friend or not. He formally shook Greta's hand, and then she left. He felt oddly guilty, as if he had been unfaithful to Sara for the first time.

After she had gone, he stood by the window watching Ron Maccione's caterpillars leveling the field, bright mechanical yellow amongst the dark trees. He lifted the gingham cloth from Greta Reuter's peach pie. It was heavily sifted with sugar and the crust was burned at the edge.

Across the top, Greta Reuter had cut out the pastry greeting, *Welcome Home.*

It took Ron Maccione six days to clear the meadow. They trucked over 150 tonnes of rocks and stones which they stacked at the far perimeter of the property to form a dry-stone retaining wall. Then they leveled the ground in preparation for Fraser and Fairmont to asphalt and mark out the courts.

Late Thursday afternoon, as the last caterpillar was loaded up on to a flatbed trailer, Richard came out with a chilled sixpack of Olympia Gold, and handed them around.

"Never shifted so many damned rocks in my natural life," said Ron Maccione, swallowing beer. "But you've got yourself a real clear site there now, Mr Palen. You could lay down a spirit-level anyplace you liked, any direction."

Richard said, "You've done a fine job, Mr Maccione. I'll go get your check."

That evening, Richard took a slow lonely walk around the meadow. The oaks were thick with shadows, like Rorschach blots. A damp, chilly wind was blowing. *Home is where the heart is, but the heart is not at home.* He stood for a long time on the stone retaining-wall, looking back toward the house.

He was just about to walk back when he heard the hollow knocking of dislodged stones. He hesitated, listened, but there was no more knocking, and the field remained silent. Silent as a closed purse.

He walked back toward the house across the finely-graded soil which would soon be his tennis-courts. As he locked the doors and went upstairs to bed, he realized that he hadn't thought about Sara and the children all day. Maybe grief did eventually die, after all.

When he slept that night in his curtainless bedroom, on his foldaway bed, he dreamed he was being pressed down on to the mattress by an unbearably oppressive weight. He

112

struggled and twisted, but the weight grew progressively heavier, crushing him, until he could scarcely breathe.

He tried to scream, but in his dream he couldn't make himself heard. The weight on top of him began to crush his feet, and then his shins, the bones crunching and splitting like bamboo canes. Then his kneecaps were edged sideways off his knees; his thighbones splintered; and finally, agonizingly, his pelvis broke apart, flooding the bed with his intestines.

He woke up shivering, as if he were suffering from a high fever. He wiped the sweat from his face with his sheet; then he turned over and checked his watch. It wasn't even midnight yet.

He went downstairs to the kitchen and poured himself a large glass of water. He stood drinking it, holding on to the faucet the way that children do, watching himself reflected in the kitchen window. He had dreamed about Sara again and again, he had dreamed about the children screaming; but he had never dreamed about himself before, being crushed.

Perhaps this was all part of the process of healing; of becoming whole again. He wasn't sure that he liked it; he wasn't even sure that he could handle it; but maybe it was what he needed.

He rinsed his glass, and set it upside-down on the draining-board, and switched off the kitchen light. As he set foot on the stairs, however, he heard a dry clonking noise. He stopped still, listening. Maybe it was the plumbing. But it had sounded empty, echoing, like two skulls being knocked together.

Two skulls, or two stones.

Ron Maccione said, "Are you trying to kid me, or what?"

Richard was standing in the hallway, his Dad U R The Greatest coffee-mug steaming on top of the kitchen stool

113

beside him. It was a few minutes after seven o'clock the sun had been up for less than twenty minutes.

"No kidding, Mr Maccione. The whole field is full of them."

"Well, that's pretty damned hard to believe, Mr Palen. We shifted over one hundred fifty-eight tonnes of stone and rock off of that field. We graded that soil fine as baby-powder."

"You want to come over and check it out for yourself?"

"Sure I'll come over and check it out for myself. But I'm pretty damned tied up today. What do you say Monday?"

"Mr Maccione I'm going to cancel your check. You promised me no stones, remember?"

"I cleared the stones, Mr Palen, so help me. When I left that field, there wasn't a single stone worth calling a stone."

Richard sipped coffee, and burned his mouth. "You said they could come back. Some kind of physics. The cereal-box syndrome."

"Well, sure, but that's only if they're *there*, Mr Palen, under the soil surface. We cleared them, Mr Palen. We cleared them good."

Richard picked up the telephone and stepped sideways in the hallway so that he could see through the sitting-room window to the gardens at the back, and beyond, to the meadow. The early-morning light was bony and uncompromising. Even though the meadow was screened by trees, the stones that were strewn across it were obvious, even from here. Hundreds of them, scattered right across the finely-graded soil from one side of the meadow to the other.

"Shit," said Ron Maccione. *"Piove sul bagnato."*

While he was waiting for Ron Maccione to arrive, Richard

walked out across the meadow, picking his way between the stones with complete bewilderment. I mean, how the *hell* – ?

Even allowing for natural geological sifting – the so-called "cereal-box" effect in which smaller particles sift and trickle downwards between larger particles, like the powdery crushed-up bits in a box of Cap'n Crunchberries – all these hundreds of rocks couldn't have risen out of the ground overnight. And yet nobody could have trucked them all back again – there were no footprints on the soil, no tiretracks.

Richard began to feel peculiarly alarmed; as if the reappearance of the stones were more than a scientific phenomenon. As if it were a threat, or a warning.

Some of the rocks were huge, four or five feet across, and must have weighed seven or eight hundred pounds. Others were not much than pebbles. He picked up one of the smaller stones and hurled it high toward the far side of the meadow.

As he stepped back to watch it fall, a tissue-soft voice said, close behind him, "You're up early, Mr Palen."

Richard turned around. Greta Reuter was standing close by, her face pale, her eyes the same crushed-sugar color as the morning light. She wore a thick maroon dress and a maroon woollen shawl.

She looked around the meadow. "I thought you were going to clear it," she said. "You can't play much tennis on this, can you? Stones trip; stones hurt the feet; stones betray."

There was something about her expression that was almost amused. Richard said, "Stones seem to have the ability to come up overnight, too. This field was cleared yesterday. Not a stone in sight."

Greta Reuter said nothing, but continued to smile.

Richard finished the last of his coffee. "You wouldn't know anything about this, would you? I mean, there isn't

115

anybody local who doesn't like the idea of a tennis-club, is there?"

Greta Reuter turned her face away. "People are very reserved hereabouts. Very jealous about their privacy."

"Jealous enough to sabotage my tennis-courts?" Richard retorted. He hesitated, and then he said, "I'm only asking. I used to be a tennis champion. I've come across jealousy before."

"I suppose it *could* be sabotage," said Greta Reuter. "But if it was, who would have done it, and more important, how was it done?"

"Witchcraft?" Richard suggested. "This is prime country for witches."

Greta Reuter stared at him mischievously for a moment, then threw back her head and let out a loud, mannish laugh.

Baffled, enraged, Ron Maccione brought two of his bulldozers back to the meadow, and spent the better part of a day and a half clearing the stones back to the perimeter.

"I don't know what happened, don't even ask me," he said. "I'm taking the full responsibility, okay? I guaranteed you a clear field, no stones, *di riffe o di raffe*. But I don't know what the hell happened." That night, Richard heard knocking noises in his sleep: heavy, hollow, knocking noises, skulls knocking together. He woke up sweating, trembling, terrified – but conscious that he hadn't been dreaming of Sara. This dream was something new; something cold; something abrasive; something to do with Preston, and the stones in the meadow; and the crushed-sugar eyes of Greta Reuter.

He sat up in bed and drank a glass of tepid water. Then he eased himself up, and found his old toweling wrap, the one that Ivan Lendl had given him after Wimbledon, six years ago, and limped downstairs.

116

He opened the kitchen door. The moon was out. Under its colorless light, the stones were back. All over the meadow, as many as before, even strewn across the garden this time, closer to the house.

Richard went to the sitting-room and opened up his half-bottle of Jack Daniel's and poured himself a glassful. He stared at his reflection in the mirror, and he looked like a ghost of himself, a badly-frightened ghost.

Sara, he thought. *Help me.*

But the night remained silent and sealed, and the stones lay scattered across the meadow and the garden as if they had been beached by a prehistoric tide.

He was tempted to call Ron Maccione straight away, but he waited until morning.

"Mr Maccione," he said. "They're back."

"What? What's back? What are you talking about?"

"The stones, they're back. In fact, they're worse."

There was a very long silence. If anybody could convey over the telephone a sense of bitterness as sharp and as rural as bitten cow-parsley, then Ron Maccione managed to do it.

"So sue me," he said.

"What?"

"You heard. Sue me. I wash my hands."

Richard spent the entire morning wheeling stones out of the garden in a squeaking barrow and tipping them on to the edge of the meadow. Even though the day was cold and thundery, with flickers of lightning in the distance, he was sweating and puffing by eleven o'clock, and he stripped off his shirt. He felt like a character in a Grimm's fairy-tale, Dick the Stone-Shifter. He was rumbling the wheelbarrow back across the garden for what he had promised himself would be the last load when he became aware that Greta Reuter was standing close to the house, watching him.

117

He set down the wheelbarrow, and wiped sweat from his forehead with the back of his hand. He said nothing.

"I see the stones are back," she remarked, approaching him along the diagonal paths, left and then right, left and then right.

He nodded, still short of breath.

"Quite a phenomenon," she said, still smiling. "Have you found out what's causing it? Or *who*?"

He wiped his chest with his shirt. "You want some coffee?"

"I brought you another pie," she said. "Seeing how much you liked the last one. It's blueberry this time. Sad, sad, blueberry."

"Thank you, you needn't have troubled yourself. I'm getting quite used to a diet of frozen pizzas and lima beans."

She accompanied him back to the kitchen. "Tell me," she said. "When you're playing a game of tennis, and you do something to deliberately frighten or unsettle your opponent, what do you call that?"

Richard glanced at her sharply. "I don't know. Psyching out, I guess."

"That's it," she smiled. "Psyching out."

It was only after she had left that he lifted the cloth covering the pie, and saw the pastry letters *Fare Thee Well*.

He was wakened by the sound of knocking. Dark, granite-hard knocking. He sat up in bed and switched on his bedside lamp. He sat listening. There was somebody in the house. Somebody, or something. He listened for two or three minutes, suppressing his breathing.

He heard the softest of crunching noises outside the door. He eased himself out of bed, and crossed the room. He had almost reached the door when it creaked sharply; and one of the upper hinges popped.

He hesitated, with his hand on the doorknob. The door

creaked again – a deep, twisted creak, as if the very grain of the wood were being tortured. Behind the door he heard a heavy grating and grinding. It seemed as if the whole door-frame were being subjected to enormous pressure.

But from what?

The door cracked. Richard stepped back a little; but he was too late. The door suddenly burst its hinges, and collapsed on top of him, followed by an avalanche of rocks. He screamed in pain as both his ankles were broken, and the stainless steel pins which held his thighbones together exploded through his skin.

He was pinned to the floor, on his back, with the rock-heaped door pressing down on top of him.

"*Aah! God! Help me!*" he screamed. "*God! Help me!*"

But nobody answered, and the door grew heavier and heavier as one more rock after another scraped itself on to the top of the heap.

The rocks were alive. They were like huge, blind, slow-creeping turtles, with a heartless and unstoppable determination to crush the last ounce of life out of him.

He felt his ribs clutching him; then crackling one by one. He felt something burst inside him, and blood and bile gushed up into his mouth. He spat, coughed, choked.

"*God!*" he gargled, with lungs that were so tightly compressed that they could scarcely take in any air.

His head fell back and his eyes rolled up; and it was then that he saw her standing over him, Greta Reuter, in a long grayish dress, her blonde hair loosened, smiling, calm, with her hands held up in front of her as if she were praying.

"Help me," he whispered. "For God's sake, help me."

Greta Reuter slowly shook her head. "William Palen didn't help George Sturgeon, not for God's sake, not for any sake. His wife Emily begged for his life, but William Palen hardened his heart."

119

"Help me," Richard repeated. "I can't – "

Again Greta Reuter shook her head.

"William Palen piled on the last of the rocks that pressed George Sturgeon to death. And now you're back in Preston, and you're William Palen's natural heir, so you must pay the price."

She knelt down beside him, and touched his forehead with cool fingertips. "Missie Sturgeon lives within me. Missie Sturgeon has lived for generations within all the Sturgeon women until the time could come when she could take her revenge. That is the way with witches."

All that Richard could do was gasp, as yet another massive rock grated its way to the top of the heap, and added enough weight to break his pelvis apart.

"Fare thee well," smiled Greta Reuter, drawing back her hair so that she could kiss his bloody lips.

Richard had never imagined that being slowly crushed could be so painful. He felt as if every nerve in his body were being stripped, like electrical cables. But he could no longer draw enough air into his lungs to cry out.

The very worst part was to feel like screaming but not to be able to. *Sara*, he thought, in agony. *Sara*.

Greta Reuter left the house like a gray shadow leaving the door open behind her. Outside, lightning danced epileptically on the horizon.

As she walked diagonally across the meadow, the stones that were strewn across it began to shift, and to knock against each other, and then to tumble.

By the time she reached the center of the meadow, with her blonde hair blowing across her face, hundreds of stones were clattering behind her, in her footsteps. The lightning flickered; her eyes shone white as milky marbles.

She had not yet reached the far side of the meadow, however, when a tall dark-haired figure materialized out of the darkness. A woman with dark eyes, and a face as composed as a porcelain mask.

"Where are you going, Missie Sturgeon?" the woman called, in a shrill, commanding voice. Greta Reuter stopped rigidly still, and her bride's train of tumbling rocks clattered into silence.

"Who are you?" Greta Reuter demanded. "What do you want of me?"

"What have you done, Missie Sturgeon?" the woman cried. Her voice like saws; her voice like seagulls.

Greta Reuter took three stiff-legged steps forward. The rocks followed. "Sara Nugent," she whispered.

"You've killed him!" Sara accused her. "You had no right to. You had no call to."

Greta Reuter took another step forward, but Sara swung her arm and crackles of lightning skipped and popped from her fingertips, real witchery; and Greta Reuter stood stiff and terrified, her hair rising and flying straight up above her, as the hair of all women flies up when they are about to be struck by lightning. Her face contorted, screaming a wide, silent scream.

"You had no right to," Sara repeated, her voice soft and blurry with static electricity. "The sin dies with the sinner, you know that."

Greta Reuter continued to scream. Then lightning struck her, directly on top of her head, and for one terrible instant her bones were visible through her skin. Then she fell backwards, in flames, convulsing and shuddering, with smoke pouring out of her wide-open mouth.

All around her, the stones cracked and split and exploded in every direction.

Sara stood over her for a long time, while the storm rumbled and gradually passed. Then she walked toward the house, where Richard at last would be waiting for her.

The Woman in the Wall

Archbold, Ohio

Archbold, Ohio, (population 3,318) is the only town in this book in which I have never spent any time (I stopped for twenty minutes for a cup of coffee and a Danish). Without being disparaging, I can think of no earthly reason why I should, and even one of the residents agreed with me. Because I have altered and fictionalized the setting, I have changed its name slightly to "Archman". But I have visited Toledo and Defiance and seen the Independence Dam, and I was so taken by the scenery and the kindness of the people I met that I wanted to set a story somewhere in the vastness of northern Ohio – with that sense of being poised in the mid-West, somewhere between Cleveland and the setting sun.

I still have a postcard I bought in Archbold, showing some outstandingly nondescript buildings. Perhaps Archbold – except for those who live there and love it – is one of those places that should forever remain in one's imagination.

THE WOMAN IN THE WALL

It was raining in cold dreary sheets that day I moved into 31 Caper Street; scurrying between the uplifted tailgate of my station wagon and the wedged-open front door, with a sodden copy of the *Archman Times* draped over my head.

And when at last it was all over, and I was sitting in my own brown dilapidated chair with rain-streaked boxes stacked around me, I closed my eyes against the raw glare of the single electric bulb and breathed relief.

But what sadness, too. Because Vicky was gone, and Jimmy Junior was gone, and here I was, alone in Archman, Ohio, on a rainy night, with wet shoes, and nothing to show for four years of marriage but old magazines and dog-eared Christmas cards and records I never wanted to listen to, never again.

I rummaged my way through four cardboard boxes until I found a half-empty bottle of Wild Turkey. There was nothing to drink it out of but a lime-encrusted flower-vase. I sat under the single bulb and drank myself a toast. To love, to life, to what-the-hell.

You threaten to walk out so many times. You rage and argue and all the time you never believe that one day you're going to do it. And then one day you do. And once you're standing on the wrong side of that door, that's it. Something irrevocable has happened, and you can never, ever go back.

125

My advice to all discontented husbands: don't argue, don't drink, don't walk through that door.

Now Vicky was working as a secretary in Toledo and Jimmy Junior was classified as the child of a single-parent family and I was preparing to start work as a geography-and-athletics teacher at Archman Junior High. Your whole life can turn itself upside-down that quickly – just because you walked out of that door.

I finished my drink, and lay back for a while, and then I decided I needed a walk, and maybe some supper, too. I left the apartment by the narrow front stairs and walked along Caper Street as far as Main.

It had stopped raining, but the streets were still wet. An occasional car swooshed past, its brake-lights bleeding into the glistening blacktop. I thrust my hands into my pockets and looked up at the rapidly-clearing sky, and felt that I was two thousand miles away from anybody I knew and loved.

On the corner of Willow and Main, there was a drug-store with steamy windows called Irv's Best. I pushed my way inside and it smelled of meatloaf and grape-flavored gum and *Elf Quest* comics. There was a rundown-looking guy behind the counter with a face like potatoes and a folded paper hat. "How about a Reuben sandwich and a lite beer?" I asked him.

He poured me the beer. "You want gas?" he said. "This'll give you gas. This, and a Reuben sandwich. You want a guaranteed recipe for gas?"

"I just want a sandwich and a beer, is that all right with you?"

He sniffed. "You headed east?" he asked me.

"I'm not headed anywhere."

He frowned. He obviously didn't understand.

"I'm moving in. I've come to live here."

"You've come to live in Archman? You out of your tree?"

"I'm teaching geography and athletics at the Junior High."

"You *are* out of your tree."

"I don't think so," I told him, and by this time he was making me feel irritated. "I wanted to find someplace quiet, and Archman looks like it."

"Well, you're right there. Archman is someplace quiet all right. Archman is so goddamned quiet they keep sending the sheriff across from Wauseon to see if we're still breathing."

He sniffed more violently, and spent some time wiping the stainless-steel counter with a smeary rag. "There's a church, and a store, and a brickworks, and a library full of books that everybody's read, and that's it."

He was silent and thoughtful for a while, and then he reached out his hand and said, "My name's Carl, by the way. Good to know you. Welcome to Archman."

"What happened to Irv?"

"Irv who?"

"This place is called Irv's Best, isn't it?"

"Oh, that Irv. He died."

I finished my sandwich and walked back to Caper Street. Carl was right. Archman was the quietest place I've ever been in, *ever*. You could stand in the middle of Main Street at midnight and you couldn't hear anything at all. It was just as if the whole town had been covered by a thick felt blanket. Claustrophobic memories of childhood, underneath a bedspread that was too heavy.

I climbed wearily up the stairs to my first-floor apartment, and closed the door behind me. I undressed, dropping my clothes on the floor. Then I took a shower. The plumbing shuddered so loud I imagined they could probably hear me all the way across town. I soaped myself and whistled a little. *The night they drove Old Dixie down . . . and all the people were singing . . .*

127

But then, so soft and indistinct that I thought I might have imagined it, I heard a noise in the apartment somewhere.

I listened, feeling that odd tingly feeling you get when your intellect is telling you to be reasonable but your instinct is more than just a little bit alarmed. I never particularly like taking a shower in an empty apartment anyway, it makes me feel *vulnerable*.

The next thing you know, Anthony Perkins is going to come slashing his way through the shower-curtain with a twelve-inch carving-knife.

I heard the noise again, and this time I shut off the faucet. I listened and listened, but all I could hear now was the soft gurgling of water going down the drain. I stepped out of the shower and picked up my towel. I opened the bathroom door.

There it was again. A soft, insistent, scratching noise. A rat, maybe; or a bird in the eaves. It seemed to be coming from the bedroom. I hesitated outside the door for a while, and then stepped in.

The bedroom was empty. There was a solid red-brick wall at one end, and the three other walls were painted white. I had set up the new divan with the brass headboard which I had bought three days ago at Sear's, but there was nothing else in the room at all. No cupboards for rats or cats to conceal themselves in. No nooks and crannies. Just a plain rectangular room, with a bed. A double bed, which one casualty from a recently-broken marriage was hoping from time to time to share with somebody else. God let there be some single women in Archman. Correction, God. Single women under the age of 60.

I listened a moment longer, but all I could hear was the muffled rattling of a distant freight-train. I finished drying myself, and then I climbed into bed and switched out the light. The ceiling was criss-crossed with squares of light from the street outside, on which the shadows of raindrops trembled. I lay with my eyes open feeling more sad and lonely than I had ever been in my whole life. I thought of Vicky. I thought of Jimmy Junior. I let out one tight sob that was more of a cough and then I didn't allow myself any more.

Sleep took me by stealth. I snored once, and jolted, but then I was sleeping again. Two hours of the night passed me by, and then I heard that noise again. A soft, repetitive scritching, like claws against brick. I lay staring at the wall, tensed-up, not breathing, and then it came again.

I reached down and switched on the lamp, half-expecting to send a rat scurrying away into the shadows. But the bedroom was bare. I listened and listened and there it was. *Scritch, scritch, scritch.*

There was no doubt about it this time. It was coming from the other side of the wall. Perhaps somebody in the next building had a pet dog that was locked up for the night. Perhaps they were doing some late-night decorating, scraping off some old wallpaper. Whatever it was, it didn't have anything to do with me – except that if it kept on, I'd have to go next door and complain about it.

I turned off the light, dragged the comforter up around my ears, and made a determined effort to go to sleep. I had almost sunk back into the darkness when the scratching started up again. Angry now, and deeply fatigued, I picked up a heavy bronze ashtray and banged on the wall with it.

"Can you hear me? There's somebody living here now! I'm trying to get some sleep!"

Almost immediately, I received three sharp knocks on the wall in reply.

"Listen!" I yelled. "All I want you to do is to shut up! Do you hear me? No more knocking! Just let me get some sleep!"

There was silence. I stayed where I was, kneeling up in bed, half-expecting to hear another knock, but none came.

After a while, I allowed myself to wriggle back under the covers and re-arrange my nest.

An hour passed. I dozed and dreamed. I heard whispering and laughter. Sometimes I was asleep and sometimes I was awake. I thought I could see someone sitting hunched in a hood in the opposite corner of the room, and it turned out to be nothing more than a shadow. Then, later, I woke up sweating and although the room was silent I knew that somebody had been speaking to me. I lay bunched up in my covers, listening, holding my breath, my brain feeling as cold as an empty linoleum corridor.

Somebody said, "*Help me.*"

I lifted my head a fraction.

"*Help me,*" the voice repeated. A woman's voice, but very faint.

I sat up in bed, listening so intently that my eardrums sang.

"*Please help me call somebody, please*".

I pressed my ear against the brick walls.

"*Help me,*" she repeated, and this time there was no doubt that she was next door, whispering to me through the wall.

"What's wrong?" I called back. "Can you hear me? What's wrong?"

" – *lp me,*" she said.

"Listen!" I shouted. "Are you locked in? What's wrong? Has somebody locked you in? What's happening in there?"

" – *me, for God's sake, hel –* "

I sat up straight. I didn't know what the hell to do. A strange woman on the opposite side of my bedroom wall was begging me for help, but she wouldn't tell me what was wrong. Either that, or she couldn't hear me. But if she were whispering, and I could hear *her*, then she must be able to hear me yelling.

I climbed out of bed. I went through to the living-room,

130

found the phone and picked it up, intent on calling the police. But then I thought I'd better make one last check. I'd called the police once before, when Vicky and I had been arguing, and that experience had been sufficient to make me feel highly prudent about summoning the law. I went back to the bedroom and knocked on the bricks with my ashtray.

"Are you okay?" I called. "Are you hurt, or anything like that? Do you need an ambulance?"

"*He's coming,*" she whispered. "*Please hurry, he's coming!*" Then she screamed, and her scream was so piercing that I shouted out, too, and dragged my pants off the back of the chair, and hop-stumbled into them, and grabbed at my shirt, and wrenched open my door and ran down the stairs to the street not even stopping to think that I was scared.

Outside it was cold and windy, with a fine flying drizzle in the air. I banged at the door of the house next door, Number 29. "Let me in!" I shouted. "Let me in! You touch that woman and I'll call the cops!"

I banged and yelled and yelled and banged, and two or three lights went on, in bedrooms across the street. I tried to wrestle the front door open with my shoulder, but even though it was old and rotten and the gray-green paint was flaking, it wouldn't budge.

I stepped panting into the street and peered up at the second-story windows. They were dark and blank. They looked almost as if they had been boarded up from the inside. I wondered if I ought to shout out again, or find an ax and try to smash the door down, but neighbors were watching me now, hostile and inquisitive, and I decided against it. If anything serious was going on next door at Number 29, I'd better call the police, and leave it to them to break in.

I ran back upstairs, and hammered at the bedroom wall. "It's all right! Hold on! I'm calling the police!"

There was no reply. My God, I thought, he's killed her. He's killed her and I couldn't stop him. I picked up the telephone with shaking hands and dialed the local police station. It was almost a minute before they answered.

The patrol car parked on the curb outside with its red-and-blue lights flashing and now the whole neighborhood was awake. A thin gray-haired police officer with a Boy Scout hat was standing on the sidewalk waiting for me when I opened the door. "You the fellow who made the complaint about twenty-nine?"

"That's right. I heard a woman calling for help. Then a scream. She said something about a man coming to get her. I tried to break into the house but I couldn't."

The police-officer tirelessly chewed gum and stared at me with interest. "You tried to break in but you couldn't?"

I nodded. "The door was locked, I couldn't budge it."

"The door was locked," he repeated. I was beginning to feel as if one of us was some kind of mental retard.

I inclined my head toward Number 29. "Don't you think you'd better try to get in there, to see what's happened? There's a woman in there and she could have been hurt."

The police-officer fastidiously adjusted his hat. "Well, you come along with me, sir, and we'll see just exactly what's been going on."

I closed the front door behind me, and followed him along the sidewalk. Several neighbors had come out into the street and were standing staring at me, their arms folded in suspicion, their faces conspicuously unfriendly.

"You lived here long?" the police officer asked me, without turning around.

"I moved in this afternoon."

"Thought I hadn't seen your face before. I know most faces. Excepting those that want to hide them deliberate."

132

To my surprise, he walked straight past the front door of Number 29 without even glancing at it. "The screaming was coming from here," I told him, trying to catch up. "It was coming from right next door."

The police officer carried on walking to the corner of Number 29. He turned into the alleyway beside it, and then turned and beckoned me.

"What?" I said, uncertainly.

"Come on here," he said. "Take a look for yourself."

I stepped after him into the alleyway, convinced that I was going to witness something terrible. Yet he seemed so calm.

"Look," he said, and pointed, and I took one last step forward and saw that behind the brick facade of Number 29 with its tightly-locked door and its blanked-out windows there was nothing but a vacant lot, overgrown with grass and dead-nettles and strewn with tires and broken bedsteads and other debris.

I raised my eyes slowly up the scabby outside wall of Number 31, and saw the patchy brickwork of my own bedroom wall, twenty feet above the ground. Nobody could have scratched or whispered or screamed at that wall, not unless they had a twenty-foot ladder. An extraordinary unbalancing shudder went through me, and I turned back and stared at the police officer in total perplexity.

He chewed his gum and smiled. "I'd say you had a nightmare, wouldn't you?" he asked me.

I stared back at the wall. It was beginning to drizzle more heavily now, and the drizzle made a soft prickling noise among the weeds.

"I don't know," I replied. "It surely didn't *seem* like a nightmare. Not at the time."

"Best get back to sleep," the police officer told me, and without another word he walked back to his patrol car, slammed the door, and drove off.

* * *

133

The next morning, at Irv's, Carl leaned across the counter and said, "Heard about your little frack-ass last night."

"News travels fast," I told him, with a mouthful of cheese Danish.

"Aint much escapes my attention," said Carl. "Jim Kelly said you heard some woman screaming, something like that, in Number Twenty-nine."

"Who's Jim Kelly?"

"Plumber, lives opposite you."

I swallowed Danish and stirred my coffee. "Yes, well, I must have made some kind of mistake. The police officer who showed up said I was probably having a nightmare."

"That's what he always says."

"What do you mean, 'that's what he *always* says'? You mean it's happened before?"

Carl nodded. "All over town. Here, there, and every-where. John Peebles heard it over on Sycamore; Mrs Dunning heard it on East Main. In the end, the Chamber of Commerce asked some professor from the University of Chicago to come down and see what the hell was going on. Collective hysterics, that's what he called it, something like that. Community guilt."

"Guilt about what?" I asked him.

"Not what, *who*. Nesta Philips, the local grade-school teacher. She was leaving school one winter afternoon four years ago and that was the last time that anybody saw her. They never found hide nor hair of her, excepting one of the combs she wore in her hair, and that was all clogged up with dried blood. They never found Nesta, and they never found who killed her, and that's why the population of Archman is supposed to hear whispering and screaming just the way you did last night. Kind of makes your hair stand up on end, don't you think? I'm surprised that Dennis didn't tell you."

"Who's Dennis?"

"Dennis is the local deputy. The fellow who said you were probably having a nightmare. You know what they say about Dennis? You can always rely on Dennis to be just. Just plain stupid." Carl snickered at his own joke, and shook his head. "He's as even-handed as the day is long, and twice as dumb."

I swallowed coffee. "It's hard to believe that what I heard last night was just an hallucination. I mean – *I* couldn't be feeling guilty about Nesta Philips, could I? I never even heard of her, till now."

"There's stranger things under the sun than you or I ever dreamed about, fair Horatio," Carl misquoted.

"But she sounded so real. She sounded just like she was right next door."

Carl made a face. "You saw for yourself. There *is* no next door."

"She could almost have been – *inside* the wall."

"You mean, bricked up?" Carl asked me. "You mean she's climbed up a whole story, right inside a cavity wall, just to keep you awake at night? Even if it was possible, it still wouldn't make any sense."

"I don't know," I told him. "*None* of it makes sense, whichever way you look at it."

It was well past midnight before I heard it again. It had taken me nearly two hours to get myself to sleep, and just when I was beginning to slide into unconsciousness, I heard a *scritch, scritch* and I sat up in bed, startled, wide awake, clutching the covers as tightly as a child.

"Is that you?" I asked, in a choked-up voice.

There was a long silence. Two or three cars swished past on the wet streets outside. "Is that you?" I repeated.

Again, there was a soft scratching, claws on brick.

I hesitated for a while, and then I said, "Are you in any kind of danger?"

No reply.

135

"Are you trapped? Is that it? Are you trapped inside the wall?"

No reply.

"Listen," I said, more boldly now, "if I'm going to help you, I have to know where you are."

There was a very long silence. I was beginning to think that she wouldn't answer me, but then I heard that fearful, electrifying whisper. *"Help me. Please, help me."*

I leaned against the wall. "But where are you?" I begged her. "I can't do anything until you tell me where you are!"

"Help me, he's coming. Please help me. Please! You don't know what he's going to do to me! Please!"

"Listen to me!" I yelled at her. "I can't do anything! I don't know where you are!"

It was then that she started to sob and scream and beg me to help her, *beg* me. There was nothing else that I could do. I galloped downstairs to my station wagon, dragged out my tool-box, and took out a hammer and a maul and a tire-iron. I made such a clanking noise with the tools that a light went on, across the street, and a voice cried out, "For the love of mike!"

Back upstairs in the bedroom, I dragged the bed clear of the wall, and immediately starting hammering at the bare brick. As I did so, the woman's voice screamed and screamed, and babbled hysterically for help. I was almost hysterical myself. I kept hammering away, dislodging the mortar with the maul, and then levering the bricks out with the sharp end of the tire-iron.

After the third brick had banged on to the floor, there was a loud knocking at my apartment door. "Hey! What the hell's going on! What the hell are you doing in there? Don't you know it's one o' clock in the morning!"

I ignored the shouting, and kept on knocking bricks out of the wall. The voice said, "I'm calling the landlord!

136

I'm going to have you thrown out of here, you inconsiderate bum!"

I dislodged half-a-dozen more bricks, and they went tumbling across the floor. Now I could see right inside the cavity of the wall. I lifted my bedside lamp and held it up, so that it shone down into the wall where it sounded as if the woman's voice had been coming from.

"Can you see this light?" I shouted. "Can you see this light?"

Silence.

"Can you hear me? Can you see this light?"

Again, silence. I began to have the dreadful feeling that she might have climbed right up inside the wall-cavity, all the way to the level of my bedroom – and that my first few blows with the hammer had dislodged her, and sent her dropping twenty feet down to ground level again. She could be wedged inside the wall somewhere, unconscious, or seriously hurt.

Yet the wall-cavity was no more than five or six inches wide. Nobody could have crawled up inside it, even if they had been deranged enough to want to. It was too narrow and too dark, and they would have been lacerated by the rough mortar and the razor-sharp edges of the bricks.

I stood staring at the huge hole in my bedroom wall, and dropped my hammer on to the floor. As I did so, I heard the front door of my apartment open. My landlord Mr Katz came in, wrapped in a green padded bathrobe, looking white-faced and furious.

He stared at the wall and spread his hands wide. "What's this? You stupid *momzer*! What have you done to my wall?"

I sat down on the bed. "I thought I heard something inside it."

He looked at me with his mouth wide open. "You thought you heard something *inside* it? Like what?"

"I don't know. It sounded as if somebody was trapped. Maybe it was all my imagination."

"An imagination like yours my brother-in-law should have! He runs a demolition company!"

"I'm sorry, Mr Katz," I said. I suddenly felt weary and stupid and very alone. "I'm really sorry."

"I should throw you out, you know that?" said Mr Katz, stepping forward in his mules and peering down into the drafty cavity. "I should throw you out right now, with all these – cardboard boxes after you."

But he turned back again, and said, "You're going to be teaching at the school, right? I know Mrs Henry, the principal, she and I are good friends. So for her sake, I'll give you a last chance. You repair this damage, you make this wall good, and don't ever again break anything else in this apartment, not so much as a lightswitch, and we'll forget it ever happened."

He picked up one of the bricks from the floor. "Get new bricks, these are all broke. And get this rug cleaned, too. Then we'll forget it."

He stared at me for a long time without saying anything. Then he laid his hand on my shoulder and said, "You got divorced, maybe that's it. Sometimes a sadness stays in your head, and then comes out some other way, like breaking down walls maybe."

"Maybe," I said, without looking up.

On Saturday morning I went down to the Archman Brickworks down by the river to pick up a dozen matching bricks to repair Mr Katz's wall. It was a damp, foggy morning. The brick-kilns smoked steadily into the fog. Everywhere around there were huge stacks of recently-fired bricks, flettons and marls and engineering bricks. I walked up to a young man who was sitting in a forklift truck reading a copy of *Guns & Ammo* and listening to tinny rock music on a Sony Walkman.

"Office?" I shouted, and he jerked his thumb toward a small shack with a corrugated-iron roof at the side of the main tunnel-kiln building.

In the office, a kerosene heater had raised the temperature until it was almost asphyxiating. A fat red-faced man was shouting at somebody on the telephone. Abruptly, he clamped the telephone down and turned to face me. "Well?" he demanded, "what can I do for *you*?"

"I'm looking for some bricks," I said, lamely.

He dragged out a handkerchief and noisily blew his nose. "I guess you came to the right place. How many do you want?"

"Eleven," I told him. I rested my brown-paper shopping sack on the table, and lifted out one of the bricks from my bedroom wall. "Eleven like this."

The red-faced man took the brick and hefted it in his hand. "This is a hand-made job. First-quality facing brick. We don't make these any more."

He handed the brick back. "We may have some left in stock. Come around to the back."

Thankfully, I followed him out of the overheated office into the chill outside. He waddled ahead of me over the gritty, brick-red ground. We passed stack after stack of different-colored bricks, until at last we reached a row of stacks that were protected from the weather by a lean-to roof.

"Here we are," said the red-faced man. "No more'n five dozen left. We used to have a guy who made them special, all by hand, but after he was gone, there wasn't no point in training anybody else to make them. It's all mechanized now. Two tunnel-kilns and a Hoffmann kiln. You can drive your car down here and pick what you want."

He waddled off again, leaving me to select my eleven bricks. I lifted them up, one by one, making sure that none of them were chipped, and that they matched the pale rosy hue of the sample brick from my bedroom wall.

I had almost finished when I thought I heard somebody whisper.

I said, "What?" involuntarily, and looked around. But the brickyard was deserted and foggy. Even the boy in the fork-lift had gone.

Then I heard it again, and it was unmistakeable. *"Help me."*

It was her. It was the woman in the wall. The skin on the back of my hands prickled as if I had been electrocuted.

"Help me. Please, Help me."

I stared down at the eleventh brick, resting in the palm of my hand. *"Help me, please, help me,"* she pleaded, and then I knew for sure. I lifted the brick up and held it close to my chest.

The bricks, damn it! She was in the bricks! Her body or her soul or some part of her last agonies alive were mixed into the bricks! That was why they had heard her whispering and pleading in different parts of town! Wherever a wall had been built or patched with any of these bricks, she was there – begging, crying to be saved.

I walked back to the brickyard office, shaken but determined. "How much for the whole stack?" I asked the red-faced man.

"Thought you only wanted eleven," he retorted.

"Well, I did. But they're such beautiful bricks."

"One hundred fifty dollars even. You'll have to carry 'em away yourself, though. My delivery truck's broke."

I counted out $150, and laid them on his desk. "Tell me," I said, as casually as I could manage. "The man who made these bricks . . . is he still alive?"

The red-faced man took out his handkerchief again. "Sure he's still alive. He didn't retire old or nothing. He was just sick of making bricks, that's what he said. His name's Jesse Franks, lives over on Sycamore, right down by the Exxon gas station. He runs his own body-shop these days."

140

"Thanks," I told him. "I'll just drive down and load up the bricks."

"Get Martin to lend you a hand. About time that boy did some hard work."

I sat in my station-wagon for most of Saturday afternoon, cater-corner from Jesse Franks' house on Sycamore Street, waiting to catch a glimpse of Jesse Franks himself. I suppose I could have gone straight up and knocked on his front door and introduced myself. After all, he wouldn't have known me from Adam. But for what I had in mind, I preferred to remain unseen and incognito, just in case it all went wrong and I was making a horse's ass out of myself.

I was frightened, too, to tell the truth, because if I *wasn't* making a horse's ass out of myself, then Jesse Franks was not the kind of man I wanted to upset.

It rained, and then the rain cleared. At four o'clock, when the clouds were scurrying like windblown newspapers and it was just beginning to get dark, the front door of his gray weatherboarded house opened, and he stepped out on to the porch. He was wearing a navy reefer coat and a brown woollen hat. He must have been forty-five years old, solidly built. He looked up and down the street for a moment, and then he came down the steps and out of his gate and started to walk southwards on Sycamore past the gas station.

He reached the bar on the corner and disappeared inside. I gave him five minutes, while the light steadily failed, and then I opened the door of my station wagon and climbed out. The suspension groaned. I still had the five dozen bricks stacked in the back: I had chosen to come here first, before unloading them and carrying them all the way up the stairs to my apartment.

I crossed the street keeping my head lowered and my coat-collar lifted. I went straight into Jesse Franks' front yard, and down the steps that led to his basement. There was a smell of cat's wee and weeds down there. I rattled the doorhandle but the door was locked. I hesitated for a moment. I could give it all up now, and forget it. Nobody would know the difference. Only Nesta Philips, whose soul was somehow imprisoned in those bricks, and who could never be free.

But she had whispered, "*Help me*," with such desperation, and I knew that I was the only person who could.

There was a broken triangle of concrete in the yard. I picked it up and, without hesitation, smashed one of the panes of glass in the basement door. I reached inside, and thank God there was the key. The door juddered as I opened it. Inside the basement it was gloomy and dusty and smelled of camphor.

I hurried upstairs, breathless and sweating. I kept imagining Jesse Franks finishing his beer and leaving the bar and walking back along the street. His house was bare and poorly-furnished. A sagging sofa with a brown stretch-nylon cover, two second-hand wheelback chairs. A television set, and a bureau with cracked veneer. No flowers, no ornaments, and only two pictures on the wall, both of waggon-trains. In the kitchen, a faucet with a blue rubber anti-splash attachment dripped into a large stained sink. I listened, and the silence was almost more alarming than the sound of somebody coming.

Up in the front bedroom, under the double-bed with the sawed-oak frame, I found what I was looking for.

My mouth was as dry as emery paper, and my pulse was skipping as I dragged it out. A cheap brown-fiber suitcase, locked. I forced open the locks with my screwdriver. Inside, a selection of knives – well-worn knives, with insulating tape around the handles – as well as a cheerfully-colored profusion of porno magazines, and a large pungent red rubber apron. Underneath the apron, a woman's dress, beige, neatly-folded; a woman's pantyhose,

142

underslip, and bra. All of these items of clothing were jigsawed with dark rusty marks.

I had been to the offices of the *Archman Times* just after lunch, and read everything I could find about Nesta Philips. On the day that she had gone missing, she had been wearing a "beige, or light-brown dress."

I closed the suitcase, and picked it up. I stood for a moment, listening; and then I hurried quickly and quietly downstairs. I tiptoed along the hall to the front door. The best thing to do was walk calmly and normally out of the house, and across the street to my car. But as I reached up toward the door-handle, the key sharply turned in the lock on the other side.

Panicking, I tried to retreat down the hallway, but the edge of the suitcase caught on the small hall table, and knives and magazines and clothes went sprawling everywhere. The front door opened and there was Jesse Franks, staring at me in complete amazement.

"Who the – ?" he began to ask, but then he saw the stained dress and the red rubber apron and the knives.

"What the hell do you think *you're* doing?" he demanded. His face was bunched-up muscle, with two glassy little pale-blue eyes.

I didn't wait to get into conversation. I shouldered him sharply in the chest, twisted away from his grabbing hands, and jumped down the front steps of the house three at a time. I ran across the road and wrenched open the door of my station-wagon.

Jesse Franks, however, was right behind. He caught my arm and swung me away from the wagon. Then he punched me hard in the ribs; and then again, and I staggered back and stumbled over a low wall just behind me.

"You interfering bastard, I'll kill you!" he panted, and he came forward to hit me again.

If it hadn't have been for dumb Dennis, I think he might

143

have done. But Dennis had been called out to Sycamore Street by a curtain-twitching old lady across the street, who had seen me breaking in. Just at that moment he came around the corner with his lights flashing and his siren warbling, and Jesse Franks spun awkwardly around as if somebody had body-tackled him.

"You bastard!" he shouted at me, hoarsely. "You called the cops!"

I was too winded to do anything but ineffectually raise one hand.

Jesse clambered heavily into my station wagon, and started the engine.

"That's my wagon!" I protested. But all he did was to give me the finger, and snarl, "If I ever get caught, bastard, I'm going to finish you off for good!"

He swerved away from the side of the road. As he did so, however, a huge gasoline truck emerged from the Exxon station and completely blocked the street. Jesse slewed my station wagon around, and came speeding back towards me.

Dennis saw what he was doing, and turned his patrol car sideways-on to block Jesse's escape.

I can remember what happened next as vividly as if it were a video-recording, which I can run and re-run and never forget. Jesse drove my station-wagon on to the sidewalk, but it bounced and skidded out of control, and collided head-on with a hydrant.

I started running towards it, but then I stopped. I couldn't believe what I was seeing. Under normal circumstances, Jesse Franks would have easily survived a collision like that. But the crash sent a furious blizzard of bricks hurtling the length of the wagon, smashing and buffeting his head and spraying blood all the way up the windows. I saw him flailing his arms, trying to protect himself, but then a single brick struck the back of his neck and his head jerked sideways at a sickening angle. Some of

144

the bricks burst right through the windshield and tumbled on to the sidewalk in a slush of glass.

Dennis came hurrying over, and tugged open the wagon door. Jesse lay slumped over the steering-wheel, with dark blood dripping on to the leg of his pants.

"He's dead," said Dennis, and he was shocked.

"Yes," I said. My stomach knotted itself up, and I had to take a deep breath and look the other way. "He was trying to get away."

"Well, get away from *what*?" asked Dennis. "I was called out because somebody was supposed to be breaking into his house."

"That was me. I was looking for something. Proof that Jesse Franks might have killed Nesta Philips. Go take a look in his hallway. All the evidence is there. Knives, clothes. I guess he was keeping them as some sort of souvenir."

"Jesse Franks killed Nesta Philips?"

I nodded. "That's right, and dismembered her, and baked her in his brick-kiln, I shouldn't be surprised, and powdered up her ashes, and fired them into bricks. That way, nobody would ever find any trace of her."

Dennis stepped away from the wagon and sniffed. "How come *you* did?"

I bent forward and picked up one of the bricks. "They say that the human spirit is immortal, don't they? They say that you never really die."

They wouldn't grant me permission for a grave at Archman Cemetery, so one day I drove the bricks out to the woods around Hamson Lake, and buried them there, neatly, under four feet of soil. I stood over the grave for a while in the chilly late-afternoon sunshine, and said the Lord's Prayer, and thought about ashes to ashes and dust to dust.

I thought I might have heard a voice, whispering to me;

but it was probably nothing more than the wind, blowing through the trees.

The next time Vicky brought Jimmy Junior around, she noticed a framed black-and-white photograph of a young woman on top of my bureau. She contained her inquisitiveness for as long as she could, but then she said, "Is it rude of me to ask who that is?"

"Oh, that's Nesta," I told her.

"Nesta? You never mentioned any Nesta."

"No, she's gone now," I replied. I picked up the photograph and smiled at it regretfully. "We were neighbors, that's all. Just very close neighbors. She lived –" and I pointed toward the wall.

Making Belinda

St Brelade's Bay, Jersey

Jersey is the southernmost of the Channel Islands, about 15 km long by 10 km wide, lying within sight of northern France. Its northern coast is characterized by high, rugged cliffs, but it slopes southwards through many pretty steep-sided valleys to St Brelade's and several other attractive and sandy bays. Jersey is a tax-haven, with its own legislative assembly (the States) and its own police. Its countryside is intensely farmed with tomatoes and potatoes and flowers under glass; while its towns are depressingly suburban, like any British seaside resort.

St Brelade's Bay, however, is one of the most unspoiled, with smooth sand and jagged rocks, and the balmy, timeless, slightly eccentric feeling of *Mr Hulot's Holiday*. In 1910, the teeth of a Neanderthal man were discovered at La Cotte, a rock-shelter in St Brelade's Bay, which gave me the first inkling for *Making Belinda*.

MAKING BELINDA

He lifted his arm in slow-motion, like a Movietone newsreel of an athlete breaking the hundred-yard sprint record in 1936, and the cocktail-waiter immediately caught the confidence in his wave, and deafened himself to the plaintive "could we have two pina coladas, please?" from the man with the brightly peeling head and the yellow Hawaiian shirt, and came weaving along the terrace to ask him what he wanted.

"The Perrier et Jouët, Belle Epoque, rosé," he said.

A frown at the wine-list. A moment's defensiveness.

"Ah. We don't sell that by the *glass*, sir."

"I didn't ask for a glass. I want a bottle. With two glasses, please."

"Of course, sir. Two glasses? May I see your key?"

It took the waiter ten minutes to bring the champagne and to make a fuss about opening it. Bryan didn't usually like fuss; but today he sat back and allowed the waiter to show off. It was, after all, Perrier Jouët Belle Epoque, in a wonderful stylized art-nouveau bottle. The man in the yellow Hawaiian shirt watched suspiciously.

A small but sharply-humiliating experience had taught Bryan a long time ago that it was naff to make a performance over opening wine. In front of a very stylish young woman, he had sniffed a Chianti cork – a *Chianti* cork – and she had flayed him with supercilious laughter. Bryan had also learned with equal pain that it was just as naff to order anything flambé, or to drink any kind of

149

coffee with cream floating on the top, or to push £10 into the maitre-d's hand in the hope of getting a good table.

These days, Bryan's motto was: don't give the bastards even the *chance* to laugh at you.

Bryan was a print rep. He had sold color printing for Johnson & Foreman for nearly nine years, driving hundreds of thousands of miles. Rain, shine, seasides, provincial cities, isolated factories. Walls, hotel kettles, florid wallpaper, sausages for breakfast. He had eaten in more hotel restaurants than he could remember, and he had learned his social graces the hard way.

His mother and father had eaten their Friday supper straight out of the *Daily Mirror*, walking along the street. His cheeks still burned when he thought about it. But he himself had learned to be self-contained, and self-disciplined, and tight. He had also learned that it's a serious mistake to pretend to be more sophisticated than you really are; because wherever you go there will always be someone more sophisticated than you, and with one small word they can make you publicly bleed. Not only can, but will. So – although Bryan himself was self-made, he had learned to despise the self-made. (How many Benidorm-bronzed print-buyers' wives, in overtight gilt evening-dresses, hysterical with a whole afternoon's gin, had massaged his thigh under how many dinner-tables?) From Newcastle to Plymouth, O Lord; from Bradford to Bishop's Stortford. Desperate for what? Not sex. They were usually too squiffy for sex. Reality, maybe.

But this evening was different. This evening Bryan was celebrating one of the most profitable print contracts he had ever negotiated; alone; on the cocktail terrace of L'Horizon Hotel, overlooking the smooth brassy sands of St Brelade's Bay, on Jersey; and this evening he could risk showing off, just a little. Shortly before lunch, after only two and a half hours, he had signed contracts for £2.3 million worth of color brochure printing; two and a half

150

hours in a bland featureless office in St Helier, all dusty yuccas and chipboard partitions and travel posters; and that was it. The deal closed, the contracts initialled, everybody happy. Mr Shah had shaken his hand. He had shaken Mr Aziz's hand. Very good, excellent, nice to do business with you. Budduh-budduh-budda, mate, and chicken biryani to you too.

From the terrace of L'Horizon it was only fifteen stone steps to the sand. In the distance, where the sea glittered, they were dragging in the last of the pedaloes, complicated silhouettes of skinny girls and skeletal machines. There was a faint smell of fish-and-chips on the wind, from one of the beach cafes; and the last children on the beach sounded as sad as distant seagulls.

Earlier in the day, when the sun was high, Bryan had seen topless girls sunbathing underneath the promenade, breasts like caramel creams. All the girls were gone now; but Bryan had asked for two champagne glasses because a thirtyish woman with a handsome face and highlighted blonde hair was sitting two tables away, wearing a pink halter-top that emphasized her heavy bosom, and bright Bermuda shorts. She was concentrating on solving the *Daily Telegraph* crossword, and Bryan found that attractive. Intellectual, but apparently alone.

He stood up, scraping his chair. He stood over her. She bit the end of her ballpen with lipstick-tinged teeth.

He was about to open his mouth and ask her if she wanted to share his celebration, when she said, "'Join to make a saving,' four letters."

"Pardon?" he replied.

She looked up. He could see himself reflected in her sunglasses. A thin, shortish man with deep-set, almost Russian-looking eyes and his black hair well cut, but somehow too thin and too shortish to be quite convincing enough. His trousers too shapeless to be provocative but too tight to be fashionable.

"'Bond,'" she said, and wrote it into her crossword. "Thank you."

He tried to laugh. "I'm not sure that I helped very much."

She paused for a moment, then took off her sunglasses. "Yes, you did. Just by being there. It always helps if I can ask somebody out loud."

"Oh. Good. Well, so long as I was useful."

Another pause, and he didn't go away. At last she looked up again. "Did you want something?"

"Yes," he said. Then, "Yes," and nodded. "I did a bloody good business deal today; and made myself a bloody good commission; and I've just ordered a bottle of Perrier Jouët rose, and I can't drink it all on my own. So I was wondering if you'd like to join me."

She stared at him without blinking. Eyes flecked; very little compassion. "I don't think so," she said.

"I don't want to drink it all on my own."

Still she didn't blink. "I'm sorry, I really don't care. *Don't* drink it on your own. But you're not going to drink it with me."

"Oh," he said. He tried to smile. Nobody had put him down quite as directly before. "Well, then . . . looks as if I'll have to find somebody else."

She didn't even answer. It was so obvious on this nearly-deserted terrace that there *was* nobody else – not unless he wanted to celebrate with a fat French woman in a catastrophic blue dress who was sitting with her legs set staunchly apart; or a malarial-looking couple who must have been over ninety, and were probably clinging to each other to stop themselves from trembling so much.

"All right, then," he said; to the terrace in general. "Sod it."

He lifted the flower-decorated champagne bottle out of its cooler, picked up his glass, and stepped down from the terrace. Then he crossed to the steps that led down to

152

the beach. Glass in one hand, bottle in the other, with sand in his white Alan McAfee loafers, he plodded to the waterline, and stood with his face to the south, to the sea, to the sun, to France, and toasted himself.

"Well-done-Bryan-you-are-a-fucking-genius, amen."

He looked back at the promenade; back at the hotel terrace; just in time to see the blonde thirtyish woman in the pink top being collected by a gray-haired man in enormous shorts and heavy-rimmed glasses.

"Sod it," he said. The gray-haired man in enormous shorts and heavy-rimmed glasses was probably the same age as him, 37; or maybe younger. He deserved a woman who couldn't solve the *Daily Telegraph* crossword without talking to perfect strangers. She probably kept on doing the crossword when he was fucking her. "'Large guns required when leaving town, nine letters'?"

Night began to flood slowly across the sky like washable ink. The sea continued to shush and fuss; but there was very little wind; and between the rocks that bordered St Brelade's Bay, Bryan felt that he could have been back in his childhood, in the seaside land of Rupert Bear or Tiger Tim, where there were always crabs and starfish and sandcastles with flags that flew. He walked along the very edge of the sea, allowing it to foam occasionally into his sneakers, £210 a pair, but who cared, this was a night for celebration.

It was almost dark when he reached the rocks on the eastern side of the bay. A faint mauvish afterlight still outlined the hills and the neighboring rooftops, but here on the beach it was chilly and damp and very black. He swigged Perrier Jouët from the neck of the bottle. It frothed violently in his mouth, and he almost choked.

He was about to turn back to L'Horizon when he saw a quick light darting across the sand, beside the rocks. Dim, diagonal, very quick, then extinguished. He peered into the darkness, wishing he weren't so drunk.

He heard scuffling noises; chipping noises; then he saw the light again.

He approached the rocks. The light was shone directly into his face.

He waited, and when nothing happened, and nobody said anything, he raised the Perrier Jouët bottle. "How about a drink?" he suggested.

A sniff. Then a man's voice, with a burry Jersey accent, "Orright then, don't care if I do."

He passed the bottle into the darkness. Swigging, sloshing noises. Then the bottle returned. "Wass that, cider?"

"Champagne, the best. I'm celebrating."

"Oh yuss?"

"I sold two-point-three million pounds' worth of print today."

"Oh yuss? That good, then?"

Bryan laughed. His laugh sounded flat against the rocks. "Good? It's not much short of a miracle!"

"Oh," said the man's voice. "You've come to the right place, then."

Bryan drank more champagne; hesitated; then passed over the bottle. "What do you mean by that?"

"Well . . . just here, after dark, in St Brelade's Bay . . . this is the place for miracles."

"I suppose it is."

Abruptly, the man shone the torch into his own face, from underneath, so that it took on all the ghastliness of a primitive mask carved out of a coconut. A thin-faced man, cavernously thin, with a prickly stubbled chin and blood-streaked eyes.

"Aint no suppose at-all. You ever seen the like of this?"

He clenched the torch between the knees of a well-soiled pair of brown corduroy trousers; and directed it toward the sand. Then, deftly, he molded the sand into

154

the shape of a smallish crab, outlining its claws with his fingernails and its shell with the ball of his thumb.

He had hardly finished sculpting it when it seemed to shift. Bryan watched in complete horror and astonishment as it suddenly released itself from the beach out of which it had been fashioned, and scuttled quickly toward the sea.

"You made a crab," he said, his lungs rising in his ribcage. "How the hell did you do that? You made a crab and it was actually alive."

The man laughed, as grating and roaring as a sink-disposal unit. Then he said, "It's the sand, ennit, this side of St Brelade's Bay. The story goes it's all the bones of shipwrecked sailors, ground up by the waves. Look how white it is, you could believe that, couldn't you? And look how red these rocks are! They say they're stained with blood. The stuff of life, this sand! The elements of life!"

Bryan swayed. He was feeling very drunk, and he wasn't quite sure if he were really here or not. "So what are you saying?" he asked the old man. "You're saying this part of the beach is *magic*? or what? I don't follow you!"

The man stood up. For some reason, Bryan could smell the drink on his breath, although he couldn't taste drink in his own mouth.

The man swayed close to him, and said, "Whatever you make out of this sand, Sonny Jim, it takes on a life of its own. Make it after dark, and it'll be yours till morning. Living, breathing, whatever you want. It's sailors' sand, that's why. Shipwrecked mariners' sand."

Bryan stared at him for a very long time without saying anything. Then he said, "Do it again."

"What?"

"Make another one. Go on."

"I'll have another drink first."

Bryan handed over the bottle and the man wiped the neck and swigged it. "Gah, bloody awful this stuff. All froth. Like drinking your own bathwater."

"Make another crab," Bryan insisted.

The man crouched down again. "What do you want, big un or little un?"

"Big un."

"How big?"

"Really big. Big as you like."

The man began to mold and pat the sand into a domed heap; and then to outline two monstrous claws. "Don't want to make it *too* big," he remarked. "Don't want to make it so bloody big we have to make a run for it." Then he laughed, and coughed, and spat into the darkness.

Bryan watched him closely as he finished the pie-crust crimping around the edge of the sand-crab's shell. It was almost a foot-and-a-half across, the biggest crab that he had ever seen, and by the erratic light of the torch it looked humped and sinister. But how could it live? It was only sand, after all, and it was so ridiculously huge that the man wouldn't be able to deceive him by substituting a real crab – which was what Bryan was beginning to suspect that he had done the first time. The crab had probably been buried in the sand all the time, and all it had needed was a quick brushing-away and a tap on the shell and off it had scuttled.

At last the man was finished. He stood up, and smacked the sand from his hands, and said, "There."

"But it hasn't come to life."

"Give it a chance. The bigger you make em, the slower."

They stood beside the crab for almost ten minutes, sharing the bottle of Perrier Jouët's best bathwater. Eventually, Bryan said, "You're pulling my leg. That's not going to come alive."

The man coughed. And, at that instant, the humped crab suddenly stirred, and swung its claw, and started to heave itself out of the surrounding sand. Bryan said,

"Shit!" and jumped back in alarm, colliding with the man, and dropping his champagne bottle.

Both of them took a few cautious paces back, well out of the crab's reach. It stayed where it was for a moment, its bead-black eyes revolving on their stalks.

"Do you think it's dangerous?" Bryan whispered.

The man shook his head. "Prolly not. It's trying to sniff for the sea, ennit?"

He was right. The crab was simply trying to fix its bearings. After a while, it began slowly to lurch toward the sound of the distant breakers. Bryan played the torch on it as it crossed the beach, and eventually disappeared into the darkness.

"Shit," he said.

He looked around. The man was already making his way back around the rocks, toward the stone esplanade, where summer lights were strung all the way from one side of the bay to the other.

"Your torch!" called Bryan. Then started to hurry after him. But he paused when he reached the steps that led back up to the esplanade, and stared at the rocks, and the sands that the man had called sailors' sand, the elements of life.

He was thoughtful all the next day. He sat in L'Horizon's health club, eating a slow breakfast of croissants and marmalade and strong black coffee. The shouts of children echoed around the pool. Last night he had dreamed about crabs, hundreds of crabs, stirring in the darkness. Then he had dreamed about the woman doing the *Daily Telegraph* crossword. She had been naked, lying back on a sunbed, with a bare-shaved vulva, sticky and pink, out of which bees had been crawling, and wiping their wings, and then flying into the sunshine. She had looked up and smiled at him, and licked her lips.

He called Roger Herbert, his sales manager in York,

157

and said that he wasn't feeling well, and that he would spend one more night on Jersey. Roger sounded irritated but there wasn't much that he could do about it. "Wasn't something you ate, was it?" he asked. "You should watch the shellfish. My mother was almost killed by a whelk."

Bryan bought himself a L'Horizon sweatshirt and pair of baggy running shorts and went for a walk across the beach.

This morning, children were building castles and roads out of the same sand from which the man had fashioned his monster crab. Bryan knelt down by the rocks and self-consciously made his own crab, only a small one, but as realistic as he could manage, patting the sand smooth and hard. He sat and watched the crab for almost twenty minutes but it didn't stir. Of course the man had told him that the sand only came to life at night, but it had been worth a try.

He spent the day sightseeing. He visited the dank warren of whitewashed tunnels that the Nazis had used during the war as an underground hospital. Then he wandered around a shoddy decrepit selection of plants and plaster statues that was supposed to be Gardens of All Lands. It was unbearably hot and stuffy inland, and so he drove to Jersey's north shore and stood on the cliffs and watched the sea.

Far below him, down on the beach, he saw a small Highland terrier dashing and up and down, just like the dog that his uncle had given him when he was a boy; and that gave him an idea.

Darkness seemed to be reluctant to fall that evening. Bryan took a can of beer on to the beach and sat on the rocks and waited. At last the pedaloes were dragged ashore; and the last of the topless girls came in from the surf, a huge-breasted blonde accompanied by a spiky-haired boyfriend who looked as if he would gratuitously garrotte anybody who even so much as glanced at her.

Then it was night, and Bryan was alone on the beach, on the sailors' sand, with the man's torch and a blue plastic spade that he had bought from the souvenir shop. He wedged the torch in the rocks, so that he could see what he was doing. Then he knelt down, and began to dig. It took him about quarter of an hour to fashion a small terrier out of sand, sitting with its paws neatly in front of it, and its ears perked up. He carefully drew its fur with a discarded lollipop stick, and gave it wide, appealing eyes. When he had finished he stood up and admired it.

He opened another can of Tennent's and stood beside the dog and waited. The wind from the sea was dark and warm; more like a restless dream than a wind. He checked his watch. It was only ten past ten. He wondered how drunk he had been last night. Maybe he had imagined that man and his monster crab. Pink champagne had always made him a little mad; even madder than Tennent's, or Carslberg Special Brew.

He waited an hour and nothing happened. The terrier remained a sand terrier. In the end, growing chilled and hungry, he left the rocks and walked back to the hotel. He went up to his room and changed into his navy-blue blazer and gray slacks. Before he went down to the bar, though, he went out on to his balcony and stared out at the darkened beach. He whistled, softly at first, then a little louder. "Come on, boy. Come on, boy!"

The sea shushed; the wind made the strings of lights dance. He closed the balcony door and went down to the bar to see if he could find himself a spare bit of talent to chat up.

Shortly after two o'clock that morning, something woke him up. He opened his eyes and listened intently. It wasn't the sea. It wasn't the awning over the hotel balcony, ruffling and slapping in the breeze. It was more like a *scratching* noise.

He sat up. He heard it again. *Skrittch, skkrittch, skkritch* at his bedroom door.

He climbed out of bed, and walked across to the door in nothing but his pajama bottoms. He listened again. *Skrittch, skkritcch, skkritch*, and a high-pitched whining.

He opened the door with a cold feeling of delight and alarm, and there it was. The sand terrier; still sandy-colored; but alive; and real; and sitting up to beg.

He knelt down in the corridor and cautiously stroked the little dog's head. It jumped up and down and wagged its tail and tried to lick his hand.

"You're real," he whispered. "I made you, and you're real."

He felt extraordinary; sober and strange and incredibly elated. "Here, boy," he called the terrier. "Here, boy, come on boy!"

He picked the dog up and it wriggled wildly in his arms, its tail lashing against his chest. "You're terrific," he told it. "You're terrific. What the hell am I going to call you? How the hell am I going to get you back to the mainland? You're amazing!"

He was just about to go back into his room when the night porter appeared at the end of the corridor. "Sir?" he called.

Bryan kept on stroking the terrier's head. "Everything's fine, thanks."

"I'm sorry, sir, but no dogs permitted."

"Oh . . . I didn't know. I'm sorry. He's only a little one, very well behaved."

The night porter looked at the wriggling terrier, unimpressed. "I'm sorry, sir. Hotel rules. No dogs; not even by arrangement."

"Well, what am I going to do with him? I can't just let him go."

"We have a kennel downstairs, sir, in the luggage room. I can take him down there for the night, but

160

you'll have to make alternative arrangements tomorrow."

"All right, then," Bryan agreed, handing the little dog over. "You'll make sure he gets something to eat, though, won't you?"

The night porter gave him a tightly-stretched smile. "I believe the grill room has some hamburgers left over, sir."

With that, he carried the dog away. Bryan closed the door of his room, and thought: I've got a dog. I've actually got a dog. I made it out of sand, and it came alive and found me.

He switched on his bedside light, and then opened up his mini-bar and took out a beer. Who cared if it was two o'clock in the morning. This called for a drink!

He was standing by the bed, swallowing ice-cold beer out of the can, when his gaze wandered across the room to the copy of *Men Only* lying open on the desk. A blonde with breasts even larger than the girl on the beach was smiling back at him, her thighs wide apart. He swallowed more beer. He didn't take his eyes off the photograph.

Early the next morning, he went down to the porter's office to collect the little dog.

"I've come for my dog," he told the sandy-haired porter.

"I'm sorry, sir?"

"The night porter took my dog last night and put it in the kennel in the luggage-room."

"Oh, certainly, sir. Please wait."

The porter disappeared, and then returned looking flushed. "I'm sorry, sir. Your dog doesn't seem to be there."

"You haven't let it out?"

The porter shook his head. "The luggage room has been locked all night, sir. It always is."

161

"Let me take a look," Bryan insisted.

He went behind the counter and into the luggage room. At the far end stood a large green-painted kennel, with a wire door, fastened with a loop and a nail. Bryan knelt down in front of it, and peered inside.

"As you see, sir," the porter remarked. "No dog."

But on the floor of the kennel was a half-eaten hamburger patty; and in the opposite corner, a small heap of dry white sand. The terrier *had* been put in here; and it hadn't escaped. But it looked as if the sailors' sand could only live and breathe by night. *Yours till morning*, the man had said.

"Do you want me to make some inquiries, sir?" the porter asked him. "I could talk to the night porter, if he hasn't yet gone to bed."

Bryan shook his head. "No . . . don't worry. I think I know what's happened." He spent all day lying on his bed staring at the girl in *Men Only*. Belinda, from Staffordshire, 40D, likes sculling. Sculling? That must be made up. But she was just the kind of girl who really appealed to him. The face of a princess and the body of a stripper. Fine cheekbones, provocative blue eyes.

And if he were to sculpt Belinda from Staffordshire out of sand, she would be real, and she would be his. She wouldn't belong to some belligerent oick on the beach; or some middle-aged businessman in heavy-rimmed glasses. She would be his. For the night, at least . . . and in the morning, she would be gone, leaving him without any responsibilities whatsoever, except to brush away the sand he had used to create her.

He stayed at the hotel all day, swimming and exercising and taking saunas. The day seemed to last for ever, and during the afternoon the sun seemed to be staying permanently high in the sky, as if it was refusing even to think about setting.

But at last he was out by the rocks, in the warm and

162

welcoming darkness, with his torch and two spades and plenty to drink.

He took his time. Belinda had to be perfect. He marked out her height on the sand, 5ft 4ins, then he carefully dug and smoothed and patted and shaped. It was almost half-past eleven by the time he had finished. He knelt in the sand beside her, and lightly ran his hand over her breasts and her stomach. In the slanting torchlight, she looked almost alive already.

"Belinda," he breathed, in her ear. "Can you hear me, Belinda? I love you already."

He had planned to wait on the beach until she came to life, and to help her back to the hotel. He had even brought a bathrobe to wrap around her. After all, she couldn't walk through the lobby naked. But after he had been sitting beside her for almost an hour, and nothing had happened, he was beginning to wonder if this was such a brilliant idea after all. Maybe the sands could only bring crabs and small animals to life. Maybe it was asking too much, to create a living, breathing human being.

He was still sitting there when he heard a shuffling noise, and he felt electric prickles all around the back of his neck. Then there was another shuffle, and the man in the brown corduroy trousers appeared from behind the rocks.

"You still got my torch," he declared.

"Yes, I have. I'm sorry."

"Well, I want it back."

"Of course."

The man came closer, and peered around the darkened beach. "What you doing out here? You aint making nothing?"

"No, of course not."

"You shouldn't try making nothing. You'll never know what harm you can do, trying to make things."

"I was out for a walk, that's all."

"Long as you wasn't making nothing."

Bryan had no choice. To divert the man away from his sculpture of Belinda, he took hold of his bony elbow and said, "Why don't you join me? I'm going for a drink."

The man coughed, and spat, and sniffed. "Don't care if I do."

Together they walked back to the hotel. The wind was rising, and it was growing chillier. Bryan glanced anxiously behind him. Let's hope that Belinda doesn't come to life before I can get rid of this bloody pest. Let's hope she doesn't start wandering around looking for me, stark naked.

He didn't notice the two joggers, panting their way across the sands in the darkness. Even if he had, he wouldn't have thought anything much about it, even when they jogged around the rocks, their training-shoes leaving deep impressions in the sand.

It took three pints of Guinness and a large Bells to get rid of his unwelcome friend. The man coughed and laughed and talked too loudly about the old days in Jersey, and how he used to play practical jokes on the Germans during the Occupation, letting down the tires of their motorbikes, and pouring yacht varnish into their coffee. Obviously he was a well-known local nuisance, because the hotel waiters treated him with contempt bordering on out-and-out hostility.

Eventually, he staggered off along the esplanade. Bryan waited until he was out of sight, then ran down the steps and sprinted across the beach. For God's sake, tell me I'm not too late. But as soon as he came around the rocks he could see that Belinda was still there – or what was left of Belinda.

The joggers had run right across her, plunging deep footprints into her stomach, her left breast, and her face. Where those big wide eyes and that upturned nose had once been, there was nothing but the impression of a size-10 sole.

Dispirited, tired, Bryan picked up his discarded bathrobe and brushed the sand off it. There was obviously no point in trying to repair the damage. The sands might be the stuff of life for crabs and puppies, but obviously its powers didn't stretch to creating human beings.

He gave the sand-sculpture a last resentful kick in the knee, and then trudged slowly back across the beach. He could hear dreary, pedestrian dance music wafting from the hotel dining-room, half-swallowed by the wind and the sea. This time he didn't look back.

He drank a beer, watched half of *Three Men And A Baby* on video, then stiffly undressed and climbed into bed. Lying in the darkness, he kept thinking about the man with his monster crab, and the terrier that he had made. He could still remember what its tail had felt like, slapping against his chest. How that could have been fashioned from sand, and then fallen back into sand, he couldn't imagine.

Maybe the man had been right. Maybe there *are* miracles.

He slept. He dreamed he was walking along the shoreline. He heard the sea, dragging and shuffling its way across the sand. Dragging and shuffling, dragging and shuffling. It sounded almost like somebody dragging themselves along the corridor outside his room. Somebody maimed, somebody disfigured beyond all human imagination.

He opened his eyes. Was he still dreaming? He thought he had heard something softly collide with his door. He listened for a while, then he switched on the light and climbed out of bed. He went close to the door, and strained his ears. He was sure that he could hear breathing

165

outside, but it was more like an animal breathing than a human. Thick and distorted and infinitely labored.

Again, that soft collision against the other side of the door.

"Who is it?" he demanded, in a hoarse whisper.

A blurred, breathy sound. Then yet another collision.

"Who is it?" he demanded, his voice tight with fear. "Belinda, is that you? Belinda?"

Eric the Pie

South Croydon, Surrey

Eric the Pie was always going to be a story that was right on the very edge of acceptability, and so I chose the most downbeat and mundane setting for it that I could. South Croydon is a cheerless suburb of London, with terrace after terrace of jerry-built Victorian houses, a bus station, several huge and miserable public-houses, and more used-car dealerships than you could drive a second-hand Ford Escort at.

However, I derive an enormous amount of satisfaction from researching places like South Croydon. It's worth stopping, it's worth looking – just to see where people live and how they decorate their houses. Not all fictional characters live in Paris, or Rome, or Bel Air. Sometimes, like Eric, they live in places where net-curtains twitch and real-estate agents fear to tread.

ERIC THE PIE

It's a very odd thing –
As odd as can be –
That whatever Miss T. eats
Turns into Miss T
    Walter De La Mare.

Eric's mother always used to tell him that "You are what you eat."

Eric, seven years old, used to eat up all his ground-beef pie at supper-time and then lie in bed, feeling his arms and his legs, to see if he were developing a crust.

How many ground-beef pies did you have to eat before you yourself turned into a ground-beef pie?

But if you ate Marmite sandwiches, as well; and fishcakes; and sweet cigarettes; and greengage jam tarts; and licquorice hardsticks; and apples; and cornflakes – what did you turn into then?

Eric used to lean on the windowsill of his high attic bedroom and look out over the slated rooftops of suburban south London and try to imagine what you turned into then.

A kind of terrible groaning slushy monster, with eyes like pickled onions and skin as black as haddock, with crusty excrescences of Hovis loaf and appalling soft cavities dripping with gravy and strings of lamb-fat.

One hot afternoon in August, Eric fell over in the playground at school when he and his friends were playing "it".

He scraped his knee and it bled into his sock. That night he lay in bed feeling the scab form hard and crusty on his leg and thought that he was turning into a ground-beef pie.

He spent hours in his room staring at his nursery-rhyme book. *"Simple Simon met a pieman."* A pieman! There was no picture of the pieman, but Eric didn't need a picture. He could imagine himself what this terrifying creature was like. A hunched, pastry-encrusted beast, dragging himself along with muffled whimpers. A man who had eaten far too many pies in his life, and had paid the ultimate penalty.

A man whose skin had gradually turned into crumbling pastry. A man whose lungs and stomach had gradually turned into ground beef. A pieman!

Eric had gone to bed and had nightmares about the pieman. He had heard the pieman's nasal begging through bubbles of gravy. *Eat me, kill me. I can't bear it any longer.*

For weeks, he had eaten scarcely anything at all. And he had always left his crusts on the side of his plate. His mother had talked to Dr Wilson; and once Dr Wilson had visited the house, and Eric had answered questions to his blue chalk-striped waistcoat and his gold watch-chain.

"Do you dislike your food, Eric?"

"No, sir."

"Are you worried about anything at school?"

"No, sir."

"Cough."

(Eric coughed.)

"Breathe in, and hold it."

(Eric breathed in, and held it.)

Then, in the brown-wallpapered hallway, next to the barometer that was always set fair, the doctor murmuring to his mother, "He's quite all right, you know. Boys of this age quite often eat very little. But when he starts to grow . . . well, he'll have to eat to live; and he'll live to eat. You mark my words, and stock up your larder."

His mother had returned to the sitting-room, and sat and stared at him; almost as if she were resentful that he wasn't really sick.

"The doctor says you're all right."

Long pause. "Oh."

She knelt on the floor next to him, and took his hand. Her eyes were so colorless. Her face was so colorless. "You have to eat, Eric. You have to build yourself up. You have to eat or you'll die. You are what you eat, Eric."

"That's what I'm afraid of," he whispered.

"What?"

"That's what I'm afraid of. If I eat too many pies."

"What?"

"If I eat too many pies, I'll be Eric the Pie."

His mother had laughed. Her laugh like fragments of broken mirror in the summer bedroom. Bright, sharp, slice your nose off.

"No you won't. Food gives you life, that's all. If you eat life, you'll have life. It's like an equation. Life in, life out."

"Oh."

Eric understood. Suddenly the pieman was nothing but a story. Pieces fell off him. Crust, base, lumps of kidney. Suddenly the pieman was nothing but pie. Eric had grown up. Now, at last, he understood the mystery of human existence. It was like an equation. Life in, life out. That was all. Nothing to do with ground-beef pies; nothing to do with fishcakes; or greengage jam tarts. It was simple. If you ate life, you stayed alive.

Next morning was sunny and suffocatingly hot. Eric, bored, and tired by the heat, sat on top of the coal-shed swinging his legs, a pale elf-faced boy with huge brown eyes and protruding ears. He had no friends to play with.

Everybody at school called him "Mekon" and bullied him. He was no good at football and when he tried to play cricket he was always out for a duck.

In the yard at the back of Eric's terraced suburban house there was a strong smell of elderflowers and cat's pee, because next door's cat used to slink into the coal to relieve itself. Eric's mother had just hung out her laundry and it dripped intermittently on to the concrete path. Above Eric's head the sky was as blue as washable writing-ink, and thinly streaked with cirrus clouds. High up, to the west, a Bristol Britannia airliner caught the sunlight. The Whispering Giant, the newspapers called it. Eric thought the idea of a whispering giant was rather sad and rather sinister.

He watched a woodlouse crawl across the hot tarpaper roof of the coal-shed. It reached his cotton shorts, and then began a long and painful diversion along his thigh.

Eric picked it up between finger and thumb. Immediately, it curled itself up into a gray armored ball. Eric threw it up a little way, and then caught it. He did this two or three times. He wondered what it was thinking about, as he tossed it up. Was it frightened? Or didn't it have enough brains to be frightened?

It was alive. Alive enough to crawl across the coal-shed roof. So it must think *something*. He wondered what it would think if he ate it. The woodlouse's life would become part of his life. His big life and the woodlouse's tiny life would be irreversibly combined. Perhaps then he would know what the woodlouse was thinking. You are what you eat, after all.

He popped the pill-like woodlouse into his mouth. It rested on his tongue. It must have thought it had discovered some damp, warm friendly niche in the coal-shed somewhere, because it unrolled itself in the cleft of his tongue, and began to crawl down his throat.

For a moment, Eric was seized by the urge to gag. But

he calmed himself, restrained himself. The woodlouse was joining his life by its own volition, and he liked the idea of that.

It crawled to the back of his throat and then he swallowed it.

He closed his eyes. He wondered how long it would take before the woodlouse's consciousness became part of his own.

Perhaps it was too small. Perhaps he needed to eat lots more woodlice. He jumped down from the top of the coal-shed and searched around the yard, picking up bricks and stones and poking in the dampest corners of the wall. Each woodlouse he found, he popped into his mouth, and swallowed. In less than a quarter of an hour, he found thirty-one.

His mother came out with another basket of washing and began to peg her slips and stockings on to the line. "What are you doing, Eric?" she asked him, one eye closed against the sunlight.

"Nothing," said Eric. While she pegged up her clothes, he quickly ate four more woodlice. They crunched between his teeth.

That night in bed he stared at the ceiling and he was sure that he could feel the woodlice's lives weaving in and out of his body and his mind. He felt stronger, more alive. If you eat life, you stay alive.

On his eighth birthday his mother gave him a bicycle. It wasn't new, but she had cleaned it and painted it blue and Mr Tedder at the second-hand car showroom had fitted new brake-blocks and a blue hooter with a rubber bulb.

He cycled up and down Churchill Road, which was as far as his mother would let him go. Churchill Road was a crescent, safe and quiet, away from the main road.

One gray afternoon he came across a pigeon, limping

and fluttering in the gutter. He stopped his bicycle close beside it and watched it. It stared helplessly up at him with a beady orange eye. Every now and then it dragged itself a few inches further away, but Eric followed it, the wheels of his bicycle tick-ticking with every step.

It was alive. It had a much larger life than woodlice (which he had been eating by the handful whenever he found them; and ants, too; and spiders; and moths.) If he ate it, maybe he could experience just the briefest flicker of what it was like to fly.

He looked around. The crescent was deserted. Three parked cars, one of them propped up on bricks, but that was all. Nobody looking. Only the distant sound of buses.

He left his bicycle propped against a garden fence and took the wounded pigeon into the alleyway between two terraced houses. It struggled and fluttered and he could feel its heart racing against his thumbs. He pressed its hard pungent breast against his mouth, and bit into feathers and meat and sinew. The pigeon struggled wildly, and uttered a throaty scream that excited Eric so much that he bit it again, and then again, until the pigeon was thrashing bloodily against his face and he was biting into bone and sinew and things that were bitter and slimy.

For one ecstatic instant, he felt its heart beating on the tip of his tongue. Then he forced its breast even deeper into his mouth, and killed it.

An elderly woman was watching him from an upstairs window. She had suffered a stroke not long ago, and she was unable to speak. All she could do was stare at him in horror as he wiped the ragged bloody remains of the bird around and around his face; and skipped while he did; a pigeon dance; a death dance.

When he got home, Eric had to sneak in by the back door, and wash his face and hands in cold water in the scullery. Blood streaked the white ceramic sink. He felt elated, as if he had learned how to fly. He heard his mother calling, "Eric?"

When he was eleven, he crouched in the fusty-smelling coal-shed, waiting for the neighbors' cat. When it came in, he caught it, and tied its mouth tight with fishing-line, knotted tight. The cat struggled furiously, hurling itself from side to side, and scratching at his face and hands. But Eric was ready for that. He chopped off its paws, one by one, with a pair of gardening shears. Then, when it was still struggling and writhing with pain, he hung it up from a cup-hook that he had screwed into the low wooden ceiling. He was covered in blood. The cat sprayed blood everywhere. But Eric liked the blood. It was warm and it tasted salty, like life.

He buried his face in the hot tangled fur of the cat's belly and bit into it. It crunched and burst, and the cat almost exploded with pain. Eric licked its lungs while they were still breathing. There was air inside them; life. Eric licked its heart while it was still pumping. There was blood inside it; life. Eric took the cat's life in his mouth and ate it, and the cat became Eric. You are what you eat. Eric was an insect, a bird, a cat, and scores of spiders.

Eric knew that he could live for ever.

Not long after his sixteenth birthday, Eric went to stay with his grandparents in Earl's Colne, in rural Essex. Hot summer days, glazed like syrup. Hallucinatory hay-fields, dotted with bright-red poppies.

Eric found a brown-and-white calf, down by the river. The calf had become entangled in barbed-wire, and was crying in pain. Eric knelt down beside it for a long time and watched it struggle. Butterflies blew by; the afternoon was so hot that it almost seemed to swell.

Eric took off his jeans and his T-shirt and his underpants and hung them up on the bushes. Naked, he approached the calf, and touched it. It licked his hand, and twisted pitifully against the barbed-wire.

Eric picked up a large stone in his right hand broke the calf's legs, all four of them, one after the other. The calf dropped to the ground, bellowing with pain. Eric forced the stone between its jaws so that it couldn't cry out any more. He was panting and sweaty and his penis was rigid, with the foreskin drawn tautly back.

He mounted the calf and raped it. Black flesh, pink flesh. While he raped it, he bit into its smooth-haired chest, and tore lumps of bloody meat away. It kicked and fought, but Eric was too strong. Eric had too much life in him. Cats' lives; birds' lives; dogs' lives. Eric was life itself. He ran the tip of his tongue over the calf's living eye and the eye slickly quivered; so Eric bit into it, so that a clear gelatinous gobbet of optic fluid slithered down his throat like a prize oyster; and at the same time he ejaculated into the dying animal's bowels.

He spent almost an hour eating and retching and smothering himself in blood. By the time he had finished, he was surrounded by swarms of flies. The calf quivered, just once. He kissed its bloodied anus, from which his own semen glutinously dripped. He said a prayer to all that was terrible, all that was wonderful. The power of one life over another.

In the far distance, the sky was very black; granite black; and thunder rumbled. A rush of warm wind crossed the hay-field, like a premonition of early death.

Eric left school and found a job at a color-separation company in Lewisham, in south-east London. He lived in a mews flat over a lock-up garage only a one-and-sixpenny busride from where he worked. He was tall now, tall and long-legged, with a strange diving stride that could only have been adopted by a man who never walked with women; because no woman could have possibly caught up with him. He wore National Health tortoiseshell spectacles and his hair was cut so short that it always stuck up at the crown, like a cockatoo.

He sat at his drawing-board at work, painting out flaws on color separations, his head bowed, his nose so close to the celluloid film that his face was reflected in its blackness. He hardly ever spoke to anybody. He brought a Thermos of Ovaltine, but nobody ever saw him eat lunch. Deborah Gibbs, who was new in accounts, thought he was lonely and strange and rather alluring. "He's Byronic," she said; and Kevin in the platemaking section wanted to know if it was catching.

Every night Eric stood on the corner outside the works and waited for the bus which would take him back home. He would sit downstairs on the 3-seats where his thigh would be pressed against the thigh of some homegoing typist or some big West Indian woman in a bright print frock, with bagfuls of Sainsbury's shopping on her lap. He liked to feel their warmth. He liked to feel their life. There were airless days in summer when his leg was pressed close to the woman next to him, and he could have ducked his head down and taken a bite out of her living flesh.

The mews was almost always deserted when he returned; the late sun hanging in the sky like a yellow badge. Occasionally Mr Bristow was tinkering with his old Standard Twelve, but usually it was Eric's echoing footsteps and Eric's jingling keys and nothing else. Only the deep ambient roar of suburban London.

He would climb the metal fire-escape stairs and let himself into the flat. A small kitchenette with a wooden draining-board and a tap that constantly dripped. A curled-up calendar for 1961, Views of the Lake District. He would sniff, whistle, switch on the electric kettle. Then he would walk through to the sitting-room; which at this time of day was always dark, and smelled of damp.

He would switch on the black-and-white television but

he would turn down the sound. Nobody on television ever had anything to say which interested Eric in the slightest. The news was all about President Kennedy and Mr K and death; or pop music, which he didn't understand. He heard it all day, every day. They played it on transistor radios at work. But he simply didn't understand it. That endless nagging bang, bang, bang, bang. It gave him a headache. It made him feel that he had been imprisoned by some primitive tribe that didn't even realize that that night sky wasn't a lid.

The only program that Eric liked was *Hancock's Half Hour*, although it never made him laugh. He liked lines like, "I thought my mother was a bad cook, but at least her gravy moved about."

In the bedroom, Eric's unmade bed. And all around it, pinned to the wall in their hundreds, Eric's drawings. Anatomical studies of insects, rats, dogs and horses. Anatomical studies of woodlice, anatomical studies of pigeons. Everything that Eric had eaten, meticulously drawn in pencil. Each one signed, each one dated, a catalog of Eric's living meals. Each one bore the legend, "You are what you eat."

Under the bed were drawings which he kept tied up in a large gray fiberboard portfolio. These were special drawings which he didn't want the landlady to see, in case she visited his flat when he was out at work.

These were drawings of things that Eric had never eaten, but which he would like to eat. New-born babies, as they emerged from their mothers, still hot, still steaming, like offerings from some sacred oven. Afterbirths, Eric would have given anything to be able to eat an afterbirth, plunge his face into hot pungent gristle. Men's faces; children's thighs. Slices of women's breasts. Eric drew them in painstaking detail, shading and shading with his 2B pencil until the heel of his hand was silvery-black with rubbed-off graphite.

178

Later, when the sun had gone down, and the mews was very dark, Eric used to go down to the garage. He would lay his hand flat against the green weather-blistered paint. He would say nothing; but close his eyes. Sometimes he felt as if he didn't belong on this planet at all. At other times, he felt that he owned it, and that everybody else was intruding on his privacy.

He would turn his key in the Yale lock, and push open the wooden concertina doors. They would always shudder and complain, even though Eric had greased them three or four times. Eric would step into the darkness of the garage and smell 1930s motor-oil and leather and dust; but most of all, blood; and despair.

He would close the doors behind him, and then he would switch on the light. Suspended from the garage ceiling by an elaborate system of weights and hooks and pulleys were six or seven animals – dogs, cats, rabbits, even a goat. Their jaws were bound with fishing-line so that they were unable to utter the slightest sound, even though they were suspended from hooks and wires that must have been causing them intense and endless agony. Most of them had been bitten here and there. A black Labrador dog had the flesh from its hind-legs missing, so that it pedaled the air with nothing but bones. The goat's eyes had been sucked from their sockets, and its udder had been opened up and partially devoured; like a huge bloody pudding.

Eric took life wherever he could find it. Eric ate everything which offered him life. He felt strong and knowledgeable and *many*, as if every animal that he had eaten had given him some of its instincts, some of its intellect, some of its individuality. He was sure that he could run faster, balance better, smell more keenly. He was sure that he could hear dog-whistles. He was convinced that if he ate many more living birds, he would soon be able to fly.

Every night, Eric would lock his garage door, take off all of his clothes, and fold them on a bentwood chair which he had placed by the wall for this very purpose. Then, naked, Eric would feed; trying to keep each of his animals alive for as long as possible. There was nothing like staring into the eyes of a living creature while you were actually chewing its flesh. And digesting it. Sometimes he would bend over naked in front of the suffering, dangling animals and excrete, so that they could witness their final fate. Dropped onto the oil-stained concrete floor, lifeless!

One hot evening in August, 1963, Deborah Gibbs came over and perched her hip on Eric's plan-chest. She was wearing a small white sleeveless top and a short green skirt and Eric, when he looked up, could see chestnut-brown stocking-tops and white plump thighs and white knickers.

Sandy Jarrett in developing had bet Deborah ten shillings that she couldn't persuade Eric to take her out for a drink. Sandy was hiding behind the reeded-glass partition and trying to smother giggles. Eric could see her ginger hair bobbing.

"I was wondering what you was doing tonight," said Deborah.

Eric wiped his brush and peered at her through his paint-freckled spectacles.

"I'm not doing anything. Why?"

"I don't know. Thought you might like to come down the Blue Wanker."

"The what?" blushed Eric.

"Oh, sorry. We all call it that. The Blue Anchor. It's the pub over at Hilly Fields."

"Why should I want to do that?" Eric asked her. His hand lying still and white on the drawing-board, as if it were something dead that didn't belong to him. Fingernails ruthlessly bitten until they bled, and formed scabs, and been bitten again, and bled again . . .

180

Deborah wriggled and giggled. Sandy giggled from the next office. "It's hot. Thought you might like it, that's all."

"Well . . ." said Eric, staring at Deborah's stocking-tops, staring at the flesh that bulged from Deborah's thighs.

They sat outside the Blue Anchor watching half-a-dozen small boys play cricket. Eric drank two halves of cider and pecked at a packet of crisps. Deborah drank gin-and-orange and chattered incessantly.

"Sandy says you're a mystery man," she giggled.

"Oh, yes?"

"Sandy says you're probably a spy or something."

"No, I'm not a spy."

"You're a mystery, though, aren't you?"

"I don't think so. I just believe in living my life my own way, that's all."

"And what way's that?"

He stared at her. She hadn't realized before how dreadfully pale he was. He smelled, too. He gave off the strangest of smells. It was sweet, yet sickening. A bit like a gas-leak. She hadn't smelled anything like it since a starling had died in her bedroom chimney.

"You can come and see my flat if my like," he told her. "Then I'll show you."

They finished their drinks and took the bus to Eric's flat. The sun was almost gone. Eric seemed to be peculiarly cheerful, and he strode along with his hands in his pockets and Deborah found it almost impossible to keep up with him.

They reached the mews. It was silent and deserted. Mr Bristow's Standard Twelve but no Mr Bristow.

"He's probably inside, having his tea," Eric remarked.

"Who?" asked Deborah. She had laddered one of her stockings and she was growing worried.

181

"Sandy thinks I'm a mystery man, does she? Well she should come and see this."

Eric unlocked the garage door and took hold of Deborah's hand and guided her inside. It was so dark that she couldn't see anything at all. Eric let go of her hand and she stood breathless not knowing what to do. But then the garage doors collided behind her, and locked, and Eric switched on the light.

He folded his glasses and set them on top of his trousers. He was white, ribby, blue-veined, but his penis stood out erect and very dark.

Deborah tried to scream, but he had gagged her so tightly that she could only shout mfff, mfff, mfff. He approached her, drawing aside the hooks and chains that dangled down from every beam on the ceiling, and peered at her from only six or seven inches away. She could smell his breath; and it smelled of unspeakable decay.

He had taken off all her clothes except for her stockings and garter-belt and he had tied her in a sitting position in his bentwood chair. He had criss-crossed her breasts with thin cord so that they bulged in diamond patterns. He peered shortsightedly between her legs and then reached out to touch her, but she mffff'd! with such ferocity that he hesitated.

"I've never seen a real girl naked before."

She tried to scream at him to let her go; but he suddenly turned away, with apparent disinterest. But then he turned back again, and he was holding a craft-knife in his hand.

"You are what you eat, Deborah. Can't argue with that. Cakes, Mars bars, you are what you eat. I always used to think that if I ate too many pies, I'd turn into a pie! Can you imagine that? Eric the Pie!"

He took the triangular-bladed craft-knife, and touched the point of it against her skin, just below the breast-bone. She saw the knife, his smile, his blue-cheese skin.

"Life, that's what it's all about," said Eric, and sliced Deborah open, all the way down to her light brown public hair.

She looked down and saw her own bloodied intestines, pouring into her lap. There was a fetid smell like nothing she had ever smelled before; blood and digestion and bile. Then she saw Eric plunge his whole head into the gaping cavity of her body, *his whole head*, and felt the unbearable tearing of his teeth. He was after her living liver. He was after her pancreas, and her stomach, and her kidneys. He was trying to eat her alive, from the inside out.

She felt herself fainting; she felt herself dying. She felt her whole world tinged with black. She did the only thing that she was capable of doing, which was to throw herself backward. Her chair fell; she fell; Eric fell. He bellowed with rage, his head still buried in the bloodiness of her body. The goat, nearly dead now, swung heavily against them on its Calvary of chains.

Deborah lay with her head against the concrete floor, quivering with agony and approaching death. Eric sucked and bit and tore at her liver, almost drowned in blood. Deborah turned her face and saw that her fall had loosened her right arm; that her right arm was free.

She also saw the hook that swung on the end of a chain, backwards and forwards.

She didn't care whether she could summon up the strength or not. She was going to do it, no matter what. She was dying; and words like "impossible" didn't mean anything any more.

She snatched at the chain, once, twice, then caught it. Eric bloodily guzzled, oblivious.

With a trembling, blood-smeared hand, she grasped the hook, and lifted it as high as she could. She couldn't scream; she couldn't cry out. She was almost dead. She probably *was* dead, pathologically speaking.

But she dug the hook in between Eric's bare buttocks as

deeply as she could; and she felt sphincter and muscle and tissue tear, and *inside her body* Eric screamed. A muffled, wet, bubbling scream.

His face rose out of the gaping lips of her abdomen like the scarlet mask of the devil himself. His eyes were wide, bloody-black liver clung to his teeth. A fine spray of blood blew out of his nostrils. He roared, hopped, twisted, and tried to pull the hook out of himself. But as he did so, Deborah seized the goat, and the goat fell on top of her, and all of Eric's weights and chains and counterbalances went furiously haywire.

Eric was yanked, shrieking, up to the ceiling, where he dangled and writhed and prayed and wept.

Deborah died. The day died. But Eric circled around all night and still he didn't die. He spun slowly around and around, feeling a pain that was almost dreamlike in its intensity. He slept, and he woke, and the pain still dominated everything.

Near to dawn, he tried to shake himself free, jerking up and down on his hook, until at last it tore through flesh and skin and he dropped heavily on to the garage floor. He lay shivering and weeping, bruised and maimed and unable to move.

The day passed him by. He heard cars. He heard Mr Bristow with his spanners, whistling and humming to himself. He slept, shivered, mumbled.

Late in the evening, he felt something tug at his left eyelid. Something sharp, something painful. He tried to brush it away, but when he opened his eyes he knew that he wouldn't have the strength to keep it away for long.

It was a massive gray sewer-rat, one of the biggest he had ever seen. It wasn't attacking him, it was simply feeding. It stared at him and he knew with a terrible certainty that Eric the Pie had met his Simple Simon; that he would soon become nothing more than pellet-shaped droppings, in some unexplored outfall; that you are what you eat.

For the very first time in his life, Eric understood the sin of being predatory, and he prayed for forgiveness while one rat, then another rat, then many rats, turned his body into a thrashing, rolling cloak of bloodied fur.

Rococo

New York, New York

Rococo could only be located in New York at the height
of Yuppie supremacy, in a high-tech building close to
Bowling Green, in the financial district. Bowling Green
is at Battery Place, at the very bottom end of Broadway,
and it was originally used by colonial bowls-players, who
played out their games under the imperious gaze of a
statue of George III. It was New York City's very first
park, and records show that it was leased in 1733 for
a single peppercorn a year. In 1776 the royal statue,
unsurprisingly, was pulled down, and a fence erected
around the green which is still there today. In recent
times, the green and its benches have been restored,
and a circular pool and a fountain added, making it
an ideal spot in summer for business persons to take a
sandwich lunch.

However, even the most innocent lunchtime break can
have horrendous consequences . . .

ROCOCO

It was such a warm spring day that Margot had decided
to brown-bag it in the plaza outside the office, next to the
ultra-modern Spechocchi-designed waterfall. The plaza
was always bustling with pedestrians, but after the high-
tension hyper-air-conditioned chill of her single-window
office in the Jurgens Building, eating lunch here was
almost as good as a Mediterranean vacation.

She was as classy at brown-bagging it as she was at her
job; and she laid out a crisp pink Tiffany napkin with
sfinciuni, the thin Palermo-style pizza sandwich, with a
filling of unsmoked ham, ricotta and fontina; a fruit salad
of mangoes and strawberries macerated in white wine; and
a bottle of still Malvern water.

It was while she was laying out her lunch that she
first noticed the man in the dove-gray suit, sitting on
the opposite side of the plaza, close to the edge of the
waterfall. Most of the time he was half-hidden by passing
pedestrians, but there was no doubt at all that he was
staring at her. In fact he didn't take his eyes away from
her once; and after a few minutes she began to find his
unswerving gaze distinctly unsettling.

Margot was used to being stared at by men. She
was tall, just over five feet nine inches, and she had
striking dark-brunette hair that was upswept into curls.
Her ex-fiancé Paul had told her that she had the face
like an angel about to cry: wide blue eyes, a straight
delicately-defined nose, and subtly-pouting lips. She was

189

large-bosomed, and quite large-hipped, like her mother, but unlike her mother she could afford to flatter her curves in tailored business suits.

She was the only female account executive at Rutter Blane Rutter. She was the highest-paid woman she knew; and she was determined to reach the very top. No compromises. The top.

She began to eat; but she couldn't help raising her eyes to see if the man was still staring at her. He was, no doubt about it. He was sitting back on one of the benches in a very relaxed pose, one leg crossed over the other. He must have been about thirty-eight or thirty-nine years old, with shining blond hair that was far too long and wavy to be fashionable, at least in the circles in which Margot moved. He wore a pale cream shirt and a dove-gray bow-tie to match his suit. There was something about his posture which suggested that he was very wealthy, and very self-indulgent, too.

Margot had almost finished her *sfinciuni* when Ray Trimmer appeared. Ray was one of the hottest copywriters at Rutter Blane Rutter, although his lack of personal organization sometimes drove Margot crazy. He slapped a huge untidy package of sandwiches on to the concrete tabletop, and sat down too close to her.

"Mind if I join you?" he asked, opening up his sandwiches one by one to investigate their fillings. "My daughter made my lunch today. She's eight. I told her to use her imagination."

Margot frowned at the sandwich on the top of the pile. "Tuna and marmalade. You can't say that's not imaginative."

Ray began to eat. "I wanted to talk to you about that Spring Flower spot. I'm working toward something less suburban, if you know what I mean. I know a bed-freshener is an entirely suburban product, but I think we have to make it look more elegant, more up-market."

"I liked your first idea."

"I don't know. I ran it past Dale and he wasn't too happy. The woman looks like she's fumigating the bed to get rid of her husband's farts."

"Isn't that just what Spring Flower's for?"

Ray bent forward to pick up another sandwich. As he did so, Margot became conscious again that the man in the dove-gray suit was still staring at her. Blond shining hair, a face that was curiously *medieval*, with eyes of washed-out blue.

"Ray, do you see that guy over there? The one sitting by the waterfall?"

Ray looked up, his mouth full of sandwich; then turned and looked around. At that moment a crowd of Japanese tourists were shuffling across the plaza, and the man was temporarily obscured from view. When the tourists had gone, so had he; although Margot was at a loss to understand how he could have left without her seeing him go.

"I don't see any man," Ray told her. He pulled a face, and opened up the sandwich he was eating. "What the hell's this? Cheez Whiz and Cap'n Crunchberries. Jesus!"

Margot folded her napkin, and tucked it into her Jasper Conran tote bag. "I'll catch you later, Ray, okay?"

"Don't you want to see what I've got for dessert?"

Quickly, Margot crossed the plaza toward the waterfall. The water slid so smoothly over the lip at the top that it didn't appear to be moving at all; a sheet of glass. To her surprise, the man was standing a little way behind it, in a brick niche where a bronze statue of a naked woman was displayed; a naked woman with a blindfold.

The man saw Margot coming and made no attempt to walk away. Instead he looked as if he had been expecting her.

"Pardon me," said Margot, as commandingly as she

could, although her heart-rate was jumping around like Roger Rabbit, "do you have some kind of eye problem?"

The man smiled. Close up, he was very tall, six foot three, and he smelled of cinnamon and musk and some very perfumed tobacco.

"Eye problem?" he asked her, in a soft, deep voice.

"Your eyes seem to be incapable of looking at anything except me. Do you want me to call a cop?"

"I apologize," the man replied, bowing his head. "It was not my intention to intimidate you."

"You didn't. But there are plenty of women who might have been."

"Then I apologize again. My only excuse is that I was admiring you. Do you think I might give you something, a very small token of my regret?"

Margot frowned at him in disbelief. "You don't have to give me anything, sir. All I'm asking is that you don't stare at women like Sammy the Psychotic."

He laughed, and held out his hand. In his palm was a tiny sparkling brooch; a miniscule pink-and-white flower, embedded in glass.

Margot stared at it. "It's beautiful. What is it?"

"It's a jinn-flower, from Mount Rakapushi, in the High Pamirs. It's extinct now; so this is probably the last one there is. It was picked high up on the snow line, and taken to Hunza, where it was encased in molten glass by a method that has been completely lost."

Margot wasn't at all sure that she believed any of this. It sounded like an extremely devious and complicated line; but a line all the same. She slowly shook her head. "I couldn't possibly accept anything like that; even if I wanted to accept anything at all."

The man said gently, "I shall be extremely hurt if you don't. You see, I bought it especially for you."

"That's ridiculous. You don't even know me."

"You're Margot Hunter. You're an account executive

for Rutter Blane Rutter. I've seen you many times before, Margot. I made a point of finding out."

"Oh, yes?" Margot snapped. "And who the hell are *you*?"

"James Blascoe."

"Is that it? James Blascoe? And what do you do, James Blascoe? And what right do you think you have to check up on me, and then to stare at me?"

James Blascoe raised both hands in apologetic surrender. "I don't really do anything. Some people, like you, are the doers. Other people, like me, are the watchers. You do, I watch. That's all, it's as simple as that."

"Well, do you mind going someplace else to do your watching, Mr Blascoe?" Margot demanded. "Someplace where you won't scare people?"

"Your point is well taken," James Blascoe told her, and bowed his head once again, and walked off across the plaza. Margot watched him go; both relieved and disturbed. He had been remarkably attractive, and he was obviously rich. As he reached Bowling Green on the far side of the plaza a long midnight-blue Lincoln stretch-limo appeared, and drew up to the curb. He climbed into it, and closed the door, and didn't look back once.

Margot returned to her office. Ray was waiting for her, with a whole sheaf of messy notes and layouts spread all over her normally-pristine desk.

"You look like you saw a ghost," said Ray.

Margot gave him a quick, distracted smile. "Do I? I'm okay."

"You want to look at these new ideas? Kenny did the drawings. They're not exactly right yet, but I think you'll understand where we're coming from."

"All right," Margot nodded. She shuffled through the layouts, still thinking about James Blascoe. *Other people, like me, are the watchers.*

193

"Neat pin," Ray remarked, as she lifted up another layout.

"I beg your pardon?"

"Your pin, your brooch, whatever it is. Where'd you get it? Bloomingdale's?"

Margot looked down at her fawn linen business suit, and there it was, sparkling brightly in the exact center of her lapel. The tiny jinn-flower, embedded in glass.

"Now how the hell did he do that?" she demanded. Then, indignantly, to Ray, "This isn't Bloomingdale's. This is just about the rarest brooch in the whole darn universe! A real flower, handmade glass."

Ray took off his spectacles and peered at it more closely. "Really?" he said; and gave Margot the most peculiar look that she had ever seen.

He was waiting for her the next morning when she arrived at the office. He was standing by the revolving doors in the bright eight o'clock sunshine; immaculately dressed, as yesterday, in gray. He stepped toward her with both hands held out, as if to say, I'm sorry, I didn't mean to impose on your life yesterday, I don't mean to impose on your life today.

"You're angry with me," he told her, before she could say anything. She had to step out of the way to avoid the hurrying crowds of office-workers.

"I'm not *angry* with you," she retorted. "It's just that I can't accept your gift."

"I don't understand," he replied. For the first time, in the morning light, she saw the small crescent-shaped scar on his left cheekbone.

"It's too much. It's too valuable. Mr Blascoe, I don't even *know* you."

"What difference does that make? I wanted you to have it."

"In return for what?"

194

He shook his head as if she had amazed him. "In return for your pleasure, that's all! Do you think I'm some kind of Romeo?"

"But why me? Look at all these pretty girls! Why choose me?"

James Blascoe looked serious for a moment. "Because you are special. Because you are chosen. Because there is no other girl like you in the whole wide world."

"Well, I'm flattered, Mr Blascoe, but I really can't – "

"Keep the brooch, please. Don't break my heart. And please . . . accept this, too."

He held out a small purse of pale blue moire silk, tied with a gold cord.

Margot laughed in disbelief. "You can't keep on giving me gifts like this!"

"Please," he begged her; and there was a look in his eyes which made it oddly difficult for her to resist him. The look in his eyes didn't match his voice at all: it wasn't a begging look. It was level and imperative. A look that said, *you will, whether you like it or not.* Before Margot had time to analyze what she was doing, and the implications of what she was doing, she had taken the silk purse, and held it up, and said, "All right, then. Thank you."

James Blascoe said, "It's an ounce of perfume created by Isabey, of the Faubourg St Honoré, in Paris, in 1925. It was specially blended for the Polish baroness Krystyna Waclacz, and there is no more left, but this one bottle."

"Why give it to me?" Margot asked him. For some reason, she felt frightened rather than pleased.

James Blascoe shrugged. "What will happen to it, if you don't wear it? Wear it tonight. Wear it every night."

"Hi, Margot!" called her secretary, Denise, as she passed close by. "Don't forget the Perry meeting, eight-thirty on the button!"

Margot looked up at James Blascoe but he was standing against the sun and his face was masked in shadow. She

195

hesitated for a moment, and then she said, "I'd better go," and pushed her way through the revolving door, leaving James Blascoe standing outside, watching her intently, his features distorted by the curved glass.

In the elevator, she felt as if she were being compressed. Breathless, squashed, tightly surrounded by people who were determined to press the life out of her. By the time the chime rang for the 36th floor, she was shivering, as if she had contracted the 'flu, and when she reached her office she stood with her back pressed to the door, taking deep breaths, wondering if she were terrified or aroused, or both. That night she was taken to see *Les Misérables* by Dominic Bross, the record producer, whom she had met while working on the Bross Records account. Dominic was 55, gray-haired, handsome, talkative, opinionated, and Margot wouldn't have dreamed of going to bed with him in a million years. However, she always enjoyed his company, and he always behaved like a perfect gentleman.

Halfway through the second act, Dominic leaned over to Margot and whispered, "Do you *smell* something?"

Margot sniffed. All she could smell was the musky Isabey perfume which James Blascoe had given her. Once it had warmed on her skin, it had started to give off the deepest, most sensuous fragrance that she had ever experienced. Maybe it had been wrong of her to accept it, but it was something erotic and very special, something that made her head spin.

"I don't know," Dominic complained. "It smells like something died."

James Blascoe was waiting by her apartment door when she returned from her dinner with Dominic. She was tired and quite angry. For some reason Dominic had been unusually hurried and offhand, and hadn't even accepted her invitation to come up for coffee. Finding

196

James Blascoe at her door didn't make her feel very much better.

"Well, well," she said, taking out her key. "I'm surprised Leland let you in to the building."

"Oh, you know me," James Blascoe smiled. "Bribery and corruption are second nature to me."

"I'm not going to invite you in," Margot told him. "I've had a totally terrible evening, and all I'm going to do is take a bath and get some sleep."

"I'm sorry," James Blascoe told her. "I quite understand, and I won't intrude. But I wanted to give you this."

He reached into his inside pocket, and took out a long black jewelry case. Before Margot could protest, he had opened it up, and shown her what lay inside. It was a shimmering diamond necklace, so bright that it was almost magical, seven diamond festoons attached to ten diamond-encrusted bows.

"This is absurd," Margot protested; although it was hard for her to keep her eyes off the necklace. It was absolutely the most beautiful thing she had ever seen in her life.

James Blascoe slowly smiled. It was like somebody slowly drawing a spoon through an open jar of molasses. "Traditionally, this necklace was supposed to have been part of the ransom offered by Catherine the Great to the Sultan of Turkey, to persuade him to release her husband Peter the Great after he was captured at the Battle of Rusen in 1711."

"Well, who does it belong to now?" asked Margot. The diamonds shone in tiny pinpricks of light across her cheeks.

"Now," James Blascoe said, with utter simplicity, "now, it belongs to you."

Margot lifted her eyes away from the necklace. "Mr Blascoe, this is ridiculous. I'm not a whore."

197

"Did I ever suggest that you were? Take it. It's a gift. I want nothing in return."

"You really want nothing?" Margot challenged him.

"Take it," he said. "I want you to have the finest of everything. That's all. I have no other ambition."

There was an unblinking look of command in his eyes. Margot knew that the jinn-flower brooch and the Isabey perfume had been one thing. But if she accepted this necklace, no matter how much James Blascoe protested that he wanted nothing at all, she would be beholden to him. It was probably worth over a hundred thousand dollars. It was certainly exquisite: the kind of jewelry which most women can never even dream of owning.

"No," said her mouth. *What am I doing?* said her mind. But her hand reached out and took it.

Two days later, at a cocktail thrash at the Plaza Hotel for Overmeyer & Cranston, one of their biggest clients, Margot decided to take a risk and wear the necklace for the first time. She matched it with a simple electric-blue cocktail dress, and wore the simplest of diamond-stud earrings.

The party was already noisy with laughter and conversation when Margot arrived. She smiled and waved to O & C's president George Demaris, and then to Dick Manzi of NBC. However, she was surprised when both of them frowned at her and gave her only a half-hearted wave in return; and she was even more surprised when the cocktail waiter stared at her in what could only be described as dumbstruck astonishment.

She took a glass of champagne, and challenged him, "Something wrong?"

"Oh, no, no. Nothing's wrong, ma'am."

A few moments later, however, Walter Rutter angled his way across the room toward her and took her arm and tugged her almost immediately to the side of the buffet table.

"Margot? What's with the necklace? You can't wear something like that here!"

"What do you mean, Walter? This necklace is worth a fortune! It was part of the ransom that Catherine the Great gave to the Sultan of Turkey!"

Walter narrowed his crowsfooted eyes and stared at Margot for a long time. Margot defiantly stared back at him.

"Catherine the Great gave that necklace to the Sultan of Turkey?" Walter repeated.

Margot nodded. "A very dear friend gave it to me."

"I'm sorry," Walter told her. He was obviously choosing his words carefully. "But – if it's worth a fortune – maybe this is not quite the place to wear it. You know, for the sake of security. Maybe we should ask the management to lock it in the safe for a while."

Margot fingered the necklace in disappointment. "You really think so?"

Walter laid a fatherly arm around her bare shoulders. "Yes, Margot. I really think so." Then he sniffed, and looked around, and said, "Those fish canapes sure smell strong. I hope nobody goes down with food-poisoning."

The next morning, James Blascoe was waiting for Margot in the foyer of Rutter Blane Rutter, with a large gift-wrapped box in his hands. Black shiny paper, a black shiny bow.

"Mr Blascoe," she said, emphatically, before he could open his mouth, "this really has to stop. You can't go on giving me all of these ridiculously expensive gifts."

He thought for a moment, lowered his eyes. "Supposing I were to tell you that I loved you, beyond all reason?"

"Mr Blascoe – "

"Please, call me James. And, please, take this gift. It's an original Fortuny evening dress, made for La Comtesse de la Ronce, one of the wealthiest women in France, in

1927. The only person in the world who could possibly wear it is you."

"Mr Blascoe –" she protested. But his eyes told her that she must accept the gown, no matter what.

"James," she whispered, and took the box.

That evening, he was waiting outside her apartment, with a black silk shoe-bag. Inside were the softest pair of pointed suede ankle-boots, handmade by Rayne. They were meticulously hand-stitched, and dyed to the color of crushed loganberries, to match exactly the color of the Fortuny gown.

"Take them, wear them," he insisted. "Wear them always. Remember how much I love you."

She was awoken the next morning by the phone ringing. Tugging her fingers through her tangled curls, she found the receiver and picked it up.

"Margot? Sorry to call you so early. This is Walter Rutter."

"Walter! Hi, good morning! What can I do for you?"

"Margot, I wanted to catch you before you left for the office. You see, the point is I'm in some difficulty here. I have to make some savings in the agency's overall budget, and that regrettably means shedding some staff."

"I see. Do you know how many?"

"Not exactly, Margot. But the problem is that it has to be last in, first out. This is nothing to do with the fact that you're a woman; and nothing to do with your abilities, which have been tremendous in the past, and have earned us a great deal of acclaim. But . . . as things stand, I'm afraid that I'm going to have to disemploy you, as of now."

Margot sat up straight. "You mean I'm fired?"

"Nothing like that, Margot. Not fired. But not continued with, staffwise."

Margot couldn't think of anything to say. She let the phone drop on to the comforter. She felt as if someone had suddenly lashed at her with a birch, stinging her face, cutting her hands, slicing her self-assurance into ribbons.

She was still sitting upright in bed twenty minutes later, when the doorbell rang.

Mechanically, she wrapped herself in her short silk robe, and went to answer the door. It was James Blascoe, with a long gift-wrapped box, and the smile of a man whose will can never be denied.

"I've brought you something," he announced.

Without waiting to be asked, he walked into the living-room and laid the box on the table. He tugged free the gift-ribbon himself, and eased off the lid. Inside, wrapped in dark brown tissue-paper, was a huge greenish scepter, almost four feet long, embossed with gold bands and complicated gold knobs and bumps. James lifted it up, and Margot saw that the scepter's head had been cast in the helmeted shape of a man's erect glans, except that it was nearly twice the size.

She stared at it, strangely excited by its decorative blatancy.

"Do you know what this is?" asked James. "The copper phallus used by Queen Nefertiti of Egypt to give herself erotic pleasure. It has been passed down from one century to another; from one royal court to the next. It has slid its way up between the thighs of more celebrated women than anybody could count.

He grasped the glans in his hand, as if it were his own. "It is said to give more pleasure than anything you could imagine, man or beast. Now it's yours; to keep; and to use."

He brought it across the room and laid it in the palms of her hands. "Tonight, at midnight, dress in the jewelry and clothes that I have given you, perfume yourself with my perfume; and then think of me, and give yourself the pleasure that only you deserve."

Margot still couldn't speak. James kissed her forehead with a cool, dry, almost abstracted kiss, and then left the apartment, and closed the door behind him.

At eleven o'clock that night, like a woman in a dream, Margot ran herself a deep perfumed bath. She washed herself slowly and sensually, rubbing the soap over her full white breasts over and over again, until the nipples rose between her fingers.

At last she rose naked from the bath and dried herself in a deep warm Descamps towel. Her apartment was filled with mirrors: she could watch herself walk from room to room.

She brushed out her curls, and made up her face, starkly, very white. Then she dropped the velvety Fortuny dress over her shoulders, and it touched her bare body like a series of soft, hurried kisses. She fastened the diamond-festoon necklace around her neck, and slipped on the handmade ankle-boots. Last of all she sprayed herself with Isabey perfume.

It was almost midnight. She went to the table and lifted the huge copper-and-gold phallus out of its tissue-paper. It was very heavy, and gleamed dully in the lamplight. *It is said to give more pleasure than anything you could imagine, man or beast.*

She knelt in the middle of the floor, and lifted up her gown. Holding the phallus with both hands, she parted her thighs, and presented its massive bottle-green glans to the dark silky fur of her vulva.

At first she didn't believe that she would be able to insert it, and she clenched her teeth. But then, little by little, the huge cold head buried itself inside her, and she managed to force it further and further up, until she was able to kneel upright, with the base of the phallus flat against the floor.

The sensation of having such a huge rod of chilled, uncompromising metal up inside her made her wince and quake with erotic anticipation. Her hands smoothed and massaged the swollen lips of her vulva, and caressed the slippery meeting-place between metal and flesh.

Think of me, James had asked her; and as she pressed her whole weight down on to the phallus, she tried to visualize his face. As flesh parted, as membranes tore, she tried to remember what he looked like. But she couldn't. She couldn't even think of his eyes.

He had been right, though. The pleasure was beyond all belief. She gasped and shook in the most devastating of climaxes, and then the blood suddenly welled in her throat and poured out over her lips.

Ray had been trying to call her all day, and when she didn't answer, he took a taxi around to her apartment, and persuaded the concierge Leland to let him in.

The living-room was dark, with the blinds still closed. In the center of the room, surrounded by mirrors, Margot lay with her eyes still open and her mouth caked with dried blood.

Around her neck she wore a piece of twisted wire, decorated with Pepsi caps and unrolled condoms. She was dressed in a frayed candlewick bathrobe and worn-down Keds. The bathrobe was stained dark with blood, and out from between her thighs protruded a long section of bloodily-fingerprinted scaffolding-pole.

Shaking with shock, Ray knelt down next to her and closed her eyelids with finger and thumb. He had realized that she had been going off the rails a little. Pressure of success, that's what Walter Rutter had called it. But he had never imagined for one moment that she would kill herself, not like this. How could any woman kill herself like this?

The room stank of sardine-oil; the same smell that

203

had been following Margot around for the past few days.

Ray stood up at last and looked around. The concierge was standing in the doorway, pale, paralyzed with uncertainty, and Ray said, "You'd better call an ambulance; and the cops."

Outside in the spring sunny street, a man stood watching as the ambulance arrived. He was unshaven and wearing a soiled gray suit. His eyes were red from lack of sleep and alcohol. He waited to see the blanket-covered body taken away, and then, as the sirens whooped, he started walking southward, sniffing from time to time, and ceaselessly searching through his pockets as if he expected to find a cigarette-butt that he had previously overlooked, or even a couple of quarters.

When he reached Times Square he stood on the curb outside Macy's for five or ten minutes. Then he saw a pretty well-dressed young girl crossing the street toward him, and he gave a last sniff, and straightened himself up, and smiled, at her.

5A Bedford Row

Worthing, Sussex

Like most of the popular seaside resorts along Britain's south coast, Worthing was nothing more than a fishing hamlet until it was favored by a visit by royalty – in Worthing's case, by Princess Amelia, the youngest daughter of George III, when she came to take the bracing Channel air in 1798. In the next 14 years, Worthing grew into the safe, dull and geriatric town it is today. It has a shingled beach, four miles of promenades, a pier, concert halls and the Connaught theater. Paintings in Worthing Museum include many fine 19th-century and Victorian watercolors.

Despite Worthing's dullness, it still has a strong sense of history and place – positioned as it is between the sea and the South Downs, where you can still find Iron Age camps, prehistoric flint mines and wild, windy views of the sea.

5a BEDFORD ROW

I saw my first-ever real-live dead body the morning I arrived at 5a Bedford Row; and if that wasn't a cue to turn right around and never go back, I don't know what else could have been.

But I was soaking wet and starving hungry and absolutely knackered after walking from the station, and I really didn't have anywhere else to go.

5a Bedford Row was about a hundred yards down a narrow sidestreet off the seafront in Worthing. It was the last week in August, 1967, and it was raining so hard you couldn't tell where the sea ended and the town began. The clouds were racing north towards the Sussex Downs like a pack of wet mad dogs. I'd only had cornies for breakfast with no milk and my unemployment money hadn't turned up before I left London. Apart from that the train had stopped for three-quarters of an hour at Christ's Hospital for no apparent reason at all, and we'd all just sat there watching the rain run down the windows.

It was nearly eleven o'clock before we got into Worthing, and even then I had a twenty-minute walk down the back streets, past the police station and the art college and the Connaught Theater.

5a Bedford Row was a flat-fronted three-story house: typical Sussex coast mid-Victorian, faced with diseased gray cement, broken guttering, slipped slates. The doorbell didn't work (or at least I couldn't hear it and no bugger came to answer it) and when I opened the letter-box to shout hallo, anybody home, I was greeted by this steady breeze smelling of damp plaster and Izal toilet-blocks and other people's stale chip-fat.

I was only a second away from seeing my first real-live dead body, though I didn't know it. Because of the rain, I hadn't seen the black Daimler hearse parked on the otherside of the Row, by the bus garage. I was still peering into the letter-box with rain running down the collar of my Millett's anorak when the front door was suddenly jostled open and this tall red-faced chap with a noseful of broken veins came struggling out backwards, carrying the end of an open coffin.

"Will you watch out for Christ's sake," he snapped at me, out of the corner of his mouth.

Then he shuffled and swayed and blinked up at the sky. "Fuck it, it's still fucking raining. And trust you to forget the fucking lid."

He was addressing this abuse to a thin waxy-faced young chap who was holding the other end of the coffin, his lank hair swinging, his forehead greasy with perspiration.

But it was the occupant of the coffin who startled me the most. My nerves thrilled as if somebody had circled my forehead with elastic bands. She was lying in this coffin and she was dead. Well, I mean, it was logical that she was dead, you don't usually lie in a coffin unless you're dead, but she was actually dead, her head nodding as they carried her in a slack way that it never could have nodded if she had been alive.

She was skinny and drawn and worst of all she was whitish-blue, even her lips. The darkness of her eyes showed through her closed eyelids like the eyes of a dead fledgling.

"I've got the umbrella, Mr Pedrick," said the young chap, in a hopeful voice.

"Oh, you've got the fucking umbrella, have you, and who's going to hold it up? Our ladyfriend in the box here?"

I don't know why, but I said, "It's all right, I will."

Mr Pedrick's gray-blue eyes swiveled into focus. "Well, that's a noble offer, now. Very noble. They may not feel it, you know, the dead" (jerking his head down at the body) "the rain" (jerking his head up at the clouds). "But they deserve our respect at the very least."

The two of them struggled across the Row with the coffin while I kept awkward shuffling pace beside them, holding up their huge black musty-smelling umbrella, which must have sheltered a thousand widows at a thousand rainy gravesides. Mr Pedrick wrestled with the hearse door and at last they managed to slide the coffin noisily into place.

The waxy-faced young chap covered the body with the coffin-lid, and then sneezed.

"Oh God where's your fucking hankie," Mr Pedrick snapped at him, and then to me, "I'm most grateful, a noble act."

"That's all right," I told him. "I've never seen one before."

Mr Pedrick rolled his eyes toward the coffin. "You've never seen a –?"

I shook my head, feeling numb and peculiarly innocent and very wet.

"There's one thing, they don't argue. They can look accusing. Oh yes, and they can look *very* resentful at times. But they don't argue." He paused, and then he sniffed. "They'd better fucking not, anyway."

From the tone of his voice, I took it that he would be quite prepared to beat up a body that even *looked* as if it might be arguing.

I stood and watched the undertakers drive away. I felt really weird, as if I'd blinked and missed a whole day out of my life. Eternity, I thought, that's what it is. It was a bit like jet-lag, except that I'd never been on a jet then, so I didn't know what jet-lag was like. I crossed the street slowly back to the house.

The door was still half-open and I could see a woman in the hall, polishing a small hall-table with a cloth that had once been a child's nightdress. She was probably fifty; and twenty years ago she had probably been quite handsome, in a chubby sort of way. Now her face was oval and featureless, like a white dinner-plate. She wore one of those floral housecoats that women wore during the war, and her gray hair was pinned up with a crisscross fence of about eight thousand kirbygrips. She was smoking as if she was in a smoking race.

"Mrs Bristow?" I asked her. "I'm David Moore."

She stared at me, sipping at her cigarette. Then she said, "Bit wet, aren't you? Where's your things?"

"Actually I haven't got any things. I mean, not as such. I thought the room was furnished."

She paused, sip, puff, sip, puff. "Well, it is. But there isn't much. I mean there's pots and pans, and a cheese-grater. But no sheets or blankets or anything. And I don't supply soap or toilet-paper."

"I, er – I left most of my stuff in London. I was thinking of buying some new sheets."

Mrs Bristow folded and refolded the nightdress. "Well, then," she said. "You'll want to see the room."

"Yes, smashing." I smiled, although I felt so cheesed off I could have burst into tears. Mrs Bristow, wide-hipped in her housecoat, led the way upstairs, smoking and polishing as she went.

There was nothing in 5a Bedford Row to cheer your heart. The wallpaper down the stairs had obviously once been patterned with roses, but time and damp had strained all the color out of it, so that the roses looked like week-old cauliflowers. The banisters were stained with dark Edwardian varnish, and the staircase creaked and groaned as we climbed it.

"I met the undertakers on the way in," I said, as we reached the first-floor landing.

Mrs Bristow stopped, and stared at me. "That was Miss Coates," she said.

"Oh," I said.

"Poor Miss Coates," Mrs Bristow repeated, louder, as if she thought I were deaf. "She used to do piecework, you know. Making up first-aid kits for some mail-order company. There's dozens of them, in the cellar. I'll have to ring up the company and get them to take them all away. She gave me a first-aid kit once, when her rent was late. Dear me, flipping useless, it was. Two sticking plasters and a tube of Germolene. Fat lot of good if you cut your head off."

"I súppose you're right," I said. Then, "What did she die of?"

Mrs Bristow didn't answer, but heaved her way up the next flight of stairs like an impatient rock-climber. Through a small window at the end of the landing, I could just glimpse a gray rain-ribbed roof and a haze of lighter greeny-grayness which I took to be the sea.

"Of course, she had Room Two," said Mrs Bristow.

"I'm sorry?"

"Miss Coates. She had Room Two. That's our best room. Sea view, self-contained kitchenette, ladies only. Newly decorated, too."

"Oh," I said.

We resumed our climb. "Of course it's very coveted amongst my lady tenants, Room Two. So much bigger and nicer. It used to be my husband and I's room."

"Oh, nice," I said. I wished she would stop puffing smoke in my face.

"Idyllic in the summer, Room Two. Absolutely idyllic.

211

Miss Coates liked it so much, she said she wanted to spend the rest of her days there."

"Well, she did, didn't she?" I ventured.

Mrs Bristow stopped again, and turned to stare at me through a sliding wreath of gray cigarette smoke. "I do expect proper behaviour, you know," she told me. "I don't expect parties and I don't expect, you know, overnight friends. Of *either*, you know, sex."

I nodded obediently. I had about three-and-six in my jacket pocket for a half of bitter and a Cornish pasty, and she expected me to have parties, and to be able to woo somebody into an overnight friendship? But I resisted the temptation to say you must be bleeding joking missis.

We were almost up at the top of the house when we heard the sound of a small child grizzling, and the sharp clatter of worn-down high heels on the stairs. As we reached the top landing, Mrs Bristow stood back against the wall, like a railway lineworker waiting for an express to pass, and I did, too. Along the landing came a rolled-up pink satin quilt, walking on long fishnet-stockinged legs. The quilt was followed by a blonde boy of about two years old in a stripey orange-and-brown T-shirt and nothing else, grumbling and crying.

"I haven't vacew-ummed Room Two yet, Nancy," said Mrs Bristow, blowing out smoke from both nostrils.

The quilt was dropped abruptly to the floor. A girl's white face appeared, with wild back-combed dyed-black hair, and huge eyes with two pairs of false eyelashes. Then a deeply low-scooped black sweater, into which were crammed the biggest whitest breasts that I had ever seen in my whole life. A wide black patent-leather belt, cinched tight. And then a cheap white cotton mini-skirt, with fraying seams.

"Oh 'allo, Mrs B. Didn't see you behind me bedding."

"Nancy, this is Mr Moore. He's coming to stay in Room Seven."

212

"David," I said, holding out my hand; and then realizing that Nancy didn't have a hand free to shake it.

"Pleased to meet you, David," said Nancy. "This misery-guts here is Simon, aren't you, Simon?"

Simon continued to grizzle unabated.

"Well, since you're so keen to move in already, I'll do the vacewming later," said Mrs Bristow, puff, sip. "Come on, Mr Moore, I'll show you your room."

"See you later, aye?" smiled Nancy, and then, "Shut up, Simon, for God's sake."

Room Seven was high in the roof, with a dormer window propped open with an old hairless washing-up brush. I had a saggy bed and a red Parker-Knoll chair and a table with a tiny cream-colored Belling electric cooker on it, and about a million cigarette burns all the way along the edge.

"It's very light in the mornings, Room Seven," said Mrs Bristow. "And you can see the Dome, too. Just a peek, anyway."

She waited at the open door. "It's two weeks' deposit and a week in advance," she said. "That's thirteen pounds ten."

"Erm, I wonder if I could pay you at the end of the week. I'm afraid my cheque hasn't come yet."

Mrs Bristow's head disappeared in a cloud of smoke, and she coughed. "I don't usually," she said.

"I'd be very grateful."

"Well, all right, then," she sighed, and disappeared down the stairs, leaving a trail of smoke behind her. "But Friday," she called back. "Or else I'm afraid you're out."

I went to the open dormer window and stared out at the rainy slate rooftops. Below me I could hear traffic on the wet roads, and the insistent shushing of the sea. I felt depressed and lonely but at the same time I felt strangely content. I had come to Worthing because it was the most depressing place I could think of, and I needed a sanctuary that suited my mood. I was broke, and out

213

of work, and my life didn't seem to be going anywhere. Nineteen-and-a-half, with no prospects. What better place to get your head together than Worthing?

The only reason I knew Worthing was because my great-aunt had lived here when I was little, and we used to come and visit. The beach was all pebbles and smelled strongly of seaweed.

Worthing has a pier, and one of those grassy municipal squares that Sussex people call a Steyne, and a bandstand, and some public toilets, and several nasty department stores full of shiny reproduction furniture and place-mats with hunting scenes on them, and EPNS cutlery. It's neither as vulgar as Brighton nor as self-consciously tight-arsed as Eastbourne. It's just a gray British suburb by the sea. *St-Despair-sur-Mer*, as my great-aunt used to call it.

I suppose I had a vague idea that I might make some money as a deckchair attendant, or working in a fish-and-chip shop, but I wasn't really sure. I'd taken my A-levels in English and Geography and French, but my marks had been so bad that there hadn't really been much point in trying to get a place in college. Lack of application, the teachers had called it. I think I'd just run out of any desire to carry on. I just didn't want to participate any more. I wanted to think, and do menial, unimportant things. If I'd been religious, I suppose I would've joined a monastery; but going to Worthing was just about the next most mortifying thing.

There was a stringy roller-towel on the back of the door and I dried myself. I had a wet paper carrier-bag with yesterday's shirt in it, which wasn't quite as wet as today's, so I changed. Then I counted out my last remaining cash, which was actually three-and-sevepence-halfpenny, and decided to go out for some lunch.

As I came down the stairs to the middle landing, Nancy was just closing the door behind Room Two.

214

"Settled in, then?" she asked me.

"Sort of. I've got to buy some sheets and stuff."

"Is that where you're going now?"

"I was going to the pub for some lunch, actually."

Without hesitation, she linked arms with me. Even in her stiletto heels, she was only about five-three. She smelled of tangeriney hairspray and Shalimar. "That's good, you can buy me some!"

"I've only got three-and-seven."

"You're *joh*-king."

"No, I'm not. Look." I held out a halfcrown, a shilling, and a penny and three ha'pennies. "The sum total of my worldly wealth."

Nancy laughed. "Looks like I'm paying then, doesn't it? Fancy the Thieves Kitchen?"

"Don't know. Never been there."

We borrowed Mrs Bristow's broken pink umbrella and scampered out into the rain. The Thieves Kitchen wasn't far, only two streets away. A large pub-restaurant offering Traditional Lunches. It was dark and smoky, with pretense oak beams and horse-brasses. We sat in a booth and ordered pork chops and fried eggs and pints of Red Barrel bitter. Nancy was chatty and flirtatious and changed the whole of my outlook on life in the space of one meal.

She talked and ate and laughed and I just ate. I watched her the whole time. She was absolutely smashing. Underneath those double sets of false eyelashes and that white pancake make-up she was deliciously pretty. She had a babyish face, with pouting lips and a little snub nose and big wide blue-lilac eyes, and I think I fell in love with her after the third mouthful of pork chop. Everything about her entranced me. Her cheapness, her outspokenness, the tiny gold studs in her ears, and that deep, pressed-together cleavage, which exuded Boot's talcum powder and unimaginable promise.

"I should never 'ave married Vince, never," she said,

215

swallowing beer from a pint glass. "I was a fool to meself. But then 'e was ever so good-looking and 'e 'ad a bike and a sidecar, and 'e was ever so *moody*, do you know what I mean? And I was only sixteen. I was really stupid then. But ever since I've 'ad Simon . . . well, you 'ave to be more machewer, don't you?"

"Where is Simon?" I asked her.

"'Aving 'is nap," said Nancy. "I give 'im 'is lunch at twelve o'clock, and then 'e sleeps through till 'alf-past two; every day, regular as clockwork."

She asked me what I was doing in Worthing; and I told her. She listened sympathetically but I don't think that she really understood. It was like trying to quote Paul Verlaine to somebody at a noisy drinks party. "*Les sanglots longs des violons de l' automne . . . blessent mon coeur d'une langueur monotone . . .*"

Nancy paid for the whole lunch herself, out of a white vinyl purse. "Oh, don't worry, Vince is ever so good to me. 'E sends me seven pounds a week and I don't usually spend it all."

We walked back to 5a Bedford Row arm in arm, under Mrs Bristow's wounded umbrella. Outside Room Two, Nancy said, "D'you want to come in for a cuppa coff?"

Room Two was almost four times larger than my room. Nancy had drawn the thin flower-patterned curtains so that Simon could sleep. He lay in his cot in the corner, his thumb planted in his mouth, his blonde hair sticky, his cheeks like fire. I stood over him and wished that he were mine, instead of Vince's. I turned back to Nancy and she was just standing there, looking at me.

"Mrs Bristow says that Room Two is idyllic," I told her.

"Can't say that I've noticed," Nancy replied, without taking her eyes off me.

"No, well," I said, uncomfortably. I looked around. The room was freshly-papered with a strange yellowish

216

crisscross pattern, Woolworths' best. There was a 1950s dressing-table by the window, with a semicircular mirror; a large cheap varnished bed; a chest-of-drawers that somebody had painted powder-blue; and a huge Victorian wardrobe, in carved mahogany.

"Fantastic wardrobe," I remarked.

"Oh, yeah, 'cept that she always keep it locked."

I tried the brass handle, but the door wouldn't budge. "What's in here, do you know?"

Nancy sat on the edge of the bed. "Personal stuff, that's all. Says she 'asn't got nowhere else to keep it."

I sat on her bed next to her. "You don't 'alf talk posh," she said.

"What do you mean?"

"Well, you're all kind of posh and poetic. Everything you say. Like the clouds being like mad dogs, that kind of thing. You ought to be a writer."

"Hunh," I told her. "There's no money in writing. I'm going to be a deck-chair attendant."

"Well, you'll pick up some girls."

There was a long silence. The room was silent; Simon slept silently. Then Nancy said, "Do you want to see something really shocking?"

I stared at her. Her eyes were deep lilac in the subdued light of Room Two.

"What do you mean, shocking?"

"Well, just look. Tell me if you're shocked."

Without hesitation, without taking her eyes off me, she lifted her black sweater and dragged it off over her head. Then she unhooked her lacy black bra, and bared her breasts. She gave a little wiggle, so that they swung and bounced.

Her breasts looked even bigger than they had before. They were full and white like two huge milk puddings; their skin imprinted with the pattern of her bra. Her areolas were wide and pale, and her nipples were crinkled

217

tight. What fascinated me, though – and what was obviously supposed to shock me – was that both her nipples had been pierced with thin gold rings.

I had heard about girls piercing their nipples, I mean everybody's *heard* about it, but I had never met a girl who had actually done it. Let along found myself face to face with one, on a double-bed, on a wet afternoon in Worthing. My cock uncurled inside my jeans, and I felt a hot flush color my cheeks.

"What do you think?" she asked me, giving her breasts another little jiggle.

"I don't know. It's fantastic."

"Vince wanted it done. I didn't want to, at first, but now I quite like it."

"It's fantastic," I repeated. I didn't know what else to say.

"You don't think it's shocking, then?"

"It's surprising."

"But not shocking?"

I shook my head.

She looked at me seriously. "You can touch them, if you like."

I hesitated; then reached out, and felt both nipples, and rings. The rings could be rotated through the nipples quite easily.

"You can lift them up, if you like."

I stared at her. It wasn't what *I* liked; it was what *she* wanted. I hooked my fingers through both rings, and lifted her heavy breasts with them, until both nipples were stretched. She closed her eyes and arched her head back, while I gently tugged at her breasts again and again, as if they were disobedient puppies.

Without a word, she lifted my hands away from her breasts, and unfastened the hook-and-eye catches of cheap white skirt. Underneath she wore fishnet tights, no panties. The dark pink flesh of her vulva bulged through the fishnet in diamond patterns. I smelled the pungent erotic smell of sex and urine.

We made love tightly, quietly, fiercely, for nearly forty minutes. It seemed like a lifetime went by. Eternity. That same eternity I had glimpsed outside, when they were carrying Miss Coates away. But then I opened my eyes and we were lying together in Room Two, with the curtains drawn, under an embroidered sampler which said, *Work Out Your Own Salvation With Fear And Trembling*.

Nancy turned her head and blurrily smiled at me. There were pearls of semen still clinging to her false eyelashes. She said, "You're good, you are, David Moore."

I kissed her. I could have married her then and there. "You too, Nancy Whatever-Your-Name-Is."

"Bright," she said, and kissed me again.

It was then that Simon stirred, and coughed, and opened his eyes.

For the next two weeks we went everywhere together and went to bed at every possible opportunity. The August rain blew over and left us with warm and windy weather, and we took the bus to Littlehampton and made love naked in the grassy sand-dunes while Simon built a castle with a real sea-water moat.

Nancy was dirty-minded and mad and she didn't care what she did. She never wore panties; she didn't even own any. She lay face-down in the dunes with her bottom lifted and her vagina pulled open with her fingers and yelped like a seagull when I pushed myself into her. She loved rolling around and filthy language and sucking and kissing, and all the delights that the flesh can be heir to.

I had never met a girl like Nancy, ever. I've never met a girl like Nancy since. Vince could keep his bike and his sidecar. Nancy was everything I could have dreamed of. Perhaps I couldn't have taken her home to meet my parents. ("Oh, mum, this is Nancy, she

219

has a two-year-old illegitimate son and she wears nipple rings.") But who cared about that? With Nancy, I was in nineteen-year-old heaven. With Nancy, I forgot about depression and despair.

I deferred looking for a job, and we spent days on the beach; or took the train to Arundel and walked around the castle; or climbed on the chalky dinosaur backs of the Sussex Downs, while the huge clouds sailed over-head and their shadows sailed across the water-meadows below. Days of sunshine and silliness and not much money. Days of country pubs and picnics with doorstep sandwiches and walks down fragrant Sussex lanes; kissing in the shadow of ancient oaks.

When the last day came, I didn't even know it was the last. We'd been to the funfair at Littlehampton, and come back by bus. We finished up by walking along the seafront at sunset, one of those gray warm evenings with the sun stirred into the Channel mist like damson jam into a pudding. Simon was riding piggyback on my shoulders and Nancy was walking beside me in white hot pants and a black nylon blouse knotted over her midriff. Somebody was playing a tranny on the pier, *Hey Joe* by Jimi Hendrix. "*Hey Joe, where you goin' with that gun in your hand . . .*" Jimi Hendrix was Nancy's favorite, after the Stones.

"Do you think you'll ever get married," Nancy asked me.

"I don't know," I said, guardedly. I suppose I was already convinced that I was going to marry *her*.

"I'm not goin' to get married again," she told me, emphatically.

"Oh."

Simon tugged at my hair, and said, "Giddyup, horsey!"

"What about Simon?" I asked Nancy.

"What about him?"

"Well, he'll want a father, won't he? Especially when he's older. My father used to take me to Farnborough Air Show."

220

"There's more to life than fathers," said Nancy. She looked away, and for some inexplicable reason I knew then that I had lost her; that something had changed between us. Simon jiggled up and down and said, "Giddyup, horsey! Giddyup, horsey!"

I galloped along the seafront with him, in that gray-plum evening light, and Nancy followed along behind us with a tight distracted smile, looking small, and different. *Goin' down to shoot my ole lady . . . 'cause she's been runnin' around with another man . . ."*

That evening I came downstairs from Room Seven and knocked gently at Nancy's door. It was half-past eight, and Simon should have been asleep by then.

Nancy was a long time answering. She whispered through the closed door, *"Who is it?"*

"It's David. Can I come in?"

"I'm not dressed."

Not being dressed had never stopped her opening the door before. I stood on the landing, hesitant and confused.

"I thought we could go to the pub."

Another long pause, then, "I haven't got any money."

"I've still got a pound."

"Oh, great evenin' out we're goin' to have on a pound."

So that was it, I thought. She was fed up with my having no money. "Listen," I called, "I'll go out and get a job tomorrow. They're looking for attendants at Peter Pan's Playground."

"Do what you like."

I ran my hand through my hair. She was beginning to make me feel distinctly desperate. "Look, can we talk?"

"What about?"

"Well, us. You and me."

"There isn't anything to talk about."

"Nancy," I said, on that gloomy wallpapered landing, "I love you."

221

"No you don't. You want somebody posh and poetic."

"I want you. I want to marry you."

"Oh, come on, Dave; don't talk stupid."

"But I do. You can take this as a formal proposal of marriage."

"Dave, for goodness' sake, go away."

I rattled the doorknob but the door was firmly locked. And it was then that I heard heavy swaying footsteps on the stairs, and Mrs Bristow hove into view, in her stage-magician cloud of Guards cigarette smoke. She stood at the far end of the landing watching me, and there was nothing I could do but retreat back to Room Seven and close the door.

I stood on my chair with my head out of the skylight, miserably contemplating the rooftops and the distant Downs. It was growing dark now, and the seafront was necklaced with sodium lights. The sea shushed, and shushed, with its hollow mouthful of pebbles; and there isn't a sound in the world more weary and lonely than that.

At about ten o'clock I heard Mrs Bristow bang and lock the back door, and so I decided to go down and give Nancy another try. Perhaps she'd been tired. Perhaps it was the wrong time of the mouth. But I missed her so much. Even after just a few hours I missed her. I couldn't bear to think that she didn't want to go to bed with me any more.

I crept downstairs, and stood outside Room Two. The timing switch on the stairs clicked off, and left me in darkness. I couldn't hear anything at first except Radio Caroline playing in Room Four. "*Waterloo Sunset . . . I am in Paradise . . .*" Then I heard somebody talking; and it wasn't Nancy. It was a man's voice: thick and breathy and crackling.

Oh God, I though, she's found somebody else. Somebody older; somebody more like her. Somebody who's not all wet and poetic like me. Perhaps Vince had come back. I'd seen a photograph of Vince, black leather jacket, quiff, sideburns, and a BSA bike with a sidecar. How could a skinny Mod like me hope to compete with a heavy-duty Rocker like him? And he was Simon's real father.

I heard Nancy saying something, but at first I couldn't make out what it was. I knelt down beside the keyhole, so that the draft blew in my ear. She was saying, ". . . for ever? 'Ow can I stay 'ere for ever?"

"*Because I want you to stay here for ever*," crackled the man's voice, surprisingly loudly and distinctly. "*Because I love you, and because you must.*"

"But what about Simon?" asked Nancy.

"*All children are damned, you should know that by now.*"

"But 'oo's goin' to take care of 'im?"

"*Fate will take care of him. He is only one more speck of flotsam on the ocean of the night.*"

I slowly stood up. That couldn't be Vince. According to Nancy, Vince had talked about nothing except Eddie Cochrane and motorbikes. And how could she say that I was too poetic if she was talking to somebody who said things like "one more speck of flotsam on the ocean of the night?"

In a fit of jealousy, I thumped at the door with my fist. "Nancy!" I yelled at her. "Nancy!"

There was a moment's silence.

"Nancy!" I yelled again. "Open this bloody door!"

To my surprise, I heard the door unlock. Then it opened, only two or three inches. Inside, Room Two was illuminated by a single beside lamp with a mock-parchment shade. The number of times I had lain in Nancy's bed and stared at the picture on that shade, the Spanish Armada in full sail. Nancy was naked; her skin was shining with sweat. Her blonde hair was stuck to her forehead in dark mermaid curls.

223

"What's the matter?" she asked me. "You'll wake Simon."

"You might have had the decency to bloody well tell me," I raged at her.

"Tell you what? What are you talkin' about?"

"You might have had the decency to bloody well tell me there was somebody else."

She stared at me. I had never seen her look at me like that before. It wasn't unloving; it wasn't angry. If it was anything describable, it was sad, remote; like somebody who's being carried away from you for ever at a railway station. *Brief Encounters*, I suppose.

"There isn't anybody else," she said, with awesome simplicity.

"Oh, I suppose I was hearing things, was I? Specks of flotsam, for instance?"

Nancy shook her head. "Must've been the radio. There's nobody 'ere."

She pushed the door open wide. I looked into the room, but didn't step inside. It was obvious that she didn't want me to step inside. Simon was sleeping in his cot with a blanket draped over one side to block out the light. But apart from Simon, there was nobody else. Nobody that I could see, anyway – although I did notice that the wardrobe door was slightly ajar.

"Satisfied?" asked Nancy.

I didn't know what to say. I felt clumsy and juvenile. I supposed I could have challenged her to fling open the wardrobe; but what if there were nobody in it? Worse still, what if there were? What would I say to Nancy's new lover, face-to-face? "Oh, hallo, I'm David from upstairs. I used to fuck Nancy but now I'm just leaving, sorry."

I looked at Nancy and her expression hadn't changed. I knew then that she didn't belong to me and that she never would.

I said, softly, "All right," I bent my head forward to

224

kiss her but she dodged her cheek away. I've really got to tell you, that hurt. I went back upstairs and sat in my Parker-Knoll chair in the dark and cried for nearly twenty minutes. Then I wiped my eyes on the bedspread and wondered what the hell I was going to do without her.

The next morning I got a job at the Ocean Fish Bar in Montague Street. It was run by a bullet-headed former wrestler who liked his staff to call him Mr George but whose fighting name had been Skull Thomson. I learned how to dip fillets of cod in batter and how to operate the potato-chipper and how to toss a whole bucketful of chips into deep boiling fat without killing myself. I also learned how to wrap a double portion of rock and chips in newspaper so that it could be dredged in salt and doused in malt vinegar and eaten while walking along the street.

After three hours of frying I reeked of fat, but at least I was getting paid, and I wasn't going to go hungry. Mr George let us have all the fish-and-chips we could eat.

That evening, when we closed, I took two cod and chips back to 5a Bedford Row, with a saveloy for Simon. I knocked at Nancy's door and waited.

She took a long, long time to answer, and when she did she sounded very tired. "What do you want?" she called.

"It's David, Dave. I've got a job at the Ocean Fish Bar. I've brought you some fish and chips, if you want some."

"No thanks. Just leave me alone."

"Listen," I persisted. "I lost my temper yesterday, I'm sorry. It was all a misunderstanding. Look, just have some fish and chips, no strings attached. I've brought a sausage for Simon."

"Leave me alone, Dave, do you mind?"

I stood in the hallway with my warm greasy newspaper package, and I just didn't know what to do. I didn't feel like going back to my room. It was too pokey; too dark. I went for a walk along Marine Parade, and gave my fish and

225

chips to an old tramp who was sitting in one of the concrete shelters with a bottle of cider and a cigarette-tip glowing.

After that, Nancy refused even to answer my knocking. I got another job, temporary carpet fitting for Vokins department store, and what with carpet-fitting in the mornings and fish-frying all afternoon and evening, I didn't get much of a chance to think about her, either. In early September all the art students came back to Union Place, and I made quite a few new friends. I went out with a thin lithography student called Sandra. She had shaggy hair and baggy sweaters and drainpipe jeans, and although she made it clear right from the beginning that she wasn't going to go the whole way, we had plenty of heavy snogging sessions. Whenever I got really frustrated, I bought copies of *Health & Efficiency*. Weekends with Sandra were all instant coffee and trad jazz and walks on the beach.

Occasionally, however, I would pause on my way back upstairs to Room Seven, and stand outside Room Two, and listen. Most of the time, I heard nothing at all. Sometimes I heard the radio, playing faintly. But once or twice I heard Nancy's voice, oddly thin and unsure; and that hoarse crackling man's voice.

On the last night of September I was passing Room Two when I heard the voice saying, " . . . *love you beyond all conceivable loves* . . ."

I hesitated, holding my breath. I heard Nancy saying, " . . . ever, not for ever . . ."

There was a muffled creaking noise. It sounded like the bed. Then some indistinct conversation, the man and Nancy both talking at the same time. Then the man saying, "*Soon and soon and soon, my beautiful darling . . . soon and soon and soon!*"

Nancy whimpered; then cried out. The she let out a peculiar strangled keening noise. I was horrified, electrified. I rattled the doorknob sharply. Then I wrenched at

it in fury and temper. I heard Nancy screaming, *"No!"* I
took a step back, held on to the banisters, and kicked at
the door with my Chelsea boot.

The door juddered open, the catch swinging broken.
Instantly, the wardrobe door, which had been wide open,
slammed shut. Nancy was standing beside it, naked, her
arms crossed protectively over her breasts. She stared at
me wildly, whimpering, trembling, unable to speak.

I couldn't believe what I saw. I knew it was Nancy,
it had to be Nancy, but she was hideously emaciated.
Her back-combed blonde hair had turned bone-white and
bedraggled; her arms and legs were as thin as chair-sticks.
I could see her hip-bones stretching against her white
blue-veined skin. Her breasts had shrunk to empty dugs,
although the gold nipple-rings still hung from her nipples,
proving beyond question that it was really her. Her eyes
were dark-circled; her lips were deeply-lined.

"Nancy?" I whispered. I was so shocked that I didn't
know how to move my legs, didn't know how to walk.
"Nancy, what's happened?"

"It's nearly over," she told me. It sounded as if she had
no saliva in her mouth at all.

"What? What's nearly over? What are you talking
about?"

She sat down unsteadily on the end of the bed, with
all the stiffness of an eighty-year-old woman. "It's nearly
over," she repeated, nodding her head.

I went across to the cot. Simon was sleeping deeply, whistling softly through one clogged nostril. A bottle of cherry
cough mixture, three-quarters empty, stood on the edge of
the basin nearby. The poor little kid was half-drugged.

I closed the door of the room so that nobody could see
in. I had kicked the screws out of the latch, that was all,
so it wouldn't take much repairing.

"Are you ill, or what?" I asked Nancy. I was both
impatient and frightened.

"Ill?" She gave a dry little smile. "No, I'm not ill. I'm in love."

"But what's happened to you? You look as if you haven't eaten for a month."

"Don't need to eat. Don't need nothin'."

I glanced at the wardrobe. "What have you got in there?"

"Nothin' in particular. Mrs Bristow's stuff. It's locked."

"It's not locked. When I bashed open the door, I saw it open."

"It's locked," Nancy intoned. "Nothin' inside it, only Mrs Bristow's stuff."

"You won't mind if I take a look, then?"

Nancy lifted her head. Her eyes reminded me of poor Miss Coates, the assembler of first-aid kits, who had been carried out of 5a Bedford Row in an open coffin, in the rain. "Forget it, Dave. It's nearly over, forget it."

"I think I've got a right," I told her, and I made my way around the end of the bed, and took hold of the brass knob of the wardrobe door.

"*No!*" pleaded Nancy. She climbed to her feet, and hobbled across to me, and seized my wrists with her claw-like hands.

Close-up, she looked as if she had walked straight out of Belsen. Her teeth were gone, her hair was coming out in clumps, her skin was scaly and blistered. She was so weak that she couldn't have hoped to pull me away from the wardrobe; but I stepped away in any case, in sheer disgust. I couldn't help it. It was almost impossible to believe that she and I had once made love in the dunes.

"It's locked," she whispered, throatily. "Please, Dave, it's locked."

I reached out again, and this time she didn't try to stop me. I tugged at the knob and she was right. It wouldn't open.

"I want to know what's in there," I demanded. "I've got a right."

"No," she insisted.

"For Christ's sake, Nancy, I wanted to *marry* you once!"

"No," she mouthed. "And that gives you no right."

"Didn't you love me, too?" I asked her.

She slowly blinked those dead-fledgling eyes. "I thought I did. But I didn't know what real love really was, did I? I didn't know what it was really like."

"And now you do?" I challenged her.

I heard the door of the room jar open behind me. I turned around, and there stood Mrs Bristow, in her brown candlewick dressing-gown, one eye squinched up against the cigarette that smoldered between her lips.

"I heard a commotion," she said.

Nancy sat down again. Mrs Bristow came across the room, picked up Nancy's nightdress from the bed, and draped it around her shoulders. "I think you'd better get back to your room, Mr Moore."

"I think I want to know what's happened to Nancy, Mrs Bristow," I replied, belligerently folding my arms.

Mrs Bristow puffed smoke. "You heard her. She's in love."

"She's half-dead, for God's sake!"

"Love conquers death, Mr Moore. You'll understand that one day."

"I don't know what the bloody hell you're talking about, and I don't want to know. But I can tell you this: Nancy's coming out of this room and she's going to stay with me, and she's going to eat properly. She's got a kid to look after, for God's sake. So, out of my way."

Mrs Bristow puffed, sipped, puffed. "She won't come with you, Mr Moore."

"Then I'll carry her."

"She'll always come back, Mr Moore. And she'll never

229

love you, never. In fact, if you try to keep her away, she'll grow to hate you."

"I'm going to call the police," I replied. "I'm going to call the police and a welfare officer, and then we'll bloody well see."

"No!" begged Nancy. "Dave, no, please, no!"

Mrs Bristow stared at me with wide warning eyes. "You shouldn't have stuck your nose where it wasn't wanted, Mr Moore. You should have stayed in Room Seven with your baked beans and your naughty magazines."

"I'm still going to call the police," I told her. I sensed that I had her worried, and I wanted to know why. Besides, if there was any chance of saving Nancy, I wanted to find out what it was.

Mrs Bristow said nothing for almost half a minute. Nancy, her bony shoulders bowed, began softly to sob. It sounded like the sobbing of an old, old woman, who suddenly and vividly remembers her girlhood. Cornflowers, sunshine, straw hats.

"Very well," said Mrs Bristow. She reached over, and opened the wardrobe door.

To my total horror, a man was standing motionless in the wardrobe. He was stocky, heavily-built, about forty-five years old. His hair was oiled and combed back from his forehead. He wore a neat little bristle mustache. He was naked, with a huge reddened penis hanging down between his thighs. His legs were shaggy with ginger hair. His eyes were totally bloodshot, totally red.

"Is he dead?" I asked, in a voice that didn't sound like me at all.

Mrs Bristow shook her head. She allowed me one last look and then she closed the wardrobe door.

"My husband, Mr Bristow."

"I don't believe this," I protested. "That's your husband, and he's hiding in the wardrobe?"

"Not hiding, Mr Moore. He lives there. Or rather he

230

ekes out his existence there. His real living is done inside his mind."

She went to the window, opened it an inch, and flickered her cigarette butt out into the night. Then she turned back, and blew out a last puff of smoke. "He's a great lover, Mr Moore. Greater than you'll ever understand. He takes a great deal out of every woman who loves him; but he gives just as much in return; if not more."

"But what the hell has he done to Nancy?" I demanded. "He's killing her!"

"In one sense, yes, I suppose he is," Mrs Bristow replied, patting the pockets of her housecoat to find her cigarettes. "But she won't know greater ecstasy, I can assure you of that. Now and forever after. Real ecstasy. I envy her. I envy *all* of them. But somebody has to take care of things on the outside, don't they? That's what a wife is for."

"He's killing her," I repeated.

"Almost gone, yes," Mrs Bristow agreed. She lit another cigarette. "Just like poor Miss Coates; and poor Miss Unwin; and poor Miss Baker; and poor Miss Dadachanji. But they're all still there; he has them all. And as long as he lives, so will they."

I stared at her. "So when you gave Nancy this room – you *knew* – you did it on purpose."

Mrs Bristow nodded. "We all have to live, Mr Moore, the best way we can."

Something burst inside my head. It was like a melon blown up with dynamite. I lost all of my reason, all of my self-control. It was bad enough that this stuffed-dummy of a man had taken Nancy away from me; but now he was killing her, too. I shouldered Mrs Bristow aside, and yanked open the wardrobe door, and confronted the naked man who stood there with his shaggy thighs and his bloodred eyes and shrieked, "*You bastard! You murdering bloody bastard!*"

I was about to grab him by the shoulders and heave him out of the wardrobe when he stretched open his mouth and he roared at me.

I stopped dead in absolute paralytic terror. It wasn't just a roar of anger. It was a roar like a blast-furnace; like the rumbling exhaust of a jet. It seemed to toss aside blankets and papers and tumble over bedside lights. It was deafening, and it went on and on and relentlessly on.

As he roared, the man's face swelled. His veins stood out like pulsing snakes. Then his face stretched and twisted, and turned into another face, the face of a pale-skinned girl. Her eyes, too, were filled with red, and she was roaring.

I took a stumbling step backward. I was full of rage, full of anguish, but I wasn't brave enough to face up to anything like this. The girl's face knotted and contorted. Her forehead bulged, her nose folded in on itself, and another girl's face appeared, slimy and dark-skinned, still roaring. I saw face after face, all women, roaring at me red-eyed, an unholy portrait gallery of hundreds of different personalities; all of them absorbed into one man's body.

Mrs Bristow had talked of ecstasy, of love. But all I saw was agony and distortion and screaming helplessness.

Stiff-legged with fear, I reached down and scooped Simon awkwardly out of his cot. Nancy, her head bowed, did nothing to stop me. Mrs Bristow remained by the wardrobe door, her housecoat fluttering in the roaring draft, expressionless, waiting for me to leave.

I took one last look at that hideous naked creature in the wardrobe with its heads twisting and changing, one after the other, and then I hoisted Simon up against me shoulder and I hurried out of 5a Bedford Row and out into the windy, brine-smelling night. I didn't realize that I was crying out loud until I was well past West Buildings.

I suppose I should have gone to the police right away.

But I was too frightened and too numb, and too worried about Simon. God knows how much cough medicine Nancy had given him, but he flopped in my arms like a little hot doll. I carried him up to Sandra's flat in Surrey Street; up three flights of stairs, sweating and gasping, and pressed the doorbell with my elbow.

Sandra came to the door in a striped man's shirt and long socks. "David?" she frowned. "What on earth's the matter?"

I spent the night drinking coffee and keeping a lonely watch over Simon. Around seven he stirred and opened his eyes and frowned at me. "Uncle Dave? Where's mummy?"

I returned to 5a Bedford Row about eleven o'clock the next morning, accompanied by two police officers. As we drew up outside the house, I was just in time to see a black pickup truck disappearing around the corner on to the seafront. I couldn't be sure, but in the back of the pickup truck, I thought I glimpsed a large wardrobe, half-covered with a sheet of tarpaulin.

On the other side of the road, next to the bus garage, a black Daimler hearse was parked without any consideration for any other traffic that might have wanted to get past.

The police officers rang the doorbell. One of them said, "D'you hear about Chalky collaring that JP for drunken driving? Laugh?"

The door was opened. It was Mrs Bristow. She looked at me sharply, and then at the two policemen. "Mr Moore? Is anything wrong?"

"You know bloody well what's wrong," I told her. "Where's Nancy?"

"I'm sorry, Mr Moore; but old Miss Bright passed away this morning, in the early hours. We think it was probably her heart."

"*Old* Miss Bright?" frowned one of the policemen.

233

We climbed the stairs to Room Two. The curtains were drawn, and the room was in semi-darkness, but I could see at once that the wardrobe had gone. Nancy lay on the bed, thin and white-haired and really dead; the same way that Miss Coates had been really dead. Mr Pedrick and his young assistant were preparing to lift her into her coffin.

"Who's this, then?" asked one of the policemen.

"The name's Pedrick," said Mr Pedrick.

"I mean the deceased."

"Oh, mistake me for a fucking corpse, please," Mr Pedrick complained.

"This is Nancy," I told the policeman.

"I'm sorry?"

"This is Nancy Bright. My girlfriend, Simon's mother."

The constable peered at Nancy closely. "Well, you'll have to forgive me, Mr Moore, but she looks a trifle long in the tooth to be your girlfriend. And she can't possible be young Simon's mother now, can she? She must be eighty if she's a day."

"That's how they killed her," I insisted. "They took everything out of her – everything. Her youth, her looks, her blood for all I know. It's Mr Bristow. Every woman he wants becomes part of him. Mixed up inside him, almost. It's really hard to describe until you've seen it for yourself."

"Too right," said Mr Pedrick.

"Where's this fellow now, then?" asked the constable. "This Mr Bristow?"

"He was in the wardrobe. The wardrobe was right there, almost exactly where you're standing. Look, you can see the mark of its legs on the carpet. And it must have been really heavy, because the marks are so deep."

"Oh, yes," said the policeman, rubbing the mark with his shoe. "Sherlock Holmes strikes again."

"So where's this wardrobe now?" asked the other policeman.

"It's gone," I admitted. "They've taken it away."

"With Mr Bristow still inside it?"

"I don't know. I suppose so."

There was nothing more that I could do. The police just didn't believe me and nothing I said could persuade them. I managed to telephone Vince and ask him to help, but apart from being ever so sorry that Nancy was dead, he didn't want to get involved. All the same, his mum and dad drove down from Thornton Heath in their Cortina and collected Simon from Worthing Hospital, and promised to bring him up like a good young South London tyke. Nancy didn't have a mother, and her father was in Hull, working as a printer. I phoned him up at his digs while he was trying to watch *Coronation Street* and he said, "I see. Well, it doesn't surprise me," and hung up.

A week later I called round to 5a Bedford Row to pick up my few belongings and Mrs Bristow had moved out. The rooms were being managed by a black-haired woman with a hairy mole and a bad hip. She didn't know where Mrs Bristow had gone, except that it was probably the seaside.

I grew up, like everybody else. I got a job. I got married. The last time I went to Worthing they had demolished 5a Bedford Row and most of the rest of the town, too. I stood for a long time looking at the waste-ground of broken bricks and thinking that was the end of it.

Last week, however, I was walking through The Lanes, in Brighton, when I stopped to look at an antiquarian book and print shop in Duke Street. Right in front of me was a Victorian poster for THE GREAT BRISTOE, Prestidigitator Extraordinaire. He was supposed to be appearing at the Palace Pier, Brighton, on, June 4, 1879.

"Man of 1,000 voices! Man of 1,000 faces! The most remarkable series of Female Impersonations ever Achieved on Stage!! No Mirrors, No Trickery!! The Secret of the

Arabian Harem Conjurors for you to witness in front of your eyes!"

Staring at me in the middle of the poster was a steel-engraved portrait of the man in the wardrobe. The man who could live for ever by absorbing the life and character of one young girl after another; the man in whose body the girl I had once loved still lay physically entangled. According to Mrs Bristow, she was experiencing some kind of unending ecstasy; or maybe some kind of unending purgatory, which is what unending ecstasy usually turns out to be.

I've never mentioned Nancy to my wife; nor to anyone else, before now. It all sounds too mad. It all sounds childish and ridiculous. But oh God, I loved her, you know; and oh God, I miss her. It hurts me so much to think of what unimaginable suffering she might still be going through now. I think of her sometimes and I still have to make an excuse and go out into the garden and sob like an idiot.

And I never, ever open other people's wardrobes, in other people's houses. He's there somewhere, in some-body's wardrobe, and believe you me, I don't want to be the one to find him.

Saint Joan

Saint-Valéry-sur-Somme, France

Saint-Valéry lies on the Baie de la Somme, on the Opal Coast of Northern France. It is famous for its annual wild bird festival, and ornithologists come from all over Europe to spot birds, drink wine, eat *moules frites*, drink more wine, and spot more birds. Saint-Valéry has a well-preserved medieval center that is almost eerie in its historical atmosphere, and the remains of a 14th-century hilltop fortress where Joan of Arc was imprisoned. But there is a sadder feeling here, too: the ghosts of all the Allied soldiers who landed here during both world wars, and those who fell on the Somme.

Saint-Valéry is an ideal location for a haunting.

SAINT JOAN

On the other side of the restaurant, a woman with blue hair screamed with laughter.

David couldn't help turning around. The whole table of old-age pensioners was rocking with amusement. "*Armand, tu es si drôle!*" cackled a woman with lavender-colored hair.

David turned back to Robert and Jeremy and shrugged. "I wish I understood French better. That was probably a cracker."

"Probably dirty," said Robert. "You know what old people are like."

David smiled, and refilled his glass with Pouilly Fumé. He was sitting with his sons at a table by the window, looking out over the silvery flatness of the Somme estuary. In the distance, across the marshes, he saw occasional glitters of sunshine; but for the most part the day was cloudy and gray.

At the moment, the only other diners in the restaurant were the rainbow-rinsed pensioners and two men with waxy breathless faces who volubly argued with each other with their mouths full of bread.

The restaurant was crimson-wallpapered and darkly-paneled, decorated with stuffed ducks and lobster pots and a waterfall that trickled over painted plaster rocks. There were three maroon-jacketed waiters: one looked like Jacques Cousteau and the other two looked like Pee Wee Herman if Pee Wee Herman had been twins.

Robert said, "Mummy would have liked this."

"Ah well," David replied. "She'll be better by tomorrow. I think it must have been that Camembert. She said it tasted funny when she was eating it."

Jeremy was trying to scrape all of the mushroom-and-onion sauce off his *poulet gran'mère*. "I wish they wouldn't put all this glop on it," he complained.

"Some gourmet you are," Robert restorted. Robert, at 17, was two years older than Jeremy, and considered himself to be totally fearless when it came to food. He had even tried snails, although he had given up after the third, saying that if he was going to eat chewing-gum, he preferred mint flavor to garlic.

David said, "Here's ours."

One of the Pee Wee Hermans brought them two huge steaming tureens of *moules marinières* and a vast plateful of *pommes frites*. "*Attention, c'est tres chaud*," he warned; but Jeremy took a *frite* straight away, and then dropped it in his beer because it was too hot.

"Brilliant shot," laughed Robert.

After that, they were quiet for a while, although the French pensioners were growing noisier and noisier, scraping their chairs and laughing and arguing at the tops of their voices. David forked out mussels and dipped his bread into the oniony liquor and felt extremely at peace for the first time in months.

There was nothing very special about this part of France, the Opal Coast, apart from its beaches and its marshes and its wildlife. They had come here for only three days, simply for the quiet and the change of scenery. The weather had been dreadful, most of the time, but they had gone for walks along the promenade and up into the cobbled medieval town, and sat in cafes watching the rain trickle down the windows, drinking wine, and that had been all that they had either expected or needed.

David had recently finished a complicated eleven-month

design project, updating the corporate identity of British Allied Fibres, which had meant producing a new company logo, new livery for the company's vans, new notepaper, and even redecorating the company's headquarters. He had just wanted to escape for a while from anything that looked like a British Allied Fibre.

He was a dark, rather Scottish-looking man of 45, a once-keen tennis-player gone to seed. Robert was unmistakably his father's son, only an inch or two taller, while Jeremy was blonde and snub-nosed and looked much more like his mother.

They finished their meal with strong cups of coffee, and then the three of them strolled back along the promenade. The promenade was almost a mile long, very straight, flanked on one side by tall, black-painted lamp-posts, and on the other by the greasy gray banks of the Somme. There were thirty or forty little fishing dinghies moored in a line on the mud, just beginning to bob and jiggle as the tide came in.

The wind came off the Channel steady and cold, and David was glad that he had remembered his raincoat.

They passed a sad, red-brick Gothic hotel, with towers and balconies and a tangled garden criss-crossed with colorless bracken. They passed a tatty casino, closed until the summer; and a small cafe called Brasserie Jehanne D'Arc where lorry-drivers sat, smoking and drinking coffee. They paused at a small marble monument with a plaque on it which read, "On this spot, on May 13, 1940, Maurice Renaud fell to the bullets of the enemy." Then they reached their hotel, La Colonne de Bronze, a nondescript yellow-stucco building on a tight corner of the town's main road.

Inside, in the small gloomy bar, *madame* was polishing wine-glasses. She was a thirty-sevenish woman with tightly-braided hair and a sharp, vixen-like face. She appeared always to be immaculately dressed: today, in one of those boxy gray suits that French women seem to like so much. *"Monsieur,"* she said tightly, as the door swung shut behind them.

The boys had brought some schoolbooks with them, and they went up to their room to revise for a while (and probably to wrestle). David thought that he would look in on Carole, to see if she was feeling any better, and then maybe take a walk up to the town's medieval gatehouse, and take a few photographs.

He climbed the narrow stairs to the landing, and eased open the door of Chambre 1. The curtains were still drawn, as he had left them, and the room was overheated and gloomy. "Carole?" he said. "Carole? Are you awake?"

She didn't answer. He closed the door behind him and tiptoed over to the bed. It was then that he saw that the orange bedcover had been neatly drawn over it, and that there was nobody in it.

"Carole?" he called. She must have felt better, and decided to get up. It was odd that she hadn't opened the curtains, though. He went to the bathroom, and opened the door. Carole wasn't there, either. The shower dripped monotonously into shower-tray.

He drew back the curtains. The room filled with wan gray daylight. From here, David could see across the road, to the cafe where the lorry-drivers were still sitting, and the nub of granite that commemorated the falling of Maurice Renaud.

He went back downstairs. Madame was still polishing wine-glasses in the bar. Carole certainly wasn't here, because there were only three tables, two barstools and a potted palm, and hardly enough room to swing *une chatte*.

He poked his head around the door of the dining-room. Perhaps Carole had felt hungry, after a whole night of being sick, and had ordered herself some lunch. But the dining-room was silent and empty, with all the cutlery and napkins set out for this evening's meal.

"*Monsieur?*" asked *madame.*

"*Je cherche ma femme,*" said David. "*Est-elle sortie, peut-etre?*"

Madame frowned at him, looking even more vixenish than ever. "*Pardonnez, monsieur, je ne comprends pas.*"

"*Ma femme,*" David repeated. "*Ce matin, elle était très malade. Elle dorme. Mais, elle n'est plus dans nôtre chambre.*" God, he wished his French were better.

Madame continued to frown. "*Je ne comprends pas,*" she repeated.

"*Madame* . . .," said David, fully aware that he was sounding more and more like an impatient Englishman Abroad. "I am looking – *je cherche, comprenez-vous?* – for my wife – *ma femme.* This morning she was sick – sick, *malade, dans l'estomac.* I left her asleep while my sons and I went *pour manger.* Now she has gone. *Elle a disparu.*"

Madame put down the glass she was polishing, went to the side of the bar, and unhooked the key marked Ch.1. Without a word, she beckoned David to follow her, and stamped ahead of him up the stairs. She flung open the door, stretched out her hand, and said, "*Voilà, monsieur.*"

David sighed. "I don't think you understand. I know that my wife isn't here. What I want to know is, where is she? *Où se trouve ma femme?*"

Madame shook her head. "*Je ne sais pas, monsieur. Vous êtes arrivés avec deux fils, n'est-ce pas? Deux fils, oui? Mais, pas de la femme.* You understand, monsieur? You arrive with two boys, two sons. But, no wife. Last night you rested in this room *tout seul.* You were alone."

"Well, that's patently ridiculous," said David. "My wife was sick all night. I just want to know where she is. Maybe she's gone to the chemist, *la pharmacie*? Or the doctor? Is there a clinic around here?"

"*Ah, oui monsieur.* A very short way along the street, only *cent metres*. But, you had no wife."

"Of course I had a wife! You saw her yourself! You spoke to her! Do you think I could hallucinate my own wife? All of her things are here – look!"

He wrenched open the door of the small brown-varnished wardrobe, and there was a discordant jingling of wire coat-hangers. Inside hung a navy-blue blazer, a two pairs of trousers, three clean shirts and two ties. On the shelves were socks, underpants, and a neat stack of four clean handkerchiefs. None of Carole's clothes at all.

For the first time, David felt a genuine sense of dread. He looked at *madame* and said, "*Je ne comprends pas.*"

Madame shrugged. "*Monsieur*, you came here with your two sons. That is all."

David hesitated, thinking, looking around. Why on earth would Carole have left like that, without telling him? They hadn't argued. She hadn't been depressed. Everything had been going swimmingly until she ate that damned cheese in Abbeville.

Madame was about to go back downstairs, but David said, "Wait, *s'il-vous plait – un moment*," and swung their suitcase on to the bed. They were due to leave tomorrow: maybe Carole had simply packed all her clothes for the want of something to do.

But when he clicked open the catches, and opened the lid, he found that the suitcase was completely empty, apart from a plastic bag crammed with soiled laundry. He tipped the laundry across the bed, but there were no bras, no lacy panties, no rose-embroidered handkerchiefs. All of the laundry was his. Socks, underpants, handkerchiefs initialed with the letter J.

"*Monsieur* . . .," said *madame*. "I regret that I am very busy."

244

"That's all right, yes," said David, and *madame* went back down to the bar, her high-heels banging on the stairs. David let the lid of the case drop; and then he stood in front of the bed and wondered what to do next.

Had Carole left him? Had she really had enough, and taken her clothes, and disappeared? But why would she do it here, in France, on a three-day holiday? She could just as easily have disappeared in England. She could just as easily have said, "David, I need some breathing-space, why don't we separate for a while?"

He knew that he hadn't been behaving very well: not as far as Carole was concerned, anyway. He'd been arriving home late from the office, elated, excited, smelling of drink. But that had been all part of the high – all part of the office adrenaline that had enabled him to finish a first-class corporate identity package in eleven months flat, right on schedule, and nothing missed out, not a single mistake, right down to the visiting cards and the British Allied Fibres ballpens.

But he couldn't believe that she would have left. Not here, not now. Not without discussing things first. And she adored Robert and Jeremy. How could she have left Robert and Jeremy, without a word?

He opened the boys' bedroom door. They were wrestling on Jeremy's bed – or at least, they had been until about a millisecond after they heard his hand on the doorknob. Now they were sitting six feet apart, reading *The Mystery of Edwin Drood* and *The White Company*, sweating, flushed, but very studious.

"Hi, daddy," said Robert, nonchalantly.

"You haven't seen mummy?" he asked them.

Robert looked up. "What do you mean?"

"I mean mummy wasn't here, when we got back." He didn't like to tell them that her clothes had gone, too.

Jeremy shrugged. "Perhaps she felt better. Perhaps she

went to that antique shop. She said she liked those china ducks."

David didn't answer. He didn't know what to say.

"She probably went for a walk, that's all," said Robert, going back to his book.

David said, "She did come with us, didn't she? I mean, she *was* here?"

They both stared at him. "Of course she was here."

"It's just that her clothes have all gone; and her make-up, too, out of the bathroom; and *madame* downstairs doesn't seem to remember her."

"But that's stupid!" Jeremy protested. "Of course she was here! Her coat's in the car, and everything!"

Together, they walked across the road. From a second-story window next to La Colonne de Bronze, a fat man in a dark-blue fisherman's sweater watched them with unabashed curiosity and smoked. In the next window, an old woman in a floral housecoat watched them with unabashed curiosity and knitted.

David opened the boot of their silver Rover and it was empty. No coat, no shoes, nothing. He opened the glovebox and there was no hairbrush with blonde hairs clinging, no eau-de-toilette, no lipstick, no tissues, no hairgrips, nothing feminine at all.

He covered his mouth with his hand while the boys watched him in bewilderment. At last he took his hand away, and said, "She *was* with us, wasn't she?"

"Of course she was with us," said Jeremy. Both of the boys' faces were very white. "I mean, she was with us, she was here. She couldn't have just disappeared."

They walked back to La Colonne de Bronze. Madame wasn't in the bar, so David rang the bell and eventually she appeared, bustling and displeased. The restaurant was making preparations for tonight's dinner.

"*Madame*, I'm sorry to trouble you, but my wife *was* here, and now she has gone. My sons are both witness to that. I mean, it's possible that *I* may have been hallucinating, but not all three of us."

Madame's face remained impassive. Either she hadn't understood very much of what David had said, or else she simply hadn't been listening.

"I am sorry, *monsieur*," she said, at last. "I do not know how to help you."

David and the boys went back up to the room, and searched it yet again. Jeremy even went down on to his hands and knees and looked under the bed. On one wall there was a very bad painting of a yacht; on the other, a reproduction of an Ingres painting of a girl reading. Neither the room itself nor anything in it gave any clue as to what might have happened to Carole. David even sniffed the pillow and the bedsheets, trying to detect Carole's perfume, but the bed had been freshly made, and it smelled of nothing but the inside of French linen-cupboards.

"Where do you think she's gone?" asked Robert, and David had never heard him sound so frightened. He put his arm around Robert's shoulders (even though Robert was taller than him) and gave him a reassuring squeeze.

"It's okay . . . there has to be some logical explanation."

"She couldn't have been kidnapped, could she?" Jeremy suggested.

"Well, no . . . I don't think so. I mean, she's taken all of her clothes and all of her makeup and everything – *and* her coat from the car. You'd think that if anybody had taken her away against her will, there would have been some signs of a fight. *Madame* downstairs would have heard something."

"I think we'd better call the police," said Robert, seriously.

They walked along the main street to the gendarmerie,

a large three-story building of pale orange brick, with a small walled courtyard, in which meticulously-pruned bay-trees grew. The sky had grown much darker now, and the stone steps of the gendarmerie were measled with rain. They pushed the heavy door open, and found themselves in an echoing mosaic-floored hallway, where a round-faced young man in a police uniform sat at a lonely desk, smoking and reading a newspaper.

David stood in front of him and coughed. The gendarme looked up, his head almost entirely hidden in wreaths of blue Gitanes smoke.

"*Parlez-vous anglais*?" asked David.

The gendarme nodded and shrugged. "If it is strictly necessary. That is the secret of France, of course. Almost everybody in France speaks English. It is just that they do not choose to. How do you say it? It is our ultimate deterrent against the English."

"My wife's missing," said David.

The gendarme blew out a last stream of smoke and crushed out his cigarette. "Your wife?"

"We're staying at La Colonne de Bronze. This morning she felt ill so she stayed in bed. I took the boys out for lunch at Les Pilotes. When we came back – well, she was missing. No sign of her. She'd taken her clothes, too. Her coat, her make-up, everything."

The gendarme listened to this with no expression on his face. Then he consulted the calendar on his desk. "*Merde*," he said, softly.

"Is something wrong?"

"No, no, *monsieur*. Of course not. It's just that I've forgotten something."

"The thing is," said David, "the landlady at La Colonne de Bronze denies that she ever saw my wife. She says I checked in by myself, with nobody else except my two sons."

The gendarme sniffed, and then wiped his nose with

the back of his hand. "Why do you think she would say something like that?"

"I don't know. I don't have the faintest idea. But we all came over on the Seacat from Dover to Boulogne on Monday . . . and my wife's been with us all the time. We've taken photographs, and videos."

"Mme Courbet, at the hotel, did she take your wife's passport?"

David shook his head. "No, no. Only mine."

"Do you have any idea what might have happened to your wife? Any clues? Any wild guesses?"

"None at all. We hadn't argued, everything was fine."

"Have you tried to telephone your home in England, to see if perhaps she has returned there?"

"I hadn't thought of that, but I will."

"Good. Meanwhile, stay at your hotel, and I will call some assistance. You understand that we are a very small gendarmerie here. Only two officers, as a rule, except in the summer months. Do you by any chance have a picture of your wife, to help with identification?"

David took out his wallet, and leafed through receipts and laundry tickets until he found the photograph of Carole which he always carried with him. The picture that he had taken on their fifteenth wedding anniversary, in the garden.

To his surprise, Carole's face was obscured by a dark, brownish mark, as if his wallet had got wet, and the dye had run. "I'm sorry," he told the gendarme. "That's the only one I have . . . apart from the pictures that are still in the camera, and the videos."

The gendarme took the picture and held it up to the light. Then he carefully sniffed it.

"You see . . . it's been scorched," he said.

"Scorched? I don't understand. It's never been out of my wallet."

"This has happened twice before, to my knowledge."

"What's happened twice before?" David demanded. "What are you talking about?"

"*Monsieur*, two English women have disappeared from St Valéry-sur-Mer in the past one hundred years. One was a very famous case, Mrs Brownlow, who came here in 1915 with the Prince of Wales to visit the Western Front. At your hotel you may have seen a brass plaque beside one of the tables in the dining-room. It was at this table that the Prince of Wales dined with Mrs Brownlow the evening before she vanished."

David was becoming increasingly exasperated. "That was nearly eighty years ago! What on earth does that have to do with my wife?"

"I don't know, *monsieur*. Perhaps nothing at all. But when the Prince of Wales returned to England, he discovered that the photograph of Mrs Brownlow which he kept in his dressing-room had been badly burned."

David took back the photograph of Carole and raised it to his nose. The gendarme was right: it did smell scorched. "Was Mrs Brownlow ever found?" he asked.

The gendarme nodded. "Yes, *monsieur*. She was discovered on the beach, just below the cliffs. Her body had been burned to ashes, and she was almost unrecognizable. In fact she was identified only by the diamonds which the Prince of Wales had given her as a gift, in the form of a brooch. The brooch itself had completely melted."

"You said you knew of *two* disappearances," said David. He didn't believe for a moment that the burned body of a woman who had been found here in 1915 could possibly have any connection with Carole's disappearance, but all the same he wanted to know what had happened.

The gendarme took out another Gitane and lit it, and breathed smoke out of his nose. "The other was in 1838 . . . another very famous case. An Englishwoman came here with her elderly mother on a painting holiday. One afternoon, while her mother was asleep, she went out to paint and disappeared. There were stories of a fierce fire that rushed through the streets of St Valéry that night like a whirlwind, but this lady's body was never found. When the mother returned to Gloucestershire, however, she found that her daughter's self-portrait had been burned black."

"Well, that's fascinating," said David. "I don't think it's very relevant to my wife's case, though, do you?"

But Robert said, very gravely, "It's seventy-seven years from 1838 to 1915 and it's seventy-seven years from 1915 to 1992."

"That doesn't mean anything," Jeremy retorted. "Mummy's just lost her memory or something or got fed up and gone home by train."

The gendarme said, "Of course, yes, you are probably right. The most mundane answer is always the most likely. I apologize, *monsieur*, I had no wish to alarm you. These are only stories . . . the sort of Gothic mysteries that we relish so much in France . . . like the murders in the Rue Morgue."

"What are you going to do now?" asked David.

"As I say . . . I will call at once for reinforcements, and I will initiate a search. You would do well to try to think of anywhere your wife might have gone to . . . perhaps a town or tourist attraction she might have mentioned. Sometimes, when people are ill, they have a tendency to act out of character."

David looked down at the brown-scorched photograph. He could just make out the very edge of Carole's smile. "Yes," he said. "I suppose they do." They spent the rest of the afternoon searching the town. Although it lay in one of the flattest parts of France, the old quarter of St Valéry-sur-Mer had been built on the side of a steep cliff, on top of which stood the ruins of its fifteenth-century castle. The streets and squares were almost deserted: a silent medieval community with cobbles and courtyards and shuttered windows. Now and then they came across an open window in which a child might stare out at them, saying nothing; or an open door which gave them a narrow view of a kitchen or a flight of ancient stone steps. But there was no sign of Carole, and the day grew grayer, and the cold breath of the Somme estuary chilled the town like the breath of some Breugelesque pestilence.

They reached the very crest of the cliff, where the dark hunched towers of the castle's gatehouse stood, overlooking the river. Far below them, in the grayness, a bulldozer toiled, leveling the beach, and occasionally they could hear the bellowing of its engine and the clanking of its tracks.

Jeremy held his father's hand. "She hasn't gone for ever, you know."

"I know," said David, although he didn't. He had never felt so alone in his life. Supposing he *never* found her? Supposing she *never* came back?

Robert was reading the plaque on the ruined gatehouse. "Through this gate . . . in 1430 . . . Joan of Arc was taken on her way to Rouen to be surrendered to the English."

They walked disconsolately back down the cobbled hill, past the castle ramparts, and down through the town. There was another broken heap of stones at the bottom of the hill, on which a plaque said, "Here, Joan of Arc was imprisoned after her capture by the Burgundians."

"What happened to Joan of Arc?" asked Jeremy.

"They tried her as a witch and a heretic," said Robert.

"Then what?"

"They burned her at the stake, of course. Don't you know anything?"

The three of them returned to La Colonne de Bronze. There was no sign of *madame* – the restaurant was being prepared for this evening's dinner, and already there was a strong smell of poaching cod. However, a young gendarme with a wispy mustache was waiting for

252

them in the bar. He stood up when they came in, and saluted.

"*Bonsoir, monsieur.*"

"Any news?" asked David, tiredly.

"I regret no, *monsieur*. But we have fifty men searching this district, and also we have sent messages to all of the ports and airports. If you can be so good as to remain here, we will contact you immediately if we have anything to report."

"Thank you," said David. Then, "What about a drink, boys?"

He tried to eat that evening, for the sake of reassuring Robert and Jeremy, but he was barely able to touch his sole in lemon sauce, and he felt sick at heart. He kept glancing across the restaurant at the brass plaque commemorating the visit of the Prince of Wales in 1915. He finished off a whole bottle of Sancerre on his own, and then he went upstairs to bed.

The room was just the same. Dark, empty, smelling of foreign hotels. Upstairs, somebody was creaking the floorboards as they undressed for bed. David didn't bother to undress. He simply prized off his shoes and lay back exhausted and drunk on the orange bedcover.

He slept heavily for a while, and he was sure that he could hear somebody snoring. He woke up to discover that it was him. He climbed unsteadily out of bed, went to the bathroom, and drank three glasses of water, one after the other. He stared at himself in the bathroom mirror. *She's gone, whether she's disappeared or dead. She's gone, and now you're all alone.*

He tipped himself back into bed, and slept for another hour. This time, however, his mind was crowded with dreams and voices and inexplicable noises. He dreamed that he was running through the streets of St Valéry, forcing his way through medieval alleyways that were so

253

narrow and twisting that his shoulders scraped against the walls on either side. He dreamed he saw a young man in a brown tunic disappearing round a corner, just in front of him. He ran to the corner, but the young man had already started to scale the hill, up toward the ruined gatehouse. He tried to shout out, but he couldn't make his larynx work.

He heard people laughing and muttering, and somebody singing a garbled hymn. He heard odd, plangent music, drums and flutes and sackbuts. He heard a woman screaming and screaming as if she could never stop.

He opened his eyes. He was shaking, and drenched in sweat. He propped himself up on his elbow, and listened, but all he could hear was the fluffing of the wind against the window and the sharp ticking of his watch. He checked the time: three o'clock in the morning. He felt terrible. His breath stank of wine and the inside of his head felt like a coalhole.

He eased himself out of bed, and went to the window. The hairpin corner of the main road was silent. Lights twinkled somewhere in the far distance, out across the marshes. He pressed his forehead against the cold glass and said, "Carole," and her name formed an evanescent oval of breath.

"Carole, where the hell are you?" God – she could be anywhere, dead, raped, tied up, imprisoned in some maniac's garage. He swallowed and it hurt to swallow but he couldn't bring himself to cry.

He was just about to go to the bathroom again when he glimpsed something in the shadows across the road. The window was misted, so he couldn't be sure. But it looked like somebody dressed in white, hurrying up the narrow alleyway that led toward the ramparts, and the castle.

"*Carole*?" he breathed, in disbelief.

With a surge of panic and excitement, he found his shoes, yanked the laces wide apart, and shoved them on.

254

He ran down the hotel stairs, colliding with the wall at the bottom, and then he wrenched at the front door. Shit! It was locked. He turned around, and hurried through to the back of the hotel, where the toilettes trickled drearily throughout the night. He found the back door, turned the key, and unbolted it. Then he ran out through the car park and into the street.

There was no sign of the hurrying white figure, but all the same he crossed the road and ran up the steep cobbled gradient. The path zig-zagged to the left, and then to the right, and then David was panting through a shadowy, echoing archway, and up past a small boulangerie, with its gray-painted shutters tightly closed.

He emerged on to the ramparts, where the wind blew steady and damp and very cold. He was gasping, and his lungs hurt. But off to his right, a curving pathway wound uptoward the ruined gatehouse, and he thought he saw the faintest flicker of white.

"Carole!" he called, his voice hoarse. "Carole!"

He struggled up the pathway, until he reached the black medieval bulk of the gatehouse. He circled the gatehouse twice, but there didn't appear to be anybody here.

"Carole!" he called again. It might be futile, it might be stupid, but so what? There was nobody to hear him.

He came around the gatehouse yet again, and it was then that he saw them. He stopped, and he stared. It was so dark that he could scarcely make them out. He said, "Carole?" once more, but he wasn't sure whether he had spoken her name out loud or not.

He was trembling, juddering – not only with cold, but with the greatest dread he had ever known.

Carole was standing by the railings overlooking the cliff, where today the bulldozer had been working. Her face was very white and her blonde hair looked white in the darkness and she was still wearing the white nightdress that she had been wearing yesterday morning. Her eyes were smudgy with fatigue and fear.

Facing her – very close, with his back turned to David, so that David couldn't see his face – was a tall youth wearing a loose brown shirt and brown leggings and boots. His arms were outstretched, like a crucifix, and he was approaching Carole with a slow, strange gait, as if he were trying to embrace her.

But there was something else. Carole's breath was visible in the cold; but the boy himself was *smoldering*. There was smoke pouring from his hair, and smoke trailing out of his cuffs; and as David gradually came nearer, he could see something orange glowing through the rough-woven hessian of his shirt. Something that crawled, and flickered, and grew brighter. *He was alight. He was literally burning alive.*

"*Carole!*" David screamed at her. "*Carole!*"

He rushed forward. The boy whipped around, and David stopped dead.

Jesus, it wasn't a boy at all. It was a girl. A young, plain-faced girl, with a straight, bony nose and a bowl-shaped haircut and eyes like nothing that David had ever seen before. They were black, as black as jet, but fire was glittering out of them like fire through a keyhole.

"What?" David shouted at her. "What do you want? Who are you?"

The girl hesitated for a long time. Then she said, "You are not welcome here, *monsieur*."

David tried to circle around her, to reach Carole.

"Carole? Are you all right?"

"*Monsieur*," the girl interrupted. "You needs must leave now."

"Oh, no," said David. "Not without my wife."

"Your wife is forfeit, *monsieur*. From the day that the Pope's council first met to rehabilitate me, one English woman was forfeit, every witch-year."

256

"What the hell are you talking about?" David shouted at her. "I want my wife, and I'm not leaving without her!"

"*Monsieur*," the girl blazed at him; and her eyes brightened now, and the smell of burning hessian grew stronger. "A witch-year is three-score and seventeen years; and Satan demands that three-score and seventeen witch-years shall pass before the settlement is finally settled; and that in every witch-year an Englishwoman shall burn as *I* was condemned to burn, in the place of my imprisonment, until the English are forgiven and the Popes are freed of their obligation."

David stared at her. He felt as if the whole world were turning beneath his feet; as if time and gravity had no meaning at all; as if Hell were real.

"You're Joan," he whispered.

She laughed, and smoke poured out of her mouth, and tongues of flame began to lick at her shirt. "*Ah, oui monsieur*, Joan, burned at the stake for heresy and witchery! And then forgiven, for my Master Lord Satan would not have me sacrificed, not without seventy-seven sacrifices to redeem me! And the Pope's council shook in their shoes, and knew no sanity, and heard the dead screaming in the night, and saw dead dogs running through the streets of Rome."

"You're not taking my wife," said David. His head pounded, his adrenaline-level was rising like a thermometer.

"I have already taken her," said Joan. "I came to her, and I talked to her, and she took all of her possessions and burned them. Now she, too, is prepared to be burned. Look at her! *Regarde!* She is waiting for that last embrace! She is impatient for it! And all I have to do is to take her into my arms!"

"*No!*" yelled David.

But Joan smiled and shook her head and fire licked out of her sleeves: David could hear it softly crackling.

257

Then Joan turned back to Carole, and raised her arms, and Carole hesitantly came towards her, as if she really wanted to be burned; as if she were really happy to be sacrificed.

David wasn't sure if he were sleeping or waking, but he rushed toward Joan and clutched her in his arms with the terrible enthusiasm of a true martyr.

He thought she might burn him. He was afraid she might burn him. But his only experience of burns was scalding his hand on a kettle. He wasn't at all prepared for the blast of heat which roared through his eyebrows and his hair and which burst his lips open and shriveled his cheeks.

She was so fiercely hot that he couldn't even scream: couldn't draw breath. But he knew that he had to hold her tight and never let go, or else Carole would die, and he couldn't let Carole die for anything.

He turned his head around, fighting for breath, too agonized even to groan. He was afire from head to foot, and the pain was greater than any pain he had ever experienced or could ever have imagined. Every nerve ending was alight. Every inch of skin was alight. He felt the insides of his thighs wrinkling with pain, and then his testicles burn. He cried out, "*God! God forgive me!*" although he wasn't sure why. Then he gripped Joan's burning body as tightly as he could, and pitched himself right through the wooden railings and over the cliff and the two of them cartwheeled through the night, fiery and screaming, until they hit the sand below and burned and burned.

The next morning Carole stood on the beach with her hair blown by the wind. Robert and Jeremy stayed close beside her. The *pompiers* had already covered the ashes with a yellow tarpaulin, and an ambulance was driving across the sand with its red light flashing but no siren. A flight of geese crossed the estuary, honking plaintively as they flew.

The gendarme from St Valéry came up to Carole and made a sympathetic face. "I am pleased that you are safe," he told her. "I am sorry for what happened to your husband."

Carole nodded, with tears prickling her eyes.

The gendarme said, "It will be impossible for other people to understand, you know that? But what your husband did was very brave. Also, it finished something for ever. It broke a chain, if you see what I mean. The burning of an English woman was necessary for this process to continue. Joan was cheated of that. His Majesty was cheated of that.

The gendarme looked around, and Carole was surprised to see that there were tears in his eyes, too. "You know something?" he asked. "When Joan was burning at the stake, a priest risked his life to mount the burning brushwood and to give her a wooden crucifix, that she might hold it, and enter the kingdom of Heaven.

He lifted his hand, and offered Carole a crude oak cross. "I found it here, on the beach, amongst the ashes. It was not burned at all. I think, you know, that it must belong to you."

Carole took the cross and pressed it close to her chest. Then she turned and walked back to La Colonne de Bronze, with Robert and Jeremy following her.

In the lounge, she found *madame*, dressed in black. "*Madame*, my husband's passport, please."

Madame opened her cashbox and handed Carole the maroon passport without a word. Carole opened it up, and saw that David's photograph was charred by a dark-brown diagonal scorch-mark.

She closed his passport, closed his life, and walked out into the gray overcast morning, where her boys were waiting for her.

The Sixth Man

Selborne, Hampshire

Although much of *The Sixth Man* is set in Antarctica, the real dark heart of the story beats in Selborne, in Hampshire. Selborne village is the birthplace of the Rev Gilbert White, 1720–93, the pioneering naturalist, and remains today very much as he knew it in the 18th century, with a giant old yew tree in the churchyard, and pollarded lime trees outside the butcher's shop. Gilbert White's 17th-century house, The Wakes, is now a museum which is jointly devoted to White himself and to Captain Oates, the ill-fated Antarctic explorer. Here you can see photographs and documents and artefacts which bring the suffering of Captain Scott's party into chilling life.

Afterward, you can climb the steep zig-zag path which Gilbert White helped to make up to the top of Selborne Hanger, and look out over the warm, spectacular countryside, and think about the meaning of ambition, and self-sacrifice, and the meaning of fear itself.

THE SIXTH MAN

We were walking back to the house when Michael said, "I've discovered something rather strange. I don't quite know what to do about it."

It was a perfect English summer's day. There was a deep, sweet smell of meadowgrass and clover, and above us the clouds lazed slowly over the Lyth like huge cream-colored comforters. Not far away, next to the split-rail fence, a small herd of Jersey cows stood thoughtfully chewing, and occasionally flicked their tails.

"Do you want to tell me what it is?" I asked. Michael was a petroleum geologist, a discoverer and an exploiter of oil-fields in far-flung and undesirable places, and not exactly the sort of chap who ever thought anything was "strange", let alone worried himself about it.

"I've found a photograph," he said. "I've looked at it again and again. I've even had it examined by the photo-lab. No doubt about it, it's quite genuine; but it makes no sense at all; and I'm afraid a lot of people are going to be quite embarrassed and hurt about it."

We reached the edge of the meadow and climbed over the stile. I didn't push Michael any further. He was always careful and deliberate in his choice of words, and it was obvious that he was genuinely disturbed.

"I think I'd better show you," he said, at last. "Come into the study. Would you like a beer? I think I've got a couple of cans of Ruddles in the fridge."

We made our way through the tangled dog-roses at

the end of his garden, past the overgrown sundial, and in through the old-fashioned kitchen. His young wife Tania was out, collecting their three-year-old son Tim from playschool. Her apron lay across the back of the chair, and a freshly-made apple-pie stood in a circle of lightly-dusted flour. I had known Tania long before I had known Michael; and in a funny way I still wished that she and I could have loved each other more. It was unsettling for me to see her carrying Michael's son in her arms.

Carrying frosted cans of beer, we climbed the uncarpeted stairs to Michael's study. There was a smell of warm days and dried-out horsehair plaster, and oak. Michael's house had been built in 1670, but his study had all the equipment that a petro-geologist needed: an IBM computer, a fax machine, seismic charts, maps and rows of immaculate files and books and atlases.

He took out a large black folder labeled *Falcon Petroleum: Ross Ice-Shelf*, laid it flat on his gray steel desk, and took out an envelope. Inside the envelope were several copies of old black-and-white photographs.

"Here," he said, and passed one over. As far as I could see, it was the famous photograph of Captain Scott and his ill-fated party at the South Pole. Wilson, Evans, Scott, Oates and Bowers, frost-bitten and making no pretense of being bitterly dejected. I turned it over, and on the back there was a typewritten label: *Captain Robert Scott and party, South Pole, January 17, 1912.*

"Well?" I asked Michael. "What of it?"

"There were *supposed* to be five of them," he said. "Actually, of course, there were originally only supposed to be four – but for some inexplicable reason Scott took Lieutenant Bowers along on the last leg to the Pole, even though they didn't have enough food."

"There *are* five of them," I told him.

"Yes, but who took the photograph?" Michael insisted.

I gave him the photograph back. "They operated the camera with a long thread, everybody knows that."

"Everybody *supposes* they used a thread. But if that's true . . . then who's this?"

He handed over another photograph. It showed Scott standing beside the small triangular tent left by the Norwegian explorer Roald Amundsen, who had beaten the British expedition in their race to the Pole by just over a month. There was Oates, bending over beside one of the guy-ropes; there were Evans and Bowers, standing close together, Bowers making notes in a notebook. But in the background, about fifty or sixty yards away, another figure was standing, in a long black coat, and a huge black hat, neither of which remotely resembled any of the coats or hats that the rest of the party were wearing.

Michael tapped the photograph with his finger. "Presumably, this picture was taken by Dr Evans. It's not the kind of photograph you could take with a thread, anyway, not with the type of camera that Scott took with him to the Pole. Too far away, too difficult. But look at the caption . . . Dr Evans hasn't attempted to give any special emphasis to this unknown sixth man; and none of the others seem to be concerned that he's there. Yet, he isn't mentioned Scott's diary; and we know for a recorded fact that only five set off on the last leg across the polar plateau. So where did he come from? And who is he? And what happened to him, when all the rest of them died?"

I stared at the photograph for a long time. The mysterious sixth man was very tall, and his hat had a wide sweeping brim, like a coal-heaver's hat, so that his face was obscured by an impenetrable shadow. He could have been anybody. I looked at the back of the photograph, and read, *R. Amundsen's Tent At The Pole, January 17, 1912*. No mention at all of the man in black. A mystery, nearly eighty years old, but Michael was right about its sensitivity. At the time, the tragedy of Captain Scott's

Antarctic expedition had moved a whole nation to tears; and there were many people in England, even today, who would find any revisionist explanations of their fate to be gravely offensive.

"Where did you find this?" I asked Michael.

"In the private papers of Herbert Ponting, the expedition's photographer. I was looking for pictures of the Ross Ice-Shelf and the Beardmore Glacier, the way they used to be."

"And you don't have any idea who this sixth man could be?"

Michael shook his head. "I went through Scott's diary with a fine-tooth comb. I checked Amundsen's account, too. Amundsen left nobody behind at the Pole; and he saw nobody else."

I held the photograph up to the window. "It's not a double exposure?"

"Absolutely not."

I shrugged, and handed the photograph back. "In that case, it's one of the great unexplained mysteries of all time."

Michael grinned, for the first time that afternoon. "Not if I can help it."

The Chinook helicopter slowly circled and then landed on the ice, whirling up a white blizzard that sparkled and glittered in the sunlight. The cargo doors were opened up immediately, and the orange-jacketed engineers heaved out tools and ropes and crates of supplies. Michael wiped his spectacles with his thumb, and then tugged the hood of his parka tight around his chin. "You ready?" he asked me.

The Antarctic wind sliced into the open cargo doors like frozen knives. "I thought you said this was summer," I told him, following him along the fuselage, and then down the steps to the ice.

266

"It is," he grinned. "You should try visiting here in June."

Slowly the Chinook's rotor-blades flickered to a standstill. Michael led me across the hard-packed ice to the largest of the nine huts that made up Falcon Petroleum's Beardmore Research Station. It looked like rush hour. Sno-Cats bellowed from one side of the station to the other, dog-teams panted past us, and dozens of riggers and engineers were working on aerials and scaffolding and two more half-finished huts.

The research station covered more than eleven acres, and the once-pristine Antarctic ice was strewn with discarded caterpillar-tracks; broken packing-cases; and heaps of wind-blown rubbish.

"I thought it was going to be all peace and solitude," I shouted at Michael.

He shook his head. "Not a hope. These days, the Antarctic is busier than a Bank Holiday in Brighton."

We entered the hut and stamped the ice from our feet. Huge fan heaters made the inside of the hut roaringly hot, and it stank of stale cigarette-smoke and sweat and something else, something musty, a smell which will always remind me of the South Pole, for ever and ever. It was almost like the smell of something which has been dead and frozen for a very long time, but is at last beginning to thaw.

Michael said, "It's a pretty gruesome life, but you get used to it. We get a regular supply of Johnnie Walker and porno videos from the Falklands."

He led me along a gloomy sisal-carpeted corridor, and then opened one of the doors. "Here, you're lucky, you can have this room to yourself. Dr Philips had to go back to London for six weeks. His wife got tired of him being away so long, and she's divorcing him."

I threw my suitcase on to the bed. The room was small, with a narrow steel-framed bed and a small desk and a packing-case which did duty as a bookshelf. On the chip-board wall was a color photograph of a large mousy-haired woman in a pale blue cardigan, with washing pinned up behind her; and next to it, a pin-up of a massively busty blonde with her legs stretched wide apart.

I thought of Tania. "What does Tania think about *you*, being away for so long?" I asked Michael.

"Oh, she doesn't like it, but she lumps it," he replied, rather evasively. He went to the window and peered out at the blindingly sunlit ice. "We all have to make sacrifices, don't we? That's what made Britain great – sacrifices."

I started to unzip my anorak, but Michael said. "Don't take it off yet. Rodney Jones can probably take us out to see the drilling site pretty well straight away. That's unless you're hungry."

I shook my head. "The chaps on the *Erebus* gave me steak and eggs and all the trimmings."

We went back along the corridor, and turned left. The first room we came to was marked *Seismic Studies*. It was large and untidy, crammed with desks and packing-cases and all kinds of flickering computer screens and noisily-zizzing fax machines. A handsome thirtyish man with a thick gingery beard was sitting with his thick oiled fishermen's socks propped up on one of the desks, reading a copy of *Woman's Weekly*.

"Hullo, Mike," he said, dropping the magazine on the desk. "I'm thinking of knitting myself a guernsey and matching scarf, what do you think?"

"You haven't finished my gloves yet," said Michael.

"I'm having trouble with the reindeer," Rodney retorted. "All those damned antlers."

Michael introduced me. "This is James McAlan, patholo-gist extraordinary, from Sussex University. He's come to look at our discovery."

Rodney stood up and shook hands. "Glad you could make it. *We* don't know what to do about it. I mean, *we're* only geologists. Is this your first time at the South Pole?"

"This is my first time at either Pole," I told him. "Up until now, the furthest south I've ever been is Nice."

"Well, you'll hate it," said Rodney, enthusiastically. He picked up his windcheater from the floor, and banged it with the flat of his hand to beat the dust off. "Borchgrevink said that the silence roars in one's ears. 'Centuries of heaped-up solitude,' that's what he called it. Borchgrevink was a Norwegian explorer, one of the first to spend the winter here. I've spent three winters here, which qualifies me as the stupidest bugger on the base."

He led us back out of the hut and across the rutted ice. Off to our left, a pack of huskies were yapping and jumping as they were fed. "Bloody dogs," Rodney remarked. "I don't care if I never see another dog again, not one, as long as I live."

It took us only six or seven minutes to reach the site of the excavation. It wasn't very impressive. A shallowish scour, surrounded by heaps of filthy broken-up ice, discarded equipment and a half-completed tower for seismological soundings. In the bottom of the scour, a green tent had been erected, to shield their discovery from the Antarctic weather, and protect it from stray dogs.

Michael led the way down to the tent, and Rodney tugged free the frozen laces, and opened up the flap. It was solid with ice, and it made a sharp cracking noise as he turned it back. "You'll have to crawl," Rodney told us.

We got down on hands and knees and edged our way into the tent. "I was out all night in a blizzard once," said Rodney, touching the roof of the tent with his gloved hand. "The snow piled up so heavy on top that the canvas was only an inch away from my nose. And to think I used to get claustrophobic in the Tube."

We shuffled ourselves into a crouching position. By the darting, criss-crossing light of Michael's torch, I had already glimpsed something very grim. But now he concentrated the beam on the center of the tent, and there was what he had brought me three-quarters of the way around the world to see.

"Jesus," I said, under my breath, and my breath froze against my chin.

Rodney sniffed. "You couldn't see it with the naked eye, but there was a deep crevasse just here. We discovered it when we started our sound survey. We dug down sixty feet or so . . . and this is what we found. We haven't touched either of them."

Tangled together in the snow lay the remains of two human beings. If there hadn't been two skulls, however, I wouldn't initially have guessed that there were two of them. There were only shoulders and ribs remaining, and ripped-open snow-jackets. But what made the sight so horrifying was that on some of the bones, there were still some fragments of flesh, tanned by age and extreme cold to the color of *prosciutto*. One of the skulls had been stripped almost completely bare of skin and flesh, but the other was practically intact – the mauvish, frozen face of a man dying in abject terror – his eyes empty, his mouth stretched wide, his lips thick with frost.

"Are you sure that it's them?" I asked Michael. Inside the confines of the tent, my voice sounded oddly flat and featureless.

Michael nodded. "Evans and Oates. No doubt about it." He inclined his head toward the frozen face – still locked in a scream that had been screamed nearly eighty years before. "There were papers, bits and pieces. Not much, but enough for us to be completely sure."

I couldn't take my eyes away from the gruesome, frost-encrusted remains. "I know that Evans collapsed and died around here, at the head of the Beardmore Glacier. But Oates didn't walk out into the blizzard until they were well down on the Ross Ice-Shelf, only twenty-nine miles away from One Ton Depot."

"That's right," said Michael. "So the question is . . . how did Oates get all the way back here? He couldn't have walked back. His feet were badly frostbitten, and the whole reason he walked out into the blizzard was because he couldn't drag himself any further. Apart from that, even if he *could* have walked back, why on earth *would* he?"

I peered at the remains more closely. "I think I can probably answer that," I told him. "These bones have been gnawed. See there – and there – definite teethmarks, although it's hard to guess *what* teethmarks. Eighty years ago, this crevasse could well have been the shelter for some predatory animal. It might have been following Scott and his party, the way jackals follow herds of antelope, just waiting for one to drop and die. Evans dropped, then Oates dropped. It dragged them both back here and used them for its winter food."

"James . . ." said Rodney. "I hate to be pedantic, but what kind of predatory animal could that have possibly been? There are plenty of walruses and seals and seabirds in the Antarctic, but there are no natural inland predators – no bears, no tigers, no snow-leopards . . . nothing that could have used these men as a winter larder."

I turned to him seriously. "A starving man is a predatory animal."

Rodney looked dubious. "Scott wasn't the kind of man who would have condoned cannibalism, surely? He was reluctant even to eat his dogs. And there's not a single word in his notes that suggests it so much as crossed his mind."

"I'm aware of that," I told him. "But you asked me what happened to these men and I told you. The probability is that some predatory animal dragged them here and ate them. Now, whether that predatory animal was a rogue

271

husky or a man who was prepared to eat anything and anyone in order to survive, I just don't know . . . not until I've made all the necessary tests."

Michael said, "You think it was Scott, don't you?"

I didn't reply. It was difficult, even now, to compromise one of the most glorious tragedies in British history.

But Michael persisted. "You think that Scott was lying, don't you . . . and that they might have killed and eaten Evans and Oates, just to keep going? All that stuff about Oates going out into the blizzard so that he wouldn't be a burden to the other three . . . you think that was so much guff . . . an inspired bit of heroic invention?"

Dry-mouthed, I said, "Yes. But I don't think you can blame anybody for what they did under extreme duress. Remember the Donner Party. Remember those schoolchildren when their aeroplane crashed in the Andes. You can't judge men who were starving to death in the middle of nowhere when you've just eaten steak and eggs on the good ship *Erebus*."

We hunched our way out of the tent, climbed out of the ice-scour, and walked slowly back to the hut.

"How long will it take you before you know for certain?" asked Michael.

"Twenty-four hours. Not longer."

Michael said, "You remember that photograph I found? The one of Scott and all the rest of them at the Pole?"

"Of course. Did you ever find out who that mysterious sixth man was?"

Michael shook his head. "I decided in the end that it was probably Evans, in a different hat, and that he'd somehow managed to rig up a very long string to take it."

"You said you found papers, bits and pieces. Do you think I could see them?"

Back in the hut, Michael brewed up some hot coffee, laced with whiskey, while I poked through the few pathetic remnants that had been discovered with Oates and Evans in the crevasse. A comb; a pair of leather snow-goggles (unglazed, and very ineffective, since plastic had not yet been invented); a single fur glove, dried up like a mummified cat; and a small snow-blotched diary. Most of the diary's pages had stuck together, but at the back there was a single legible entry . . . not in Scott's handwriting, but presumably in Oates'.

It said, simply, *Jan 18, now for the run home but Despair will soon overtake us.*

I sat sipping my coffee and frowning at the diary for a long time. The entry seemed simple enough, but the phraseology was odd. Apart from the capital "D" for "Despair", why had he said that "Despair will soon overtake us"? Despair was an emotion that might certainly have overtaken anybody who found themselves at the South Pole, with 800 miles to walk to safety, and scarcely any hot food. But you didn't normally talk about it overtaking you until it actually did.

It was as odd as saying "Tomorrow, when we climb the mountain, we will be overtaken by fear." The chances are that you certainly *will* be overtaken by fear, but you just don't express it like that.

I said to Michael, "Can we go to the Pole, and then slowly fly back over Scott's route?"

"If you think it'll help. I was going to take you to the Pole anyway. Bit of a letdown to come all this way and not quite make it."

We left the research station at the head of the Beardmore Glacier at a little after seven o'clock the next morning. The Chinook lifted itself diagonally into the sunlight, and across the peaks of the Queen Alexandra Mountains, toward the polar plateau. The wind had been rising throughout the night, and when I looked down at the ice, I saw long horse's-tails of snow waving across the ice.

"Unlucky for Scott he didn't have a helicopter," Michael shouted, above the roar of the engines. He passed me a ham roll, wrapped up in cling-film. "Breakfast," he told me.

It was about three hundred and fifty miles to the South Pole from the research station, and the flight took us low over the icy plateau. "Terrible terrain for man-hauling sledges," Michael pointed out. "Dragging a sledge across those ice-crystals is like dragging it across sand. No friction at all."

We were only twenty minutes away from the Pole when the pilot turned back to us and remarked, "I'm getting some adverse blizzard reports, Michael. Looks like we won't have too long."

"That's all right, we just want a quick shufti," Michael told him. "Besides, it's tripe tonight, and I don't want to miss that."

As we circled around the Pole, however, the winds began to buffet the Chinook violently, and I heard the rotor-gears whining in protest.

"Are you sure it's going to be okay?" I asked Michael. "We can always come back when the weather's better."

"Don't worry, we're going to be fine," he reassured me. "Here you are, Andy, put her down wherever you like."

"Is this really it?" I asked. "The actual South Pole?"

"Didn't expect to see a real pole, did you?" laughed Andy.

We were almost down. Michael had unbuckled his seatbelt. Then abruptly the Chinook lurched and banged, and I heard metal screeching hideously against metal. I was hurled sideways, my shoulder colliding against the seat next to me. I heard somebody shout, "Jesus!" and then the whole helicopter seemed to tear open all around me, like a theater curtain being parted, and I was dropped face-first into the shatteringly cold snow.

It was a long time before I realized what had happened.

I thought I was dead; or at least that my back was broken. But gradually I was able to creep up on to my hands and knees, and then sit up, and look around.

A sudden gust must have caught the Chinook just on the point of landing – either that, or her rotor-gears had sheared, which had occasionally happened with Chinooks, and her two synchronized rotor-blades had enmeshed. Whatever it was, she was lying on her side, split apart, with her rotors sticking up into the Antarctic air like abandoned windmills. There was no sign of Michael, and no sign of Andy or his co-pilot. All I could hear was the rising wind.

I crept cautiously back into the wreckage, sniffing for aviation fuel, in case of fire. I found Andy and his co-pilot sitting side by side, both with their eyes open, both plastered with blood, as if they had emptied pots of red paint over their heads for a joke, both dead. Shaking, I retreated from the cockpit and climbed back outside. It was then that I saw Michael standing about thirty yards away, without his glasses, looking stunned.

"Are you all right?" I asked him.

He nodded. "Are they dead?" he whispered.

"Yes," I told him. "I'm afraid they are."

"Oh, hell," he said. It seemed to be the worst expletive he could think of.

In the first two hours, our moods swung dramatically from hysterical relief to deep, silent moodiness. It was only the shock, and it soon began to wear off. We climbed back into the helicopter, trying not to look too closely at Andy and his co-pilot, and attempted to get the radio working. But one of the rotors (apart from shearing off the lower half of Andy and his co-pilot's bodies) had cut right through the wiring, and it would have taken an honors graduate in popular mechanics to get it going again.

"Still, they'll come out looking for us pretty well

immediately," said Michael. "And we always carry a tent and emergency rations and survival kit."

We manhandled the bright orange tent out of the helicopter and set it up. It wasn't easy, because the wind had risen to even great ferocity, almost a blizzard, and neither of us were particularly brilliant at playing Boy Scouts. However we managed to climb inside, and zip it up, and light the butane heater which was part of our survival kit. Michael managed to brew up two tin cups full of passable tea, with lots of sugar in it.

"I reckon it'll take them three hours to find us, at the outside," said Michael, checking his watch. "We should even be back in time for supper."

But outside the tent, the blizzard rose to a long and unearthly scream, and we felt snow lashing furiously against the fabric. I opened the vent just a couple of inches, and all we could see outside was howling white.

"Looks like we're getting a taste of Scott's expedition first hand," Michael remarked, wryly.

We both assumed that, since it was summer, the blizzard would have died away by morning. But it screamed all night, and when we woke up at eight o'clock the next day, the tent was dark, and it was still screaming. I tugged open the vent and a heavy lump of snow dropped in. During the night, the tent had been totally buried.

"This can't last much longer than twenty-four hours," Michael said, confidently. "How about some morning tea?"

But throughout the long hours of the day, the wind and the snow never abated once. It was well up to Force 8 – "blizzing like blazes," as the ill-fated Bowers had described it. By six o'clock that evening, we were feeling tired and cold and depressed. What was more, our butane gas was running low.

"There's another two cylinders in the back of the stores locker," Michael told me. So I tightened the laces of my hood, and scooped my way out of the tent, and into the storm.

I had been in snowstorms before; in Aspen, and in the Swiss Alps. But I had never been in anything like this. The wind was screeching at me as if it were human, but insane. It actually had a *voice*. I was barely able to stand up, let alone walk, and all I could see of the crashed Chinook was a hunchbacked tomb of white snow and four twisted rotor-blades.

However, I managed to plant one boot in front of the other, and with curses and grunts I began to traverse the space between the tent and the helicopter.

I was less than halfway across it when I saw the sixth man.

I stopped, staggering in the ferocity of the blizzard. I was already cold; but now I was chilled with an extraordinary dread; a fear that I had never experienced before in my life.

He was standing so that he was just within view behind the whirling snow. Tall, with a black cloak that silently flapped, and a huge black hat. He said nothing, he didn't move. I stood and stared at him and didn't know whether to stagger back to the tent, or to shout out to him, or what.

Hallucination, I thought. *How could he possibly be real? Nobody could survive out in this weather . . . and besides, the last picture I had seen of him had been taken eighty years ago. No doubt about it – he's an optical illusion. A snow-ghost.*

Still, I kept a close eye on him as I battled my way to the helicopter and back. All the time he remained where he was, sometimes standing in plain sight, sometimes almost invisible behind the snow. I heaved myself back into the tent and zipped it up.

"What's the matter?" asked Michael. His lips looked blue and he was chafing his hands.

I shook my head. "Nothing. Nothing at all."

"You've seen something."

"Of course not," I told him. "There's nothing to see but snow."

He looked at me narrowly and wouldn't take his eyes away. "You've *seen* something."

The next day the blizzard was worse and we were almost out of butane. The temperature dropped and dropped, like a stone thrown down a bottomless well, and for the first time it began to occur to me that we might not be rescued – that the blizzard might go on for ever and ever, until we starved or froze, whichever came first.

Michael volunteered to go back to the Chinook to see if he could rummage any more food, and anything that we could burn for heat. I helped him to crawl out of the tent, and then lit the lamp and started to brew up some drinking-chocolate, to warm him when he came back.

But he was back almost at once, and his eyes were wide in their snow-rimed lashes. "He's there!" he croaked.

"Who? Who are you talking about?"

"You know damn well who's there! The sixth man! You must have seen him yourself!"

He could see by the expression on my face that I had. He scrambled awkwardly back into the tent.

"Maybe he can help!" Michael suggested. "Maybe he can help us escape!"

"Michael, he can't be real. He's some kind of hallucination, that's all."

"How can you say he's not real? He's standing right outside!"

"Michael, he simply doesn't exist. He *can't* exist. He's in our minds, that's all."

But Michael was too excited. "The South Pole only exists in our minds, but it's still the South Pole."

I tried to argue with him, but both of us were hungry and numb with cold, and I didn't want to waste energy, or hope. I brewed up the chocolate on the last few beads of dwindling gas, and we sat close together and drank it. All the time Michael kept staring at the tent-flap, as if he was gathering himself together to go out into the blizzard and meet the sixth man face to face.

The blizzard had been screaming relentlessly for nearly five days when Michael grasped me by the shoulder and shook me awake. His eyes glistened red-rimmed in the dim light of our failing flashlight.

"James, there's no hope, is there? We're going to die here."

"Come on, don't give up," I told him. "The blizzard can't go on for very much longer."

He smiled, and shook his head. "You know it's all up, just as well as I do. There's only one thing left."

"You're not going outside?"

He nodded. "I understand now, who he is, the sixth man. Oates understood, too. He's Despair. He's the total absence of human hope. The Eskimos always used to say that in some intensely cold places, extreme human emotions could take on human shape. So did the Kwakiutl Indians."

"Come on, Michael, you're losing your grip."

"No," he said. "No! When Scott got to the Pole and found that Amundsen had got here first, he despaired. He knew, too, that they probably couldn't get back alive. And that was the sixth man, Despair; and Despair tracked them down one by one; and you know what they say about Despair? Despair tears the very flesh, right off your bones."

Michael didn't look mad; but he made me feel mad.

He kept smiling as if he had never been happier. *Despair will overtake us*, that's what Oates had written, and Michael was right. It did make some kind of inverted sense.

He hugged me tightly. "I want you to look after Tania. I know how much you care about her." Then he opened the tent flap, and crawled outside.

Slitting my eyes against the blisteringly cold wind, I saw him trudge away, in the direction of the helicopter. Scarcely visible in the snow, I saw the tall man in black waiting for him, unmoving, infinitely patient. *In some intensely cold places, extreme human emotions could take on human shape.*

Michael stood in front of the man like an obedient soldier reporting to his captain. Then the man raised both hands, and plunged them into the front of Michael's anorak, plunged them right through fabric and skin and living flesh. With a grisly cracking noise that I could hear even over the screaming blizzard, he literally ripped Michael inside-out, in a storm-bloodied chaos of lungs and heart and wallowing stomach.

The blizzard blew even more fiercely then, and obscured them. Trembling, muttering with fright, I closed the tent-flap and sat huddled in my anorak and my blankets, waiting for one kind of death or another.

I said the longest prayer that any man ever said, and hoped.

The tent flap opened and I found myself sitting in a triangle of sunlight. There was no blizzard, no wind, only the distant whistling of helicopter rotors, and the sounds of men shouting.

It was Rodney. He said, "James! My God, you're still alive."

I sat with Tania on top of the Lyth, looking out over

280

Selborne. It was one of those still, hot, timeless August evenings.

She said, "Mike used to love these summer days."

I nodded. Two house-martins swooped and dived just above us. Very faithful, house-martins, always return to the same house to build their nests, every year.

"Sometimes I get the feeling that he's still with us," she remarked.

"Yes," I said. "He probably is."

"He didn't suffer, though, did he?"

"No," I told her. "All three of them were killed instantly, no pain. They wouldn't even have felt the fire."

"You were lucky," she said, a little sadly.

"Come on," I coaxed her. "Let's get back."

I helped her up from the grass, and together we made our way down the hillside, between the gorse-bushes and the brambles. At one point, Tania went on ahead; and I stopped for a moment and looked back, at the warm and fragrant woodland, and those peaceful summer slopes, and at my own shadow, tall and black and motionless, like a memory of something that has never been.

Beijing Craps

Las Vegas, Nevada

No city in the world combines fun and panic in such a heady mixture as Las Vegas. I don't gamble, but I was completely won over by the glitter, the glitz and the sheer hysteria. Even when people are having a wonderful, wonderful time in Las Vegas, they seem to be conscious that the cold breath of death is blowing down the backs of their necks. It's not just the desert that surrounds Las Vegas that makes it so surrealistic. It's not just the lights and the wedding-chapels and the Jetson-style architecture. It's the feeling that people have come here because they're desperate, because they need a short-cut to wealth and happiness or whatever other joys that life has never dealt out to them.

BEIJING CRAPS

Like all professional gamblers, whose days are measured only in throws, and rolls, and hands, and spins, it had never seriously occurred to Jack Druce that he would ever have to face death. But that Friday morning at the Golden Lode Casino, at the exact instant when the second-hand swept silently past 1 a.m., he shivered, and lifted his head, and frowned, as if he had been momentarily been touched by the chilly breath of impending extinction.

Alert to the slightest tremor in mood at the craps table, the croupier noticed his hesitation, and said, "Intending to shoot, sir-r-r?" His "r's" rolled as hard as dice.

Solly Bartholomew noticed Jack's hesitation, too, but didn't lift his eyes from the layout.

Jack nodded, and scooped up the dice, but didn't speak.

He had already stacked up eleven thousand dollars' worth of chips in three hours' play. But for no reason at all he suddenly felt as if the layout had gone cold, the same way that (seven years ago) his wife Elaine had grown cold, lying in his arms, asleep first of all, breathing, then not breathing, then dead.

Jack guessed that he and Solly could make two or three thousand more. Solly was the only other professional at the table; a neat man who looked like a smalltown realtor, but who threw the dice with all the tight assurance of a practised arm. Cautiously, showing no outward signs that they knew each other, or that they were working together, he and Jack were carving up the amateurs between them.

There was money around, too. Not yacht money, for sure, but lunch money. They had just been joined by a tall horse-faced over-excited man from Indianapolis in a powder-blue polyester suit who was placing his chips on all the hardways bets, and a redhead with her roots showing and a deep withered cleavage who yelped like a chihuahua every time Jack threw a pass. Divorcee, Jack calculated, splashing out with her settlement. She wouldn't stop playing until every last cent of it was totally blown. It was a form of revenge. Jack knew all about women's revenge. Elaine had stopped breathing while he was holding her in his arms, and what revenge could any woman have exacted on any man that was more terrible than that?

Jack blew softly on the ivories, shook them twice, and sent them tumbling off across the soft green felt. "Nine," commented the croupier, and pushed Jack another stack of fifty-dollar chips.

"I'm out," said Jack, and began gathering his winnings in both hands.

Solly hesitated for a moment; then said, "Me too."

"Aw shit," said the tall horse-faced man.

The croupier's eyes flicked sideways toward the pit boss. Jack said, "Something wrong, my friend?" He had spent thirty years of his life dealing with men who communicated whole libraries with the quiver of an eyelid.

"Pit boss'd like a word, sir. And –" turning toward Solly, "– you, too, sir. That's if you don't mind."

"I have a plane to catch," Solly complained. Solly always had a plane to catch.

"It's ten after one in the morning," the croupier told him.

"Well I have to catch some sleep before I catch my plane."

"This won't take long, sir, believe me."

Jack and Solly waited with their hands full of chips while the small neat pit boss approached him. White tuxedo, ruffled pink shirt, smooth Sienese face, eyes like slanted black olives, black hair parted dead-center. The pit boss held out one of his tiny hands, as if to guide them away from the table by the elbow, but he didn't actually touch them. Players were not to be physically touched. It was bad karma.

"Mr Newman presents his compliments, sir."

"Oh does he?" asked Jack, sniffing and blinking behind his heavy-rimmed eyeglasses. Beside him, he heard the redhead yelping again.

The pit boss smiled, and went along with the pretense. "Well, sir, Mr Newman is the joint owner of the Golden Lode, sir. And he would like to see you."

Jack held up his chips. "Listen, my friend, I have my winnings here."

Solly said, "Me too."

"Of course," said the pit-boss. His smile slid out of the side of his mouth like the cottonseed oil pouring out of a freshly-opened can of sardines. "We'll take care of your winnings, sir. Carlos! Here, take care of these gentlemen's winnings."

"Twelve and a half k," said Jack, pointedly, as if it were more money than he had ever possessed in his life.

"Five," said Solly, without expression.

"Don't worry, sir. Carlos will keep it in the safe for you."

With a great show of reluctance, Jack handed over his chips. "Twelve and a half k," he repeated. "What do you think of that?"

Behind his well-pumiced acne craters, the stone-faced Carlos obviously thought nothing of it at all. One night's winnings for a mid-Western mark, that was all. The casino would have it all back tomorrow, or the next night.

"Please . . . this young lady will show you to Mr Graf," said the pit-boss, still smiling. From somewhere behind him, like an assistant in one of those corny Las Vegas lounge magical acts, a Chinese-looking girl appeared, in a skin-tight dress of cerise silk, with a split all the way up to the top of her thigh.

"Please follow," she said, and immediately turned and began to walk ahead of them. Jack glanced at Solly and Solly glanced back at Jack. They could cut and run. But Jack had heard of Mr Graf; and Mr Graf had a hard, hard reputation; and if they ran away from Mr Graf, then the chances were that they would have to keep on running, for the rest of their natural borns.

Whatever had to be faced, had to be faced. Jack and Solly had both been beaten up before, more than once.

The Chinese-looking girl was already halfway across the casino floor, headed toward the wide violet-carpeted staircase that led down from the restaurant and the offices.

Solly said, "After you, sport," and Jack shambled after her like an obedient mutt, tugging the knot of his necktie, although it was already too tight. During his gambling career, he had deliberately cultivated the dislocated mannerisms of a Rube, freshly off the Piedmont redeye from the rural mid-West with a billfold crammed with ready money and no idea of how to play the tables.

In reality he had been born in Providence, Rhode Island, the son of a high school principal, and he was both well-educated and extensively-traveled. He had lived in Florence, in Aqaba, and Paris; and in the 1950s he had spent nine miserable months in London. But in the late 1960s he had spent six weeks living in Bellflower, Illinois, painstakingly imitating the local mannerisms and the local speech. These days, only a fully-bloomed Bellflorian could have detected that his accent wasn't for real. He still said "grass" instead of "grayce."

288

He had altered his appearance, too. He had cropped his hair short and bought himself a vivid chestnut-brown toupee. He had adopted thick-rimmed eyeglasses and sunbathed in his T-shirt, so that he had acquired that farm-style tan, face and neck and forearms only. Every morning he squeezed lumps of modeling clay in the palms of his hands, to give himself cheesy-looking crescents of dirt under his fingernails.

When he was working, he assumed a crumpled seer-sucker suit in brown-and-white check, a brown drip-dry shirt, and scuffed tan sneakers. At least, he liked to think that he "assumed" them, and that his "real" clothes were the clothes that hung in the closet of his suite at the Sands hotel. A single gray Armani suit, three handmade shirts, and a pair of polished English shoes.

In reality, however, the "real" clothes had scarcely been worn, because Jack was always working. Even the soles of his "real" shoes remained unscratched. He spent all afternoon and most of the night as Jack Druce the Rube. The rest of the time he spent sprawled on his back on his hotel bed with his sheet knotted around his waist like a loincloth, dreaming of Elaine going cold in his arms and whispering numbers to himself. But he needed the "real" clothes to be hanging there waiting for him.

If he ever discarded his "real" clothes, then the "real" Jack Druce would cease to exist; and all that would be left would be Jack Druce the Rube; Jack Druce the Chronic Gambler. The laughing, sophisticated young college graduate would have vanished for ever; so would the husband of Elaine; and the father of Roddy, for what that was worth.

On the last day of May, 1961, Jack Druce had been a mathematical whiz-kid, the youngest research team-leader that San Fernando Electronics had ever employed. On the last day of May, 1961, San Fernando Electronics had brought two hundred seventy employees to Las Vegas, for the company's tenth annual convention. That night, Jack Druce had played dice for the very first time in his life, and doubled his annual salary in four-and-a-half hours.

Jack Druce had woken on the first day of June, 1961, with the certain knowledge that he had been hooked.

Now his house was gone and his car was gone. Not because he couldn't afford them. Most days, technically, he was very rich. The simple fact was that houses and cars didn't figure in his life any more. He lived in hotels; he walked to work; and he subsisted on free casino snacks and Salem Menthol Lights. His home was the Pass line. He never looked at his watch.

The Chinese girl led Jack and Solly through thick suffocating velour curtains, and then through double doors of heavy carved Joshua wood.

"I'm not so sure about this," Jack told her; but she turned and half-smiled and said, "Don't be afraid."

Solly said nothing. Solly had an especially sensitive nose for danger. Solly was sniffing the atmosphere, checking it out.

Beyond the double doors, they found themselves in a large gloomy room, ferociously chilly with air-conditioning. In the center of the room stood a gaming-table, lit by a single low-hanging lamp of bottle green glass, a dark secretive lamp that scarcely illuminated the table at all, and gave to the six or seven men and women who were hunched around it a ghastly green look, as if they had been dead for several days.

Jack frowned at them. Two of them looked as if they had one foot in the grave for real. Their white hair shone silvery-green in the reflected light from the lamp; their skin was shrink-wrapped over their skulls, and thick with wriggling veins.

Yet three of the players were almost children – a spotty boy of sixteen or seventeen; a young girl of not much more than twelve; and a blond-headed boy who was so small he could scarcely throw the dice.

All of them, however, shared something in common. They all wore loose Chinese robes, of gleaming black silk, with fire-breathing dragons embroidered on the back, and the name Nu Kua in red silk italics.

"Come," said the Chinese girl, and led Jack and Solly toward the table.

Jack was fascinated to see that the dice appeared to glow fluorescently in the darkness; and that when they were thrown, they left glowing patterns in the air. Solly watched the game over his shoulder for a while, and then murmured, "What the hell kind of craps is that?"

Jack looked around the table. "I'm supposed to be talking to Mr Graf," he said, loudly.

The blond-headed boy left his place and came around the table, smiling and holding out his hand in greeting. He looked no older than five or six.

Jack smiled. "How's tricks, kid?"

"I'm Nevvar Graf," the boy told him, in an unbroken but carefully-modulated voice.

"Sure and I'm Tammy Wynette."

The boy continued to hold out his hand. "You don't believe me?" he asked, tilting his head to one side.

"Nevvar Graf has owned the Golden Lode Casino for twenty years, minimum. He's just about old enough to be your grandfather."

The boy smiled. "There are more things on heaven and earth, Horatio."

"Oh, sure," Jack nodded. "Now is Mr Graf here, because if not, I intend to leave."

"I told you, Mr Druce, I'm Nevvar Graf."

There was something in the tone of the boy's voice that caught Jack's attention. Something far too commanding for a boy of five. And how did he know Jack's name?

Jack took off his spectacles and folded them and tucked them slowly into his pocket.

The boy said, "I'm Nevvar Graf, and you're Jack Druce. I've been watching you for years, Mr Druce. You're good, one of the best arms in the business. Everybody knows Jack Druce. It's always beaten me why you dress so crummy, and talk so dumb, when everybody knows who you are. You saw Carlos downstairs? The minute you leave the Golden Lode, Carlos always gets on to the radio-transmitter and warns the doorman at the Diamond Saloon."

Jack said, hoarsely, "Young fellow, I don't know what the hell you think you're playing at, but my name is Keith Kovacs, and I came here from Illinois for the week to gamble a few hundred dollars, just like I've always promised myself; and when my money's all gone, I'll be gone, too.

"Jack Druce?" he added. "I never even heard of anybody called Jack Druce."

The boy popped his knuckles, one by one. "You see that game going on behind me?"

"I see it," said Jack. "Some kind of fancy dice."

"Beijing Craps," the boy told him, with a smile.

Jack shook his head. "Never heard of it."

"Never heard of it, huh?" The boy turned to Solly, and said, "Have you heard of it? Beijing Craps?"

Solly nervously sniffed, and lowered his eyes. "Sure. I've heard of it."

The boy circled around Jack and took hold of Solly's hand. "Solly Bartholomew," he said, in that piping voice. "The greatest arm in the east. The scourge of the Atlantic City boardwalk."

Solly didn't attempt to deny it. He stood holding the boy's hand with his eyes on the carpet and said nothing.

"Beijing Craps," the boy repeated. "The legendary magical mystical Beijing Craps. Banned in China since

292

the revolution; banned in Thailand where they don't ban nothing; punishable by flogging in Japan; punishable by death in Viet Nam. Illegal in every country in the world, with the exception of Pol Pot's Cambodia, and that's where these dice were smuggled in from."

He tugged Solly's hand. "Come on, Solly, come closer. Take a look."

Solly stayed where he was, his head still lowered. The boy tugged his hand again, then smiled. "You don't want to take a look? You don't have to play."

"You know just what the fuck you're talking about," said Solly, his false teeth clenched together. "If I look, I'll have to play."

The boy laughed. "That's up to you, Solly. You're ready for it. You know that you're ready for it. That's why I asked you up here, you and your friend Jack Druce. I've been watching you two lately and you're the cream de la cream. But you're getting bored, too. You're too damned good for your own damned good. What's the fun, when you don't play the game to the limit – can't play the game to the limit, because the pit boss is going to suss you out and then you're finished at the Golden Lode; and then you're finished at Caesar's Palace and Glitter Gulch and even Sassy Sally's, and before you know it you're finished in Vegas altogether, then Reno, then Tahoe, then Atlantic City.

"That's when clever men like you start to play Russian Roulette, and hoping you'll lose. But Nevvar Graf here has an alternative for you, a different way out, a new life maybe, leave the old life behind, all or nothing. Beijing Craps."

Jack said, dryly, "You're Nevvar Graf, aren't you? You really are."

The boy released Solly's hand and came back to Jack, and looked up at him, his eyes bright with mischief. "I really am. And what you're looking at is proof. Look at me, I'm five years old! And that's the magic of Beijing Craps. You win, you can live your life all over again!"

Solly nodded toward the table, where the white-haired men and women were rasping their breath on to the dice. "What if you lose?"

"You won't lose. You're too good. You know you're too good."

Jack stepped up to the table, and inspected the layout. "So what's in it for you?" he wanted to know. "Why'd you want me to play?"

The boy smiled more gently now. "Same as always, Jack. The odds favor the house; and I'm the house."

"Explain it to me," said Jack.

The boy came up and stood beside him. "It's pretty much the same as a regular dice game. You pick up the dice, you make your bet, you shoot; and other players fade your bet. The only difference is that we use special dice, you want to take a look?"

Jack looked across the table at the withered yellow-faced old man who was holding the dice. He had never seen such an expression of dumb panic in anybody's eyes in his whole life; not even on the faces of trust-fund managers who had just gambled away their clients' investments, or husbands who had just lost their houses.

"Mr Fortunato, will you pass me the dice for just a moment?" asked the boy.

Old Mr Fortunato hesitated for one moment, the dice held protectively in the cage-like like claw of his hand.

"Come on, Mr Fortunato," the boy coaxed him; and at last he dropped them into the boy's open palm. The boy passed them carefully to Jack.

They were greenish-black, these dice, and they tingled and glowed. Holding them in his hand, Jack felt as if the ground were sliding away beneath his feet, like jet-lag, or a minor earth tremor. Instead of numbers, they were engraved with tiny demonic figures – figures whose outlines crawled with static electricity.

"There are six Ghosts on each dice," the boy explained. "If you shoot Yo Huang – this one – and Kuan-yin Pusa – this one – that's roughly the same as throwing a seven in craps; and if you shoot Yo Huang and Chung Kuei – here – that's just about the same as throwing eleven. In either case, these are the Beijing equivalent of naturals, okay, and you win.

"Yo Huang was the Lord of the Skies; Kuan-yin Pusa was a good and great sorceress. Chung Kuei was known as the Protector Against Evil Spirits."

Jack slowly rubbed the dice between finger and thumb. "That's three Ghosts. What are the other three?"

"Well," smiled the boy. "They're the bad guys. This one with the hood is Shui-Mu, the Chinese water demon; and this little dwarf guy is Hsu Hao, who changes joy to misery; and this is Yama the judge of hell, who was the first mortal ever to die – and do you know why?"

"I have a feeling you're going to tell me," said Jack.

The boy smiled. "He was the first mortal ever to die because he traveled down the road from whence there is no return."

Solly licked his lips. "The road from whence there is no return? What's that?"

The boy turned and looked at him slyly. "You're traveling down it already, my friend. You should know."

"Let me feel those dice," Solly demanded.

Jack closed his fingers over them. "Solly . . . maybe you shouldn't."

"Oh, yeah? And any particular reason why not? Seeing as how I'm already supposed to be taking the hike with no return?"

There was such a crackling charge of power from the dice that Jack felt as if every nerve in the palm of his hand was wriggling and twitching, centipedes under the skin. He had the irrational but terrible feeling that the dice wanted Solly very badly. The dice knew that Solly was there; and they were hungry for him.

Solly held out his hand, and Jack reluctantly dropped the dice one after the other into his palm. Solly said nothing, but something passed across his eyes like a shadow across a doorway. There was no telling what Solly could feel. Jack suspected that the dice felt different for everybody who held them. It depended on your needs. It depended on your weaknesses.

"So you place your bet," said Jack, without taking his eyes away from Solly. "What do you bet? Your soul, something like that?"

"Oh, no, nothing as melodramatic as that. Anyway, what's a soul worth? Nothing. A soul is like a marker. Once the guy's dead, how's he going to pay?"

"So what's the stake?" Jack persisted.

"Months, that's what you bet," the boy told him. From the other side of the table, Mr Fortunato hadn't lost sight of the dice for one moment, and when the boy said "months", he shivered, as if the boy had said "millions".

"Months?" asked Solly.

The boy nodded, and then held out his hand for the dice. "The shooter bets as many months as he wants, and the other players collectively put up an equal number of months that he's going to lose. Lunar months, that is, Chinese months. The rest of the players can bet amongst themselves, too, whether the shooter comes or don't come, except in Beijing Craps we say dies-a-little or lives-a-little; and there are hard-way bets, too, just like regular craps, whether the shooter throws two Yo Huangs or two Chung Kueis or whether he digs himself a grave and throws two Yamas."

"But if you win, what?" asked Solly, hoarsely.

"If you win, you win months, that's what. Two, three

296

months; maybe a year; maybe two years, depending what you've bet."

Solly looked around, found himself a chair, dragged it over, and sat down. His breathing was harsh and irregular. "You mean you actually get younger?"

The boy giggled. "Look at me, Solly! Nevvar Graf, five years old!"

Solly rubbed his mouth with his hand, as if he were trying to smear away the taste of greasy hamburger. "Jack," he said. "Jack, we got to give this a shot."

Jack shook his head. "Forget it," he said; although his throat was dry. "I play for money. Months, what's a month? Who wants to play for months?"

The boy shrugged. "What do they say? Time is money. Money is time. It's all the same. You ought to try it, Jack, you'll like it. I mean, let's put it this way. Keeping yourself in toupees and hotel-rooms is one thing; but being ten years younger, that's something else. How about fifteen years younger, Jack? How about twenty years younger? How about walking away from this table tonight the same age you were when you first started gambling, with your whole life ahead of you, all over again? No more crap tables, no more cards, no more cigar-smoke, no more shills? How about a wife and a family, Jack, the way your life was always meant to be?"

"How the hell do you know how my life was always meant to be?" Jack retorted.

The boy's eyes gleamed. "I've been working in this business all my life, Jack. You're just one of a million. The International Brotherhood of Optimistic Suckers."

Jack looked at the table; at Solly; at the mean green lamp; at the strange assortment of faces around the layout. He knew with suffocating certainty that he would have to play before he left. Elaine had died in his arms; Roddy had dwindled to a Kodak photograph tucked in his wallet. The chance of starting over burned in the darkness of his

297

present existence like the molten line of the setting sun, burning on the western horizon. To go back! To catch up the sun!

He heard himself saying, "Solly and me, we'll watch for a while."

"Hey, you can watch," Solly told him, abruptly standing up, and sniffing, and clearing his throat. "Me, I'm going to play."

"Solly –" Jack warned; but the boy touched one finger against his lips.

"We're all playing for time here, Jack. We're playing for life. It's your own decision; it's Solly's own decision."

Jack looked at Solly – tried for the first time in a coon's age to look like a friend, somebody who cared; although he didn't find it easy. To the professional craps player, no expression comes easy.

The boy said, "You'll have to change. There's a Chinese screen in the corner, with plenty of robes."

"Change?" Solly wanted to know. "Why?"

"You might win, Solly," the boy smiled at him. "You might win big. And if you win big, you might find yourself ten years old, all over again. And how would a ten-year-old boy look, hmh? in a 38-chest sport-coat like yours?"

Solly nodded. "Sure. You're right. I'll change. For sure. If I lose, though – you won't take my suit for collateral?"

"You're a kidder, Solly," the boy grinned at him. "You're a genuine platinum-plated kidder."

Solly disappeared behind the Chinese screen; and while everybody edgily waited for him, the boy whistled, She's My Jeannie With The Light Brown Hair, over and over.

At last Solly emerged in his black silk robe. He looked like an invalid, on his way to hydro-therapy. He smiled nervously – first at the rest of the players, then at Nevvar Graf, then at Jack.

Jack hesitated, and then stepped back. He didn't shake Solly's hand. He didn't say a word. He knew that – inside of himself – he was just as much of a victim as Solly.

"All right," said the boy, smacking his hands. "Let's play Beijing Craps!"

From out of the shadows at the back of the room, three Chinese and a Burmese appeared, dressed in the Golden Lode uniform of overtight black tuxedo and frilled shirtfront. The boy said, "Same as regular craps, a boxman, a stickman, and two dealers. In Beijing Craps, though, we call them Tevodas, which means witnesses who can testify to somebody's sins."

It was Mr Fortunato's turn to roll. Solly stood beside him, watching him with naked eagerness. "Six months," Mr Fortunato declared, and placed six shimmering gold tokens in front of him; tokens that shone brighter than the bottle-green lamp.

"Two weeks he dies-a-little," whispered a white-haired old man from the far corner of the table.

"One month he lives-a-little," said the twelve-year-old girl. Jack looked at her closely for the first time and realized that her hair had been permanent-waved in the style of a woman who was old enough to be her mother.

"One week he dies-a-little," said one of the oldest players, a woman whose skull was showing through her skin. Her shriveled hand placed one of her last gold tokens on to the square marked with the face of Yama.

When all the bets had been placed, Mr Fortunato gasped on the dice, and rolled them. They sparkled and bounced, leaving fluorescent after-images of Chinese ghosts melting in the air over the tabletop. Yo-Hang and Kuan-yin Pusa. Mr Fortunato had won his six months.

"Mr Fortunato lives-a-little," intoned the Tevoda, the stickman, and collected the dice and handed them back. Mr Fortunato breathed a little more easily on to the dice this time; but the old woman who had lost a week betting

299

that he would die-a-little had begun to shudder. Jack swallowed and looked at the blond-haired boy; but the blond-haired boy simply grinned.

Mr Fortunato bet another six months, and rolled again. He threw Kuan-yin Pusa and Shui-Mu. The blond-haired boy leaned toward Jack and whispered, "He's won again. In Chinese magic, Kuan-yin Pusa trapped Shui-Mu by feeding her with noodles which turned into chains in her stomach and locked her up guts up for good. Throwing Kuan-yin Pusa and Shui-Mu is like a point in craps; and what Mr Fortunato has to do now is to throw them again. But if he throws Yo-Hang and Kuan-yin Pusa again, he loses."

Jack watched every roll of the dice intently; and especially the side bets. Some of the players were picking up weeks here and there with easy bets; others lost one month after another with hard-ways bets. Live-a-little, die-a-little. Their lives ebbed and flowed with every roll.

Mr Fortunato bet a whole year, threw a crap, and lost it. Twelve months of his life, swallowed in an instant. Who knows what age Mr Fortunato had been, when he had started playing this game? Forty? Seventy? Twenty-two? It didn't matter. His age was determined by the dice now; his life depended on Beijing Craps. He coughed and wheezed with stress and badly-concealed terror, and passed the dice to Solly with fingers that could scarcely manage to open. Nobody else at the table showed any compassion. The blond boy had aged by three years since Mr Fortunato had started to play, and was far taller and more composed; although the woman with the skull-like face seemed to have shrunk in her black silk robe almost to nothing, more like a bewildered vivisected monkey than a human.

Jack caught Solly's eyes but he remained impassive. They were professionals, both of them. They helped each other on the tables when the dice were rolling, but they

300

never ventured to give each other criticism, or personal advice, or to warn each other to back off, no matter how cold the table, no matter how vertiginous the bet. You want to fly, you want to die? That's your business. Under the lights, out on the center, there was nobody else but you, and Madame Luck.

"Solly," said Jack; but the adolescent Mr Graf shot him a glance as hard as a carpet-tack, and he said nothing else.

Solly bet six months. He jiggled the dice in the palms of his hands, and breathed on them, and whispered something, and then he rolled. They had once called Solly the Arm of Atlantic City; and his arm didn't fail him now. The dice bounced, glowed, and tumbled, and came up Kuan-yin Pusa and Yo Huang.

Next, he bet a year, and threw another natural. He threw again, and won again. Roll after roll, he played like a genius; played like Jack had never seen him play before. With each win, he gradually began to look younger. His gray hairs wriggled out of sight, his wrinkles unfolded like a played-back film of crumpled wrapping-paper. He stood taller, straighter, and played with even more confidence; and all the other players bet along with him, hardways bets, right bets, they shed years and years in front of Jack's eyes. After twenty minutes, he was watching a game played by young, good-looking, vigorous people: attractive young women and smiling young men. Their shriveled skin was plumper and pinker; their hair was thick and shiny; their voices roared with vigor and health.

"How about some champagne?" called Mr Fortunato.

A twelve-year-old Mr Graf snapped his fingers stickily to one of the girls. "Bring these people champagne."

Jack didn't bet. Not yet. He was tempted to. But he wanted to bide his time. He wanted to see the losing side of this game, as well as the winning side. He wanted to work out the odds. And although Solly was winning, and

301

consistently winning, it occurred to Jack that the younger he became, the less experienced he became, the more risks he was prepared to take, the wilder his arm.

"Ten years!" grinned a 24-year-old Solly, shaking the dice in his hands. "I'm betting ten years! Fourteen again, and screw the zits!"

He rolled. The dice glowered, shimmered, sparkled. They bounced off the cushion on the opposite side of the layout, but then they seemed almost to slow down, as if they were bouncing through transparent glue. The Ghosts glowed malevolently for all to see. Yama and Shui-Mu. Craps. An entire decade was silently sucked from Solly's body and soul; and he visibly shuddered.

After that – as far as Solly was concerned – the table turned as cold as a graveyard. Mr Graf was shooting, winning a little here and a little there; but Solly was stacking his counters on all the impossible bets, trying to win time, trying to win time, but losing it with every roll. When Mr Graf finally missed, Solly was white-haired; on the verge of respiratory collapse. He sat hunched over the opposite side of the table, his hands dry like desert thorns, his head bowed.

Jack approached him but didn't touch him. Bad karma to touch him; no matter what affection he felt.

"Solly," he said thickly, "pull out now. You've lost, Solly. Call it quits."

Solly raised his head and stared at Jack with filmy eyes. His neck hung in a brown-measled wattle.

"One more bet," he whispered.

"Solly, for God's sake, you're falling apart. You look about a hundred years old."

Solly wasn't amused. "I'm eighty-seven, two months, and three days exactly, you unctuous bastard, thanks very much. And if I win another thirty on the next roll, I'll be only fifty-seven. And if I bet another thirty after that . . . well, then, I'll be happy to quit. Life was good to me when I was twenty-seven. Twenty-seven is a pretty good age."

Jack said nothing. If Solly bet thirty years and won, then Jack would be happy for him. But if he bet thirty years and lost . . .

He looked at Mr Graf. Mr Graf had lost six or seven years betting on Solly's last roll, and was looking much older again, and more like the Mr Graf that Jack had seen hurrying in and out of the Golden Lode, hedged in by minders and shills and hard-faced accountants. Mr Graf's eyes turned like a lizard's toward Solly. What could he say? Solly had lost and those who had lost were always hooked. Those who had won were hooked, too. So what could he say?

"You're not playing, Mr Druce? It's your roll, if you're playing."

"If it's all the same to you, I think I'll stay out of it," said Jack, although perspiration was sliding from his armpits and his fingernails were clenched into the palms of his hands.

"Sure thing. It's all the same to me," said Mr Graf, immediately offering the dice to Mr Fortunato. With the unashamed greed of the truly fearful, Mr Fortunato held out his hand.

"Wait, Jack!" wheezed Solly, and took hold of Jack's sleeve, and twisted it. He bent his head close, so that Jack could smell his unexpected age, chalk and cloves and geriatric staleness. "Jack, you're the best arm there ever was. If anybody can win back those years for me, you can. Jack, I'm begging you, Jack. We never did nothing for each other, did we? Never expected nothing, never asked for nothing. You know that. But I'm asking you now, Jack, I'm down on my knees. If you let Fortunato shoot next, I'm dead meat, Jack. I'm gone. You know that."

Jack sniffed, the way that a heroin addict sniffs. He feared this game of Beijing Craps more than any game

303

he had ever come across. It had all the glamor of punto banco and all the fascinating horror of standing in front of a speeding express train. He knew that if he rolled those dice just once, he would be caught for good.

Mr Graf sensed his hesitation, however, and held the glowing dice suspended in the air, just two inches above Mr Fortunato's open hand. Jack could almost see the nerves that crawled with anticipation in Mr Fortunato's palm.

Solly tugged his sleeve even tighter. "Jack, for old time's sake, I'm pleading with you now. I never pled before. I never pled to nobody. But please."

Jack hesitated for one more second. He didn't need to look at his watch. He never did. He knew what time it was. He loosened his necktie and said, "Give me a minute to change, all right?"

He undressed behind the screen. The black dragon-robe was cold and silky on his skin. He tightened the sash, and then he reemerged, and Mr Graf was still waiting, still smiling.

Jack approached Nevvar Graf and slowly held out his hand. Mr Graf smiled secretively, and dropped the dice into Jack's palm. They tumbled and turned as slowly as if they didn't particularly care for gravity. When they touched Jack's palm, they felt like fire and ice and naked voltage.

The players gathered around the table again. The lamp was so dim that all Jack could see of their faces was smudges of paleness in the shadows. He shook the dice and tiny grave-worms of bluish fluorescence wriggled out from between his fingers. He bet six months, and stood back waiting while the side-bets were placed.

He threw the dice across the table. They jumped and sparkled with even more brilliance than they had before.

"You see that?" said Mr Graf, slyly. "Even the *dice* know when an expert is throwing."

Jack had come out with Chung Kuei and Yo Huang. Solly clenched his fists and breathed. "All *right*! You goddamned brilliant son-of-a-bitch!"

Jack threw again, Kuan-yin Pusa and Chung Kuei. He threw them again the next throw, and picked up a whole year. He didn't *feel* any different, but it was stimulating to think that he was a whole year younger.

He continued to win, again and again and again; living-a-little and living-a-little more, throwing naturals and points as swiftly and confidently as if the dice were loaded – which, in a strange way, they were. The years fell away from him with every win, until he was betting two and three years at a time, and his black silk robe began to hang loosely around his slim twenty-two-year-old frame.

Solly placed numbers to win with almost every throw, and gradually won back the years he had lost before. He played cautiously, however, and didn't risk more than a year a time, until he reached forty-five.

Then – just as Jack was about to throw again – he placed a hard-ways bet of twenty years.

Jack looked at him sharply, but Solly grinned and winked. "One last throw, my friend, and then I'm going to walk away, and never come back."

But Jack felt something in the dice; as if they had shrunk and tightened in the palm of his hand; as if they had suddenly gone cold. The dice were not going to let Solly go.

Jack said, "Twenty years on one throw, Solly? That's a hell of a bet."

"That's the last bet ever," said Solly. "You just do your bit, and let me take care of myself."

Jack threw the dice. They dropped leadenly onto the layout, scarcely bouncing at all. They came up Shui-Mu and Hsua Hao, a win for Jack; but Solly had bet Shui-Mu and Shui-Mu, and he was immediately aged by twenty years.

305

Jack was only a little over twenty years old now. He stood straighter and taller, and his hair was thick and wavy and brown. He took off his toupee and crammed it into the pocket of his robe. Mr Graf smiled at him. "Hair today, gone tomorrow, huh, Mr Druce?"

Jack scooped up the dice and prepared to throw them again. As he did so, Solly put down the gleaming tokens that showed he was staking another twenty years.

"Solly!" called Jack.

Solly looked up. "Don't do it, Solly," Jack warned him, in a clear and youthful voice; although he found that he didn't really care too much whether Solly lost another twenty years or not. Look at the guy, he was practically dead already.

"Just throw, will you?" Solly growled at him.

Jack threw; and won; but Solly lost yet again, and so did two or three of the others at the table. Jack heard from Solly a sharp harsh intake of breath, and then Solly staggered, and gripped the edge of the table to stop himself from falling.

"Solly? You okay?"

Solly's eyes bulged and his face was blue from lack of oxygen. "What do you care?" he gasped. "Will you shoot, for God's sake? Just shoot!"

Mr Graf was very young again, a small boy peering over the dimly-lit center of the table. He said to Solly with utmost calmness, "Do you want an ambulance, sir? Or maybe I should call the house physician?"

"Shoot, that's all," Solly insisted, and placed another twenty years on the table.

Jack slowly juggled the dice. Fire and honey in his hand. "Solly . . . you understand what could happen if you lose?"

"Shoot," hissed Solly, through false teeth that were too large for his shrunken gums.

"Go on," urged Mr Fortunato; although he too was

306

ancient, with sunken ink-stained eyes and wispy white hair.

Jack shrugged, shook the dice, and threw.

Suddenly, the dice crackled with new vitality. They bounced on the opposite cushion, and tumbled across the table in a cascade of glowing Chinese images. They came to rest right in front of Solly.

Yama and Hsua Hao. Solly had lost.

"I –" he gargled. But traceries of light had already crept out of the dice, trembling and flickering like static electricity. They forked across the baize to the tips of Solly's fingers. Silently, enticingly – right in front of Jack's eyes – the light crept up Solly's arms, and entwined themselves around him in a brilliant cage.

"*Solly!*" Jack shouted.

But Solly began to shudder uncontrollably. His hair was lifted up on end, and white sparks began to shower out of his nose and eyes. He looked as if fierce fireworks had been ignited inside his head.

Jack heard a noise that was something like a sob and something like a scream, and then Solly collapsed onto his knees, although his fingers still clung to the edge of the table.

Twitching electricity streamed out of his body, shrinking down his arms and pouring out of his fingertips, back across the craps table and into the dice. They vanished into the Ghosts on the dice like disappearing rats' tails. Solly dropped backward onto the floor, his skull hitting the polished wood with a hollow knock.

The dice remained on the table, softly glowing, as if Solly's life had given them renewed energy.

"Well, Mr Druce?" asked Nevvar Graf. "We're waiting."

Jack looked down at Solly's crumpled, dried-up body; and then at Nevvar Graf; and then back at the dice. The haunted circle of faces watched him expectantly.

Then – "No," said Jack. "That's it. I'm out."

"You still have five years on the table, Mr Druce. You'll lose your five years. Rules of the game."

"I'm only twenty-two now. What do five years matter?"

Mr Graf smiled. "Ask Mr Fortunato what five years matter. It's an education, Beijing Craps. It teaches you that the time you throw away when you're young, you'll bitterly regret when you're old. Beijing Craps teaches you the value of life, Mr Druce. What does a month matter, to a bored teenage kid? Nothing: he hopes that month will pass as soon as possible. But tell me what a month matters to a man with only one month left to live."

Jack took a deep, steadying breath. "Whatever, I'm out."

"You'll be back."

"Well, we'll just have to see about that."

"All right," shrugged Mr Graf. "Carlos – will you escort Mr Druce out of the casino? And make sure you pay him his winnings. Thank you, Mr Druce. You have a rare skill with the ivories."

Jack changed back into his loose seersucker suit. Before he left, he nodded to the circle of players. One or two of them nodded back; but most of them seemed to have forgotten him already. Carlos took his arm, the first time that anybody in the casino had touched him, and he was led back out into the bright glittering world of the Golden Lode.

When he had cashed his winnings, he went across to the *punto banco* table. He watched the game for a while, considering a couple of bets. A bleached-blonde girl standing next to him was screaming with excitement as she won her first hand. But after Beijing Craps, the idea of playing for money seemed absurdly petty. He glanced back toward the staircase that led up to Mr Graf's private craps game. Carlos was still standing at the top of the stairs, and he smiled back at Jack with a smile like curdled milk.

Jack knew then that he would never escape. He would be back at that table, no matter how hard he tried to resist it. Maybe not tomorrow; maybe not next week; maybe not for years. But he would be back. No real gambler could resist the temptation of playing for his very life.

He left the Golden Lode and stepped out on to the hot, brilliantly bright sidewalk. He had started playing Beijing Craps at two o'clock in the morning, and now it was well past nine. For the first time in a long time he felt hungry; and he decided to go back to his hotel room and shower and change, and then treat himself to a meal of prime rib and fried zucchini. He could wear his Armani suit, his *real* suit.

The sidewalk was crowded with shuffling tourists and squalling kids. Las Vegas wasn't what it used to be, back in the days of the mob. Bugsy Siegel would have rolled over in his desert grave to see creches and stroller parks and family restaurants, and hookers being turned away from casino doors. But Jack didn't care. He had found himself the ultimate game, even in this sanitized Las Vegas, and he was twenty-seven again. He had forgotten how much strength and energy he used to have, at twenty-seven – how light and easy it was to walk.

He went up to his hotel room humming along to the Muzak in the elevator. *Raindrops keep fallin' on my head . . . they keep fallin' . . .* He boogied along the corridor, chafing his feet on the nylon carpet, so that when he reached out for his doorhandle, there was a sharp crackling spark of static.

To his surprise, however, his door was half-an-inch ajar. He hesitated, then pushed it wide. The room appeared to be empty, but you never knew. There were plenty of scumbags who followed gamblers back to their hotel rooms, and forcibly relieved them of their winnings.

"Anybody there?" he called, stepping into the room. The bed was made, and there was no utility cart around, so it couldn't have been the maids. Maybe the door had been left open by accident. He went over to the bureau and tugged open the drawers. His gold cufflinks were still there; so was his Gucci ballpen and five hundred dollars in small bills.

He was just about to turn around and close the door, however, when he heard it softly click shut by itself. A voice said, "Freeze, buddy. Stay right where you are."

He stood up straight. In the mirror on top of the bureau, he saw a young man step out from behind the drapes, holding a handgun, .32 by the look of it, although Jack didn't know much about guns.

"Looking for some loose change?" the young man asked him.

"Maybe I should ask you the same question," Jack replied. The young man came around and faced him. He was pale and thin-faced and haggard, and he was dressed in worn-out denims.

"I'm not looking for trouble," he told Jack. "Maybe you should turn around and walk back out of that door and we'll forget the whole thing."

"I'm not going anyplace," Jack retorted. "This is my room."

"Unh-hunh," the young man grinned. "I know whose room this is. This is Mr Druce's room, and you sure as hell aren't Mr Druce."

"Of course I'm Mr Druce. Who do you think I am?"

"Don't kid me," the young man told him, raising his pistol higher. "Mr Druce just happens to be my father; and there's no way that *you're* my father, buddy."

Jack stared at him. "Mr Druce is your *father*?"

The young man nodded. "You sound like you know him."

"Know him? I *am* him."

"Are you out of your tree or what?" the young man demanded. "You're not much older than me. How the hell can you be my father?"

"How the hell can you be my son?" Jack retorted. "My son is three years old."

"Oh, yes? Well, that's very interesting. But right now, I think you'd better *vamos*, don't you, before Mr Druce gets back and finds you here."

Jack said, "Listen, I think we've gotten our lines crossed here. You must be looking for the wrong Mr Druce. I'm Jack Druce, this is my room, and there's no way in the world you can be my son, because look – "

Jack reached inside his suit for his wallet, and his Kodak photograph of Roddy by the pool. But the young man instantly cocked his handgun and tensed up, and said, "Freeze! Freeze! Keep your hands where I can see them!"

"But if I showed you –" Jack began.

The young man screamed *"Freeze!"* at him, and fired. The bullet hit Jack in the right side of his head, and burst out through the back of his skull. Blood and brains were thrown against the yellow flock wallpaper.

Jack thought, *He's killed me. I can't believe it. The punk's gone and killed me.* He opened and closed his mouth, and then his knees folded up under him and he collapsed on to the floor.

The hotel dwindled away from him like a lighted television picture falling down an endless elevator shaft. Until it winked out.

Shaking, the young man hunkered down beside him, and reached into his blood-spattered coat for his wallet. He flicked through it. Over ten thousand dollars in thousand-dollar bills. Jesus. This guy must've made some killing.

He found a creased Kodak photograph of a small boy next to a swimming pool. He stared at it for a long time.

311

For some inexplicable reason, he found it disturbingly familiar. Must be the guy's son. It was weird, the way that he'd kept on insisting that his name was Jack Druce.

The young man stood up, unsure of what to do next. He couldn't wait here for his father any longer, and he didn't really have to. He'd only come to Las Vegas to ask him for money, and now he had all the money he could possibly want.

He crammed the bills into the pocket of his denim jacket, and stuffed his handgun back into the top of his jeans. He took one last look at the man lying dead on the carpet, and then he left.

He walked along the sidewalk glancing at every middle-aged man who passed him by. He wondered if he would recognize his father if he ever chanced to meet him. He wondered if his father would recognize *him*.

He passed the Golden Lode Casino, and standing on the steps outside was a young boy, no more than seven years old, wrapped in a black Chinese robe. The young boy was smiling to himself, almost beatifically, as if he were a god.

Roderick Druce smiled at him, and the boy smiled back.